Praise for the work of Carlos Cisneros

"There is a slightly subversive element here that gives the novel zip; it has all the same elements as a traditional legal thriller, but it's less predictable, more ethically ambiguous . . . keep your eye on Cisneros."
—*Booklist* on *The Case Runner*

"Cisneros has written a fast-paced novel exposing wrongdoings and political pay-offs. The various subplots blend seamlessly, causing the book to be a real page-turner. This legal thriller is sure to please and is recommended for both public and private libraries."
—*Review of Texas Books* on *The Case Runner*

"This thriller lands firmly in John Grisham territory. But Cisneros, a practicing attorney in Texas, makes the material his own. The novel isn't merely a fast-paced legal thriller; it's also a thoughtful rumination on the conflict between ambition and morality."
—*Booklist* on *The Name Partner*

"Readers who enjoy mystery and suspense storylines with a rapid pace will absolutely find *The Name Partner* to be a true page-turner."
—*Review of Texas Books* on *The Name Partner*

"Cisneros continues to impress with his sharp characterizations and thoughtful, many-layered stories."
—*Booklist* on *The Land Grant*

"In the troubled, dusty border region of South Texas, corruption and violence aren't isolated forces to be wrestled with and conquered by our hero but a pervasive condition. Alex is no white knight, but he's sympathetic enough that the harsh denouement will leave readers shaken."
—*Publishers Weekly* on *The Land Grant*

"Cisneros hits his stride when the legal machinations and dark conspiracies start to emerge. [He] deals with important and timely topics, and you can tell he has a fundamentally optimistic view of the justice system and people's capacity for change."
—*Kirkus Reviews* on *The Paper Lawyer*

THE PAPER LAWYER

Carlos Cisneros

Arte Público Press
Houston, Texas

The Paper Lawyer is funded in part by a grant from the National Endowment for the Arts. We are grateful for their support.

Recovering the past, creating the future

Arte Público Press
University of Houston
4902 Gulf Fwy, Bldg 19, Rm 100
Houston, Texas 77204-2004

Cover design by Mora Des!gn

Names: Cisneros, Carlos, 1963- author.
Title: The paper lawyer / by Carlos Cisneros.
Description: Houston, TX : Arte Público Press, [2019]
Identifiers: LCCN 2019010948 (print) I LCCN 2019012794 (ebook) I
    ISBN 9781518504310 (epub) I ISBN 9781518504327 (kindle) I
    ISBN 9781518504334 (pdf) I ISBN 9781558858497 (alk. paper)
Subjects: LCSH: Attorney and client—Fiction. I Mexican-American
    Border Region—Fiction. I Texas—Fiction.
Classification: LCC PS3603.I86 (ebook) I LCC PS3603.I86 P36 2019
    (print) I DDC 813/.6—dc23

LC record available at https://lccn.loc.gov/2019010948
∞ The paper used in this publication meets the requirements of the American National Standard for Information Sciences—Permanence of Paper for Printed Library Materials, ANSI Z39.48-1984.

19 20   5 4 3 2

This book is dedicated to Lisa García, a beautiful friend and colleague, and to all the other angels that left us too soon.

ONE

At only thirty-two years of age, Camila Harrison was known around legal circles as a talented and dedicated advocate who never backed away from a challenge. No exceptions. No matter the circumstance.

Everyone in Austin knew of Harrison, both the tough-as-nails reputation and the captivating woman who carried it; she lived in the affluent West Lake Hills, was considered a legal rock star by many—the new face of the legal profession; she sat on boards, was politically active and ran the Austin Chapter of the Young Republican Lawyers.

Harrison had made a small fortune for her white-collar law firm by representing commercial developers and landlords all throughout the Southwest. Recently, her engagement to Texas Supreme Court Justice Paxton "Pax" Thomas, III, had blown up all over the local papers, and with good reason. Harrison and Thomas weren't just a power couple, but a Texas-sized power couple, perhaps the biggest in recent memory. Her wedding promised to be Austin's "event" of the year.

One by one, all of Camila's dreams were coming true; attending Rice University for undergrad, where she'd obtained a degree in political science, with honors; thereafter graduating from the University of Houston's Bauer College of Business and Law Center *summa cum laude*, where she'd received a joint MBA and JD; landing a job at Hulse, Munson & Offerman—one of the oldest and most prestigious law firms in Austin—where she had found her niche representing commercial land developers and individual investors with real estate holdings.

To top it all off, living in Austin was a reward in itself; it was a happening place, a bustling city that attracted five thousand new residents, every month. This, in turn, translated into *more*: more construction, more apartments, more highrises, more homes, more businesses, more clients, more evictions, more zoning and variance hearings, more legal work and more money. More. An entire life filled with more. Not bad for a *gringa* born and raised in Mexico City. And now, with a high-profile wedding in the planning stages, things looked to be getting *even better* if that was even possible.

"Camila?"

James Levinson, the firm's managing partner, appeared in the entryway to her corner office. His face was serious, a cell phone in his right hand.

Camila looked up from the computer monitor.

"That was Tim Zuckerman, one of your clients, I believe? I don't know why his call went to my voice mail, but it sounded important."

"Did he say he needed to speak with me?"

"Sounds like it . . . something about some emails? He sounded worried. He mentioned the T. G. Mod litigation."

"Emails? I'm not even handling the T. G. Mod case." Camila frowned, not really understanding her client's message. "He's got outside counsel for that."

"I'm only the messenger, Cam." He raised his hands in mock surrender. "Call him when you get a chance."

Camila smiled. "I will."

"Thanks," answered Levinson as he disappeared down the hallway. A few minutes later, the managing partner poked his head in again.

"Yes?"

"Hey, remember how I was a hero a few minutes ago and passed along a client's message? I have a favor to ask. Can you cover for me this evening?"

Camila rolled her eyes dramatically and smirked. "What's going on?"

"I had promised the Austin Young Lawyers Association that I would do the CLE this evening at Joel's, but my daughter and the grandkids are in town from New York. Maddie and I want to take them to dinner."

"Sure," replied Camila, "what should I talk about? What's the topic?"

"Anything, whatever. Just recycle one of your old presentations. It's informal."

"I'll figure something out."

"Thanks," replied Levinson. "I owe you one."

"In conclusion, the courts continue to grapple with the question of whether an attorney may reveal privileged attorney-client communications . . . even years after the client has died or the illegality has come to light. Ask yourselves . . . when, in fact, does attorney-client privilege end? At the end of the case? At death? When judgment is pronounced? Never? Should there be an exception? Should confidentiality give way to national security issues? If the alternative is grave harm? Why? Or *why not*?"

The complimentary "Bats, Burgers & Beers CLE" was held every Thursday during the month of August. They reserved tables at Joel's La Parranda, a funky bar with a huge roof deck and amazing views of the Austin skyline. To the young male attorneys in the crowd that evening, Camila looked polished and beautiful. With her hair now pulled into a ponytail, she sported a pair of pressed khakis, a white polo and penny loafers. She paused to see if she was still holding the crowd's attention. She was.

"I leave you to ponder the following hypothetical: Think of your days back in law school . . . the final exam from hell."

The crowd laughed.

"What if your client confessed to you, his lawyer, to having committed a white-collar crime? Let's say your client was a fat cat from Wall Street, responsible for the global meltdown of 2008. He confessed to you in no uncertain terms that the mortgage-backed bonds his bank was selling back then were shit. Worthless. He knew full-well investors were being defrauded left and right. He also tells you that he was the one that paid money to the bond-rating agencies in New York in exchange for favorable ratings for the junk bonds his bank was selling. He's now remorseful because somebody else got thrown under the bus by the bank and was recently convicted for it. That somebody else is just a few months away from being sent to prison for twenty years. Should you, his lawyer, come forward and reveal what you know? Or would you be fiercely loyal to your client and take his secrets to your grave? Knowing without a doubt that an innocent person is going to prison for a crime he or she did not commit."

Camila paused and sipped from her margarita. She smiled as she studied the crowd. The twenty or so participants appeared stumped.

"Now, change the facts around a bit. What if it was a homicide? Your client confesses to you that it was he who committed the murder, but somebody else was convicted for it. That other person is thirty days away from being sent to the death chamber. Does that change anything? Is one case more compelling than the other? Why? Or *why not*?"

Silence.

"I invite all of you," continued Camila, "to email me your thoughts on the subject. I'm interested in hearing what you have to say. You can find my email address on my firm's website."

She winked at those in attendance and flashed a wide grin. Her green eyes sparkled under the neon lights.

The crowd broke into applause.

Camila finished her margarita, threw on her cotton blazer and prepared to leave Joel's. She was to meet Pax for dinner.

A female organizer with the state bar's CLE Planning Committee took the microphone and pointed to Camila.

"Let's give a great big thanks to attorney and volunteer Camila Harrison from the Austin-bred Hulse, Munson & Offerman Law Firm. Thank you, Ms. Harrison, for that very informative and thought-provoking presentation."

Camila finished gathering her purse and keys and mouthed a great big *thank you* back to the young organizer. As the applause died down, Camila quickly checked her iPhone and saw that she had two missed calls, one from Tim Zuckerman and the other from Pax. Pax had also texted that he was stuck at work, postponing dinner. She put her phone away.

"Don't forget," followed the presenter while addressing those still milling about the rooftop, "if you want to get credit for this CLE, you have to fill out a Scantron and provide us with your Bar card number. You may drop the Scantrons over in those boxes by that table near the jukebox. You'll receive your one hour of CLE credit in a week or two."

"Ms. Harrison, wait!" yelled the man near the bar exit. It was *Austin Chronicle* reporter Andy McCormick rushing toward Camila, anxious to put a question to her as she waited for the valet to bring her Audi around.

"I have some questions about the proposal being circulated by the city council members to have Austin adopt ordinances on rent control and eviction protections."

"I would not know anything about that," said Camila flatly, avoiding eye contact with the reporter. McCormick had always rubbed her the wrong way.

"Don't you represent some of the biggest land developers in Texas? Doesn't your firm represent the Central Texas Apartment Owners' Association?"

"We do," admitted Camila.

"Well, do you care to comment about those new proposals circulating in front of the city council?"

"We shouldn't interfere with free markets," volunteered Camila, "and neither you, nor I, nor anybody else should tamper with the laws of supply and demand."

"So, you're against rent and eviction controls?"

Camila spotted the valet coming around 5th Street, stepped off the curb and signaled for the driver to hurry.

"I'm sorry, I'd love to stay and chat, but I really have to go."

She didn't want to be rude, but McCormick was known around town as an agitator who loved controversy.

Undaunted, McCormick again tried to push Camila's buttons. "Who are you going to evict next, Camila? How many other poor renters will be out on the street this time next year? How many other Austinites will soon find themselves without a place to call home, huh? Without a roof over their heads?"

The valet drove up to Camila's spot. *Thank God.* She quickly shoved a five-dollar bill in his hand and jumped in her car.

Before hitting the gas pedal, she rolled down the passenger side window and shouted back to the pesky reporter, "Hey, I'm just doing my job, amigo. Why don't you go and find a real story for a real newspaper, huh?"

Her shiny SUV took off like a rocket down 6th Street toward the hills of West Austin.

TWO

The Hulse, Munson & Offerman Law Firm occupied floors 23 through 33 in the Trump Business Tower in downtown Austin. Hulse was one of the oldest and largest legal firms in Texas. Its positions were sought after by many, and not solely because of prestige; Hulse offered its first-year associates an annual base salary of $150,000. The four-hundred-lawyer firm also gave each of its new associates a sign-on bonus of $30,000 to help with moving expenses or to use for housing in the tight Austin real estate market. Junior partners were known to make as much as $250,000 a year, senior partners earned nearly twice that on average, with spring, summer and fall bonuses thrown in for good measure, along with other perks such as private country club and athletic memberships. The youngest senior partner in the history at the firm was Camila Harrison. She had held the position for two years, bringing in well over $450,000 annually, with bonuses more than double what her fiancé was making as a Texas Supreme Court Justice, which was why she hadn't asked him to help pay for the wedding.

Though Big Law was starting to lose its charm, Camila still loved her corner office and its panoramic view over Town Lake, Zilker Park and Barton Springs. On clear days, she could also enjoy the most spectacular sunsets in all of the Hill Country. She was not particularly fond, however, of the way her office had been decorated: the rich wood paneling, the heavy desk, the aged leather sofa and chairs, but she couldn't deny the large-framed picture of herself on the cover of *Super Lawyer Review*. It was the magazine's "Real Estate" edition featuring the 100 Most Influential Lawyers in Texas. She couldn't help but swell each time it caught her eyes.

"Ms. Harrison?"

Camila turned to face her secretary, Cassie, who was in her late fifties. She stood squarely by the door, holding a small package in her hands.

"Yes?"

"Justice Thomas is holding on line two. Also, your mother called; she asked to please call her when you get a chance. And Drew West wanted to know if you filed the evictions and if everyone in his trailer park had been served. Mr. West said that he 'now has the funding lined up to develop the property and is ready to go.' He made it a point to say he is ready to start the demolition and needs an update."

"Has Mr. Zuckerman returned my call?" asked Camila, somewhat preoccupied.

"Not today. Would you like me to call him?"

"Yes, please. He called Mr. Levinson and indicated he was looking for me, I called him back but he didn't pick up. Phone tag. I haven't been able to reach him by email either."

"Okay." Cassie paused. "I don't mean to pry, and I know this is none of my business, but are you ever going to return your mother's calls?"

"Lorena's?"

"Yes."

"I don't have time to deal with that woman," snapped Camila. "Besides, she knows she's not supposed to call me at work. And I have nothing to say to her."

"What am I supposed to tell her, Ms. Harrison? I've run out of excuses By the way, she mentioned the wedding."

"She was pumping you for info, wasn't she?" Camila threw her arms up in the air. "That lady! Why won't she get the message? What does she want now?"

The calls from Lorena were always untimely interruptions that reminded Camila of an uncomfortable and bitter past. A past too painful, too sad. She'd left home at eighteen thanks to a full-ride college scholarship, and had vowed to keep her distance. In her mind, she was collateral damage left behind by Lorena's betrayal and Darin's blind trust, a casualty of a marriage built on half-truths, unrealistic expectations and contrasting cultural values.

"What happened between you two, if may I ask?" Cassie pressed for an answer.

"It's a long story, and we don't have the time."

No matter how hard she'd tried these last few years, Camila could not make the anger and resentment go away. Her therapist had said that many emotions take hold after a traumatic experience, such as the death of a loved one or a tragic event. That people develop different coping mechanisms to deal with these experiences. That she would have to experience the entire cycle of grief before she could get better. Except, Camila could not get past the guilt and anger, despite her therapist's assurances that she would if just worked on it. But for all the money and time spent on counseling, yoga and therapy, Camila Harrison just could not move on. She was stuck, trapped in a never-ending labyrinth of resentment. And her mother, Lorena Cantú, was responsible for her condition.

"What do I tell her if she calls again?"

"Lie to her," Camila instructed, "make something up, I don't care. Tell her I'm out of the country, doing a due diligence study in Europe for a client . . . that you don't know when I'll be back . . . to call back in six months."

Cassie let out a sigh of frustration and said, "Okay."

Camila could not tell if Cassie was sighing because she felt bad for her mother or if she was getting frustrated with having to constantly run interference. In any event, nobody needed to know why she had issues with her mother. Besides, she could not control the past. That was then; another world, a different set of circumstances. This was now. Camila Harrison was a successful lawyer living the American dream, loving the present and all it had to offer. She was in control of her own destiny and ready to reap all the good things the future promised. In fact, her life was so perfect she even had a Texas Supreme Court Justice holding for her on line two.

"Ms. Harrison?" interrupted Cassie. She was back. "I forgot to give you this." She waved the small package in her hands.

"Yes," answered Camila, annoyed at the third-degree Cassie was intent on giving her today, "they're wedding invitation samples. Just put it over on the coffee table. Thanks."

Cassie did as she was told, turned and marched out the door.

Camila punched the blinking light.

"Hey, pumpkin," said Camila, glad to hear from her fiancé, "to what do I owe this honor?"

"*Mi ahmoor*," blurted Justice Thomas in mangled Spanish, "*tee keeahro muuucho. Te extrahnyooh.*"

Camila giggled. "What are you doing, silly boy?"

"I'm practicing my Spanish," Pax announced proudly. "I want to learn. I want *you* to teach me."

"Why?" asked Camila, suddenly defensive.

Speaking Spanish, unfortunately, always had a negative effect on Camila. It reminded her of her mother.

"Why not?" followed Pax.

"You know I don't like to speak Spanish. We're in America. Everybody needs to speak English."

"So, you're not going to want our kids to speak *espanyohl*? To be more diverse? More knowledgeable? More *marketable*? You know, studies have shown that executives and professionals that speak various languages make more money in their lifetimes over counterparts that only speak one language."

"Honestly? No," replied Camila, sternly. "I want them to be American. You're American, I'm American, they are going to be born in America. They're going to behave, act and talk like Americans. My kids are going to speak only the best English; no Spanish, no Tex-Mex, no Spanglish. Not any shit like that."

"Okay," Pax muttered, "you win."

He wondered what was up with his fiancée, who was one-half American and one-half Mexican. It was obvious that Camila carried emotional scars stemming from childhood, a childhood spent in vibrant Mexico City. *What could have been so bad?* Every time he'd tried to pry, she'd quickly shut down, unwilling to talk about it.

"Look at the world around us," Camila followed. "Look at what's happening in this country. Racism and prejudice. The divisions. Why would I want my kids to be shamed or ridiculed? Besides, we don't live in some bordertown. We don't live down in Mexico, or South America. We live in Austin. *Austin Goddamn Texas, U-S-A.*"

"Sorry I brought it up. . . . "

"Anyway," Camila continued, "is that why you called?"

She wondered why her fiancé liked to get her riled up. Why did he insist she claim her Mexican heritage? Didn't he know that as a woman she'd had to work twice as a hard as her male counterparts to find success in the workplace? That if she wanted to make her mark in the legal arena, it was always preferable to be white. That she had first-hand knowledge on the topic. When she had applied for work using the name Camila Cantú, there were no callbacks, no follow-up interviews. Nothing. But the minute she applied for any legal position using the name Camila Harrison, the offers came pouring in. That's the way it was. No use pretending. Besides, she already had two strikes against her: being a woman and being part Hispanic. Worse, she resented anybody or anything that reminded her of Lorena and everything she represented.

"No, I called you because of our wedding. I've looked at the court's calendar. We could have the wedding on Saturday, June 27. I can take off the following week and wouldn't have to get back to work until July 7th. How's that sound?"

"Let me look at my calendar . . . I have a light schedule the week before and the week after. That could work. And if anything comes up, I'm sure I can have someone cover for me."

Pax was relieved. "Good. I'll let my colleagues know that I'll be out of pocket on those days."

Camila was thrilled. "So . . . June 27 then?"

"June 27 it is!"

"I love you, pumpkin," whispered Camila back into the receiver.

"I love you, too," Pax whispered. "I've gotta go. Call you later."

"Bye."

"Bye, baby."

Camila let out a big sigh, held the receiver close to her heart and blew a kiss toward their picture on her credenza. She could not be happier. She had a wedding to plan, and quickly. The big day was less than ten months away.

⸺ ⸺

"Ms. Harrison!"

Camila was waiting by the elevator in the lobby of Chase Plaza, on her way to see Drew West to discuss the re-development of a six-acre trailer park. She was ecstatic, ready to personally deliver the good news to her wealthy client. Her team of process servers had just reported back; every single tenant, along with every other occupant, had been served with eviction notices, and now the Justice of the Peace courts were starting to schedule the eviction hearings. The first batch of forcible-entry-and-detainer cases were already set to begin in two weeks.

Those renters that failed to hire a lawyer to fight the evictions would be out within three weeks of their day in court. Those who still refused to vacate would be thrown out by deputies from the sheriff's office. A few would appeal the evictions to county court, and maybe delay their departure by two or three months. Those that hired counsel were buying more time, but ultimately would also find themselves on the street. After all, the law in Texas only protected a renter so much, and even those with valid lease agreements were no match for a powerful landlord with unlimited resources and access to a team of savvy lawyers.

Yvanka Stern caught up to Camila.

"I've been trying to reach you," said the petite wedding planner. "I got your message. June 27?"

Camila nodded, glowing with excitement. She then checked her phone. It was 11:00 a.m.

"Yes, that's the date. I'm sorry I've been out of the loop. I've been swamped with work. As a matter of fact, I'm going into a meeting with Mr. West right now. How did you track me down?"

Yvanka smiled. "Cassie."

She handed Camila a thick packet of pamphlets for reception halls, events centers, country clubs, caterers and wedding cake bakers. There were restaurant recommendations for the rehearsal dinner, potential musical ensembles, decorators, flower shops, photographers, wedding dress designers, printers, limousine services and even more. With a budget of $200,000 at her disposal, Yvanka was ready to make it rain. All she needed was for Camila to finalize the guest list and choose among all of the options represented in the packet.

The doors to the elevator opened and the two jumped in. Camila finished stuffing the packet in her purse.

"I'll look at it when I get home."

"One of the things we need to narrow down, now," added the wedding planner, "is the guest count. Any idea how many we're looking at?" Yvanka took out a small notepad, pen at the ready.

"Two fifty. Maybe three hundred," answered Camila.

"Do you want me to book blocks of hotel rooms? For the out-of-towners."

"I'd have to check with Pax. I'd imagine we would have some folks coming from out of town. How many exactly, I couldn't tell you."

The elevator doors opened, and Camila made her exit.

The wedding planner yelled as the elevator doors closed behind Camila. "I'll be waiting for instructions, but please hurry. June is right around the corner."

The elevator doors closed. Yvanka was gone.

Camila walked into Drew West's lobby area. Whenever Camila visited Mr. West, she felt she was walking into a World War II museum. There were black and white photos of the D-Day invasion, the Battle of the Bulge, Pearl Harbor and other battles. Bronze soldier sculptures sat atop pedestals. There were Hollywood movie posters of famous films such as *Patton*, *From Here to Eternity*, *The Dirty Dozen*, *Valkyrie*, *The Bridge on the River Kwai*, and *Saving Private Ryan*. The receptionist's desk was a Pentagon relic, made of blocky, institutional metal, but accentuated with modern touches. The couches and sofas in the waiting area were made of green canvas. And on the wall above the receptionist hung Mr. West's most prized possession, the fully restored nose of The Betty Sue, a B-24 Liberator flown by Mr. West's grandfather during WWII.

As soon as the receptionist noticed Camila, she dropped what she was doing, picked up the phone and announced that Ms. Harrison had arrived.

"Mr. West is ready to see you. Please go right in."

She hit a buzzer and Camila walked into Mr. West's office.

West was forty-nine years of age and had been voted most eligible bachelor in Austin six years in a row. He wore horn-rimmed glasses, dressed in jeans and T-shirts and had an air more akin to a Silicon Valley entrepreneur than a rich real estate investor. He kept fit by running triathlons on weekends and loved to travel. When he was not putting real estate deals together, or partying in Austin, he would fly himself to various destinations around the globe. Like his grandpa, flying was in his blood. He owned a fleet of airplanes.

"Have a seat, Camila."

"I would say in six months we should be breaking ground on the West End project," Camila announced with a smile. "Things should move pretty quickly after that." She expected a clap of excitement, a long sigh of relief or some positive reaction.

Drew was, instead, distracted. His eyes darted around the room, his mind was far from business or the potential future tenants of his commercial plaza.

"I know things are rolling along. I wanted to talk to you about something else," said West as he tossed an envelope across his desk.

Camila read the return address. It was from Trey Collins, a famous, hardcore trial attorney from Houston. Camila had heard of him.

"What does he want?"

"He wants to sue me!"

Camila didn't bother pulling out the contents of the envelope. She said calmly, "Sue you for what?"

"He says I knowingly exposed his client to HIV."

Camila bit her lower lip, but otherwise remained composed. Never in a million years would she have suspected that Drew West had the HIV virus.

"Are you HIV-positive?" Camila asked.

Drew could not look up.

"Are you?" Camila insisted.

"Yes," Drew finally admitted.

"How long have you known that you have the virus?"

"Five years."

Camila needed to know more. "What's her name?"

"His name."

"Excuse me?"

"*His* name, Ms. Harrison. I'm bisexual. His name is Gene Vogel."

Camila tried to remain stoic. She reached for the envelope, removed its contents and perused the demand letter. Trey Collins was giving Drew thirty days to compensate his client, otherwise a lawsuit would be filed in Travis County. Collin's letter also hinted at the possibility of bringing criminal charges against him. Surely Mr. West didn't want his booking photo splashed all over the *Austin American-Statesman*'s police blotter section, did he?

Drew said, "Is this something you can help me with?"

"Collins, huh?" Camila scratched her head. "Guy's a son-of-a-bitch. Ruthless. He popped somebody in a similar situation here in Austin. It was a couple of years ago. The defendant was the owner of an internet start-up. A girl claimed the defendant gave her genital herpes, a jury believed her and Collins got a ten-million-dollar verdict. Wanna know what's the saddest part of the story?"

"What?"

Camila got up and walked toward the large window behind Mr. West's desk. Down below, she could see the business lunch crowd already filling up the parking lot of a shopping complex called The Arboretum. Camila sighed. "Collins' client was willing to take one million to go away quietly, ride into the sunset never to be seen or heard from again."

"So, what are you saying?" asked Drew, looking mortified.

"You should settle the case, give Collins what he wants," announced Camila. "Quickly."

"Just like that?"

"I'll call Collins," Camila promised as she gauged her client's panic level. Usually, the more worried a client became, or the more exposed he or she felt, the better the legal fee. "I'll let him shoot us a number first, make a demand. No use betting against ourselves."

"Do you think you can keep it under three hundred thousand?"

Camila turned away from the window and locked eyes with her client. "Haven't you heard anything that I've been saying?"

"What?"

"You want Collins to do to you what he did to that other schmuck? You want him to smack you with a five- or six- or ten-million-dollar verdict? Not to mention the seven-figure punitive damage award he'll get, since you've known you've been HIV-positive for five years and you did not disclose that little fact to Vogel?"

"Can you make it go away?" pleaded Drew, fear in his eyes.

Camila thought about it for a second. "I'll need to bring in Schwarz; he's the head of the litigation department. Are you okay with that? Hell, we don't even know if it's true you gave him the virus!"

"No, don't do that. I only trust you, Camila," replied Drew. "Plus you need to know that if word gets out that I'm HIV-positive, if the banks are homophobic or concerned with family values the funding for the new development will dry up. I know you'll keep all my secrets safe. The more hands involved, the greater the risk that word will get out."

Camila considered Drew's last comment. "Okay. How much money do you have to make this thing go away? And don't bullshit me. I want an honest answer."

"I would need to move some funds around . . . sell some stocks and bonds . . . I think I can put together one million. That's all my liquidity. Everything else is tied up in real estate."

"How long will it take you to put the money together?" Camila asked.

"Two, three weeks."

Camila looked at her hands. She played with her engagement ring. "We need to sweeten the deal."

Drew was now massaging his temples. "How so?"

"I need to make Collins understand that trying to get more than a million dollars from you might take two or three years, four even, of highly contentious litigation. And even if he gets a jury verdict, he needs to know that you're prepared to then appeal and delay any collection efforts for another three to five years. Hell, I'll even drop a hint that you've been talking to bankruptcy lawyers. The idea is for Collins to convince his client to get reasonable, that way we can have this unpleasant episode put behind us and his client can get a million dollars in less than fifteen days. There's more value to getting your money now versus having to wait for it."

"Do you think he'll bite?"

"What other choice do we have?" asked Camila.

"Do it," ordered Drew. "I'll come up with the money. I can't afford a scandal."

Camila placed the envelope back on Drew's desk and headed out the door. "I hope this was an isolated incident, Drew . . . for your sake."

Camila marched past the receptionist and rushed into the elevator. On her ride down to the lobby area she wondered how it was possible that sophisticated business people, capable of thinking several steps ahead of the competition, could commit such acts of sheer stupidity.

The elevator came to a stop in the lobby. Right before the doors opened, Camila flashed a grin from ear to ear. *What would the legal profession do without clients like these?*

The encounter with the wedding planner had forced Camila to face an ugly reality, so after the meeting with Drew West, she went for a walk in the Arboretum. As she strolled past the stores and restaurants in the open-air shopping center, she realized that compiling a list of guests to invite to her wedding would be no easy task. In an empty ice cream shop, she forced herself to call her dad.

Darin Harrison had once been a loyal US government employee, whose career in the Foreign Service had taken him around the world. With a background in electronic engineering, Darin Harrison had been recruited by the Department of State, right out of college and had been assigned to the US Embassy in Mexico City with the title of Security Engineering Officer.

Stationed in Mexico City, Darin had been part of a team that traveled to all the US consular offices in the Mexican Republic developing security policies and practices. While her father was leaping from job assignment to job assignment, Lorena raised Camila while pursuing her own banking career. If Darin and Lorena had disagreements, Camila never witnessed them. Darin was, for the most part, unavailable.

At some point, Camila could not exactly remember when, a young man had entered the picture: Luis Pablo. His arrival on the scene had triggered a series of complicated events. At first, Darin had suspected Lorena was having an affair, then a midlife crisis and, after Lorena's sudden bout with depression, Darin's suspicions could no longer be ignored. He had confronted his wife, who had denied at first anything was wrong, but had finally admitted that she had a son. Luis Pablo was his name. As a teen mother, Lorena had been forced by her parents to give Luis Pablo up for adoption and was forbidden to mention his existence. The half-brother's existence had become known when Lorena received news that Luis Pablo was in a coma, clinging to life, after an auto-pedestrian accident. Unbeknownst to Darin, much less to Luis Pablo's adoptive parents, Lorena had been secretly keeping tabs on her son for many years.

The existence of Camila's half-brother had forced Darin to question many other aspects of his marriage to Lorena. The hurt and betrayal ultimately strained the marriage to the breaking point. By 1998, her parents' marriage had collapsed. It was followed by a contentious divorce. Overall, it had taken three years for Lorena and Darin, and their Mexico City lawyers, to conclude the ordeal. Yet, it had only taken Camila Harrison a few short months to hate her mother for breaking up the family.

"Hello?" Darin answered.

"Dad?"

"Cam?" answered Darin, "is that you?"

"Are you sitting down?"

"Yes, is everything all right, honey?"

"Yes, Dad, everything's fine. I'm fine."

Silence.

"I'm getting married next year," Camila whispered into her cell phone. "I wanted you to be the first to know, surprise you. And I'd like for you to give me away. Will you be able to come to Austin?"

"Honey, I'm so happy for you. Of course, I'll give you away," said Darin, sounding choked-up. "I would be honored. You know I'll do anything for you. When is the wedding?"

"Next year in June. The 27 to be exact."

"Are you still with Mr. Thomas?" asked Darin. For some strange reason, her father had never been able to call her fiancée by his first name.

"Yes, Dad. We're still together. We are going to do it. I wanted you to hear it from me."

"Have you told your mother?"

Silence.

"Do you want me to tell her? I can call her, you know? However, I'm sure she'd rather hear it from you than me," suggested Darin.

"I know," muttered Camila, "I'm just not ready to talk to her . . . not yet."

"Hey, we should take a trip to Mexico City. Just you and me. Go deliver invitations to your aunts, uncles and cousins."

Camila scoffed at the idea. "I don't think I can invite them, Dad. I never kept in touch with any of them. I really don't know them that well." The sad truth was that she felt no connection to her relatives living in Mexico's capital.

"Well, I'm okay with whatever you decide," said Darin, "but don't forget to invite Grandma Harrison and my folks in Indiana."

Camila wanted to laugh because it had been decades since she had seen any of her relatives on either side. Yes, there had been a few short summer vacations to Indiana when she was a kid, but other than that, her childhood had been spent in Mexico City, with the occasional holiday weekend escape to Acapulco, Valle de Bravo or Cuernavaca.

"Both your grandmothers should get an invite, at a minimum," ordered Darin. "I'm just saying . . . they love you more than you'll ever know."

"I have three grandmothers, remember?"

Darin did not appreciate the snide comment, which was a reference to Luis Pablo's kin.

"Listen," continued Camila, "I'll call you in a couple of weeks with an update, okay?"

"Great. Keep me updated . . . let me know what you decide."

"Thanks, Dad. I will."

Perhaps her dad was right. Maybe it was time to wave the white flag, make up with Lorena. Perhaps not. Right now, she just wanted to savor the moment. She finished paying for her pralines and pecan ice cream and walked outside. She roamed the Arboretum trying to clear her head.

Camila found herself in front of a Brazilian *churrascaría*, and for a moment, caught herself looking in. Her first date with Dante had been at a *churrascaría* in Houston. Friends from Rice University had introduced them. He was a Brazilian international business student working on his PhD, and she was a senior studying to take the LSAT. They had been dating for a few months when they got engaged, but then Lorena had intervened, with tragic results. This had been the last straw, and Camila had never been able to forgive her. Since then, she had never been able to see the world in the same way she had experienced it with Dante. Everything had changed in an instant.

She may have been able to forgive Lorena under a different set of circumstances. After all, some would argue that Lorena had only her daughter's best interest at heart. That she had not caused Dante's death. Except at the time, Camila had been blinded by hate, rage and despair. Now, almost ten years later, the wound was still tender.

She threw her ice cream in the trash, walked away from the restaurant window, and went to find her Audi.

THREE

Camila and Pax were holding hands, staring deeply into each other's eyes. They were tucked away in a booth at the Driskill Grill, a favorite of the Sunday-brunch crowd. After a romantic meal, complete with rounds of mimosas and bloody marys, the pair found themselves making plans for the future. It was a long-overdue break from their hectic schedules. In the semi-darkness and out of view of most patrons, Camila ran her toes up and down her fiancée's calves.

"You do know what that does to me, don't you?" whispered Pax.

"What?" giggled Camila. "*This?*"

"Yes, *that.*"

She pressed her toes against his flesh, inching closer to his inner thigh.

"Stop!" he said, embarrassed, "not here. I have to maintain a certain level of decorum, pumpkin. *Pleeease.* I have an image to keep."

"I can't wait to be married," Camila said, "have you all to myself."

He smiled and shifted in his seat so as to avoid more of Camila's advances. Every time she drank champagne, it caused her to behave in totally unexpected ways.

"Please, pumpkin," said Pax again, "not here. Let's wait till we get home. How would it look for a Texas Supreme Court Justice and maybe a future governor of Texas to be seen carousing in a public place? We can't afford any scandals."

Camila got the message. On the one hand, it was glamorous to be engaged to the youngest Supreme Court Justice in the history of the great state of Texas; on the other hand, Pax was a politician with big ambitions, and as such he always steered clear of any improprieties. He had worked tirelessly to make a name for himself as a jurist, and had worked even harder to catch the eye of Republican Governor Wayne Patterson. One controversial post on social media could derail all of it in an instant.

"Aren't you excited we're getting married?" asked Camila. "Starting our lives together?"

"Of course, I am, pumpkin," Pax said, happy to focus on another topic. Truth be told, Paxton Thomas III wasn't exactly *thrilled* with the idea of getting married, but he knew that married men were more electable in the eyes of the media, which then translated to the public at large. "And now that you mention it, we need to work on the guest list. I need to set aside at least fifty invitations for the governor, my friends in the legislature, my friends from my old law firm and the top lieutenants that helped me win my last race. Oh, and don't forget, I have to invite the heads of Prudential, Exxon, Dell, BP, USAA and HEB—along with their spouses."

"Why can't we just keep it small?" Camila asked, "just us, our families, a few friends . . . "

"You don't want me to invite my supporters? The friends that helped me get elected to the court of appeals *and* pushed for my appointment to the Texas Supreme Court?"

"It's not that," said Camila. "It's just . . . "

"Yes?"

"It's supposed to be *our* day, *our* wedding, and you're turning it into a political event, a fundraiser. It makes it feel more like business, that's all."

"Honey," replied Pax, "it's part of the package. This 'business' is how we keep moving up."

"Why do you want more? I guess what I'm asking is . . . when is it gonna be enough?"

"You know I want to be governor." Pax took a bite out of his celery stick and sipped his bloody mary. "In another two years, when I've finished the term I was appointed to, I'll be up for re-election. I need to put one more term in the supreme court and then I'll run for governor. If I don't invite these folks to my wedding they could very well resent it, and that could spell a catastrophe. If not now, then further down the road, when the stakes are even higher. You know how much money I'm going to need to get to the Governor's Mansion? You know how much it's going take to make you the First Lady of Texas?"

Camila perked up, liking the sound of that. "How much?"

"I'm going to need at least twenty million in my coffers. Who knows? By the time I throw my name in the ring, I may need more. So, it wouldn't be good to upset my supporters and most generous contributors at the outset. You can understand that, can't you?"

"I suppose being the First Lady of Texas wouldn't be such a bad thing," Camila sighed. "By then we would have a couple of children, I would have probably stopped working at Hulse. I'd spend my time doing what first ladies do." She sat up, her back straight. "I could get used to it, I suppose." Her face lit up in a smile.

"That's the spirit, pumpkin. What do you say we get out of here, go by and say hi to Mother?"

Camila's expression went from dreamy to a frown. "Really? Right *now*?"

He smirked. "I promised her a Sunday visit. She's been so lonely since Daddy passed away."

"You don't want to go to my place first?" Camila's eyes grew sultry. She blew him a kiss across the booth.

Pax shook his head. "I can't. She's expecting me, and I don't want to keep her waiting. You know how delicate she can be."

"You mean demanding." Camila exhaled long and loud, full of disappointment. "Why do you let her manipulate you like that?

You're a grown man. You're a Texas Supreme Court Justice, for God's sake!"

"Hey," Pax snapped back, "just because you have a shitty relationship with your mother doesn't mean I have to have one too."

"What's that supposed to mean?"

"Since the day we met, I have never heard you talk about her in any kind of meaningful way. You always talk about your dad. I know they had a bad a marriage and you blame her for breaking up the family, but you need to let bygones be bygones." His voice softened. "It's not healthy, pumpkin. Wouldn't you like your dad to give you away, and for your mother to be part of our special day? You're her only child."

"I don't know," answered Camila. She thought of her older half-brother living in Mexico, Luis Pablo. Her mother's secret had destroyed her parents' marriage and ruined Camila's relationship with her.

"Her only *daughter*. You know what I meant."

Camila studied Pax. "In case you forgot, those two can't be together in the same room. Besides, that woman is dead to me, you hear?"

"You should cut Lorena a break," Pax argued. "What happened between you two? Are you ever going to tell me? You can confide in me, let me help you. Didn't we make a promise that we would be honest with each other, pumpkin?" He put his hand on hers. "Holding a grudge can't be good for you, Camila. You should reach out and forgive her. This isn't healthy."

Camila thought about Paxton's words. She stared into his eyes. How could she ever open up to him? Explain that discussing Lorena meant having to talk about Dante, the love of her life. To this day, she still thought of him and the way he made her feel. That no one had ever made her feel that way. At times she felt that she was settling.

"What are you thinking?" he asked.

"About Lorena," she lied.

He was right, she had to admit. When they started dating they *had* promised that they would always be honest with each other.

There would be no secrets between them; the clients, their fellow ladder-climbers—of course. But never them. Whatever curveball life threw at them, they would talk about it, work through it and move forward. They were both lawyers, both adults and pragmatic problem-solvers, not to mention highly intelligent professionals who could talk over almost anything and everything without getting overly emotional. So why couldn't she bring up the topic of Lorena? Leave Dante out of it. Why couldn't she confide in Pax and trust that he would understand? What made it so hard to come clean?

"Are you going to call her?"

"I'm not ready to go there," Camila said, "it's just not the right time."

Pax was starting to get annoyed. "Let's pay the check and get out of here. Maybe after Mother, we can go catch a show. Would you like that?"

Camila reached under the table and put her shoes back on. "I will respectfully decline. You go see your mother, give her my best. I'm going to run to the office, get things ready for tomorrow."

"C'mon, pumpkin. Don't be like that."

Camila got up, reached for her keys, her purse, making sure her phone wasn't left behind. "It's okay, really. I have some work to do anyway. No big deal."

"Why are you being like this?"

He reached out and tried to grab her gently by the arm. Camila was having none of it.

"C'mon, sit down," begged Pax, "tell me about the grievance hearing you handled the other day, uh . . . what was his name?"

"Manny Valdez," she said, arms crossed. "Guy's out in the weeds and there's really nothing left to say. We're recommending he be disbarred. Just another dumb Mexican who somehow managed to throw away the American dream."

"Shhhh," Pax put a finger to his lips. "Careful. People can hear you, pumpkin. Don't use words like that."

"Why not? It's the truth!"

"Yes. It is. But you know how touchy people have become. The whole nation. It's not good politics, pumpkin. Why push a red-hot button? Besides, you're half-Mexican yourself."

"Watch your mouth. I'm not Mexican."

Pax was ready to scream. "Okay . . . Hispanic, Latina, whatever you call it."

"I'm American." Camila stood firm. "And in case you've forgotten, it's called the First Amendment; I can say whatever the hell I want!"

Pax turned to see if people were paying attention. "Shhhh . . . keep it down, momma. Please, don't make a scene."

Thankfully, no one was looking in their direction.

Though both Pax and Camila were members of the Republican Party, he had always wondered how it was that his fiancé had derived her ultra-right wing views and disdain for immigrants—namely Mexican immigrants. Nobody liked to admit it, but the truth was that they were the little engines that kept the Texan economy churning. They were indispensable to food service, hospitality and construction industries, as well as farming, shrimping and even the oil exploration and refinery business. Without such an abundance of cheap labor Texas' cost of living would be through the roof. If they were to vanish overnight, folks would be fleeing Texas, not flocking to it. Pax was able to see the big picture, unlike many of his counterparts; he knew that immigrants were here to stay, like it or not. A dyed-in-the-wool republican, he wasn't in love with the idea, but he had learned to accept that the demographics, and the voter base along with it, wouldn't remain the same for long. The shift was coming—no ifs, ands or buts. Hell, Justice Paxton Thomas III was just months away from marrying into it! He was prepared to do whatever was necessary to get the Latino vote.

Pax tugged at Camila's hand. "C'mon, pumpkin, don't be upset . . . sit down. *Please.* What's really bothering you? You can tell me. Is it Mother, or was it something else I said?"

She gave him an icy stare and pulled away. "We'll talk tomorrow." She turned around and marched out of the restaurant.

Pax sat there, confused, annoyed and frustrated, all at once. He flagged Terry, their waiter, and ordered another drink. *Damn women.*

Back at her office, the champagne buzz was short lived.

"We need to talk. Get ready, it's bad," Zuckerman had said over the phone. "I'm coming by to pick you up."

After ending the call Camila had run to the ladies' room. *What was the crisis in his tone?!* She was in panic mode, her mind was playing tricks on her. The room started spinning. She had even started hyperventilating, feeling sick to her stomach. The eggs benedict, waffles and shrimp cocktail had come back up in the stall.

Camila exited the restroom, taking time to straighten herself up, talk to herself in the mirror. She stepped almost drunkenly into the elevator and made her way to the lobby, was still feeling dizzy, wobbling as she gave a fake smile to the lone security guard at the information booth there. She decided to sit by one of the windows facing Cesar Chavez Street. She waited to spot Zuckerman's silver Range Rover. Nothing.

After waiting for what seemed like an eternity, she walked outside to the curb to try and catch a breath of fresh air. She had almost gotten her heartbeat to a regular rhythm when Zuckerman pulled up in an old, beat-up Chevy pick-up and set it thumping all over again.

He threw the door open. "Climb in."

Zuckerman punched the gas and sped down the boulevard toward I-35. Camila latched onto the door like a ten-year-old riding a roller coaster.

"What's the problem, Tim? How bad is it?" Camila's voice betrayed her worry, and she felt an icy shame because of it.

"It's bad."

"Something I can help with?"

"It's about *you*, Camila."

She felt the world pause all at once, then come back at twice the speed. "Me?! What?!"

"Somebody with the opposing law firm leaked a few of your emails. The private ones, intended for me."

"*Leaked* them?"

"Yes, ma'am." There was a strange finality to his words that made her shake her head in disbelief.

"You can't be serious!"

"I thought I had a handle on it," explained Zuckerman, "that's why I hadn't bothered you."

"But how could they even get a hold of on your emails?"

"I'm so sorry. I still don't know how it happened," Zuckerman said, glancing at his sideview mirrors and merging into north-bound I-35 traffic. "Andy McCormick got his hands on your emails."

"*The* Andy McCormick?" Camila asked, a wave of sheer terror running down her spine.

"Yes. Word on the street is there's a scathing article coming out tomorrow in *The Austin Chronicle*."

"That's all attorney-client privilege!" screamed Camila. "Didn't anybody at your *other* defense firm read the files before *they* turned them over to the other side? Those emails were for your eyes only!"

"You know how many thousands of emails are stored in our servers?" countered Zuckerman, afraid Camila was going to have a meltdown.

"But your attorneys should have purged the emails that contained attorney-client communications!" Camila wanted to punch the dashboard. She was ready to draw and quarter whoever had dropped the ball.

"I'm sorry."

"Jesus! I insulted every single type of immigrant in some of those emails . . . at least that's how it'll be interpreted. The press will make me look like a fucking bigot!"

"I'm gonna make it right," blurted Zuckerman.

"How?!" screamed Camila. "You can't unring this bell! I'M SCREWED!"

"There's gotta be something we can do, right?"

"It's Sunday evening," Camila cried. "Even if I e-filed a lawsuit tonight and requested a restraining order, I can't get *The Austin Chronicle* served in time. Every Tom, Dick and Harry in Austin will have read the story by then, will have taken the emails out of context, and my life as we know it will be over. It's all too late."

"But . . ."

Camila cut him short. "Haven't you been reading the news?! I'm about to become another casualty of outrage. What do you think happens to people whose very private, very inappropriate emails, get leaked? You think they get to apologize and move on? That they are forgiven? This could very well be the nail in the coffin, and I'm holding *you* responsible! "

Zuckerman didn't know what to say. He took the MLK exit, made a U-turn under the expressway and headed toward Barton Springs. The new plan was to stop at Zilker Park, find a bench somewhere, breathe some fresh air and come up with a strategy. He always did his best thinking outdoors or away from the office.

"Take me back," ordered Camila.

"Are you sure? I thought we could go to Zilker . . . put some sort of plan together. Mitigate the damage."

"I need to get back now." Her words were a cold curse in his ears.

"Are you sure?" asked Zuckerman.

"Of course, I'm sure. Take that exit! Now! I'd rather be anywhere than here with you in this piece-of-shit truck. You can understand that, can't you?"

"Yes."

Zuckerman stared straight ahead and kept driving. There was no way of telling how all of this was going to play out. On the one hand, not too many people read *The Austin Chronicle*. On the other, there was always the chance that the story could go viral, pick up a major following. The whole thing could be wrung out by the major networks and thought of as just another boring political fumble, but then again who knew what hit with the public and what didn't? It wouldn't be the first time that leaked emails had destroyed someone's career. It had happened to government and university officials, titans of industry, even presidents and army generals. The email had become the modern-day smoking gun.

"Okay, here we are," said Zuckerman as he pulled up to the Hulse offices.

Camila threw her door open.

"What are you gonna do?" asked Zuckerman.

"Brace myself," announced Camila as she jumped out and slammed the door behind her. "Wait for the tsunami to hit."

He shut off the truck. "Camila! Wait!"

She stopped, let out a heavy sigh. Tim's face looked hopeful when she turned around.

"At the very least you can spin it, bring up the sensitivity of outrage culture, how it's ruining the country our forefathers left to us, and state *very strongly* that you were exercising your free speech as an American . . . under the protection of the First Amendment!"

"Tim? Go fuck yourself."

He watched her strut away. Zuckerman turned the ignition half-heartedly. Who was he kidding? Camila Harrison's life was about to come undone.

***

Camila was frantically seeking out Pax down the quiet corridors of La Querencia, the assisted-living facility where her future mother-in-law had resided for the last year. Considered Austin's best life care community, the facility, more akin to a country club, was located in the rolling hills of southwest Austin. It offered its residents everything from bingo nights to wine tasting excursions to regular dances and social mixers.

Camila rode the elevators up and down all five floors, walked all the hallways, but could find neither Pauline nor Paxton. Although it was Sunday evening, she could see the staff tending to the residents, picking up laundry, delivering meals and making the rounds. Camila dreaded this place but she needed to find Pax. It felt like a matter of life and death.

As Camila rushed across the grounds in and around the facility, trying her best not to look like a crazy person, she wondered why she had included racist humor in her emails to Zuckerman in the first place. Was it because she wanted to feel like she was one of the boys? Someone they could trust? True, the emails did not contain graphic photos or demeaning videos, but she had mocked blacks, Mexicans, the poor and other minorities. In today's climate, she may as well have taken part in a beheading. What were her law partners going to say? Her clients? The public? How was Paxton going to react? How could she have been so irresponsible? So reckless? An image of Drew West popped into her head, stopping her dead in her tracks.

A familiar voice shook her out of her stupor. "What are you doing here?"

Pax and Pauline were sitting under one of the arbors located throughout the grounds, watching the sunset, enjoying the soft, evening breeze. *No,* Camila thought, looking at the two of them. *I'm nothing like Drew West. He has no one. I have them.*

Camila bent down to kiss Pauline on the cheek. "You don't mind if I steal him for a minute, do you? It's important."

"No, dear. Of course, not," said Pauline with a look of concern. Old as she may have been, not much got by her.

Pax was now more curious than ever. "What's going on, Camila? Is everything okay?"

"Walk with me," she said, her heart pounding. She pointed to another arbor about twenty feet away. "We'll keep an eye on Pauline from over there."

The two sat. On any other day the arbor would have seemed like a serene place to sit at the end of the week. Now it just felt like a precursor to the end of everything. "Have you heard of the Katy Wallace scandal?"

"Oklahoma Attorney General Katy Wallace? The one that's being recalled from office?" Pax asked.

"Yes."

"Who hasn't? It also involved two Oklahoma Supreme Court justices who were forced to resign for using state computers to exchange porn."

"Correct," replied Camila.

"Why are you bringing it up?"

"And you know how Madame Secretary of State also got in trouble over some emails?"

"Get to the point, Cam." Pax was growing uneasy.

Camila gulped hard. She rubbed her sweaty palms and bit her lower lip. "I think I screwed up."

"Excuse me?"

Camila fanned her face with her hands. "It's getting hot. I'm sorry. Give me a second."

"You're worrying me, Camila. What's going on?"

She blurted it out. "One of my clients who's in litigation inadvertently produced to opposing counsel some private emails in discovery. The other side leaked the emails to the press. Some of those emails were mine . . . and they had offensive material in them."

Pax was stunned. He got up and started pacing around. "Come again? Offensive material?"

"Yes."

"What kind?" followed Pax, "Sex pictures? Are you cheating on me? Are you?"

"No! Baby, of course not. I love you. Nothing like that."

"Then what are we talking about?"

"Well . . . " muttered Camila, wringing her hands, "I didn't use the N-word . . . but I did refer to some minorities as 'scum,' 'beaners,' 'flamers' and made fun at their expense. I think one of the emails made a reference to a 'towelhead.'"

"You're kidding me." Paxton was in shock. It was worse than he'd first imagined.

"I'm sorry, baby," Camila said, tears in her eyes. "I never thought something like this could happen."

Pax began pulling his hair. He wanted to scream, kick or punch the arbor until it came crashing down, but Pauline was watching. He struggled to restrain himself. "Okay, so somebody leaked them. Now what? How do we stop it?"

"That's just it," admitted Camila, completely out of ideas. "I called *The Austin Chronicle*'s editor at home, about an hour ago. I threatened to sue her and the paper if they ran with the story. I told her that those emails contained attorney-client communications, that they were private. She didn't buy it. In fact, she laughed at me, said that unless I had served her or *The Austin Chronicle* with a lawsuit and a restraining order, they were going to run with it. She said there was no way of stopping the publication; the edition had been printed and it was already being distributed. She hung up on me."

Pax ran his hands through his hair, turned to Camila. There was nothing but contempt in his eyes. It was a look she had never seen on his face before. It was clear; a chasm had opened between them. "How many times have I told you that you need to watch what you say and how you say it? But you just can't fucking listen!"

He turned to make sure Pauline had not heard, then continued.

"Now it's come to bite you in the ass! And no one's gonna save you, Camila Harrison. No one! Not your friends, not your law partners, not your clients, certainly not Austin. And not me."

"But . . . but," cried Camila, "we're a team, no? We can get through this together, right, baby?"

She tried to grab his hand, get him to sit down next to her. She needed assurances. She needed to know that everything was going to be okay, that they could work through this minor crisis together, like loving couples did.

He pushed her away.

Paxton Thomas knew that scandals like this had spelled the end of many political careers. He was not about to let the same happen to him. He'd worked too hard to get to the Texas Supreme Court. Emails with obscene words by themselves could be construed as offensive enough, but emails mocking and demeaning

Jews, Muslims, Mexicans, African Americans, the poor or the une-
ducated were a black hole, with *no* chance of escape. And even
more damning coming from a successful, educated, white
female—and half-Mexican or not, she would be branded by the
media as an elite white woman. As soon as her firm's clients found
out about the emails they would run for the hills, switch firms.
Hulse was about to take a major hit in the pocket, and Camila Harrison was going to pay dearly for it. Scandal was inevitable.

Paxton started crying, uncontrollably. He could see the sharks
circling, and he and Camila were right in the middle.

"Why are you crying, baby?" asked Camila, confused. "I'm the
one in trouble here."

"Because . . . " sobbed Pax, "this means you and I are finished.
I have to call it quits. And even then, my name is still muddied.
I'm sorry. *Res ipsa loquitur.*"

"What do you mean? You can't be serious?!"

"It is what it is. I knew it was too good to be true. How could
I not see? How could I be so stupid?" Pax was sobbing and shaking his head. "Just my freakin' luck! I finally find the girl I want
to build a life with, and she turns out to be dumb as dirt. What the
hell were you *thinking*?!"

Again, Drew West entered her mind.

"It was just a slip," indicated Camila, "a freak accident. How
was I supposed to know that West—I mean Zuckerman—was so
stupid as to let something like this happen?"

"You know that clients do stupid shit," countered Pax. "Hell,
without stupid clients you and I would be unemployed. You yourself have said it. Why would you assume those emails wouldn't be
leaked? Are there more emails?" Pax was incredulous; instead of
taking responsibility, accepting her guilt and apologizing, she was
trying to deflect blame.

"I don't think so."

"You know what?" asked Pax.

"What?"

"I'm glad this happened now, when I have a chance to get in
front of this, to get away. If we had been married for years or

shared a child—a few children, then I'd never be free of the stig-
ma. Mother had warned me that there was something odd about
you. Now we know. Now I see your true colors, Camila Harrison.
You're a racist."

"You are too!" she cried, denouncing him, watching him gather distance between them. "My law partners are too. The business
and legal worlds are *full* of racists and hypocrites. So, what's the
difference?"

"The difference is you got caught! Sure, society may suspect
it, may *expect* it even, but society doesn't like to hear it proven, out
in the open. You went too far. You lost. I mean, you know we're
not supposed to put anything in writing. You're a lawyer, for God's
sake! I don't wear my racism on my sleeve . . . for the world to see.
There's a place and time for everything. Unfortunately for you, us,
our time is up. I'm sorry."

The words lingered in the air for what seemed like an eternity.

"Are you shitting me? You're gonna stand there and act all
high and mighty?" Camila stood there, arms crossed and tears
flowing down her cheeks. "I thought you loved me. My flaws, my
strengths . . . everything?"

"I loved the smart, savvy professional who knew how to control herself, who knew how to rise," muttered Pax, sounding
almost impersonal. "You know, I always wanted to go further than
my dad. Do more than just help a small farming community. I
decided to do something great for the State of Texas, and I've
worked really hard to get to where I am today, to make that dream
come true. But I swear to God, Camila, I'm not gonna let some
bimbo ruin it for me."

He turned around and shuffled back to Pauline.

"Oh, so now you run to mommy?" yelled Camila, betrayed.

He never looked back, simply smoothed his hair, his shirt as
he made his way to Pauline. As if Camila was a ghost, lost to some
other realm and unable to be heard or felt. As if they had never

really existed in the same place at all. Cut off, just like that. She could only stare at him in disbelief.

She snapped back to reality when she heard Pauline's voice in the distance: "And don't you think you're keeping that engagement ring! *Com-pren-day*?!"

FOUR

Levinson stood by his office window, watching the US and Texas flags fly over the Texas Capitol. Across the spacious office, Lindsey, his paralegal, was carrying in a stack of *The Austin Chronicle* newspapers. "Mr. Levinson, where would you like me to put these newspapers? These are from the dispensing machine outside our building."

"Latest edition?"

"Yes, sir, just delivered," answered Lindsey.

Levinson continued staring out the window. He let out a sigh full of frustration, followed by curse words, then turned around. "I want the head of HR and Donald McCombs in my office, ASAP! And I want you to track down Ms. Harrison and have her attend this meeting. It's important. Tell her to drop everything she's doing."

"Yes, sir." She set the stack on the conference table and made her way out.

A moment later, the door to Levinson's office flew open. It was Donald McCombs.

"Jesus Christ!" cried McCombs, "My wife just called. I went online. What a shitshow!"

McCombs was the firm's media relations officer, the de facto crisis manager when problems arose. He looked more annoyed than angry.

Levinson growled at Lindsay through the desk intercom: "Go get Harrison. Get her ass in here!"

He pointed McCombs to a chair.

"You might want to turn on the TV," indicated McCombs as he took his place at the circular table with the stack of *Chronicles*. "My wife said they're talking about the scandal on channel eight."

Rob Oliveira, the creator, producer and host of the public affairs TV show *Buenos Días, Austin!* was interviewing none other than local beat reporter Andy McCormick. During the interview McCormick discussed some of his past investigative exploits, the corruption in the judiciary, how the local DA had recently gotten arrested for drunk driving and the allegations leveled at the Texas attorney general, stating that he was involved in investor and securities fraud.

After allowing McCormick to bolster his own image for about ten minutes, Oliveira cut in. "This morning, your paper, *The Austin Chronicle*," Oliveira held a copy of the local newsweekly, "ran a story on some leaked emails you were able to get your hands on. Why don't you tell us a little bit about that. What's in those emails? Why did you think writing the article was important?"

"Well," said McCormick, tugging at his suspenders, "more than anything the emails are a window into the way lawyers at some big firms here in town view the lower ninety-nine percent of society."

"Really?" Oliveira turned to look at the camera with wide eyes. McCombs cracked a knuckle. *That's right. Sell it, Rob.* "Are you saying lawyers are part of this nation's one percent?"

"I'm saying they're an embarrassment. To think that this level of bigotry still exists today, in one of the most liberal cities in the United States . . . and we have very telling, very revealing emails that show how these folks, the people in power, the one-per-centers—the movers and shakers of Austin—really feel about the average . . . José."

McCombs had to smile at that one. Levinson, on the other hand, wanted to punch the walls.

"Were the emails the result of a hack? Were they attained through illegal means?"

"Oh no," said McCormick, "let's be very clear: There was no hack. These emails were voluntarily produced and turned over pursuant to discovery in a public lawsuit, a contentious lawsuit involving one of the largest developers of commercial properties in Central Texas and a national clothing chain. The emails are from the developer's attorney—one in particular."

Oliveira took a breath, on approach. McCombs could practically hear the host winding up. It never failed to make him shake his head; the fact that a bad actor on the big screen was laughed at, but a bad actor behind a news desk was trusted. As if on cue, Oliveira looked right down the barrel of the camera, a dime-store expression of innocence on his face, as if he hadn't been given her name hours ago, practiced it to himself during make-up hundreds of times. "And who might that be?"

McCormick seemed to be relishing his fifteen minutes of fame. McCombs had heard through the grapevine that just a few days earlier, big-firm attorney Camila Harrison had given him the cold shoulder when he'd approached her to ask her some simple questions about the ordinance on rent control. And now he was about to get his payback. Revenge was best served cold . . . in front of thousands of TV viewers.

"The attorney at the center of this major controversy is a partner at Hulse," said a smiling McCormick.

"*The* Hulse law firm?"

"*The* Hulse," replied McCormick, "Austin's own and oldest."

"No!" said Oliveira, as he covered his mouth, sounding horrified. *And the Oscar goes to . . .*

"Yes, the emails involved came from one of Hulse's top attorneys, Camila Harrison—the youngest person to ever make partner, I believe."

McCormick nodded his head.

"Not the Camila Harrison we all love and admire? Are you sure?" Oliveira pretended his shock was now tinged with a sliver of betrayal. "The attorney that's engaged to be married to . . . to Texas Supreme Court Justice Paxton Thomas III?!"

McCormick smiled for the audience at home. "The one and only."

"But what's in those emails? What could be so damning?" followed Oliveira, as he pointed to his show's producers to project the actual emails onto a large screen.

The emails between Harrison and Zuckerman painted a sad picture for the commercial developer and Harrison's firm. The racial epithets that would fill the home viewer's TV screens were stark and damning on the white electronic background.

Oliveira shook his head, palm cradling his chin. "I would just like to take a moment to apologize to our viewers for some of the language there. What is Hulse saying?"

"Not much," said McCormick, flashing a wide grin. "They're keeping mum, as you can imagine."

"Tell you what, let's take some time to go to commercial," announced Oliveira. "Don't change the channel, folks. When we come back, we're gonna go in-depth on this latest scandal to rock the city of Austin. I tell you, I am just dumfounded by these developments, just completely bowled over. And later you'll also hear from Chef Alejandro Zisnèr! He'll teach us how to make the quickest, simplest recipe for tandoori chicken tacos. You won't want to miss it. It'll be delicious."

"They *sound* delicious, Rob," McCormick added.

The show's theme music came up as Oliveira and his guest leaned forward and whispered into each other's ears.

Camila sat alone on one side of the conference table. Facing her from the other side were Managing Partner James Levinson with phone to his ear, media relations officer Donald McCombs, and Minnie Crane, the head of HR. The air was tense. In the middle of the table sat a large stack of *The Austin Chronicle*.

Levinson finished the call and asked Camila, "You know who that was?"

"No," she said, close to trembling.

"That was Texas Supreme Court Chief Justice Bronte Dominguez. He and Justice Thomas just finished reading and discussing the article. The justices, Thomas in particular, want to distance themselves from you. Justice Thomas is putting out a press release later on today stating the engagement was called off. My condolences," he added with a sniff. "You have brought shame on the court, shame on the profession, shame on this firm. Look at you; a triple-threat girl."

McCombs and Crane stared at her, their approval of Levinson's statement was palpable.

Levinson pounded the conference table and growled, "What exactly were you thinking?"

"I wasn't," apologized Camila, sinking deeper into her chair.

"What a scandal this is!" muttered Levinson.

McCombs and Crane nodded.

"A nightmare. My God, Camila, why would you want to throw it all away? Why would you say such things in an email, exposed, our ass hanging out in the breeze?"

"I've heard you use those same words," pointed out Camila, "the exact same words."

"But not in a goddamned email!" Levinson's fist came down on the table once more.

Camila was treading water. "Those were confidential and privileged communications between a client and his counsel. No one had the right to see them."

"Sure," said McCombs from across the table, "in your dreams."

"In a perfect world," added Crane.

"You let your guard down, Cam. Pure and simple." McCombs exhaled.

"You should have known better, Counselor," added Crane. "That's the number one rule in this business: Watch what you write."

"Exactly!" barked Levinson. "You don't think that all of the classified information that Assange and his associates stole from the NSA was top secret? And what about all of the counterintelligence material leaked by Bradley Manning and others? Of course it was! But once John Q. Public gets a hold of them, confidentiality means nothing! You can't unring that bell."

"Hey!" snapped Camila, "I didn't cause this problem. It was my stupid client who turned over those emails to the enemy lawyers. A client, which if I recall correctly, was shoved down my throat by the assignment committee when nobody wanted to deal with him because he was a 'moron with millions.' Those were the chair's words, not mine."

Levinson was about to get in Camila's face when his cell phone rang. "Yessir?" he said and headed to the window. It was Texas Governor Gwayne Patterson, Levinson's close friend. Levinson silently nodded his head in agreement while the others watched. "Okay. Yes, sir. Consider it done, Governor."

He hung up and walked away from the window.

"*The* Governor?"

"Camila," started Levinson, ignoring her question, "I think you know why we had to call this meeting. My phone has been ringing off the hook. You can see that. I'm getting calls from everywhere."

At that very moment, Levinson's phone rang again. He looked at the screen and showed it to Camila. "See? That's US Senator Branson."

He looked over to McCombs and Crane.

"I need to call him back. *Outside* my office," said Levinson. He turned back to Camila. "When I come back, I need you gone. Get your severance package from Mrs. Crane here, figure out your 401k situation . . . Talk to Don about any other potentially damaging emails that can come back and bite us in the ass AND LEAVE!"

A silence, a stillness filled the room in the wake of his explosion.

Levinson took a breath, cleared his throat. "Oh, and do leave without making a scene, Cam. It would not go well for you otherwise." He moved toward the door.

"But, but . . . " muttered Camila, eyes pleading to McCombs and Crane, "you can't fire me just like that, can you? I just took out a home equity loan on my Westlake house to pay for my wedding! I need this job . . . I've got student loans and credit cards. I already paid the deposit on a banquet hall for the wedding . . . ."

McCombs and Crane stood and looked away, embarrassed.

Camila stood up and begged Levinson, "Don't I deserve a second chance? I gave this firm my blood, sweat and tears."

Levinson stared away, considering. The voice that came out was that of a disappointed patriarch. "And to top it off, you go and write those emails on our firm's email account. I can see a situation where maybe it had been your own personal account that you were using to communicate with your clients, after hours. But you put all of us at risk. You exposed the firm to shame, ridicule and contempt. Our reputation is the only thing this firm has that's above-reproach, Camila, and now you've ruined that for all of us."

McCombs and Crane looked at Camila, and shrugged. They were not about to stick their hands in the fire for anyone, much less a disgraced lawyer.

"In fact, after you clear your office and leave this building," said Levinson, cell at the ready, "I would also recommend you leave Austin. Don't stick around. Do us all a favor, move as far away as you can."

He turned and strolled out of the conference room. McCombs and Crane followed suit.

"Yes! Senator Branson," Levinson announced loudly to everyone within earshot, "what can we do for you? Oh, you've heard? Sorry about that. Don't worry, though, we've taken care of the problem."

FIVE

Houston, Texas. One month later.

"How nice of you to join us, Ms. Harrison," uttered Administrative Law Judge Harlan Murray, without looking up from the computer monitor perched on his bench. "How's Houston treating you?"

"Good morning, Your Honor," Camila replied, taking her seat next to a smelly client, a broad smile plastered to her face. "Houston's great! Glad to be here."

Since landing in Houston, she'd hired on with Alan Sorelle and was starting make some headway into the world of social security disability law. Sorelle was a family friend of Thelma Issa, Camila's closest friend. It was not a glamorous job by any means, but at least it gave her a foot in the door. Plus, the other social security disability practitioners in town had apparently never heard of Camila Harrison, the email scandal or her legal troubles. For now, she would eat humble pie and go about the business of reinventing herself. Such was life.

Judge Murray looked away from his monitor momentarily. "Since the previous hearing cancelled . . . I figured we'd get started . . . get the preliminaries out of the way. Did you see the waiting area when you came in?"

"Yes, I did, Your Honor."

How could she not? Camila had gaped at the large crowd; some people waited in wheelchairs, others in crutches, they were hooked to portable oxygen tanks, a few also sported neck braces, arm slings and head bandages. The Office of Hearings and Appeal's reception area looked more like a makeshift ER in a war-torn country than a federal office building. This was a far cry from representing millionaire land and urban developers in Central Texas.

"That's why I started early," Murray followed, "got to move those cases. Social security claims are—I hate to say it—society's new bite at the welfare apple."

Although folks thought of the rooms where the hearings were conducted as small courtrooms, the reality was that these proceedings were rather informal and nothing like a real trial. Conference Room No. 5, where Murray presided over the disability hearing, was nothing more than a converted conference room with an elevated bench platform for the judge to sit on.

Abutting the judge's bench was a large, rectangular table where the participants sat. On one side of the table, a vocational expert and a medical expert, the two experts retained by the government to testify on behalf of the Social Security Administration; across, facing the experts, sat Mr. Todd Richardson with his counsel, Camila Harrison, Esquire.

"Before you came in, Ms. Harrison," explained Judge Murray, "the medical expert already concurred that your client's herniated disks do, indeed, meet the guidelines. So, I was asking Mr. Richardson about his background, work history, job duties, skills, qualifications, things like that . . . the vocational expert has yet to testify."

The vocational expert was none other than Vernon VonWagner, a very fit sports psychologist with a Ph.D. in physical therapy and rehabilitation. Before letting Camila loose to try her hand at the hearings, Alan Sorelle had said that VonWagner liked to gather his own evidence in an effort to discredit all claimants. He was tough, tactical. Alan had joked that VonWagner had never met an octogenarian that couldn't climb Mount Everest or drive an eighteen-wheeler.

"Did we miss anything?" asked Judge Murray. "Is there something you would like to add?"

Why is VonWagner smirking? thought Camila. *What is he up to?*

"I can take it from here, Your Honor." Camila cleared her throat and gathered her thoughts. "Did Mr. Richardson tell the court that he worked as a cook all his life? That the only two places he worked at were at the Olive Garden by Reliant Stadium and the Popeye's on Wheeler Street? That he's got a limited set of transferable skills and two herniated disks? That he's going to need surgery?"

"He did. If I understand correctly, he's saying he can no longer do his job. He can no longer cook, correct? Or stand for long periods of time?" asked Judge Murray. "Thus, he's unable to maintain substantial gainful employment?"

Mr. Richardson nodded his head.

"Correct. And he takes pain medication—every day—which would make him drowsy and a danger to himself and others in the kitchen. Also, the combination of pain medication and anti-inflammatories force him to have to lie down and take a nap every four or five hours. No employer out there will hire a man such as Mr. Richardson, and . . . "

"Well, that was going to be my next question," the judge interrupted Camila, "have you seen these?" Judge Murray was waiving a stack of photos with his right hand. He handed the stack to the assistant on his right, who presented them to Camila. "Take a look at those . . . please show them to your client."

VonWagner suddenly displayed a proud, wicked smile. The pictures had been his doing.

"Okay," Camila muttered as she glanced at the pictures. She tried to remain composed. *So this is what Alan had been talking about. That sick little bastard. Shit . . . now what?*

In the photos Richardson could be seen tending with ease to a large barbecue smoker mounted on a trailer. The portable pit sat in the parking lot of a church. He was surrounded by members of the church's men's club, apparently having a great time—laughing, smiling, holding up pieces of smoked chicken—while bending, stooping, even standing with and carrying ice chests full of cooked chicken to a work station. Other photos showed Richardson moving large pots of food from one place to another.

"Would you mind asking your client about those?" asked the judge.

The others in the room sat up straight, eagerly awaiting Richardson's response, practically salivating.

Camila cleared her throat, her head spinning as she tried to assess the situation and do some quick damage control.

I got this, thought Camila. *No need to panic.*

"Counselor," Judge Murray called out, "are you going to ask him about the photos? We're waiting."

Camila fumbled with the pictures in her hand and could feel her anxiety level starting to climb. Finally, after about thirty seconds, she calmed her nerves, turned to face her client and asked, "Is that you in these pictures?"

Judge Murray rolled his eyes.

Mr. Richardson grabbed the stack, pulled it close and examined a few photos carefully. "Yes, I think so. But if not he's a handsome devil."

Judge Murray leaned forward, unamused, so did VonWagner and the female medical expert.

"And when were these photos taken?" asked Camila, trying to find a way to dig herself and her client out of the hole.

"That's our church's yearly fundraiser. We sell barbecue plates to raise money for the pantries and soup kitchens in our area of town."

"What month was it?" followed Camila, trying to get the juices flowing, rehabilitate her client, as well as buy some time to think and get her own nerves under control.

"Uh . . . oh! Last February. It was cold . . . see here? We're all wearing winter clothes. Underneath my jacket I'm wearing a brace, a support belt for my lower back. Of course, you can't see it; in the pictures I've got my bulky jacket on, plus the apron. That back brace is so uncomfortable I can usually only wear it for an hour or two."

Now we're making headway. Camila quickly realized the photos did not show the complete picture, an accurate representation. There were always two sides to every story.

"And I had taken probably twelve ibuprofen or Aleve pills . . . .
I always carry them with me." Mr. Richardson shifted in his chair
and pulled a large bottle of pain medication from his pant pocket.
"That day, I'd skipped the prescription painkillers and anti-inflammatories . . . so I wouldn't get drowsy. The pain was continuous,
but it was the only way I could help my church. When I'm in such
pain, I offer my suffering to God. I ask God to protect my loved
ones, my grandchildren . . . . I can put up with a day of horren-
dous suffering in exchange for the Lord keeping my loved ones
safe. I've even prayed for you recently, Ms. Harrison . . . that you
find your rightful place here in Houston."

VonWagner scoffed. Judge Murray gave him a stern look.

Camila ignored VonWagner. "Thank you, sir. I sure could use
some prayers. Now," she pressed on, seeing a tiny opening to sock
it to Murray and the two experts, maybe the entire Social Security
Administration even. "So, are you saying that when you take the
prescribed pain medication, combined with the anti-inflammato-
ry, you can or cannot work? Can you elaborate?"

Judge Murray inched forward, so did the others, save Von-
Wagner, who was now pretending to be bored and had started
yawning.

Richardson smiled. "I can work in spurts . . . I cannot work a
regular eight-hour shift. I have to nap constantly throughout the
day. The hydrocodone makes me clumsy and sleepy." He then
pointed at the pictures sitting on the table. "Those pictures are
very deceiving. The day of the fundraiser . . . the pain was severe.
Think of someone stabbing you with screwdrivers all around your
lower back . . . that kind of pain. The only thing that made it bear-
able, other than the brace and the ibuprofen, was the friends
around me, making me smile."

"How would you label the pain, on a scale from one to ten?"
followed Camila.

"A fifteen . . . just horrible," answered the client without hesitation.

Judge Murray paid special attention, gauging Richardson's
credibility.

"But I always help my church. Like I said . . . I just figure I'd offer my pain to God. What the pictures don't show . . . " Richardson paused, then looked to Judge Murray. "Can I get up and stretch a bit, Your Honor? I can't sit for too long. My back grows stiff . . . my legs start to tingle, like a burning sensation."

"Please," allowed Murray.

Richardson got up slowly, pushed his chair back, obviously in pain. He leaned on the conference table for support. "As I was saying," he struggled to resume his testimony, "that day I helped for about three hours, then I was spent. After I got home I soaked in a hot bath for hours, took more pain medication . . . and then went to sleep for two whole days, trying to recover."

Judge Murray and the others in the hearing room appeared to be impressed with Richardson's sincerity.

Everyone but VonWagner, of course.

"I'm sorry Murray started the hearing without me," Camila apologized. The pair headed out of the building, slowly walking toward the parking garage across the street. "Overall, I think it went well, don't you?"

"I thought Mr. Sorelle was gonna represent me," Richardson said bluntly. "Last time I talked to him, he didn't say anything about an assistant handling the hearing."

"I'm going to be helping Alan," Camila explained, "for a while, anyway . . . . I'm the new associate at his firm."

"Well, I'm just glad somebody showed up. I was getting worried. How long before we get a decision?"

"Alan says six to nine months. The judges are swamped and sometimes it takes them a while to get around to writing their decisions. I mean, you saw the waiting area . . . I don't have to tell you."

Richardson stood there, scratching his head, not really liking the lawyer's explanation. He had first applied for disability benefits from Social Security two years ago now and was getting tired of the unnecessary denials, reconsiderations and appeals. "Is it more like six months? Or nine months? Any idea?"

"I couldn't really say. I've heard of people having to wait *eighteen months* to get a decision . . . and sometimes, it isn't even a favorable one."

Richardson looked as if he was about to cry, but before he could say anything else, two attorneys stopped the pair. Camila motioned to Richardson to go on without her, seeing the recognition in their eyes. She would call him later.

"Hey, aren't you the attorney from Austin that leaked emails?" asked the male attorney. "Didn't you get in trouble with the State Bar?"

"Yeah," followed the female lawyer, "we thought we'd recognized you . . . ."

"That's me," Camila replied, embarrassed. "Privileged attorney-client communications . . . should have never been leaked."

The male stepped in. "Oh, well . . . shit happens."

"Tell me about it. Sure learned a valuable lesson," followed Camila.

"By the way," asked the female, showing genuine concern, "are you coming out to Vegas? For the annual SSA Disability Practitioners' convention? We'd love to have you."

Camila hesitated, unsure of how to respond. She could not believe how direct, yet friendly, the attorneys were. Years earlier, after struggling to finish law school while helping Darin recover at the Texas Heart Institute, she'd sworn never to return to Houston. But now, the way everyone was making her feel, she was starting to feel different about the city.

"I don't know. I'll have to think about it. It's just . . . I've got some stuff cooking on the back burner. Thanks for the invite, though."

"What kind of stuff?" asked the female lawyer. "Can you say?"

Camila smiled a polite smile. "I'm trying to pick up some criminal appointments in federal court . . . do something different . . . . I don't know that Social Security disability law is for me."

"You're also doing criminal law?" asked the male attorney. He looked surprised, but reached out. "Do you happen to have a business card with you?"

"That's good to know," followed the female. "We sometimes get calls at the office and we don't know who to refer them to. This is all we do; disability hearings."

Camila took a card from her purse and handed it over.

"Hey, I'll hang onto this. If something pops up," said the male attorney, "we'll send them your way."

"Sure," said Camila, pleasantly surprised to have two complete strangers go out of their way to make her feel welcome in the Bayou City. "Thank you."

SIX

The office-sharing arrangement involved a converted triplex with saggy hardwood floors, creaky doors and rattling AC window units installed throughout. There was a reception area and a conference room, along with six bedrooms converted to attorney suites. It was a far cry from Camila's former castle in the sky.

The building's foundation was pier and beam, which over the years had created serious structural and support issues. It also needed a new roof, the old one having been replaced twenty years earlier, during which time it had been damaged by at least two hurricanes. With an insurance settlement to compensate him for the exposed roof beams and broken windows, Alan Sorelle decided to invest the money in stocks instead of repairing the building. It was a move he regretted more than once over the years as, one by one, the majority of the old tenants moved out due to the building's bad plumbing and worsening state of disrepair.

"Hey," said Julio, the receptionist, when he saw Camila slide by on her way to her suite. "How did it go with Mr. Richardson?"

Julio also hailed from Austin, Texas. Camila discovered that Julio had been in a toxic ten-year relationship with a man named Brandon. They had met at Red Lobster, where Brandon tended bar and Julio waited tables. When things had not worked out between them, Julio moved to Houston, where he started working with Sorelle. After six years, he ran the day-to-day operations at the office with ease.

"No issues," replied Camila, politely.

"Do you want your messages?" Julio asked, waving two pink slips in the air.

Camila paused. "I've got messages? *Really?*"

"And you have mail. You want it?"

"Mail?"

"Papers bundled together, usually small and white, with your name on them. You want it?"

Camila rolled her eyes. Julio came out from behind his desk, grabbed a half-inch stack of letters from a tray nearby and looked for the mail addressed to Camila.

"You know what? I remember now . . . Alan has your mail, or at least I wanna say I saw some letters addressed to you. Hmm . . . either way Alan said he wanted to talk to you."

"Thanks," said Camila.

"But here are your messages."

Camila grabbed the pink slips from Julio's hands and scanned his handwriting on the pieces of paper. "Okay, Thelma called. I'll get back to her in a bit." She stuffed the message in her coat pocket, then read the other slip. "Pax decided to show his face too, huh? Interesting."

"*The* Paxton Thomas! He was sobbing when he called, FYI. I mean, he wasn't crying hysterically or anything. He was more like sniffling. Yes, that's it. Sniffles."

"Guy suffers from allergies," said Camila. "He's super allergic to cedar. I'm sure that's all it was."

"No," Julio corrected her, "he wanted to say something about a funeral."

Camila read the rest of the message. "Pauline?"

"Yes, that was it. Pauline."

Camila turned around, crumpled Pax's message and shoved it in her pants pocket. She would have to think about this one. The wounds were still too fresh.

⁎⁎⁎⁎⁎⁎⁎⁎⁎⁎

Alan Sorelle was in another world entirely, distracted, watching the world financial markets on his computer screen. While it was almost dinnertime in Texas, the markets in Australia and Asia would be up and running soon, and Alan Sorelle was anxious to invest, strike it rich, put some money away and retire early. He'd kiss the legal profession, and all its accompanying headaches, goodbye.

Camila quietly studied Alan as he stood glued to the monitor, mouth agape, oblivious to everything and everyone. *I guess this is part of my penance.*

Alan felt Camila's presence and finally looked away from the monitor. "Hey, how did the hearing go?" He flashed a warm smile.

"Fine. I think the client will get a favorable decision. VonWagner came in with pictures that showed our client smoking chicken at a church fundraiser . . . but I was able to clear it up. It was just like you predicted."

"That miserable punk," said Alan. "He's always pulling stuff like that."

"Did any mail come in for me? Anything from the State Bar?"

"No, nothing from them yet."

A few days earlier, Camila had gotten wind that her old law partners in Austin had filed a grievance, accusing her of unprofessional and unethical behavior. It was nothing more than a way to deflect negative attention from the firm and further distance themselves from their former law partner.

Alan noticed Camila's frown and quickly changed the topic. "But look!" He waived a couple of small manila envelopes in the air.

Twice a month, a trickle of US Treasury checks arrived in the office from disability cases that had been won months back. To Alan, opening the little manila envelopes always felt like opening a Christmas present or birthday gift; it meant having money to invest, throw around and buy toys. *Splurge galore!*

"Is *that* what they look like?"

"Yup, like a tax refund check from the IRS," said Alan. "Same look, same feel, same thing really." He then reached for a white envelope from a pile of mail on his desk. "This also came in for you."

"What is it?" Camila stretched out her hand. "Let's see . . . "

Alan shook his head. "Guess."

He threw the envelope inside his desk's top drawer.

"It's from federal court, isn't it?"

"Right you are. Sure you're up to it?"

"I've practiced plenty in federal court before," replied Camila. "I figure a criminal appointment here or there can't hurt. Besides, it was you who suggested I go by and see Judge Yamamoto. Are you saying I shouldn't do it?"

"I'm not questioning your abilities." Alan retrieved the envelope from the top drawer. "I was wondering if you're ready to play in the big leagues again. Emotionally, mentally . . . that old chestnut."

Camila hated to admit it, but maybe getting booted out of Austin had been God's will. Maybe it was for the better. Maybe there was a bigger plan that, at the moment, was not very obvious to her. But what was the message God was sending? Had she gotten too big for her own britches? Had money and success gone to her head? Why had she landed in Alan's office, in Houston of all places? There had to be a reason.

"It's not a level playing field, you know that." He rubbed his neck. "And the stakes are high. Plus the government always wins. It's what happens. All I'm saying is, it's not for the faint of heart. Some folks can't handle that on their best day."

"Well," she said, "I guess there's only one way to find out."

Alan handed Camila the envelope and returned his attention to the computer screen. "How does it feel to have to start from the bottom up? Picking up appointments in federal court?"

"It's all right." Camila shrugged, "but have you seen some of *your* firm's clients? Not exactly *crème de la crème.*"

"You're right," said Alan, as he studied some graphs and charts on his computer screen. "But they need us, Camila. They have no one else to turn to. You do this long enough, you'll realize why you had to come back here to Houston. Maybe right now it's not obvious to you. I mean, it isn't very glamorous. It's not dinner at Eddie V's, or inauguration balls at the state capital, but you'll feel a great deal of appreciation. You're very lucky. You just don't know it, yet."

"Lucky, huh?" Camila let the words sink in. She studied the envelope.

"Open it," said Alan.

"Here goes nothing." She let out a big sigh.

Camila tore into the envelope, pulled out its contents and started reading.

"What is it?" Alan asked.

"You were right. Federal Judge Colt Yamamoto . . . has just appointed me to my first criminal case." Camila studied the notice of appointment and the complaint. "Is he nice?"

"He's very fair . . . and believes in giving everybody a chance. He has no favorites. If you do a good job, he'll send you more appointments," explained Alan. "That's why I told you to go see him. He was one of my professors in law school, many years ago, before he got appointed to the federal bench."

"I didn't want to believe you. I didn't think it would be that easy."

"There are still some decent federal judges left, believe me. Anyway, you have your federal license, right? Why not use it."

"Yes," answered Camila, waving the notice and envelope in the air, "but it's been a while since I've touched a real criminal case. The last case I helped with in federal court involved a group of San Antonio doctors who got in trouble for over-billing Medicare. I was an associate then, and we all had to take a condensed refresher course to be able to participate in federal court."

"You'll figure it out." Alan looked ready to get back to investing. "There's not much to it, really." Alan turned to the other computer monitor on his desk, becoming distracted again. "Just plea your client out and be done with it; don't sweat the small stuff."

"Just sell him down the river, huh?"

Camila didn't necessarily think that was such a bad suggestion. She was ready to head back to her small office, lock herself up and get busy emailing resumes. Maybe she could land a better job in Dallas, or Washington D.C., maybe even the West Coast. Something with more class. Get out of the muddy trenches. Get some semblance of her old life back.

"Sure, Alan said."

"I like that idea; get in, get out. Dispose of the case quickly. For now, I'll stick with the appointments and see what happens. Maybe something better will come along."

"That's the spirit . . . make the best of it."

"I just hope I don't disappoint my client," said Camila, glancing again at the papers in her hand.

Alan shook his head. "You can't think that way. You're a smart lawyer, and right now you've suffered a small setback. Soon folks will forget about your troubles in Austin and you'll be back on top. Besides, you're learning new things, not to mention learning to deal with a new type of client. Who knows what new door is going to open with those new skills?"

She came back, "I guess you're right."

"You know what the difference is between those that lead successful lives and those who don't?" Alan stared at Camila, waiting for an answer.

"Hard work? Smarts? A narrow vision? Knowing what you want and going for it? Uh . . . winning?"

"Nah," he said as he sat down behind his desk. He invited Camila to do the same.

She accepted the invitation. "Working twice as hard?"

"Look around this place," Alan said, smiling as he pointed to the four walls in his office. "What do you see?"

"Squalor?" she giggled.

Alan chuckled. "What else?"

"An office building that has seen better days? Hmm . . . a lawyer that would rather make his money some other way than practicing law?"

"You're half-correct," said Alan. "It's true, many of my tenants have left because this is an old building with maintenance issues. But, did I get upset? Did I panic? Did I get mad because they breached their leases and left in the middle of the night and stole some of my clients . . . along with some furniture, stuff that I paid for?"

"I don't know, did you?"

"Nah. Maybe a tad disappointed," replied Alan, "but that's not what I'm really asking."

"What are you asking, then?"

"What's the major difference between those who have found success and those who haven't? And I'm not talking about money, power or fame necessarily."

"How are you defining success?"

"Being happy," replied Alan, as he reached for his cell phone and looked at the screen briefly, " . . . feeling fulfilled, productive, accomplished."

"I don't know, Alan." She hated guessing games. "They quit the legal profession! Is that it?"

"Nope." Alan quickly glanced at his computer monitors, then refocused on Camila. "The difference is the way they react to a problem. The way they approach a difficult situation. We all have problems, it's part of life, and no two ways about it. But the difference is how they react to a problem and go about solving it. You can choose to throw a bucket of water on it. Or you can douse it with a bucket of gasoline and make it worse. It's all about perspective and context."

"What are you saying?"

"Think about it. You landed in Houston," Alan pointed out, "in this office, referred by a mutual friend. You should make the best of it. Like I have. Sure, I'm burned out, and there are days when I hate being a lawyer, but I have found other ways to make money. I can quit the practice of law at any time, if I really want to. I'd just have to keep an eye on finances more than I want to. Your prognosis for the future will depend on how you approach whatever problems you face, at any given time. Remember that. Bucket of water or bucket of jet fuel? You know, actually, just regular gasoline . . . jet fuel doesn't burn in the open that easy like in the movies."

Camila shifted in her chair. "Are you saying maybe I should have stuck it out in Austin? That I over-reacted?"

Alan smirked. "Nah, I think jumping ship and coming to Houston was the one thing you did right."

"I tell you what," Camila said, "I also learned a very important lesson . . . don't ever put anything in writing that you don't want people to read."

"That's good," Alan agreed. "Imagine you had not learned any-thing and kept putting damning stuff in your emails, making the same mistake over and over again."

"That wouldn't be good."

"See? So, let me know if you need help with the appointment from Yamamoto. In my day, I used to do a lot of criminal work, federal appointments and such. I still remember a thing or two."

"Well, you want to see the complaint?" Camila unfolded the papers in her hand and handed them to Alan.

Alan tried to read the complaint along with the top portion of the notice of appointment. "Here it is . . . *Beezhantah Haldema*. . . . Shit . . . I can't even pronounce your client's name. It's something or other."

"Let me see that." Camila giggled. She leaned over and looked at the appointment form still in Alan's hands. "The name's *Vicente Aldama*, Counselor."

"Well, go talk to him. Stroke him, calm him down and tell him everything's gonna be okay, all the things he wants to hear. Man-age his expectations, then plea him out. Get him sentenced and submit your payment voucher. It's not complicated just explain to him what's going to happen."

"You don't think I should fight? Take it to trial? Take the gov-ernment to the mat?"

Alan clenched his jaw. "You don't win in federal court. It's a losing proposition—always. You're going up against the govern-ment, Counselor. The *United States of America*. Give it up. Besides, who needs the aggravation?"

Alan sighed. Apparently, the earlier advice that he had freely dispensed to Camila had been lost on her. What part of 'bucket of fuel or bucket of water' had Camila Harrison not understood?

"Maybe my guy has a chance. I haven't even seen the evidence. Why are you being such a downer?"

"Don't make it difficult," followed Alan. "It doesn't have to be."

"But I want to do a good job."

"Trust me on this." He flipped the top sheet and glanced at the complaint stapled behind the first page. "It's a simple money-laundering case. It'll be a quick plea. And then you can get back to the exciting world of Social Security disability law. Your guy got caught with his hands in the cookie jar. He has no defense. Besides, it says here that your guy has an ICE detainer. He's not getting out because he's in the country illegally."

Camila studied Alan. Was he serious?

"Just like that?"

"Sure, just get him the best deal possible and plea him out. Move on to the next one."

"Bucket of water, huh?"

"Look, I know how cold that sounds, I've been there. But it's a quagmire, pure and simple. All you have to do is get him to agree to debrief, cooperate and point the finger at a few other criminal targets. Do that, and he'll get a great deal with very little prison time—you'll reduce his sentence from a maximum of twenty years to six or seven. He'll be happy, you'll make a little money. Presto!"

"I'll keep that in mind." Camila got up to leave. "I'll speak with him, see what he wants to do."

"Look, the guy's here illegally. After he finishes his sentence he'll be deported. You'll never see him again. What do you care?"

"I hope you're right." Camila hesitated. "I just never felt very comfortable in federal court. Doing civil work was hard enough. And now, doing criminal, something I haven't done in years, it's kind of scary. And to top it all off, I'm probably dealing with an illegal alien."

"You're just being paranoid," Alan answered, trying to figure out why Camila was suddenly so concerned. The forty-five-year-old attorney tossed the envelope back on top of his desk, where Camila could reach it. He opened the top drawer, found a roll of Tums and popped two in his mouth.

"What an opportunity!" cried out Alan. "You are very blessed. You haven't been in town a month, and you're already handling disability cases and picking up appointments in federal court. Some lawyers never see the inside of a federal courthouse, never get to see the bowels of the beast. You're very lucky, and so is Mr. Aldama. He needs you."

"Next, you're going to say I need him too, right?" Camila rolled her eyes, ready to be done with the pep talk. "Is that what you were going to say?"

Alan shrugged and smiled. "I didn't say it. *You* did."

SEVEN

"Hi Camila, I'm returning your call," said Houston Pan American School of Law Professor Thelma Issa.

"Oh, Thelma, I wanted to let you know that I got appointed to a case in federal court."

"And?"

"I was thinking . . . I could use some help. It's been a long time since I've touched a criminal case. I thought of you. You know, if a legal issue comes up?"

"Sure . . . I'll be glad to help. Whatever you need."

"Alan suggested—although I have my doubts—to just plea the guy, get him a deal and be done. He thinks the experience will get me out of my comfort zone."

"Well . . . I guess that all depends on the particulars of the case . . . ."

"Yeah," agreed Camila, "Alan said most of these are lost causes."

"He would know, he used to do a lot of criminal work. Just keep me posted," said Thelma. "I'll be glad to help. Oh, and when can we get together?"

"I'll call you."

"Promise?"

"I will . . . I promise."

Camila had received Thelma's call while at a bar, where she was mulling over her change of station in life and reacquainting herself with cheap beer. On a TV mounted behind the bartender,

Anderson Cooper was covering a scandal involving a confidential informant who had been exposed for lying on the witness stand. The CI had been caught lying at least thirty times, yet had received thousands of dollars in payments from the DEA and the FBI. In a separate interview with US Senator Phil Branson, chairman of the Senate Committee on Organized Crime, the politician expressed great shock when told that a known perjurer was being put back to work in the judicial system. The senator promised to conduct hearings and to get to the bottom of it.

"How could the government stoop so low and use known liars to secure questionable convictions?" asked the Texas senator. "What's happening to our criminal justice system?"

"Oh, c'mon!" screamed Camila Harrison. The beer buzz she'd been enjoying as she strolled to her car was gone as soon as she spotted a tow truck hooking up her Audi. Its driver was making the final adjustments to some chains, about to jump in the cab, when Camila approached him.

"Hey, man! That's my car! What are you doing?"

The burly driver continued going about his business, but paused to say, "You were parked in an illegal zone."

"Are you serious? I was gone less than fifteen minutes." Camila started pacing back and forth, trying to figure out a way out of the costly mess. "C'mon, cut me a break! What will it take for you to give me my car back?"

"You have to get it from the impound lot, lady." He reached into the pocket of his denim shirt and pulled out a business card. "Company policy. Call this number, they'll tell you what to do."

"You gotta be kidding," complained Camila. She looked toward his name tag. "There's gotta be something we can do . . . Roscoe, is it? Let's come to an agreement, right here, right now, you and me. How much do you need? One hundred bucks?"

The guy walked around his tow truck, giving the setup one final cursory inspection.

"If you give me a minute, I can go inside and use the ATM. What do you say?"

He opened the cab door, pulled out a clipboard and began filling out some forms.

"Please?" begged Camila. She was desperate. She needed her car, especially in Houston, where the distances were vast.

"No can do."

Camila wanted to scream. "I can't believe this. At least let me get a file out of the car."

Roscoe jumped into the cab, gunned the engine and started pulling out with Camila keeping alongside, banging on the passenger door, yelling and trying to get him to stop.

"I need it for federal court, asshole! I will sue you!" threatened Camila as she went around the wrecker and planted herself firmly in front of it.

"You and what army?" yelled the driver. "Move, lady! Get out of the way!"

"Look, I'm a lawyer!" screamed Camila as she banged on the tow truck's hood.

"You're no lawyer."

"Ever heard of a 'peaceable repossession,' asshole?!" yelled Camila. "That's the law in Texas, my friend, and if you keep this up, you'll lose your license and I'm going to shut down your employer. Trust me, you don't want to go there."

Roscoe gunned the engine, trying to get Camila to back away, but she held her ground. She was face to face with the chrome grill of the tow truck.

"Go ahead!" screamed Camila, her blood boiling. "Tap me with your front bumper, dickhead. I'll have you arrested for assault with a deadly weapon."

"Look, lady," yelled Roscoe, throwing his arms up in the air, waves of frustration overtaking him, "I don't know who the hell you think you are, but you need to get out of the way. I'm taking this car, with or without your permission. Get out of the way, or I'm gonna call a cop and have you arrested!"

Just then, when the confrontation was at its zenith, a police cruiser pulled up to the scene. A Hispanic officer in his late thirties with salt-and-pepper hair got out and approached them.

The tow truck driver jumped out of the cab and rushed to the policeman. He read the tag on the officer's uniform. "Officer . . . Castro, this lady is interfering with my job. I need you to have her arrested."

The officer signaled for Camila to come to where he was standing. She obeyed.

"Ma'am, is this your car?"

"Yes, officer," replied Camila. "We have a problem here. I understand this gentleman has a job to do, but the law in Texas states that if the repossession becomes hostile, is carried out in a non-peaceable manner, then the repossession becomes illegal and cannot continue. It's all in the UCC, Chapter 9. I can cite you the case by the Texas Supreme Court, *MBank v. Sanchez*, which discusses peaceable repossessions. You want me to pull it up on Google?"

"Are you a lawyer?" asked Officer Castro.

"She's right," said a female voice.

The trio turned around.

"Who are you?" asked Officer Castro.

"I'm a law professor and a friend of Ms. Harrison," said Thelma, who just happened to walk up. "I'm not here to interfere with your duties, officer, but . . . "

"What about this so-called 'peaceable repossession' bit I just heard from your friend?"

"It's the law in Texas. Once things escalate, the law requires the truck company to back off," Thelma said. "If they don't, that's fine, they will lose in court and pay out the wazoo!"

Officer Castro then turned to the tow truck driver. "Listen, sir, sounds like you have a choice to make; you can take the car against the ladies' wishes, but you're gonna get sued, so is your employer and you could get tagged for a lot of money; or you can unhook the vehicle and turn it over to the owner. What do you want to do?"

Camila shoved her phone in the cop's hand. "Here's the Texas Supreme Court opinion, officer. I'm not pulling your leg, look how much was awarded to the plaintiffs for the wrongful repossession."

Castro tried to find his place on the small phone screen. "1.2 million dollars?!"

"That's correct," Thelma said.

Officer Castro handed back the cell phone. "I suggest you put the car down," said Castro, turning to the tow man, "but it's up to you. I can't stop you, but you know what's gonna happen. You decide."

The driver swallowed his pride, headed toward the back of his tow truck and started lowering the ramp to release Camila's Audi.

"Thank you," said Camila.

"Thank you," added Thelma.

"You think you can email me a copy of that Supreme Court decision?" Castro asked Camila.

"Sure," said Camila, as she gave a look to Thelma.

Thelma nodded 'yes.'

"Here's my email," said Castro, as he handed Camila his business card.

Camila couldn't help but notice the officer's dimples. She shoved his card in her jean's pocket, without looking at it. "I'll email it to you."

Castro got back in his police cruiser, turned off the overheads and merged into traffic.

Thelma and Camila gave each other a "Did you see that hunk?" look.

"He wasn't wearing a ring," observed Thelma.

"Stop!" replied Camila, as they both broke into laughter.

EIGHT

Camila was living in a one-bedroom garage apartment in an area of town called The Heights. Her landlady, Heather Landry, lived alone in a 1930s bungalow in front of the property. At sixty-two years of age, Mrs. Landry had been widowed for a number of years and occasionally relied on her home health provider to drive her to dialysis treatments and the grocery store.

When Camila pulled into the driveway, Mrs. Landry was sitting in her rocking chair on the porch, reading a book and enjoying the breeze. Camila collected her things from the backseat of her car and walked onto the porch.

"How was your day, dear?" asked Mrs. Landry. She put away her novel and pulled out a thin stack of mail from underneath the chair's cushion. "How are things at the office?"

"Great! My car almost got towed, but other than that, I had a good day. I still have to go see my client at the jail for the new court appointment I got," explained Camila.

"You got a new case?" Mrs. Landry remembered the stack of mail in her hand. "Oh, by the way . . . these came for you."

Camila took the stack of envelopes without looking at them. "Thanks." She dropped her purse on the floor and plopped herself down on the wooden steps leading up to the porch. "Didn't I tell you I got appointed to a case in federal court?"

"No, when did that happen?" Mrs. Landry rocked in her chair, happy to hear the news.

"Earlier today," Camila replied, massaging her temples. "Should be interesting."

"That's great news!" Mrs. Landry replied, clutching the paperback close to her chest. Camila tried to feel excited, but just couldn't. She missed Austin. She missed her clients. The city, the energy, the hustle-and-bustle of the big firm . . . she missed it all. She missed Paxton and the idea of getting married.

"Sounds like I'll be representing a guy who's charged with money laundering and possibly illegal re-entry. I haven't even met him . . . but I will, hopefully first thing tomorrow morning . . . find out what's going on."

Mrs. Landry could tell Camila was still hurting from everything that had happened to her. Since Camila had moved in, she had taken a liking to the attorney. At her age, there wasn't much she'd not seen or experienced; she had lost friends to cancer, others had undergone painful divorces or had succumbed to alcoholism, drug addiction, even suicide. She herself had suffered loss as well. Where Camila had lost her fiancé, her job, her impeccable image and reputation, Heather Landry had never been able to experience motherhood. The fact that she'd never been able to get pregnant had impacted her emotionally; the waves of guilt, depression, frustration and anger, had ruled the early years of her married life. After years in therapy, she'd finally realized that God had not wanted to punish her, that God had nothing to do with her inability to have children.

"Let me ask you," said Camila, breaking the silence, "why are there days when I hate being a lawyer? I've been having doubts, something that's never happened before."

"Doubts?"

"Maybe I chose the wrong profession," griped Camila.

Mrs. Landry was perfectly aware of what she meant. Her dad, also an attorney, had always remarked on how many of his lawyer friends felt dissatisfied, unhappy and even inadequate as legal professionals. Her father, fortunately, loved what he did, but he considered himself one of the lucky few.

"Life isn't perfect, Camila. Lawyering isn't easy, either. If it was, every Tom, Dick and Harry would be doing it. Think about it."

"I guess it takes a special kind of person . . . a glutton for punishment."

"That's what dad said his friends used to say," Mrs. Landry recalled, "but he always felt privileged. He felt honored that people would trust him and put their lives in his hands."

Mrs. Landry leaned over and touched Camila on the shoulder, then she placed her hands, slightly touching each other, on her knees, palms up, ready to listen and share.

"Dad often struggled as he prepared for trial," continued Mrs. Landry. "He never failed to get nervous before the big fight. He would have doubts too, but would find a way to put them aside. I guess he could have quit, gone on and found something else to do. But he used to say that living the rest of his life thinking about 'what may have been' would have been worse."

The compassionate landlady paused to see if her words were sinking in, then continued. "Dad would say that the big question was: Would you let others dictate how you lived, or were you ready to create your own experience? It was up to you. The power to change was inside you, all you had to do was decide. Dad always thought he could make a difference. How about *you*, Camila? Are you going to let your past control the rest of your life?"

Camila looked down, considering.

Mrs. Landry looked out into the distance, past the park and jogging trails across from her property, and cracked a smile. "It was never easy for him, even with his strong belief. I would hear him throw up the night before trial . . . he'd even develop a terrible sweat . . . but by the time the first witness took the stand, he was back to normal. The nerves never really went away, but he never quit . . . he kept trying cases until the day he died. He knew the only way to grow and change was to get out of his comfort zone. Maybe you don't hate being a lawyer, maybe you're just scared because you're now out of your comfort zone. You're no longer in Justice of the Peace court, much less state court. You're in federal court now, in *Houston*, about to do a criminal case. You're a litigator now."

"Maybe . . . maybe it's nerves."

"What matters is that you're willing to get back in the saddle."

Camila remained quiet, digesting her landlady's words. *From representing millionaires to indigent illegal aliens—I wouldn't call that getting back in the saddle.*

Mrs. Landry stopped talking and looked down at her hands. She was gauging Camila, who, by now, was also looking out into the distance.

※

Back in her apartment, Camila stood in front of the full-length mirror in her closet. She was half-naked, turned away, studying her back by looking over her right shoulder with a small hand mirror. In her left hand she held an envelope from the State Bar of Texas. Probably the notice letter that a grievance had been filed against her.

She continued taking inventory: Growing up in Mexico City, her parents' divorce, the move to Austin, Rice U, rooming with Thelma, Dante de Melo, law school, the engagement to Paxton, her wedding plans, her soaring legal career, the leaked email scandal. The fall from grace. She was amazed at how fast the tables had turned. And now, the most interesting and ironic twist was that she had just been appointed to represent an undocumented man. In federal court, no less.

She turned and studied her face in the full-length mirror. Where did these feelings come from? Paxton had always wanted to know, but she had refused to answer his questions. He had warned her to be careful, to show restraint, to watch her words, but she had refused to listen. How long could she go on like this? Could she ever let go? Forgive? One thing was clear: things had taken a turn for the worse after Dante's passing.

As she studied her reflection in the mirror, Camila felt the painful sting of irony. Had Lorena not meddled and allowed the marriage to go forward as planned, Dante would still be alive, and the couple would be living happily-ever-after down in Rio de Janeiro. Instead, Camila had allowed Lorena to convince her, manipulate her and make her wait until Dante finished his studies and Camila had graduated from law school. But then, the unthinkable had happened. The week that would have found the couple enjoying their honeymoon, away from Houston, had been the week that Dante had crossed paths with Miguel Lazcano, a twenty-something Mexican national fleeing from the police.

Lazcano had blown past a stop light. Her fiancée never stood a chance. The blood tests revealed that Lazcano had cocaine in his system and a blood-alcohol content three times the legal limit. In years past, Dante's killer had been deported to Mexico three times, yet had managed to come back. During this time, Lazcano had racked up multiple convictions for drug possession and burglary. Despite having been expelled from the United States—and warned never to come back—the murderer had paid no heed.

To add insult to injury, Lazcano had managed to squeeze out on bond, right before ICE could place a detainer on him. By the time the intoxicated manslaughter case landed in court, and people figured out what had happened, Lazcano was long gone back to Mexico. He would never face justice.

After the accident, with Thelma by her side, Camila had been tasked with identifying her fiancée at the morgue. That was the first time in her life she had felt real pain. And masked behind the pain, she felt something she had never felt before; it was hate. Waves and waves of it, swelling up inside her. The kind of hate that words cannot describe. It was not the kind of hate that gnawed at your insides, clouded your mind and made you want to grab a gun and go after the person that had caused you such misery. No, it was the kind of hate that was still raw and cruel, festering in the background, that would not let go.

Would it ever end?

NINE

The visiting room was a large rectangle with rows of chairs out in the open for the inmates and their family members to use. Along two of the walls were ten attorney interview rooms. At the opposite end, Camila could see two attorneys visiting with their respective clients inside the soundproof glass cubicles. From her leather courier bag, she pulled out a yellow pad and a pen, as well as her client's file, complete with the complaint and the notice of appointment.

She had written a small outline of things she needed to cover with her client: *immigration status, criminal history, client's version of the events, the legal process, sentencing guidelines and plea options.*

"Your client," interrupted the guard. "Vicente Aldama."

Tall and muscular with short hair, Aldama looked like a scruffy day laborer waiting to do demo work for forty bucks a day.

"*Hola,*" said Camila as she got up to shake his hand. She sized him up. "*Soy su abogada de oficio, Camila Harrison. La corte me asignó su caso para que lo represente.*"

The guard proceeded to remove Aldama's handcuffs. He rubbed his wrists and reached for Camila's hand. "Hola," he replied. He took his seat across the table from her.

The guard turned and walked away. "You want the door open or closed?"

"Closed," said Camila. She clenched her jaw. Here she was, face-to-face with her court-appointed client. The undocumented man, someone who obviously had no regard for the laws of the

United States of America, someone that in all likelihood was here simply to milk the system, avoid paying taxes and commit all sorts of crimes. A deadbeat that had already been deported before and told not to come back. Obviously, the warnings had gone in one ear and out the other. She caught herself and made a mental note to put those feelings aside. *Be objective. Be professional.* She promised to make an effort, keep an open mind and not rush to judgment.

"Okay," replied the guard. "No funny business."

Camila and her client waited until the guard was gone.

"*¿Habla usted inglés?*" asked Camila.

"Yes," replied Aldama with a slight Spanish accent. He was surprised to find out his court-appointed attorney spoke perfect Spanish. After all, she looked like a *gringa* with green eyes, reddish-brown hair and alabaster skin.

Camila looked at her notes, Aldama and the codefendants had already attended the initial appearance. It had been at this hearing that the court determined the trio could not be represented by the Federal Public Defender's Office, alone, because of potential conflict. Thus, McKenzie would be appointed an attorney from the FPD office, while Aldama and Barrera would get their own court-appointed attorneys. The co-defendants had also been advised of the charges against them.

"I'm Camila Harrison, your court-appointed attorney. I want to ask some questions . . . about you *and* the case. Can you tell me everything that happened?"

"Okay," replied Aldama, looking relieved. "Where do you want me to start?"

"From the beginning," followed Camila, "or wherever you feel most comfortable, it doesn't matter." She was surprised to find out that her client could actually carry on a regular conversation in English.

"I've already been interviewed by pre-trial services," explained Aldama. "Do you know if they're recommending I get a bond?"

"I haven't seen their report, but I can tell you what the answer will be," Camila said. For a guy that looked like a day laborer, Aldama appeared to be intelligent and even somewhat familiar with the American judicial system. "I read somewhere that you're in the country illegally?"

"Yes," replied Aldama, "I was living in Dallas for some time. I went home to check on my daughter—I had not seen her in three years. On our way back, the border patrol arrested our group as we crossed the King Ranch, down in South Texas. I served some time and was deported, but then snuck back in."

"I see . . ."

"What are the chances I can make bail? I need to get out. My daughter needs me, that's why I came back. I have to work."

"That's something I wanted to talk to you about," Camila stared intently into Aldama's eyes, "we're due back in court to have your detention and preliminary hearings."

"What are those?"

"At the detention hearing, we would be discussing whether or not you're a flight risk and whether or not you should get a bond . . ."

"And?"

"At the preliminary hearing," continued Camila, "the court hears evidence from the prosecutor to determine whether or not there's valid grounds to believe you have violated the laws of the United States. If the court finds there's evidence and probable cause, your case will be set for trial."

"Can I get a bond?" asked Aldama.

"Zero chance, I'm afraid," answered Camila without sugar-coating anything. "First of all, you have an ICE detainer. Even if you posted bond, ICE won't let the jail release you because you still have immigration issues. You would have to face the immigration judge but before you do that, you have to finish *this* criminal case. So there's that. Plus, since you're facing a lot of years, the presumption is that you'll skip bail, go back to Mexico and never come back. Where's your daughter? What's wrong with her?"

"She's back in Mexico. She has ALS and can't get out of bed. My parents help me take care of her. I had to get back somehow, make it to Houston so I could work and send money home for her care. I had to do something. I couldn't just sit with my arms crossed and watch her die."

"I'm sorry to hear that. In any case, I think we should waive the detention and preliminary hearings," suggested Camila.

"Why?"

"Because there's no reason to go through the detention hearing . . . you're not getting a bond. Now, let me ask you . . . "

"Yes?" asked Aldama, shoulders hunched.

"You guys were caught with almost a million dollars? Can you explain to me where the money came from?"

"What do you mean?"

"Was it obtained legally?" asked Camila, "can we establish it came from some legitimate source? A legitimate business? Can YOU prove to ME it didn't come from some illegal activity? In other words, do you have receipts, deposit slips, something to show it was earned legally?"

"No, I can't."

"See," followed Camila, "even if we have the preliminary hearing, I think the judge will find that those monies, quite probably, came from some illegal activity. The hearing will be a waste of time, but it's up to you. We could go through the hearings, if you'd like."

Aldama let out a big sigh, "I'd rather not."

Camila switched gears, "tell me about your daughter."

"She needs an operation . . . a tracheotomy, so she can breathe . . . ." He pointed at his neck. "And she needs the machine, which is expensive. I was hoping to put enough money together to get it done. If she doesn't get the operation, she might suffocate and die. Doctors said that the procedure needs to get done this year. I'm running out of time."

"Look, I've got to be honest," said Camila, suddenly realizing that she had started to feel for her client, "you probably need to make your peace with God and try to get used to the idea that it might be a long time before you see your daughter again. Money-laundering cases sometimes carry a maximum sentence of twenty years."

Aldama's eyes grew wide. "Are you serious?!"

"You're lucky they haven't charged you with illegal re-entry." Camila pulled two papers from her satchel. "Here's the money-laundering statute, and here's a copy of the sentencing guidelines."

Aldama took them and began reading, trying to make sense of what his attorney was saying.

"If we cut a deal, you'll reduce your exposure, and will probably get between six and ten years in prison."

Aldama's jaw was on the floor.

"Now, if you don't want to spend a whole lot of time in jail, there is a way to try and reduce your sentence. But you will be asked to play ball," explained Camila.

"'Play ball?'"

"Yes. You agree to a plea, forget about a trial and come clean with everything you know about the folks who wanted you to move the money. You'll have to debrief . . . cooperate."

"You mean snitch?"

"Yes. If you provide *substantial assistance* you can qualify for a 5K, which means that your jail sentence will be significantly reduced. You might be able to get out in under five or six years, it just kind of depends. Do you have any criminal history?"

"Just the prior deportation."

"So, who put you up this?" Camila asked. "How did you get involved in moving cash?"

"I worked for a landscaping outfit. When I came back to Houston, I got into construction," replied Aldama, sighing as he looked up at the ceiling. "That's what I've been doing since I snuck back across. Lalo, a guy I work with, offered to help. He knew I needed money for my daughter's operation. He said I could probably make a quick ten thousand dollars; maybe more. I just had to drive a car to the border."

"And you agreed?"

"Yes. I was willing to take the chance for my daughter, Alicia," he said, rubbing his neck with his right hand, as if digesting the magnitude of his predicament. "I knew once I got to South Texas that I might not be able to return to Houston. I was gonna go home, to Veracruz, and see my family . . . take care of Alicia and get her the operation she needs."

"A one-shot deal?"

"Sí," acknowledged Aldama.

Camila hadn't reviewed all of the discovery in the US attorney's file yet, but she had a sneaking suspicion. "You didn't know who the money belonged to, right?" she asked. "And I suppose Lalo is probably not the guy's real name, correct?"

"Correct." Aldama popped his knuckles as he continued to gaze at the complaint and the sentencing guidelines in front of him. He kept shaking his head, looking upset.

"Did you see where they loaded up the car?"

"No," said Aldama. "They brought the Tahoe to the parking lot outside of a Buc-ee's in South Houston."

Camila prodded some more, trying to find something she could use, something she could hang on to, a scintilla of hope. She needed to know if her client had any useful information that the feds could use to bring other criminals to justice.

"Who delivered it? Did you get a name? A description?"

Camila knew that it was valuable "intel" that the feds were after. The more one knew, the better the deal. For better or worse.

"Lalo gave me a number to call . . . I called that number. The guy who answered said to be at Buc-ee's on this date, at this time, and to wait inside. As I waited, I received a text. The instructions were to take the black Tahoe parked at Pump 6. Keys would be under the mat. I'd be given a driver's license. When we got to Brownsville, we were supposed to call another number."

"You would then receive further instructions?"

"Correct."

"You said 'we.' Who were the others in the car?" asked Camila.

"They were lookouts. I didn't know they would ride with me. They showed up in a different car and were dropped off at Buc-ees."

"Did you know *them*?"

"Nah."

"So what happened after you guys drove off?"

"We drove awhile, everything calm, ordinary, but then, out of nowhere . . . some dude wearing jeans, a T-shirt and a baseball cap pulled us over."

"Where did this happen?"

"Just north of Victoria. Honestly, I think we were set up."

"How much money was in the Tahoe? Do you know?" asked Camila as she thought about her client's last comment.

"I couldn't tell you, but I'd heard Lalo brag that these guys always moved three to five million, and that each million-dollar bundle of hundred-dollar bills weighed twenty pounds. He said the trips happened once or twice a month."

Camila pulled the asset forfeiture petition and a set of discovery from the file. The US government had now filed a civil lawsuit against Aldama and the co-defendants to seize and forfeit $850,000. The same amount was pled in the complaint. She figured Lalo was probably bragging or exaggerating.

"Okay, let's see about getting you the best deal possible," Camila said, feeling relieved that the interview was coming to an end.

"What happens if there's no deal and we have a trial?"

"You don't want that." Camila gulped and felt her pulse quicken. "Don't worry, they'll offer a deal, I'm sure. Maybe not the *best* deal, but it'll be better than going to trial." Camila could see that he wasn't convinced. "Let me ask you; do you really think an illegal alien, caught with over three-quarters of a million dollars near the border and unable to trace the source of the money . . . do you really think that person stands a chance in front of a Houston jury?"

"I guess not, but you're supposed to help me. That's your job, isn't it?"

"I *am* going to help you, but I cannot perform miracles. And I'm not going to lie to you. That's why I'm telling you that we have to plea you out, get the best deal possible and reduce your exposure as much as we can. The only way we would stand a chance at trial would be if we found a constitutional violation."

"What kind of violation?"

"Like . . . a bad traffic stop, a warrantless search, something like that. For example, did you give permission to the agent that pulled you over to search the car?"

"I may have. I don't know for sure," said Aldama. "I was really nervous."

"Well," Camila said, "we'll have to look into it."

"Please, I beg you, get me the least time possible. I need to get out, help my daughter," cried Aldama.

"How old is she? Where's her mother?"

"Alicia's nine. Her mother left us. *Esa pinche vieja no quería batallar.* She didn't want to have anything to do with Alicia or her ALS. She's out of our lives."

"Before I forget," said Camila, glad to get the ball rolling and Aldama closer to the exit, "how long have you been in this country?"

"I came to Dallas five years ago . . . then went home to Mexico for a while, got busted trying to re-enter . . . so they sent me back. A week later, I snuck back in and landed in Houston and then moved to Dallas."

"Dallas; is that where you learned to speak English?"

"Yes."

"I see . . . keep going."

"After I snuck back in, I stayed in Houston close to a year, just working construction. I'd get up, go do my demo work, head home to my little apartment and keep to myself. I'd Western Union whatever money I made to Veracruz every week," explained Aldama, peering out of the interview room and glancing at the clock on the wall above the guard station. "I didn't even have a girlfriend, I never went out. Alicia is my world. I just wanted to pay for her operation. That's why I thought Lalo's connection could help me make some quick cash."

"Do you think Lalo works for the folks that move money?"

"I don't know. I think he just knows who they are, but I really couldn't say for sure."

"How do I know you're telling me the truth?"

"Because I am," he said and then asked, "can you call my parents in Mexico, explain what happened?" Aldama paused and thought about it some more. "You know, I really didn't think I'd get caught. The whole thing sounded so easy."

"Too good to be true."

Aldama cursed his luck. "I just had to drive! Be really careful, deliver the car and get paid. *¡Híjole! ¿en qué mierda me he metido?*"

"Those are the breaks. How do I get in touch with your parents?"

"Wait! I think it's better if you call my sister, Angélica. She lives in Dallas."

"Hold on. You have a *sister* who lives in Dallas?" Camila was quite surprised. Aldama seemed like a lost soul, who wouldn't know *any* friendly faces on this side of the border.

"Yes, that's who I lived with in that city."

"And is she here illegally as well?"

"Nah. She's married to a US citizen. He was a missionary. That's how they met; he did mission work in Mexico. But Danny teaches high school now."

"Okay," said Camila, pen in hand, "let me have her number."

———

"How was your drive?" asked Camila.

Angélica and Danny had left their kids with his parents and hit the road before noon in an effort to arrive in Houston before rush hour traffic.

"Fair. We came as soon as we could," said Danny. "How can we help?"

"We don't have much money," added Angélica. "Danny is a teacher, but hardly makes enough for *our* family, let alone . . . and, well, I take care of the house and kids and pick up some odd jobs when I can. Can we go see him, visit him, comfort him?"

"First, please take a seat," said Camila, motioning to the two chairs in front of her desk. "Catch your breath. I'll explain everything to you, but please sit down and don't worry about the money."

Mr. and Mrs. Dawson sat down and held hands. Daniel Dawson was tall, lanky and bald-headed, he wore glasses that slid down his nose. Angélica was short, about five feet tall, and a little Rubenesque.

"Vicente," started Camila, "is facing charges of money laundering. The US government believes he was transporting monies that were obtained illegally, probably from drugs. They found

$850,000 in cash in secret compartments in the Tahoe he was driving. He's facing up to twenty years in prison. It's a serious situation."

"Oh my God!" Angélica covered her face with both hands. "This can't be, this can't be."

Danny patted her on the shoulder. "He's in good hands, Angie. I'm sure Ms. Harrison can help him. Remember what we said on the way over here?"

She nodded from behind her hands.

"We said we would trust the Lord. And prayed to have the Lord give Ms. Harrison the wisdom to help Vince . . . that we would be strong for him. We have to be."

"I'm not going to sugarcoat it," said Camila. "This looks grim. But if we play our cards right, I think I can reduce the amount of time he'll serve in prison, from twenty years to maybe eight. Ten max."

"Ten years?!" cried Angélica. "But he's innocent, I'm sure of it. Vince would never do such a thing. I know my brother."

Camila felt bad for Angélica, but she knew the truth. Vicente, in an act of desperation, had violated the law. He now had to pay the price. "Look, I can't share with you what my client told me, but I *can* tell you that he only had his daughter's best interest in mind."

"Are you saying . . . ?" Danny paused.

"No!" Angélica cried as she shook her head, still in denial. "It can't be."

Camila brought them back into focus. "Look, I want to plea him out and get him the best deal possible. If we push for a trial, it will be worse. If he isn't acquitted, then it's a sure bet he'll be looking at over ten years in jail. Now, if thing's go terribly wrong, he could get the maximum twenty."

"We don't want that," said Danny, fully aware now that his brother-in-law did what he did to help his daughter back in Mexico. "A plea bargain is always better . . . in these situations."

"Correct," confirmed Camila, happy to see that Danny was getting the full picture. "With a trial, all bets would be off. We'd have absolutely no safety net."

"We don't want that, Ms. Harrison," said Angélica. "Please get him out as quickly as possible, get him the best deal. Alicia needs him. Our parents back in Mexico struggle to care for her. We send what we can, but it's nowhere near enough for that operation she needs. She also needs her dad. I beg you."

Danny nodded in agreement, holding his wife's shoulders.

"I will do absolutely everything I can to reduce his jail sentence as much as possible and plea him out quickly," Camila said. "The quicker he serves his sentence, the quicker he'll get out and be with his daughter. That's what we need to focus on now."

"Please, please . . . I beg you," implored Angélica, "help him. We trust you. I know you'll . . . you'll—"

"I'll do my best," Camila muttered.

Facing impossible odds, and unable to concentrate after her meeting with the Dawsons, Camila sat in her cramped office staring at a stack of law books. Could she really get her client a good deal? What if the US attorney didn't want to plea bargain? Why would they even *want* to plea bargain? Her client was dead in the water. No Houston jury was going to feel sorry for him. He'd been caught red-handed. Plus, he was in the country illegally. No matter how she sliced it, the whole thing seemed hopeless.

Her rumination was interrupted by Julio. "Here are the standard motions for Aldama. Are you going to want me to e-file them?"

"Let me look at them first. I'll file them after the indictment comes down and I talk to the assistant US attorney. Maybe we won't have to file anything."

"Do you think they'll offer him a good deal?" asked Julio as he plopped himself down in a chair across from Camila. "Is he even willing to debrief and cooperate?"

"Oh, he's willing. Problem is, he doesn't know diddly-squat," Camila said. "Poor guy. He's just stuck between a rock and a hard place."

"How so?"

Camila felt odd opening up to Julio, but whatever she shared with him was protected under the attorney-client privilege since Julio was an employee of the office.

"He did it because he needed money to send to his daughter down in Mexico. Her name is Alicia. She needs an operation."

Camila pulled a picture of the girl from the file and showed it to Julio. The Dawsons had brought pictures of her, the grandparents and other family members to share with Aldama's attorney.

Julio couldn't take his eyes off the picture. "Jesus! *Pobrecita.* What's wrong with her?"

The picture showed Alicia being hoisted up from a hospital bed as her grandparents gave her a sponge bath.

"ALS, and without the operation she doesn't have long. Pretty soon she won't be able to breathe on her own. She needs a tracheotomy or she'll asphyxiate."

"That's . . . that's fucking awful!" snapped Julio.

Camila nodded her head.

Julio stood up and turned to leave. "I can't handle it—it's too much. That kind of suffering, for no good reason?! Bye. Just . . . bye."

"Bye . . . " Camila answered as she contemplated Vicente Aldama's fate. Why had their worlds collided?

There had to be a reason.

TEN

Barton Nutley, US Attorney for the Southern District of Texas, Houston Division, was considering a doughnut. It was Saturday morning. The hard-nosed fifty-nine-year-old was in conference with one of his top lieutenants, First Assistant Dot Griffin, a career prosecutor with political aspirations, just like her boss. If Nutley made Texas attorney general, Griffin would certainly be appointed his chief of staff.

"Dot, before I state publicly that I'm running for AG," indicated Nutley, "I'd like to put away some bad apples, make front-page news. We need something big before I renounce my position and *announce* my intentions."

Sporting a flat top, aviator sunglasses and a matching aviator sports watch, Nutley stood at one end of the conference room, near a window, holding a cup of coffee. Any time the pair worked on Saturdays, Nutley could count on Griffin showing up with a selection of Krispy Kreme doughnuts.

Despite an occasional indulgence, Nutley kept fit by playing weekly rounds of squash at the Downtown Club. The upscale racquet club was located on the sixth floor of the Bayou Center Complex, across from Houston Pan American School of Law, Nutley's alma mater.

"Anything juicy coming up on the docket?"

"Well . . . if you really want headlines," suggested Griffin, "prosecute the two Mexican governors taking bribes from the cartels and kickbacks from their *compadres* who were awarded government contracts. Now *those* would be attention-grabbing headlines."

Nutley smiled at the suggestion but shook his head. "That pair has protection from somebody high in Mexico City. Oh, the Mexican authorities have our extradition warrants . . . but won't turn those guys over. We might never get a shot at them."

"A girl can dream."

"What other cases do we have that we can try? There's got to be a wave-maker somewhere." Nutley took a gulp of coffee.

"No big headline-grabbers to speak of really . . . "

"Well is there anything worthwhile, with potential?"

Griffin tapped her iPad, clicking on the latest lists of cases parceled out to the different assistant US attorneys. These were batches of cases of the recently indicted that had the potential to go to trial.

"Bunch of alien-smuggling cases, some illegal re-entries, transporting, harboring . . . medicaid fraud, drug possession, drug trafficking. . . Oh! Here's an interesting one."

"Oh, yeah?" Nutley perked up. "How so?"

"It's laid down. An easy conviction, and you'll look like a champ! Wyatt Fox ended up with it."

"Tell me more."

"The trio that got arrested by the Odessa unit, the one with the Tahoe stuffed with cash," explained Griffin. "It got some play in the news. Juries love to convict on those cases; they're simple, and the defendants can never explain how in the world they ended up with all that cash. They're doomed from the get-go. You get yourself a couple of jurors making minimum wage, barely able to pay their bills, and they'll take out all their frustrations and resentment on the defendant. It'll be a walk in the park."

"Money laundering, huh?" Nutley cracked a smile. "I like it. I haven't tried one of those in a while, and it sounds like a home-run to me." He made his way to the center of the table, opened the box and took in the variety of sweet, fried goodness.

"There you go. Plenty of opportunity for media build-up, a criminal without a pot to piss in," Dot encouraged him. "You want me to pull it from Wyatt?"

"Do we know who's been hired to represent the defendants?"

"Looks like Burwell from the Federal Public Defender has already been appointed to represent one of the co-defendants. Another's attorney is Camila Harrison. And the third co-defendant has Bruce Michaels. Both Harrison and Michaels are court-appointed."

"No private counsel, huh?" Nutley pulled a butterscotch icing from the box. "Well, well, well . . . "

"I heard that Harrison's facing some grievances, but she's still practicing law. She got into some kind of trouble up in Austin."

"Alright now! Let's go with that case," Nutley ordered. "Tell Wyatt I'm taking the lead. He'll have to settle for second chair." Nutley brought the doughnut up to his mouth.

"There's only one problem," Griffin said.

Nutley sighed, the doughnut momentarily forgotten. "What's that?"

"It's a case from Odessa's HIDTA, the High Intensity Drug Trafficking Task Force," replied Griffin. "Those guys have been known to cut corners. The case might have issues. Could be a dog with fleas, you know?"

"Well, if that's the case, public defender Burwell will be overworked, won't pay attention and won't catch it. Michaels is deathly afraid to try cases and sells all his clients down the river sooner or later. And Harrison's probably a burnout, with a ton of personal issues. Doubt she'll even put up a fight."

"Odessa has been known to botch things, just saying. No telling what we might find."

"If it comes to that," Nutley offered, "we'll abort the trial and offer everybody time they could do on their heads. And then we'll find ourselves another windmill to turn into a goddamn giant." He took a hearty bite out of the sweet pastry, a large bulge filling his cheek.

"Or if we encounter resistance, we could always play co-defendants against each other. *And* bolster the actions of Odessa in the process," suggested Griffin.

"You mean turn them against each other?"

"Yes," Griffin replied. "One on one. Two on one. Whoever wants to play ball."

"That's why you're my *first* assistant." Nutley smiled, taking another bite. "I've always admired the way you think."

Assistant US Attorney Wyatt Fox barged into Barton Nutley's office. He was tailed by DEA Special Agent Larry Blackwell and two other young agents with the Office of Foreign Asset Control. Both Fox and Blackwell held yellow pads, case folders and bottles of water. The other two sported windbreakers with the initials OFAC printed on their backs.

"We're back," said Fox as he set the Aldama file on top of Nutley's desk and took a seat.

Blackwell set his materials down on the desk as well, then pulled up a chair and sat next to Fox. The other two remained standing.

"We talked to the guys at Odessa, like you suggested. And we also had the guys at OFAC look at the case," Fox said, pointing to the special agents standing behind them.

"Forget all the reports, Wyatt," growled Nutley. "Here's what I want to know, especially since all of you will be participating in this prosecution, one way or the other. And you, Wyatt, in particular, you'll be helping me try the case."

Fox and Blackwell sat up straight.

"In no uncertain terms, dollars to doughnuts . . . if the case goes to trial, the government wins, right? Can we get the jury to convict all defendants?"

Blackwell cracked up. Was that a rhetorical question? In all his twenty years as an agent, he had never seen anyone accused of money laundering escape conviction. Like child pornographers, money launderers always got hammered. Jurors didn't like people who cheated the system and made buckets of money while the rest struggled to make ends meet.

Fox thought it was a good question and was ready with an answer. "Yes. The case is laid down for us and the conviction's in the bag. I guarantee it."

"What about the fact that the case originated with the Odessa unit? Should we be concerned at all? Dot thought there might be issues.

Fox turned to look at the OFAC boys, then turned back to face his boss. "We talked to the Odessa agents at HQ. Looks like the traffic stop will withstand judicial scrutiny."

Blackwell interjected, "It was a clean stop, no doubt about it."

"And the driver consented to the search anyway," added Fox. "Plus, the K9 hit on the money. So, there are no unlawful search issues. Case looks solid."

"I ask again: Are we sure?"

Fox looked Nutley right in the eye. "Yes."

"Are there any other issues with the case? What was the reason for the traffic stop?'"

"A busted rear plate light," said Blackwell.

"Anything else?"

"None that we can see," answered Blackwell.

Nutley seemed satisfied. "Who's the judge?"

"Yamamoto," replied Fox.

Nutley smiled. "Hmm . . . Colt 'Maximum' Yamamoto. I guess we're in good hands, then."

"We are," Blackwell and Fox agreed, simultaneously.

Nutley had one final question for his second chair. "Have we heard from defense counsel?"

Fox looked at his notes on the yellow pad. "Burwell says his guy, McKenzie, is gonna enter a plea and is willing, ready and able to come clean. Michaels is still talking to his guy, but he's convinced, ultimately, Barrera will also buckle and take whatever deal we offer."

"And Harrison?"

"No telling what she's up to," answered Fox, "but I don't see her putting up much of a fight. She doesn't strike me as a brawler . . . someone that wants to get her hands dirty. This is her first solo in federal court. Just a few months ago Harrison was pushing paper, working on real estate deals, doing transactional work."

"A paper lawyer, huh?" Nutley smiled. He gave the team their marching orders. "Start prepping the case as if it is going to trial, leave no stone unturned. If it does goes to trial, I want to make sure we come out on top. No excuses. Got it?"

"Yes, sir," replied the bunch and marched out of Nutley's office.

ELEVEN

"Hear ye! Hear ye! Hear ye!" announced the young US marshal standing by one of the side entrances of the grand courtroom. "The United States District Court for the Southern District of Texas, Houston Division, is now in session. The Honorable Judge Colt Yamamoto presiding. God save the United States and this Honorable Court."

"You all may be seated," declared Judge Yamamoto as he took his seat at the bench. He glanced at the computer on top of his bench, straining to see the screen until he found what he was looking for. "Let's see, the court calls Case No. 2014 CR-3456-3, *The United States of America v. Vicente Aldama, et. al.* What says the government?"

"Good morning, Your Honor," announced Barton Nutley. He was standing by the prosecution's table, surrounded by Fox, Griffin and two other assistants from his office. "The government is present and ready."

"What says the defense?" asked Yamamoto.

Camila got up slowly, the butterflies playing havoc in her stomach. Here she was, going up against the United States government all alone. Where were Burwell and Michaels? Or Alan and Thelma, for that matter, the crazies who pushed her to pick up appointments? She cursed them all. She wiped her sweaty palms on her jacket, as inconspicuously as she could, anyway. "Good morning, Your Honor. Attorney Camila Harrison on behalf of Vicente Aldama."

At that moment, the US marshal brought Aldama over to the defense counsel's table and ordered him to sit down. Aldama still wore a green jumpsuit. He was handcuffed to a chain around his waist as well as shackled at the ankles.

Camila waited for her client to sit down next to her. "We're present, Your Honor."

"Please bring me up to speed, Counsel. What are we doing with this case?" the judge asked as he addressed both Harrison and Nutley.

"My understanding," said Nutley, as he turned to check with Fox, "is that two co-defendants are planning to enter pleas. I think they've already called the court to ask for re-arraignment dates for next week. We don't know what Ms. Harrison has planned for her client."

Fox stood up and addressed Judge Yamamoto, "Your Honor, Wyatt Fox for the government. Good morning."

"Yes, Mr. Fox?"

"I had a conversation with defense counsel, Mr. Michaels and the federal public defender, Mr. Burwell. Their clients will enter pleas by the early part of next week. They picked up their clients' plea packets yesterday. We don't anticipate any changes on that."

"And you, Ms. Harrison?" asked Yamamoto. "What about your client? What are we doing with him? Do we arraign him? Or is he waving the reading of the indictment?"

"Waive the reading, your Honor," Camila answered, "and enter a plea of not guilty."

"Very well," said Judge Yamamoto, "let the record reflect Mr. Aldama's decision. Now, Ms. Harrison, do you have an idea what's going to happen with your client's case?"

"Uhm, yes, Your Honor" Camila cleared her throat. "I filed several discovery motions. Standard stuff. *And* a motion for funds to hire an investigator; I'm urging the court to consider it."

"I see that. I usually don't get many of those in my court. I think everybody knows how I feel about wasting the taxpayers' money."

"Yes, could we talk about that?" Camila felt her hands get clammy.

"Why do you need an investigator?" Yamamoto asked. "Hasn't the government given you everything you need already? They have an open-file policy, and I hear they're pretty good about allowing defense counsel to conduct extensive discovery."

"We've emailed all the defense attorneys in this case their discovery, Your Honor," indicated Nutley. "And Ms. Harrison has come by our office to look at the file. I don't understand what else she could possibly want."

"I'm just prepping the case like I would any other, Your Honor," Camila tried explaining. "I have to do, at a minimum, *some* investiga—"

Yamamoto cut her off, "But this is a money-laundering case, Counselor. It's black and white. Is your client willing to lose the two points for acceptance and responsibility and the additional point for an early plea?"

"I still have to look at everything, Your Honor, before I can properly advise Mr. Aldama either way. The arrest happened less than a month ago. I can't be rushed just because the government wants my guy to roll over and plea, like the other two."

"What do you want to know?" asked Yamamoto, showing signs of impatience.

Camila stammered. "In cases . . . such as these, dealing with drug-trafficking and money-laundering organizations and such . . . I believe it's always important to know if there's a confidential informant involved . . . or not. Your Honor, I believe we're entitled to find out more."

"Okay," Judge Yamamoto said as he made some notes on the file. "But you don't need an investigator for that. I can just ask the government right here, in open court, to see if there's an informant. Mr. Nutley, is there an informant involved in this case?"

The question threw Nutley for a loop. He had to caucus with Fox and Griffin.

"We're waiting," Yamamoto huffed. "Mr. Nutley?"

Nutley looked up from the huddle. "The CI's identity is not discoverable, according to Mr. Fox, Your Honor."

Fox jumped in. "Let me clear something up, Your Honor. This case doesn't involve a confidential informant, but even if there was one—and we're not saying there is or was or wasn't—they would not be called to testify."

Yamamoto seemed satisfied with the response. "Well, there you are, Ms. Harrison. The government has represented to the court that there's no informant. And if there was one, he or she was not transactional, that is, would not testify to facts of the case. Either way, you don't get to discover the identity."

"What kind of answer is that? Your Honor is going to take the government at its word?! Just like that?"

"Are you accusing Mr. Nutley of wrongdoing on this matter?" Yamamoto's feathers appeared somewhat ruffled. "Of misleading the court?"

"We should have a hearing then, just to be on the safe side," suggested Harrison. "At least make a record, that way we would really know for sure whether the informant was or wasn't transactional, or if there even was one, period. My client is at least entitled to a hearing on the topic, Your Honor."

Yamamoto looked over at Nutley's table; again Nutley, Fox and Griffin were in a huddle. This time they were joined by the other two assistants. Yamamoto didn't like this.

"We will not have a hearing, Ms. Harrison," indicated Yamamoto. "I'm satisfied with the government's explanation. But I'll tell you what I'll do . . . "

"Yes, Your Honor?" Camila kept reminding herself to play nice. She forced herself to keep her composure. After all, this was her first meaningful appearance in a Houston federal court. No use burning any bridges, and especially not at the outset.

"The court will give you funds to use an investigator to properly prepare your case," Yamamoto promised, trying to play fair. "You will have $2,000 at your disposal, but with a caveat. This court does not like to waste the government's money for the sake of wasting money. I suggest you use it wisely because there will not be any extra. Do we understand each other?"

"Yes, Your Honor," Camila replied, happy that she had been granted at least one of her motions. Her strategy had worked: Shoot for the stars, land on the moon.

"We will conduct final pre-trial three weeks from now, on October 27, 2014, at 1:30 p.m. Jury selection will be on Monday, November 3, at 8:00 a.m. Motions *in limine* will be heard the day of jury selection. Trial shall commence on Tuesday, November 4, 2014, in the morning. You have four weeks to get ready. Also, the parties' proposed *voir dire* questions and jury charge will be due the day of the final pre-trial, on a flash drive, in Word format. Any questions?"

"No," said Nutley.

"Um . . . Your Honor," Camila struggled to find the right words, "I have a special request. If I may?"

"What is it?" Yamamoto asked, ready to move on to the next case.

"Late last night, I also filed a motion for continuance . . . "

"Let me get this straight: You want an investigator *and* a continuance?"

Camila rubbed her chin and bit her lower lip. "Thirty-some days is not enough to adequately prepare, Your Honor. Not for a case like this, where my client is exposed, potentially, to a twenty-year sentence."

"Did you ask the government if it was opposed to the continuance?"

"Yes, and Mr. Nutley opposes it."

"Then your request for continuance is denied, Counselor. Anything else?" Yamamoto asked as he looked out at the other groups of attorneys present in his courtroom, who were waiting to be called upon.

Nutley looked at Fox, who shook his head. "Nothing else, Your Honor. We would appreciate Ms. Harrison letting us know the name of her investigator, in case we need to evaluate credentials and prepare a proper cross examination. That's all."

"It's so ordered," Yamamoto said. "You're all excused."

<hr />

"The task forces were the brainchild of the Office of National Drug Control Policy," Dennis Gosling explained. "They operate in sectors designated as 'High Intensity Drug Trafficking Areas' throughout the United States—what we've come to know as drug corridors. Interstate route I-10 is such a corridor. So are I-35, US 77 and 59."

Camila and Gosling, the private eye hired to help with the Aldama case, walked down San Jacinto Street, heading toward Texas Avenue in downtown Houston. The idea was to introduce Gosling to Camila's client and explain to him the role Gosling was to play in the case. He'd indicated that he wanted to hear first-hand, straight from the client's mouth, the background story leading up to the arrest.

"The agents in the Odessa Unit are SWAT-trained and operate between Victoria and Houston. They patrol a portion of a larger drug corridor that stretches from Brownsville all the way to Houston. It's a drug interdiction task force drawn from various county sheriffs' offices and police departments along US Highway 59. They're one of several HIDTA Task Forces units operating throughout Texas. The problem is that these task forces have very little oversight."

"How's that a problem?"

"Because they answer only to themselves . . . they're not accountable to anyone, which is actually good for *us*."

"You think we'll find something?" Camila asked.

"Oh yeah . . . we'll find *something*. If they're anything like the other HIDTAs around Texas."

"What do you mean?" Camila asked as they approached the entrance to the federal detention center, a twenty-story building that housed federal inmates awaiting their day in court.

"Does the Panama Unit in South Texas ring a bell?"

"Um, not really . . . "

"Those guys would take money from the drug dealers they were supposed to be putting away. They routinely used their badges and guns to rob the traffickers who did not pay for protection. Then they would turn around and sell the seized drugs to 'friendly' drug gangs. And if they seized money . . . they kept chunks of it."

"They were worse than the bad guys, huh?"

"Apples and oranges as far as I'm concerned. Drug traffickers aren't exactly subtle when they make examples of the competition. But the Panama Unit was not the first to get in trouble. Other task forces in North Carolina, Arizona, New Mexico and Florida have also been caught red-handed."

Camila let out a big, "Really?"

Gosling enjoyed having a captive audience. "But that's not the worst part. Some, like myself, believe the higher-ups knew, and were even in on it. But this has never come out."

"You really believe corruption went up the ranks?" Camila was wide-eyed.

"Had to," said Gosling. "I'm telling you, we shouldn't plea our guy. I'd bet money Odessa is dirty, the traffic stop was illegal or that there was an informant involved. Hell, the officers may have even lacked probable cause once they stopped the vehicle, or there was no consent to search—they made it up. If we look hard enough, we'll find something. Could even be racial profiling . . . who knows?"

"You sound so certain." Camila wasn't totally convinced, but if she was going help her client, she needed something to believe in, something that could maybe turn the case around. Anything, really.

"I know what I'm telling you," Gosling reassured her. "We're going to find *something*, and once we have them cornered, either Nutley will have Fox dismiss the charges against your client, or they'll offer him a misprision of felony."

"I doubt it!" Camila giggled. "A misdemeanor? In federal court? That'll never happen."

"Look," said Gosling, getting serious, "what are they offering the co-defendants?"

"Eight years, but they have to cooperate, point fingers. If they won't cooperate, just want to take an early plea, everyone is looking at fifteen years . . . a hundred eighty months."

"Don't plea our guy," insisted Gosling, "I know what I'm telling you. I'll find something that we can negotiate with . . . you should be able to get him a misdemeanor, and he'll be out before you know it. Nutley is not going to take the case to trial."

Camila was still doubtful. "I'll do whatever the client wants us to do. Ultimately, it's his case. If he wants to plea, he'll plea; if he wants to go to trial, I'll take the case to trial."

Gosling shook his head, disappointed in what he was hearing.

Right before going into the Federal Detention Center, Camila turned to Gosling and asked, "Why are you doing this?"

Gosling reached for the door, but didn't pull it open.

"I was an honest cop," he said as he stared into Camila's eyes, "and I loved my job. I worked hard. I worked with integrity, honesty, but I was surrounded by scoundrels. Outlaws. Everywhere you'd look they were all around you. Either you joined them or you kept your nose clean and looked the other way. Ever heard of Conrado Gómez?"

"Not really."

"He was the sheriff in South Texas who went away for 38 years. I worked in his office," Gosling said, grimacing. "When the corruption got to be too much, I left and went to work with Sheriff Jesse Aguilar, but it was the same thing. He *also* went to prison. That guy used to make a lot of his cases with snitches . . . confidential informants. Once the informants his department routinely used ran out of useful intel, they started targeting innocent people. Some went to prison for crimes that were total fabrications, lives were ruined. His luck ran out when those same informants turned on Aguilar."

"You don't say," commented Camila, unable to believe what she was actually hearing, " . . . talk about being railroaded."

"Lie with dogs, wake up with fleas . . . I couldn't work like that. I always felt dirty when I came home at night. So, I quit the sheriff's office and came to work at the Houston PD. I moved hundreds of miles to get away from the corruption, but it was waiting for me here too. So I left, ended up leaving the one thing I loved the most; being a cop. An honest cop. A good cop."

"Sorry to hear that. I guess there's bad apples everywhere."

"I started doing PI work and never looked back, but I still have my share of regrets."

"Like?"

"I should have done or said something, but I didn't. That's always bothered me. Now, looking back, I realize that I chose to do what was easiest and just quit. I was really no different than the jerks I worked with. By not saying anything and looking the other way, I was also part of the problem. Guilty by omission. You get what I'm saying?"

"I can see where you're coming from," replied Camila. "I guess you see a plea as taking the easy way out?"

Gosling wouldn't come right out and say it, but instead replied, "Ms. Harrison . . . you now have the opportunity to do the *right* thing. Expose them bastards!"

"You really think so?" Camila asked, thinking the whole thing sounded ridiculous.

"I'm here, aren't I?"

"But I don't necessarily want to expose 'them bastards,'" countered Camila. "I just want do a little prep work, get my client to the best outcome possible, close the file and be done with it."

"I see what you're doing," Gosling had a sudden epiphany. "You're trying to avoid having to defend a claim of ineffective assistance of counsel, correct? That's your deal, isn't it?"

"Well," she caught herself. "I really feel for this client and would like to get him as little time as possible. But, yes, I'm trying to keep my license. I, too, have enough problems as it is. The last thing I want, or need, is for an ex-client to lodge a grievance against me because I didn't do enough for him. You know how it is, clients are never happy. You never do enough and it's never *their* fault! It's always the soulless, blood-sucking lawyer's fault."

"Gotta blame somebody," Gosling pointed out.

"I suppose."

Gosling smiled and opened the heavy glass door. He let Camila through and followed her in, happy that they understood each other this early on.

It was time to go over the client's version, once more, and start putting together a game plan.

They were on their way back to the parking garage. "Something doesn't smell right," Dennis Gosling said as he studied his notes from the meeting with Aldama.

"I'm gonna beat the bushes," followed Gosling, "see if Odessa is using confidential informants, see what my sources tell me. I would also like to look at the Tahoe, make sure everything was in working order . . . like Aldama said."

"You think Bergendahl made up probable cause for the traffic stop. In his report, he said the Tahoe's license plate light was out."

"Are you going to take him at his word? Is there a video of the traffic stop?" Gosling inquired.

"No."

"Exactly. This wasn't a traffic stop involving a state trooper. DPS always uses mounted video cameras and they record all traffic stops, equipment permitting."

"I see," said Camila.

"Which begs the question," continued Gosling, "how come Odessa doesn't videotape *their* traffic stops? 'Cause they don't want you to see there was no probable cause! It's your word against theirs, and there's ten of them. You see how they work? It's like a pack of wolves . . . you stand little chance if you're outnumbered, none if you're undocumented."

"I'm starting to get the picture," Camila admitted, images of a take-down swirling around her head.

"It's the whole wolf pack modus operandi. For them to show up, just like that, somebody must have tipped them off. And I'm sure they got a tip from a CI. Nutley is not going to like that we keep bringing that up."

"I hope you're right," said Camila as she found the keys in her purse. They had finally reached the parking garage and were about to part ways.

"Let me do some ground work," said Gosling, "and let's meet in three days. How's that sound?"

"Okay," Camila agreed. "I'll go back to the US attorney's and look at the file again. Make sure we're not missing anything."

Gosling started to walk away. "You've got my number. Text me or call me, it doesn't matter the time of day."

Back in her Audi, Camila checked her phone messages. She had a missed called from her former assistant Cassie that had gone to voice mail. In her message, Cassie explained that the bosses up in Austin were conspiring to rile up some of Camila's past clients to also come forward and file grievances against her. James Levinson had asked Cassie to download all of Camila's emails and pull all her old files because he had hired a group of auditors and examiners to go through everything with a fine-tooth comb, hoping to find material that could be made into an ethics complaint.

Cassie warned Camila to watch her back. She would call back soon with more information. Finally, Cassie had ended the call with the news that Andy McCormack's body had been found floating in Town Lake with a note tied around his toe. However, the police were not releasing any details of the note's contents.

Foul play was suspected.

TWELVE

Camila was surfing the web in her office, looking for information on the HIDTA Task Force, but all the articles she'd found touted their successes. Other than a tiny mention in a narco blog, saying that the Gulf Cartel had put a price on Bergendahl, there was really nothing negative out there. She wondered if Gosling had it right; to an impartial observer, the Odessa Task Force appeared to be clean as a whistle. Doubt came at Camila hard, forcing her to worry.

I'll have to talk to Nutley, maybe even apologize. Get him to offer my guy the same deal he offered the other two. I hope it's not too late. Gosling's reassurances seemed so minuscule in the moment.

Camila searched for her purse and car keys, was about to push the intercom button to speak with Julio, when he buzzed *her*.

She picked up the receiver. "Hey, I was just about to ring you, see if you wanted to go grab some lunch."

"You have a visitor," replied Julio. "We might not have time to do lunch—you don't want to be late to your meeting with the guys from Blackwell's office to review the evidence."

"Who is it?" Camila asked over the intercom.

"Says he's with Mexico's Consulate General. A Mr. Govela. Says he needs to talk to you."

"About?"

"Will only say it's official business."

Camila rolled her eyes, tossed her purse under her desk and threw her car keys inside the top drawer. "Okay, send him in. I only have five minutes."

Camila had mixed emotions as Gustavo Govela stretched his hand out to shake hers. There was a solidness to him, a directness in his demeanor that underscored his dark eyes and hair, his brown sugar complexion and handsome face. Were those butterflies in her stomach? For a *Mexican*, no less?

Govela flashed an official-looking ID from the consular office and then reached for a business card from his shirt pocket. He placed the card on top of Camila's desk.

"Please . . . sit down." Camila cleared her throat, felt a sudden warmth in the room.

She examined the card, also taking time to study the man now sitting across from her. He appeared to be in his late thirties, early forties, and fully comfortable in his skin.

Lic. Gustavo M. Govela
Agregado para Asuntos Judiciales Extranjeros
Consulado Mexicano
Secretaría de Relaciones Exteriores

"I'm sorry," said Camila, "you're going to have to be brief. I have a meeting in less than thirty minutes and I have to beat traffic to get to it . . . you know Houston traffic."

Govela just sat there.

"Did you hear what I said?" followed Camila. "I only have a few minutes."

"Oh . . . I'm sorry," apologized Govela. "I've never seen emerald eyes like yours . . . it's hard not to notice. Even harder not to get lost." He smiled, a playful wink following. "Anyway, the reason I'm here . . . "

"Yes?"

"It's to offer any assistance my office might be able to provide you in connection with the defense of Vicente Aldama. He's a Mexican national, being prosecuted for money laundering. I believe you represent him."

"That's right."

"I was informed that you asked the court for funds for an investigator. Our office has resources precisely for these purposes."

"Really?"

"We lend a hand to our nationals when they get in legal trouble in the States. I'm here to help with anything you might need."

"Anything?"

"Within reason," Govela said as he continued to study Camila's facial features. He also noticed she wasn't wearing any type of ring. "We have *some* funds to use for the defense of our Mexican citizens here. I'm not talking about a whole lot of money, but there are resources available."

"Don't you guys only get involved when the death penalty is in play?"

"We used to . . . " Govela leaned forward. "But this case is different. Your client's sister . . . Angélica Dawson, does that ring a bell?"

"Yes, of course." Camila said.

"Well, she took it upon herself to contact the *cancillería* in Mexico City. The *cancillería* contacted our office here in Houston to see if there was anything we could do. It's a hardship case, because of Aldama's daughter, and it's gathering some interest in the capital."

Camila listened intently.

"It's not unusual. We get calls like this all the time. Sometimes we can help, sometimes there's nothing we can do. In this instance, since we have orders straight from Mexico City, we can at least look into it. Under the Hague Convention, Mexico has the right to assist any of its citizens who get into trouble, in any signatory country," Govela explained. "Obviously, if we had a bigger budget, our involvement would be more visible. As it stands, we have to pick and choose the cases we get involved with full-bore."

"Makes sense," said Camila.

Govela played with his goatee. "Look, whatever you can do to quickly resolve Mr. Aldama's unfortunate situation, the Mexican government thanks you in advance. And if you need our help—don't take it the wrong way, I'm sure your skills as an attorney are top-notch—please give me a call. Give *us* a call, I mean. We're here to help. That's all, that's it, that's my whole spiel." Govela flashed his smile once more.

Camila was pleasantly surprised. It seemed like *everybody* was trying to help.

Flashing a big smile of her own, Camila said, "Thank you, Mr. Govela. I'll sure consider it."

He grinned from ear to ear. "Call me Gustavo."

"Okay. Gustavo."

Govela got up from his chair, looked at the time on his watch and pulled his car keys from his pants pocket. "Thanks for giving me a few minutes. Please keep in touch."

Camila and her client sat alone in a large conference room. Aldama was wearing civilian clothes, the same clothes he had been wearing the day of his arrest. He was still handcuffed and shackled at the ankles. It was 1:45 p.m. The meeting with Special Agent Blackwell was not to start for another fifteen minutes.

"In a few minutes," started Camila, "the assistant US attorney helping Mr. Nutley will walk in here and present you with a proffer letter. That's in case you decide to cooperate and avoid a trial. It's up to you."

Despite Gosling wanting Camila to push for a trial, she was still, in her heart of hearts, leaning toward the possibility of a plea bargain.

"Is that the letter you discussed with me the other day?" Aldama asked.

"Yes. It sets out the terms and conditions of your deal. The most important thing that's contained in the letter is the language that specifies that nothing you say, nothing you admit to, in connection with whatever crimes you have participated in or know about, can been used against you."

"Nothing?"

"Nothing . . . except . . . "

"¿*Excepto*?" questioned Aldama.

"If the feds find out other things that you were involved in, and you did not cover those here today—in other words, you kept things from them—then those crimes will not be covered under the proffer letter. They can still prosecute you if they want for those other criminal acts," explained Camila. "That's why it's important to tell the feds everything you know, even if we don't finish today and we have to come back."

"Tell them everything?" Aldama gulped.

"Everything," Camila said, "but that's only if you decide to take the deal and enter into a proffer. For now, let's just listen, and after our meeting, you and I will talk and figure out what should be our next move. Okay?"

"Okay."

It was then that Assistant US Attorney Wyatt Fox barged into the conference room. He was tailed by Special DEA Agent Larry Blackwell and the same two agents with the Office of Foreign Asset Control.

"Good afternoon," said Fox, setting the proffer letter down in front of Aldama. He then went around the conference table and took his place. Blackwell set down his materials next to Fox, pulled up a chair and sat down. The OFAC agents remained standing by the door.

"Take a moment and read the proffer letter, explain it to your client, Ms. Harrison," said Fox. "Make sure we're all on the same page. These other special agents," Fox pointed at the two young investigators, "work in the financial crimes' unit with OFAC. They're very interested in talking to your client as well."

The two just nodded at Aldama and Camila, stone-faced. She dismissed them and started reading the letter to herself.

She was about to lean over and explain its contents to Aldama, when Fox spoke up. "We can leave the room if you want us to.

That way you can explain the terms and conditions of the letter to your client in complete confidence."

"We've already gone over it. I printed the copy you emailed me a while back," replied Camila, "but what about the evidence? Weren't you going to show us all the evidence you intended to use at trial?"

"In the event there *is* a trial," clarified Fox.

"But," continued Camila, "we understood we'd get to go over the evidence at this meeting. That's what I told my client."

"Not so fast," countered Fox. "You get to see the evidence once we ink the proffer letter, to satisfy your and your client's curiosity. But not until then."

That was not my understanding, Camila thought. "I see."

Aldama was getting nervous. He didn't like the way the meeting was going. He kicked Camila under the conference table.

"Can you give us a moment?" asked Camila.

"Sure," nodded Fox.

Once alone, Aldama broke the silence first. "I can't do this. I can't. I don't have anything to say unless I make stuff up, and I'm not about to lie. *No puedo*, sorry."

"Look," followed Camila, "you can tell them about your role, your involvement, and tell them about Lalo; where you saw him last, what company he worked for, what he looks like. Little details like that. They want leads, so they can see who else might be involved. We can always reschedule if you need more time."

Aldama struggled to respond. He started rubbing his temples. "Everything's happening too fast."

"Look," Camila explained, "the reason this case went federal is because the government believes these monies belong to the Gulf Cartel or the Zetas . . . that's why they're interested in talking to you . . . see what else you know."

"But I don't know anything . . . really, I don't."

"If you want to think about it some more, that's fine," interrupted Camila, "just remember that US attorney Nutley gave us a deadline: 5 p.m., today. He wants to know if you're going to cooperate and debrief or if you'd rather take your chances and go to trial, that's the only decision you need to focus on right now."

Aldama had a worried expression, was shaking his head. "I don't know. Jesus, I'm so confused. Scared."

Knock. Knock. Knock.

"Where are we?" Fox stuck his head in the room. "What are we doing?"

Camila looked to her client, but he remained silent.

Fox then addressed Aldama. "Stop wasting everybody's time, Mr. Aldama. It's real simple; shit or get off the pot. If you're not going to debrief and cooperate, that's fine. Just be advised there won't be any other offers from the government. You'll have to plea cold, or go to trial."

Camila just stared back at Fox and sank in her chair, reeling. She was not happy with the way Fox had upended the meeting, creating confusion, tightening the vice. She was about to say as much, but chose to ride it out. Maybe a push from opposing counsel would force Aldama to plea.

"Well?" asked Fox, staring at the defendant.

Aldama looked at Camila, Camila at Fox.

Finally, Aldama broke the silence. "I want a trial."

THIRTEEN

Camila Harrison was dreaming that she was the keynote speaker at the annual state bar convention in Austin. She was halfway through her presentation on the latest developments in the area of zoning and urban development, when she noticed McCormick sitting in the crowd. Was he back from the dead?!

Her mind went blank.

She stared out into the crowd, a knot in her throat, beads of moisture forming along her forehead, her mouth dry as cotton. The three hundred lawyers in attendance grew more impatient with every passing moment. McCormick was thoroughly enjoying the raw spectacle.

She glanced down at her notes, looking for a way to get back on track, but the pages were blank. She turned around to look at the PowerPoint presentation on the large screen behind her, but the screen was blank as well. She cracked her knuckles. She tried to apologize, but there were no words. Nothing came out. Nothing.

She couldn't breathe. What was happening?!

"Oh my God!" she screamed in horror. She was finally awake, dripping with sweat. She sat up on the bed and looked at the clock on the dresser. It was 4:44 in the morning.

What happened? She tried to put two and two together. Where did the night go? Was that the right time on the alarm clock? Had she drank more than one shot? Was the pressure getting to her? She reached for her cell phone to double-check the time and noticed she had a missed call. The call had originated from a restricted number, but there was a message.

Ms. Harrison, this is Investigator Murphy with the State Bar's Office of the Chief Disciplinary Counsel.

I'll be in Houston next week for business and I want to see if you're available for an interview.

As you know, there are several unresolved grievances and I just wanted to make sure you have a complete grasp of the allegations.

Also, the CDC would like to know if you want your case to be reviewed in district court or by an evidentiary panel. We haven't heard from you, and we'd like to know.

And if you choose to have the complaints aired in front of an evidentiary panel, do you want that to happen in Austin or Houston? The CDC will accommodate you either way. Call me, my number is 800-555-5555.

Thanks.

<hr />

The black and white aerial photo of the city of Houston hanging in Dennis Gosling's office showed a vast area that stretched for miles. The enormous six-by-eight picture hung on a wall behind a small sitting area comprised of three retro chairs, a small sofa and a coffee table.

Size: Six hundred square miles
Population: Six million
Counties: Harris, Fort Bend and Montgomery
Ranking: 4th largest city in the nation

Camila studied the image while Gosling rifled through stacks of papers and files sitting on his cluttered desk.

"Here they are," smiled Gosling, waving an old *Rolling Stone* magazine and several clipped newspaper articles about law enforcement agents being sent to prison for all kinds of wrongdoing. "People don't want to believe our HIDTAs are a mess, but here's the proof. Did you ever read the story on the Panama Unit in *Rolling Stone?*"

"No. Panama slipped my mind. Is it a good article?"

"Read it sometime," Gosling said, handing her the magazine, "very enlightening."

"So . . . why do you think Nutley and Fox are being such assholes?" Camila asked, switching topics. "Any idea?"

"I think they're playing hardball to put the fear of God into you because they really don't want to try this case. There's probably a CI somewhere in the background. There always is." Gosling limped over to where Camila was standing. "They're going to do whatever it takes to protect him or her since you've made the informant an issue." He started coughing, reached for a yellowish handkerchief in his rear pants pocket and covered his mouth. "Tell me something . . . "

"Yes?"

He composed himself and gathered his thoughts. "Have you tried criminal cases in federal court?"

Camila shrugged her shoulders. "Sort of . . . I helped my old partners defend a Medicare fraud case in San Antonio sometime back. Why?"

"Just wondering," said Gosling. "Anyway, I'd make Nutley sweat and keep pushing for a trial. They'll regroup, come back and offer something better."

"You sound really confident."

Gosling was now going through an old rolodex on his desk. "We have to find a way to nail them bastards. When I was on the force, I worked with a guy who quit HPD to go work at Odessa. I think I wrote his info here somewhere."

"Do you have a name?"

Gosling tried to remember. He kept flipping through the rolodex. "Green? Cowen? Jaramillo? I remember his last name had a curve to the beginning. Shit, what was the guy's first name? Randolph? Roberto? Jody! There it is . . . but his *real* name is . . . it's gotta be here somewhere."

"How long ago was that?" asked Camila. "Would he still be working at the task force?"

"I'll have to check. Have you gotten all the discovery in your case?"

"Yes. Some of the officers involved were Bergendahl, Rico, Rabinovich, Wolf, González and Leal. Do any of those names ring a bell?"

"Nah, but make sure we ask for the complete file," suggested Gosling. "And also ask for the A file. There's the prosecutor's file and there's the A file, which belongs to the agents making the case. Sometimes one has stuff in it that the other is conveniently missing. They will fight you, but you need to make a strong effort to get it. It's important. They'll claim it's *work product*."

"Okay then," agreed Camila, "let me go to work."

Vicente Aldama felt angry, dejected that he would no longer be able to earn a living in order to support and care for Alicia. He was lying on the bunk bed in his cell, unable to nap, dissecting piece by piece the events leading up to his arrest. He cursed his luck.

He considered the pros and cons of debriefing or accepting the plea and ended back at square one. If he went to trial, he could get up to twenty years in prison. And what was worse? Being trapped behind bars or being trapped in a body being ravaged by paralysis? He pictured his Alicia, slowly deprived of the power to move, speak, breathe or eat. How could he prepare himself to let his little girl go—or worse, be absent when she took her last breath? He would never be able to live with himself.

The thought of losing his daughter had pushed him to the brink. He wanted to scream, pound the walls. Could Camila Harrison deliver a miracle? Was there such a thing? Why couldn't the US government see that he was not a criminal, that he had come to work? He'd never been in trouble before, at least not unforgivable kind of trouble. All he was trying to do was to send money home so Alicia could get the treatment and medications she needed. Why could nobody see that? Why?

He massaged his temples in the semi-darkness. He was in a bad place, and he knew it.

FOURTEEN

As Nutley walked into the US attorney's office, Joanna quickly tossed her nail file into a drawer and sat up straight in her chair. She buzzed her boss in, past the front door and into a world of small office suites connected by narrow corridors and open work spaces where law clerks, secretaries and paralegals cranked out most of the legal work.

In any given week, some eighty assistant US attorneys slaved away at the Houston office, defending lawsuits against the government, handling criminal prosecutions, filing and responding to appeals, conducting white-collar crime investigations, and even pushing whistleblower lawsuits.

Nutley threw his blazer on one of the chairs around the conference table and started rolling up his sleeves. Three assistant US attorneys, one special agent with OFAC and DEA Special Agent Larry Blackwell were already waiting for him, holding various files in their hands.

"What did we find out?" Nutley asked the group. "Should I be worried about Camila Harrison? C'mon, people, jury selection is in less than a month. Why won't her client roll over and plea? Does she know something that we don't? We were willing to offer Harrison the same-plea bargain—even a 5K—but her client is still unwilling to take the deal? What's wrong with this picture?"

Fox walked in flanked by Hillary Smith and Constance Washington, seasoned federal prosecutors.

Washington, tasked with digging up dirt on Aldama's attorney, broke the ice. "Camila Harrison won't pose a threat. She's not fit to try a case. She's a transactional attorney, handled evictions in JP courts and meaningless hearings in front of variance and zoning boards, but no big jury trials."

"Anything else?"

"She probably has confidence issues too. Even she has to realize she's not a 'real' trial lawyer. She sat in on a few trials with her Austin firm, sure, but never had a lead role. Plus, she's facing several grievances and complains with the State Bar. She's been seen talking to Ned Pruitt. We also found an old marriage license, but there's no record of a marriage . . . probably something to do with her fiancée losing his life in a car accident."

"Big deal!" Nutley remarked. "Anything else?"

"Yes, that's it. And her mother was married to a US Foreign Service officer, Darin Harrison. Camila has dual citizenship, being born *in* Mexico to a Mexican mother. She speaks perfect Spanish, so uh . . . watch what you say, *hombre*."

The group snickered.

"What else?"

"Found a couple of old college classmates . . . apparently her mother, Lorena, did not approve of her fiancée. Mom's a naturalized US citizen, lives in Marble Falls, about an hour outside of Austin. Those two don't get along. Anyway, after leaving Austin, under the circumstances we're all aware of, Camila landed in Houston, where she's been trying to survive by doing Social Security disability law with a bottom-of-the-barrel attorney named Alan Sorelle. The guy's a dork, owns some shabby rental properties around town. A real ham-and-egger. Anyway, this is Harrison's first appointment in federal court."

"She's an infant," Fox chimed in.

"She's a freaking *zygote*," Smith added. There was another small outbreak of laughter.

"You understand that doesn't mean anything," Nutley said.

"I don't follow," said Smith, the other career prosecutor.

Nutley started pacing back and forth. "But why isn't her client taking the plea? She must have ideas at least, pulling some shit like that. If I'm going to litigate this case, I want to be one hundred percent, absolutely sure that the government will win. I want a slam dunk conviction! Leave nothing to chance."

"This is the state bar's discipline file," said Constance Washington. She slid a fat folder towards Nutley and pulled out another. "And *this* has all of her college and law school transcripts. Oh, one more thing. Not that it means much, but she did pull a 150 in the Multistate Professional Responsibility Exam, a perfect score."

"So she's good at multiple choice tests," said Nutley. "So what?"

Everyone laughed.

"Or at the very least, she's ethical. And?" Nutley picked up the file and glanced inside. He threw it back on the table. "People, all I'm saying is look alive. All this could mean nothing or everything. We catch her on a good day, she could find us flat-footed, knock our asses to the ground. I've seen it happen before. The case against Aldama is not open-and-shut by any means. Especially if the jury gets to hear we had to cut deals with the co-defendants to get them to point the finger."

Wyatt Fox spoke next. "As far as Odessa is concerned, we've covered all the bases, boss . . . crossed our T's and dotted our I's. We've interviewed every agent that participated in the takedown. They're going to say the Tahoe had a light out—that's the reason it got pulled over—and that Aldama gave consent to search. And don't forget, Rocky, the K9 also alerted the officers to the contraband. Everyone's on board and their stories line up. Pretty maids, all in a row."

"And McKenzie and Barrera can corroborate this as well?" asked Nutley. He fired another question before anyone could answer: "What are the chances McKenzie and Barrera will recant and refuse to flip?"

"They're locked in," Fox said, smiling. "They've pled guilty already, the only thing pending is their sentencing. They know that if they want that additional one-third reduction they have to come through for us, and we've asked Yamamoto to delay their sentencing 'til after the trial with Harrison. They're in the bag."

Nutley wasn't convinced, "what do McKenzie and Barrera say about the rear plate light?"

"What do you want them to say?" followed Fox.

"Was it out?"

"For sure," said Fox, "that's what they're going to say."

Special Agent Blackwell took the next shot: "We've scoured Odessa clean . . . Gosling is not going to find anything."

"Should I be worried about Gosling?"

The other agent from OFAC put in his two cents. "He can be neutralized . . . if need be, sir."

Nutley was processing all the information, staring at President Obama's picture up on one of the walls. "What else?"

"Aldama," replied Wyatt, "was sending money to his family back in Mexico. We've obtained Western Union records. Here they are. They're small wires. One hundred to two hundred dollars a week, without fail. We have them all, for the years he's been in the states."

Blackwell interrupted. "He has a young daughter who's disabled . . . we suspect that's who the Money Grams are for. . . "

"That's irrelevant. What else?"

The agent from OFAC looked at his notes. "We also think these guys were hired to move money for the Merida Cartel. We don't have anything to make us believe they were connected to the Gulf Cartel or the Zetas like we initially thought."

"How's that?"

Blackwell pointed at a section on his report. "We know pretty much all the players for the Cartel del Golfo and the Zetas. But the names Barrera and McKenzie have provided don't pop up anywhere on our radar. The monies were for somebody else. A new organization."

Nutley looked squarely at Blackwell. "Can we prove Aldama knew the monies were in the SUV?"

"Yes," interjected Washington, "*if* the co-defendants point the finger at Aldama and say that, through *their* conversations with him, Aldama revealed that he knew the car was loaded with money."

Nutley pressed further. "Can they also say that Aldama told them they were moving the $850,000?"

The assistant US attorneys and special agents looked at each other. They knew it was always better if the government proved that the occupants of the car not only agreed to move the car, but that they knew the car was loaded with a certain amount and that the proceeds came from some unlawful activity.

Blackwell volunteered the answer: "The co-defendants claimed they didn't know the exact amount, but they will say they knew they were moving money. The way these guys operate, some folks load the car, others pick up and deliver it to remove the drugs or unload the money. And others actually drive the longer distances. The whole operation is compartmentalized."

"Wyatt," said Nutley, "I want you to call Ms. Harrison and ask her for reciprocal discovery, again."

"Yes, boss."

"We have to find out what she's up to," Nutley ordered. "And we need to show that Aldama knew for certain. Wyatt, Larry, I need you both on this. If we're to prove the charge of money laundering, we need to prove that the money came from some illegal activity. I don't want to leave anything to chance. Jurors always expect more proof than is necessary. I want to show that they knew the money was stashed and that the money came from the sale of drugs. That way Aldama's counsel has no room to wiggle."

The prosecutors and special agents sprang to their feet, gathered their notes and left the war room, marching orders in hand.

⁂

"Your client is forcing the government's hand, Ms. Harrison. Does he know what's going to happen when the jury convicts him?" Barton Nutley asked, pretending to be annoyed at the lawyer sitting in front of his desk. "What's gotten into him? I thought the eight-year offer was very generous."

"He knows he can get the max, I've explained that to him," Camila replied.

"Does he think that you're going to find some technicality, and he's going to skate? If that's the case you need to bring him back down to earth, Counselor, or he's going to be toast."

"Don't you think I've tried like crazy to convince him to cooperate, reduce his exposure? Get him to plea? Nothing has worked," replied Camila. "He has a sick daughter and wants to be able to attend her funeral. . . . He's holding out for *that*."

"I'll tell you what I'll do, and I'll do this because of his daughter and for *no* other reason. I guess you could say this would be the humanitarian thing to do," said Nutley, looking as forthright as he could, in a pose that suggested a virtuous man running for public office. One would never sense that earlier in the day he'd found out that the sequence of events that led to Aldama's arrest had, indeed, originated with a tip from a known corroborator.

Camila sat up straight. "Yes?"

"When I took this post," continued Nutley, "I took an oath. My oath was not to send everybody to jail, or to prosecute every single case, to ask for the maximum sentence or keep a tally of all my convictions. I didn't sign up for this in order to win some trophy or medal or high position. No, the oath I took . . . you know what it was?" He gave her his full gaze. Someone looking in on the scene would almost expect a father to be imparting wisdom to a daughter.

"I have no clue," said Camila.

"My oath of office," explained Nutley, "was to do justice . . . justice for the victim, for society, even for the defendant. Every case is different. I have to balance the rights of the accused versus the rights of society. I have to consider any mitigating evidence when such evidence is available. I also have to consider the seriousness of the offense, any collateral damage and any evidentiary issues that may arise in order for the government to prove its case."

"I hear you," Camila replied, then thought: *What's going on?*

"So, as much as I would like to try this case," Nutley laughed nervously, hoping Camila wouldn't get wind of the latest developments, "your client is in luck. I'm willing to reduce his sentence to just sixty months . . . five years."

"Okay . . . " muttered Camila, quite surprised. "That's very generous."

"Look," continued Nutley, "he would just have to plea to some other sort of violation."

"You're willing to drop the money laundering, the most serious charge?"

"Yup." Nutley smiled a warm smile. "He must agree to avoid a trial and enter a plea by this Friday. With credit for time served and good conduct, he'll probably only serve forty months, somewhere around three and a half years, half of an eight-year sentence. I'll let him plea to transporting cash in bulk . . . it's less serious."

"That's a good plea bargain," Camila declared. "Let me tell him . . . see if he'll take it."

"You do that. You tell him that the alternative, should he choose to fight and get convicted, is that I'll make sure Yamamoto gives him the max. No person in his or her right mind would chance it, unless they're reckless or stupid."

Camila was digesting the information when she blurted out, "This reminds me of the Robledo case that I tried in the Alamo City with my old firm."

"Come again?"

"It was a case my old firm in Austin defended. We represented Mr. Robledo, pro bono. I was co-counsel in the case. We tried it in state court in San Antonio. We contended that the cops had manufactured probable cause in order to avoid having to go to the judge for a search warrant."

"I'd like to hear about it," Nutley replied, playing nice. He wondered how come none of his assistants had caught the CI issue earlier.

"We should have fought harder for our client. Once we made the government aware of the bad search, they offered Mr. Robledo the moon and the stars. Ultimately, my client took the deal, but the whole thing always bothered me, you know?"

"Why?"

Camila looked into Nutley's eyes. "Because our firm became part of the problem, don't you see? Instead of making sure those dirty cops never worked again, we simply took the deal and didn't kick up any dust. Those cops continued to work the streets. We never fixed the underlying problem. They're probably still out there now, cutting corners, cheating the system, maybe even sending innocent folks to jail."

"But y'all got your client a great deal," said Nutley, with what Camila thought looked like a car salesman's smile.

"I guess," muttered Camila.

Nutley gulped hard. Was Harrison onto them? How much did she know? "Let me ask you," he said. "Was Robledo a drug dealer? A true criminal?"

"Of course," said Camila. "He'd buy marijuana in South Texas, then re-package it and FedEx it to different places all over the country."

"There you have it. He caught a break, and so did they. Two wrongs don't make a right, sure, but those officers have the capacity to do more good than harm in the long run. Meanwhile, Robledo . . . a criminal is a criminal, dyed in the wool. He should have gotten lots more years, but y'all got him a better deal. *You* spotted the manufactured probable cause. *You* played that angle. The system worked for *you*, you see?"

"There are similarities here. Why are you being so generous? Tell me."

Nutley started stuttering, "Well . . . you see . . . uh . . . . There's mi-mitigating circumstances . . . and . . . "

"You're throwing us a bone because there's an informant, isn't there?"

Nutley leaned forward, squinting, as if staring into the sun. "Well, yes, I mean . . . technically there is, but it's not a transactional informant. More like a tipster, an asset of sorts."

"That's what they're called now? An asset!" Camila squinted. "*That's* why you're being so kind, that's what this is: Same shit, different case. *Don't make waves. Take the deal and go away quietly,* huh?"

Nutley looked offended. "Well, if I were you, I wouldn't make a big deal out of it. And I certainly wouldn't overthink it, Counselor. Go take the plea offer to your client, see what he says. You have a duty to present it to him."

"Oh, I'll take him the offer." Camila started to rise. "I'm even going to suggest he takes it. Just don't think for one second you pulled the wool over my eyes."

"Counselor," said Nutley, "this is a good result, a fair result. Justice. So maybe the Odessa Unit falls short on occasion, but at the same time, your client *was* caught violating the law. The US government is willing to compromise. I suggest your client does the same."

Camila stood there, internalizing Nutley's last comment.

Nutley stared back, undaunted. He would never admit there was an actual CI. He would fudge the truth instead, label him a tipster, some stranger that had called the Crime Stoppers hotline.

"You'll hear from us before Friday, Mr. Nutley. One way or another, you'll have our answer. I promise."

FIFTEEN

"Well, this is a treat," Thelma said. She and Camila sat down at a little place called Catalina Coffee House on Washington Avenue, an up-and-coming area of town destined to become Houston's very own version of 6th Street, an Austin mecca. Thelma had agreed to meet Camila after she had called and left a message saying that she needed to pick her brain—something regarding the Aldama case was troubling her.

"All of a sudden, Nutley is bending over backwards to help my client," started Camila as she poured a packet of Truvia into her cappuccino.

"Really?" replied Thelma, surprised by this latest revelation. "Why do you think that is?"

"The whole thing is fishy." Camila tasted her cappuccino. She blew on it. Still too hot. "I have a feeling that there's a hole in their ship. Now, Nutley admits there was a tip that came in. I'm sure there's more, I just don't know how much more. I'm starting to think maybe I should really take the case to trial . . . but even if there's a chink in their armor it's still a gamble."

"And your client? What is he saying?"

"He wants to get out—really, really, badly. I tell him we should keep pushing, force a dismissal or a better deal. Well, you already know . . . he has a daughter with ALS, she doesn't have long to live. They've offered him five years—three and change if he can keep on the straight and narrow—but he's afraid his daughter will be dead by the time he gets out. We're stuck between a rock and hard place."

Thelma rolled her eyes, sipped at her chai tea. "What if there *is* a trial and they convict him? Is he willing to roll the dice and end up doing a couple decades in prison?"

"I think he thinks that the gamble can only help him. Five years, twenty-plus years . . . his baby will be gone either way."

"So he thinks he's really got nothing to lose by pushing the trial," figured Thelma.

"And everything to gain."

"But that's not going to happen, *amiga*," said Thelma. "You and I both know that. This is federal court. The little guy never wins in federal court, much less if the little guy also happens to be undocumented."

"What would you do?" Camila asked, looking stressed. "I kind of want to get to the truth, find out why Nutley is bending *so far* over backwards."

Thelma sipped her tea. "Is that it?"

"I don't know anymore," Camila moaned. "That's part of it. Deep in my heart of hearts, I know the arresting agency botched things up. I want to expose them."

"Sixty months is a very good deal, Camila. Never mind that it's *too* good. You should be pushing him to take it. And besides, the decision doesn't belong to you, no matter if you think you can win the case. Sure, you push him this direction, you push him that direction, but in the end you've told him all the facts and he knows exactly where he stands. It's *his* call when it's all said and done."

Camila stirred her cappuccino, trying to make the foam blend into the hot liquid until you'd never be able to tell it was there, the same way she wanted all her troubles to disappear.

"Are you listening to what I'm saying?"

"I was kind of hoping you would tell me to go for it . . . push me to do it," Camila answered from behind her drink. She licked her lips as she put the cup down. "Build me up . . . encourage me. You know, *not* shoot me down."

"This is a different kind of animal, Camila. I know everybody wanted you to get back in the saddle, take a case and work out the nerves. But there's a huge difference between plea-bargaining a case . . . and trying a case."

"Five years or twenty." Camila paused. "His daughter *is* going to be dead either way. Don't you see? Besides, I think I can win the case."

"You think?"

"I know it!"

Thelma was stunned.

Camila nodded. "Yup. I feel pretty good, Gosling is right."

Silence.

Thelma was worried. Was Camila coming unglued? Was it the Houston air? What had happened to the old Camila Harrison? The one that, not long ago, wanted to stop practicing law altogether? The one who was just going to plea her client, get out and run for the hills?

Camila kept going. "I know I can win the case, Thelma. Alicia deserves to see her dad again before she dies." Her eyes filled with tears. "I know what it's like to be apart from the ones you love."

Thelma reached over and touched Camila's hand. "I know the whole story, okay? I know this makes you think of Dante . . . but you need to take the deal, Camila. Deep down you know that's better for your client. I know you don't want to hear it, but that's my advice."

"But . . . "

"You're playing with fire, Camila."

"There's a confidential informant! My investigator confirmed this. Nutley calls him something else, but basically has admitted it. They don't want to burn him, probably wants to keep using him for other cases. If I push for a trial and they don't want Yamamoto to order the government to produce the informant, they're going to have to dismiss the case. That's why I need to take it to trial. My investigator says we can win this! He says that Odessa is dirty. It needs to come out, the whole truth."

"Forget this truth business, Camila. You're an attorney, for Christ's sake!"

"But I . . . thought . . . maybe . . . "

"This is the federal government. Nobody wins, Yamamoto is not going to let you win. It's Yamamoto's job to send the message that nobody can win in federal court. Nobody can beat the United States of America. Not the little people, anyway. Don't you see that?"

Camila played with a napkin. "I've decided. I'm not going live the rest of my life looking the other way, standing on the sidelines and doing nothing."

"You're being irrational, Camila."

"I'm going to take the case to trial, Thelma. And I need you to back me up. At least support me, encourage me . . . don't fight me."

Silence.

Thelma poured herself more tea from the small, metal tea pot. She took a deep breath. It was time to switch the focus of Camila's attention. "Just promise me you won't try to change his mind if he decides on the plea. You hear his choice, and you go along with it. Promise?"

Camila smiled from ear to ear. "I promise."

Thelma studied Camila's face. "I'm serious, Camila! Nutley wants to run for Texas Attorney General and he's not going to put up with any negative headlines. He *will* beat you, one way or another. He'll do whatever he needs to do to win. I beg you, come to your senses."

⁂

Camila Harrison faked a smile as Alan Sorelle came into her office and sat down. "Whatcha working on?"

Camila put the Aldama file off to the side and picked up a letter. It was an unfavorable decision from the OHA in a case she had handled a while back. She pretended to be reading the judge's opinion. "Just clearing my desk, trying to get organized. Why?"

"I just got off the phone with Thelma. She sounded concerned."

"She doesn't want me to take the Aldama case to trial . . . but there's nothing I can do if my client instructs me to try the case. I have to honor his wishes."

"What happened to getting rid of the case quickly? Doing the plea and getting out? Submitting your voucher for payment?"

"My investigator," Camila said impatiently, "stumbled onto some good evidence. I think my client has a shot. At a minimum, I think if I push for a trial Nutley will offer me something better than the sixty months that are on the table."

Sorelle studied Camila's body language. "And if he doesn't? What if he withdraws the offer? Are you telling me your client's so stupid that he'd rather get popped for twenty years?"

Camila made a face. "I'm getting sick and tired of naysayers. We have a shot. I know I can win the case, I can feel it. I'm intimately familiar with the facts surrounding the arrest of my client; I've read the file, the reports. All I have to do is go by Buc-ee's!"

"What have you been smoking?" Sorelle scoffed. "Your guy was in a Tahoe with close to a million dollars in cash! He's a day laborer. Everybody on that jury will know it's drug money. You wanna be slapped with another grievance? Take the plea, everybody wins; forge ahead, you're more lost than you were at the outset."

"Ha!" laughed Camila. "You'll see."

"C'mon! Get real, Camila! The jury will believe the cops, the arresting agents. These guys are going to show up to court in their uniforms, with their weapons and badges, looking like the real shit, the protectors. These are the good guys. Jurors will be smitten out of basic patriotic duty. And what does your client have, huh? You think he'll get by on the average Joe's love of *churros*? What are you thinking? Have you lost your mind? You and your client don't stand a chance—"

"Get out!" ordered Camila. "I thought you'd support me. You wanted me to get back on the horse, and now that I'm doing exactly that, you've decided to turn against me? Start giving me shit? The hell with you! The hell with Thelma, too! My client wants a trial and that's what he's going to get. I've got work to do, so get out of my office!"

"Bird in the hand . . . always better than the two in the bush," mumbled Sorelle. "Just remember that."

"Kiss my ass!"

With that, Sorelle left Camila's office.

Camila was checking her emails, still fuming. She wondered if Vicente Aldama had what it took to face what was to come. She needed to come up with a theme for the case and develop a favorable juror profile. She needed jurors who did not trust the government, folks who were skeptical of cops and had been wrongfully arrested, ticketed or charged with a bogus crime in the past. People who had been vindicated in court, who had been exonerated. She needed jurors who believed the system was easily manipulated by those in charge. She didn't need friends, spouses or relatives of personnel in law enforcement.

She was still deep in thought when she noticed an email. It read ALDAMA, URGENT! in the subject line.

Camila clicked it open.

It was AUSA Fox, saying that Mr. Nutley wanted to know if Aldama was going to take the deal. The trial was right around the corner.

So, you want a reply, huh?

She looked at her watch, then clicked on the COMPOSE button. She started typing away:

Dear Mr. Fox,
Thanks for staying on top of this case.
I've spoken to Mr. Aldama and explained to him the government's generous offer. Unfortunately, at this time, we're rejecting the plea and the five-year jail sentence.
Mr. Aldama insists on going to trial.

Sincerely,
Camila Harrison

She did the sign of the cross and hit the SEND button.

They met for dinner in midtown Houston, a mom-and-pop Greek diner with the smell of oregano and wood-fired pizza float-

ing in the air. The old waiter with the heavy Greek accent handed
the pair menus and took their drink orders. Camila played with
the basket of warm pita chips and the small dish of olive oil in the
middle of the table.

"I wanted to see you and tell you that I went ahead and
pawned my engagement ring. I figured since he called off the wedding, I did not have to give it back. So, I'm ready to hire you. Or
at least give you seven thousand dollars to get started. Can you
work with that?"

Pruitt put down his menu and smiled. "Absolutely."

"It was worth at least twice that," said Camila, as she handed
Pruitt a cashier's check, "but it was time to let it go. Besides, I need
to take care of you, so you can help me take care of the State Bar
and Hulse."

"I got the materials you sent me," said Pruitt, as he stashed
away the check inside one of his coat's pockets, "and had a chance
to review Hulse's complaint. My take on your case is that it is very
defensible . . . in fact, the remarks you made to your clients in the
emails are more of a violation of the Texas Lawyers' Creed than a
violation of the rules of ethics."

"Is that a good or a bad thing?"

"It's a good thing," Pruitt answered, "and I think I can get the
grievance dismissed . . . but here's where we have to be careful."

"I'm listening."

"If I was Hulse . . . and the State Bar didn't do anything . . . but
I lost some big clients because of something a partner did, or
didn't do . . . I might sue that partner for breaching his or her fidu-
ciary duties to the partnership."

"Are you saying Hulse might still come after me?"

"It's possible. You might want to put your insurance carriers
on notice . . . just in case."

Both attorneys glanced at each other, as if acknowledging that
there was a real possibility that Hulse's grievance could snowball
into something more. A real problem.

"Shit!" Camila said, "I hope it doesn't come to that. My
deductible is twenty-five. I don't have that kind of money."

Pruitt stared at Camila, intensely. "I'm going to share with you a small piece of free legal advice."

Camila's eyes opened wide. "File for bankruptcy?"

"No," said Pruitt, "fight fire with fire."

"What do you mean?"

"If we beat this grievance thing," Pruitt started before taking a swig from his beer, ". . . and Hulse insists on coming after you, personally. You'll need some ammo. Something that will make them stop and reconsider, stop them dead in their tracks. Anything that might give you leverage . . . gender discrimination or pay discrimination . . . sexual harassment, affairs with the staff . . . you get what I'm saying?"

"Yes, I do."

"Something that you can hold over their heads . . . stuff that will make them think twice before they continue to lock horns with you. You have to be proactive . . . find ways to protect yourself from any eventuality."

The waiter came by to take their order, but Camila was no longer hungry.

SIXTEEN

"What do you mean she rejected the government's offer? What does Bart have to say about all this?" Bruce Michaels asked. He was flabbergasted. "Who does that insolent little twat think she is?"

Assistant US Attorney Wyatt Fox was making the rounds, visiting the co-defendants' counsel, bringing them up to speed on the latest developments surrounding the Aldama prosecution. Fox was in Bruce Michaels' office, located in a highrise next to Joel Osteen's Lakewood Church. The place was decorated with colorful Mexican wrestler masks, framed wrestler capes in different fabrics and sizes and blown-up photographs of a younger Michaels wearing hot pink tights, doing aerial maneuvers from the wrestling ring's top rope. He'd been known as El Sicario.

"Can you believe the gall?!" asked Fox as he focused on a movie poster hanging on the wall behind Michaels' desk.

Right underneath the poster was a small plaque documenting Bruce Michaels' work as a stunt coordinator for the movie, Nacho Libre. Next to the poster was a framed picture of Michaels posing with actor Jack Black.

"Do you need me to prep my client?" Michaels asked. "Is that what Bart sent you to discuss?"

Of the other two co-defendants, Michaels had been appointed to represent Barrera. In his mid-fifties, Michaels had his long, dirty-blond hair tied in a ponytail; there was a large scar over his right eye. Just minutes earlier, he'd been at his desk listening to a conservative shock jock on his computer while eating a tuna salad sandwich and potato chips. Despite his age, Michaels still looked to be in great shape.

"Yes. We need your guy prepped and ready to testify," said Fox. "We're going to try and visit with Aldama's counsel one last time. Sweeten the deal some more, see if she takes it."

"And if she doesn't?" asked Michaels, licking his grease-covered finger tips before wiping them on the faded jeans he wore.

"We'll have to try the case. That's where you and your client, as well as Burwell and McKenzie, come in. We'll need all the co-defendants to come through for the government."

"Remind me again, what exactly do you need my guy to say?"

"That Aldama knew the car had money," said Fox, becoming impatient. "That he was aware they were moving $850,000—that figure is important. Don't worry, we're gonna help you with the prep."

"Done." Michaels flashed a warm, although distorted, smile, probably from years of taking flying kicks to the head. "I'll go talk to my guy, again."

"Good."

"Let me ask you," said Michaels, scratching a faded skull-and-dagger tattoo on his right forearm, "what was the last offer this Harrison chick rejected?"

"Sixty months."

"Lordy, Lordy!" exclaimed Michaels. "What did she do to deserve such a good deal? Are there issues with the case? With Odessa?"

"Nah, not Odessa in particular, but she's pushing to discover the informant's identity, and he's *quasi* transactional. Anyway, we'd rather not burn him. Yamamoto opened Pandora's Box when he agreed to give her money for an investigator. Guy's filling her head with ideas."

"Who's the investigator?"

"Gosling," said Fox.

"Doesn't ring a bell," Michaels replied. "I'll talk to Barrera, bring him up to speed. Do you think I should speak to Burwell also? Line up our stories?"

"Yes, a united front. Also, they need to say that they heard Aldama explicitly give consent for the agents to search the Tahoe. Don't forget. And remind your clients they will be rewarded accordingly."

"You guys are too much." Michaels got up from his desk and walked toward his mini fridge. He reached inside and pulled out a chilled Monster Energy drink, popped it open and took a swig. "You tell Nutley not to worry, that Barrera is going to testify that Aldama was the boss and that he moved millions every year."

Fox smiled. "That's the ticket."

"Friends helping friends." Michaels studied Fox's expression. "Don't you just love our criminal justice system?"

"Listen up, people!" yelled Barton Nutley, commanding everyone's attention. "We have a lot of work to do. The trial is quickly approaching, and Harrison is starting to annoy the shit out of me. There's something going on, and I don't like it."

Wyatt Fox, Blackwell, Dot Griffin, three investigators and five more attorneys from the US attorney's office were sitting in the war room.

Nutley stood, ready to commence the prep session. "Mr. Fox has already approached Jeremy Burwell and Bruce Michaels with instructions on getting their clients ready. Isn't that correct, Wyatt?"

"Correct. Burwell and Michaels have been briefed."

"When are we going to work with the agents who busted Aldama and the other two?"

"Wyatt and I," indicated Special Agent Blackwell, "have scheduled the entire crew to come in this weekend and go over everything; their testimony, their reports and the evidence."

"Great!" replied Nutley.

"What about any weaknesses in our case? What are we doing about that? Anybody? Have we pulled the evidence from the locker room?"

"The bundles of money have been accounted for—no chain of custody issues," replied another one of the assistant US attorneys.

"Good," said Nutley.

Another attorney spoke next. "We have enough evidence to prove all the elements alleged in the indictment. We can prove our case beyond a reasonable doubt."

"This is what I want to see happen!" yelled Nutley. "Investigators, I want two of you to stay on top of Gosling, track his every move. And one of you has to stay on top of Harrison, see what *she's* up to."

"Yes, sir," answered the trio of PIs.

"Wyatt," continued Nutley, "get together with Dot and run some good stories in the local papers about the success the Odessa unit has had in recent years. I want a front-page article in the *Houston Chronicle* showcasing drug busts and other accomplishments. See if we can have *Texas Monthly* do a feature. I want good press everywhere: radio, Facebook, newspapers, social media, Twitter . . . "

Everybody nodded in agreement, excited about the upcoming trial. Camila Harrison was not going to know what hit her.

SEVENTEEN

Camila, Thelma and Gosling found themselves eating lunch together at Mai's, a popular Vietnamese eatery located a few blocks from Sorelle's office. The place was packed with college kids and young professionals.

"Camila tells me you were a cop?" Thelma asked. She dipped a springroll in the fish and peanut sauce bowls in front of her before taking a small bite.

"That's right," Gosling replied, keeping a close eye on the peanut sauce dripping from Thelma's springroll. "I put in close to fifteen years, got tired of working with dirty cops . . . so I quit."

Camila was busy eating a bowlful of Mai's fried rice.

"Camila tells me you got wind that there's a confidential informant. Is that *all* you guys got? Do you have a name? Is he transactional? Was he present when the car was filled with cash? Did he prep the car?"

Gosling put his spoon down. He looked slightly irritated.

Thelma continued her questioning. "What have you uncovered? Where did you hear this? How is it going to help the case? Do you know where they prep the cars? Do you have any other leads? What's the approach, the strategy? Who's your source?"

"Jesus Christ! Give me a second." Gosling took a deep breath, wiped his mouth with a paper napkin and said, "The source . . . it's a guy . . . a guy I know. I've worked with him before . . . I can't reveal his name. I don't burn my sources."

Thelma kept pressing. She did not like what she was hearing. Was Camila's lead investigator stringing Camila along?

"Hey, let me ask you . . . have you ever had your license suspended? Any grievances filed against you?"

Camila sat up, stopped eating. She wanted to hear this.

"Well, there was this one instance, but nothing came of it," Gosling acknowledged.

"I'm sure it was nothing," Camila remarked. She put down her fork. "Your license is in good standing, right?"

"Last time I checked," chuckled Gosling. He continued spooning and slurping his Pho.

"So what happened?" Thelma asked. She wasn't about to let it go.

"Some crazy lawyers said I took their money," Gosling explained, "and that I didn't do the job. But I was cleared of any wrongdoing. This was long ago. We went in front of the licensing agency and nothing came of it."

"What lawyers?"

"The firm is now defunct, but they were called Rosenthal & Associates, out of Williamson County. I think one partner committed suicide. The other went to prison."

"Why did they say you took their money?"

"They hired me to find a witness in Mexico, so I made them pay me in advance. When nothing turned up, they wanted their money back," answered Gosling. "They didn't want to hear that all the money had been spent crisscrossing Mexico, following leads, encountering dead-ends, greasing palms and chasing red herrings. Without the witness, they couldn't make the case, a big case. They were mad, but I did my job to the best of my ability. It wasn't my fault there was nothing there to find."

Thelma felt somewhat satisfied with his explanation, but probed in another direction. "You must certainly have a Plan B," offered Thelma, "in case the informant angle doesn't pan out, huh? What if Judge Yamamoto says you don't get to talk about that and the jury never gets to hear anything about the source, then what?"

Gosling looked at Camila. Thelma looked at Camila, then to Gosling, then back at Camila.

Camila blurted out, "Yeah, what *is* Plan B?"

"Don't worry," smiled Gosling, ready with an answer. "My contact tells me there was nothing wrong with the rear plate lights that the guys from Odessa used as a pretext to pull the Tahoe over."

"*That's* your plan B?! You're counting on there being no probable cause for the traffic stop?"

"That's what I hear . . . "

"Do we have the Tahoe?"

"Not the actual vehicle," Camila admitted. "We're being told that all that remains are the *photos* of the vehicle. Nutley claims they auction off seized vehicles, and Fox said he believed a used car dealer bought it."

"Well, do the pictures show the condition of the plate lights? Can we tell?"

"No," Camila said. They're taken from different angles, but none show the rear plate area."

"Well, isn't *that* convenient?" marveled Thelma.

Gosling looked at a text message on his cell phone screen and suddenly sprang from the table. "Speak of the devil! I've gotta run, ladies. My contact thinks he's found the Tahoe. This is the guy who knows this *other* guy in the used car business."

"Good news," replied Thelma.

Gosling put away his cell phone, chugged his iced tea and said, "Possibly. We'll see."

Thelma and Camila watched the private investigator bolt from the restaurant.

⁜

Thelma and Camila paused outside the entrance to the Harris County Law Library, located catty-corner from the old county courthouse now housing the 1st and 14th District Courts of Appeals.

"Okay," started Thelma, "I'll drop the Gosling topic once and for all, but don't you come back and say I didn't warn you. I think the guy's a con man. He rubs me the wrong way."

"Okay," winced Camila, "you've made your point. I get it, you don't like him."

"And another thing," added Thelma, "if I'm going to help you do legal research and prepare for trial, you have to promise me one thing."

"What's that?"

"We're going to do it my way."

"What do you propose?"

Thelma looked straight into Camila's eyes. "We're going to start with the jury charge and work our way backwards. That's the only way to do this. Got it?"

"Okay . . . "

As a seasoned trial lawyer and professor, Thelma knew that jury charge provided a blueprint of the things needed to be proved by the prosecution and the defense. "I mean it," she said.

"So do I," answered Camila, "really."

"We're not going to deviate from the plan: We start from the end of the case and work our way backwards to jury selection. There won't be any jumping or skipping around, doing a bit of this or a bit of that. It's either my way or the highway. If you don't like what I'm offering, then you can do it alone. "

"I understand," answered Camila, clutching the overstuffed satchel under her shoulder. "It's a deal."

The friends shook hands.

"Here's the check from Drew West," a satisfied Camila Harrison announced, as she handed Trey Collins an envelope containing a certified check for a million dollars. "Do you have something for us?"

After the prep session at the law library, Camila had rushed to meet Trey Collins. They were on the 50th floor in a large conference room inside his office. After much back and forth, Camila

Harrison had agreed to continue to help Drew West, in secrecy, to negotiate a settlement with the lawyer representing Gene Voguel. The secret settlement negotiations had been ongoing for several weeks, now. Thankfully, West and Voguel had finally reached a compromise.

"Here's my client's signed release and confidentiality agreement," Collins smiled, delighted, pushing a stack of documents across the conference room. "Glad to see your client came around. Have Mr. West sign the counterparts and return the originals to me. You can keep a copy."

Camila grabbed the stack and started flipping some pages. Everything appeared to be in order. She looked at the clock on the wall. It was almost midnight. "And the other stuff?"

Collins pulled out a different envelope from his coat's pocket. "You mean this?"

"Yes."

"There's a flash drive inside. I believe its contents should help. Who else do you anticipate will see what's in it?"

"Just Ned and me."

Collins got up and poured himself a drink from the whiskey decanter set on top of a table over by the corner. "Good. I don't want any issues with Hulse. They can never find out where you got this."

"I won't say a thing."

"What they did to you was unforgivable," followed Collins, "I hope you kick their asses."

She stashed away the settlement documents and the envelope in her satchel and got up to leave.

"Aren't you forgetting something?" Collins asked.

She stopped, turned around, and started digging in her satchel. "You mean this?" She waved the ownership papers to one of Drew's planes. It was a Cirrus 2012 SR 22T. "That should cover your attorney's fees."

"A pleasure doing business with you," Collins said raising his glass, toasting another well-deserved victory.

EIGHTEEN

Luzatto's was one of Houston's popular Italian grills, where Mexican attaché Gustavo Govela always came to dinner when business called.

"How many?" asked the pretty hostess with a cute smile and freckles.

"There'll be two of us," Govela smiled back, not completely sure if Camila Harrison would show up to the impromptu rendezvous.

The place was packed. It was 6:00 p.m., the dinner hour, and Govela could see there was nowhere to sit in the main dining room.

"It's a forty-five-minute wait," announced the hostess. The manager came up from behind and waved for a party of five to follow him to a table that had just been reset.

"That won't do . . . " said Govela.

"We do have the communal table out in the *cortile*, our patio. Or, if you'd prefer, you could eat at the bar if you don't want to wait. It's up to you," suggested the hostess.

"Communal table will do," answered Govela, and off they went.

"Sorry I'm late . . . " apologized Camila as she took her place across from Govela.

The *cortile* was a replica of a Tuscan covered patio. Located off to one side of the restaurant, it was paved with flag stone, its walls lined with flowering vines. The rustic communal table sat underneath strings of lights which lent the place an air of intimacy. Two young couples, out on a double date, were already working on their main entrées a couple of seats down from where Govela and Camila sat.

Govela put down his dirty gin martini. "I'm just glad you made it!"

"Thank you," replied Camila. She was wearing jeans, tall leather boots and a pretty sweater. "Have you been waiting long?"

"No . . . just sat down."

"That looks good. What are you drinking?"

"This is a dirty Bombay martini," Govela said, raising his glass.

"I want to thank you for inviting me out. This is very nice," she said as she looked around the place. "I needed a break. The Aldama case is consuming my life. Every single day, hour, minute, second . . . I really needed this."

"Don't mention it," replied Govela, ready to shower Camila with compliments. "*Te ves guapísima.*"

Camila blushed. It had been months since anybody had paid her a compliment, or had anything nice to say about her at all really. And, she realized that Govela's Spanish did not bother her at all.

The waiter suddenly appeared table-side and addressed Camila. "Can I get the beautiful lady something to drink?"

"I'll have a lemon drop martini, with Tito's vodka, please," said Camila, "and make it straight up, very chilled."

"And I'll have another one," instructed Govela.

The waiter wrote the order down on his pad. "Twist, no twist?"

"Twist," answered Camila while studying Govela. "Thanks."

"Very well," said the waiter, and scurried away.

"Not to completely kill the mood," Govela said, "but how are things with the case?"

"Looks like we're going to trial," explained Camila, reading the menu. "We are scheduled to start in less than two weeks."

"Is there something we can help with? Do you need us to try and bring his parents up from Mexico for the trial? We might be able to get a waiver . . . if they don't have a visa."

"Oh," answered Camila, "they don't have a visa, trust me. They're very poor and they have their grandaughter to take care of. They can't leave her alone."

"We've done a lot of research on the applicability of the Hague Convention in cases where Mexican nationals get arrested over on this side. Let me know if you need me to research any issue or if you want to use our investigator. I mean it."

The waiter showed up to deliver the drinks and a basket of warm bread, with a ramekin of homemade, honey-lavender butter.

Camila sipped her drink. "That's so nice of you to offer, but Judge Yamamoto gave me funds to hire a PI; I think we're okay. And my best friend, Thelma, she's also helping. Thanks, anyway."

"Aw, shucks, and here I was . . . hoping I could help out a beautiful lady." Govela looked her in the eyes, all hunger beneath his calm voice, a smirk on his face.

Camila stared back, eyebrow raised. "I said I have an investigator, not that you couldn't help me."

"Ready to order?" interrupted the waiter.

"I think so," answered Govela, his eyes still on Camila.

⁎⁎⁎

They were tangled in a mess of bed sheets back at the Hyatt Hotel, in a luxury suite that the Mexican government rented year-round for consular official business.

Strewn about on the floor were socks, shoes, pants, panties, a sweater and boxers. The clock on the nightstand showed 4:00 a.m.

"Are you sleeping?" asked Camila as she played with Govela's hair.

The double curtains in the room were drawn shut. The pair was surrounded by complete darkness. The only sound coming from the AC blowing gently through the vents.

"No, ma'am."

After dinner, Gustavo Govela and Camila Harrison ended up back at the suite. One thing had led to another, and now they were both trying to work through the awkwardness that always followed a new lover.

"By the way . . . you didn't have to borrow my shirt or turn off the lights," said Govela. "You know that, right?"

"I didn't want you to see me," whispered Camila. "I haven't been with many men."

"Well, go find you a few more. I'll wait here. When you get back you can turn the light on and give my shirt some rest."

Camila slapped him playfully on the arm.

"You're perfect in my book," Gustavo whispered.

"You're sweet," said a surprised Camila. "I wish more people were like you."

"Lemme tell you, it's easy with a woman like you."

Camila smiled in the dark. "It's just . . . Paxton often made fun of my breasts because the left one is smaller than the right. He could be such a jerk."

"I'm sorry to hear that. I don't understand why some people have to be so cruel." He kissed her hand. "Or so intolerant."

"Thelma has helped me a lot. She's been by my side every step of the way. Alan, too. We fight, go round and round, but I know, deep down inside, he cares. He's a good guy. I can see why Thelma, her husband Omar and Alan are good friends."

"I'm glad . . . "

"And you? What's your story?" asked Camila.

Gustavo sighed and reached for a pack of Benson & Hedges on the night stand. He lit one up. "You really want to know?"

"Sure . . . I've got a few hours."

"Did I tell you I *run* the foreign prosecutions department?"

"Yes."

"And that we get involved in all kinds of cases, not just death penalty ones. That's the public's misconception."

"Yes, you did, and you've already explained that, when the death penalty is in play . . . obviously those cases are headline-grabbers, and that's why people notice your involvement. So people think that's all you do," Camila followed. "But that's not what I'm interested in. You know what I'm asking."

"Okay," said Gustavo, "here it goes: I was married once. Her name is Vanessa. We got married when we were young, both in college. We had two children; Gustavo and Frida, they're both teenagers now. They live in Puebla, outside of Mexico City. I get to see them during the holidays. Occasionally, they come up here to visit. That's pretty much it, in a nutshell."

"What happened?"

"Work . . . I'm always traveling . . . didn't get to spend enough time with them. And Vanessa didn't want to move the kids anymore; we'd lived in Ecuador, Australia, Belgium, Denmark and Ireland. We were like gypsies. She felt the kids needed a stable environment and chose to stay put in Mexico. Anyway, that's what happened."

"You miss them?"

"Every day."

Gustavo put out his cigarette and held Camila close to him.

"But I also enjoy what I do," he added. "I wouldn't change a thing. I still believe I can make a difference."

Camila liked what she was hearing. "My father had a job like yours."

"Really?"

"Yup. He was in the foreign service. His name is Darin Harrison. He worked for the US Embassy in Mexico City, that's how he met my mother, Lorena. She was a bank teller. For the longest time, I held a grudge because he moved to Switzerland without us. I thought he had abandoned us. After college, I finally learned the truth. Then, I held a grudge against my mother."

"What happened?"

Camila let out a big sigh. There was a long silence. "Sometimes I wish I had not asked for the truth. You know what I mean?"

"It hurts, right? Especially when you're not ready to handle it."

"It's worse than that. Talk about feeling betrayed . . . "

Gustavo held her tight, waiting.

She suddenly realized she liked being in his arms. She composed herself, gathered her thoughts. "Okay, here it goes: My mother met my dad in church, just a regular Sunday, nothing out of the ordinary, nothing all that special, except that he fell in love with her, and she was smitten as well. But there was one problem. When my mother was young, she'd had a son she'd been forced to place for adoption. It was a shameful secret, which she kept to herself."

Camila could feel her mouth getting dry, just retelling the story. "Darin was madly in love with her, and had no clue. He wanted to marry her and start a new life."

Gustavo grabbed a cigarette and played with it in his right hand. He was dying to know where this was going.

"So they got married, and after years of marriage, I was born." Gustavo gulped.

"How old were you when you found out you had a half brother?"

"Eighteen."

"Ouch!"

"But that's not the half of it. Darin never came back for us after he left. The sad part is that I always believed that the reason my dad didn't come back was because of something I did. Years later, I found out that Lorena had been the one who had not wanted to move to Europe. She'd refused. She started by making excuses . . . that she didn't want to be away from her family . . . that she didn't know anybody in Switzerland . . . that she didn't think she could adapt, it was going to be too cold, too much snow. It was excuse after excuse after excuse . . . until the truth comes out."

"And let me guess," said Gustavo, "the real reason she couldn't leave Mexico was because . . . "

"Luis Pablo, of course," finished Camila. "She wanted to be close to the family that had adopted him. All that time she'd kept tabs on him. We never knew. No one ever suspected a thing. Why would we?"

"I'm sorry to hear that."

"That was the real reason my parents divorced," added Camila. "My dad felt betrayed. He couldn't handle it, and he stayed away, far away."

Gustavo stroked her hair, letting the silence be until Camila was ready to continue.

"So, you could say that I've had my share of issues with Mom and Dad. First with Lorena for causing the divorce, then with both of them for the half-brother bomb they dropped on me. And then when Lorena refused to give me and Dante her blessing to marry."

"Dante?"

"That's another story, for another day," reminisced Camila. "Dante de Melo. My Dante. He was a good guy. I was madly in love with him."

He kissed her forehead.

"I get to Rice University and that's when I met Dante. He was working on a PhD. Everything is going great, things are falling into place and everything is making sense. My life made sense. We made sense."

Camila got quiet.

"Years later, I realized that it had not been Lorena's fault. It had not been Dad's fault, either. It was nobody's fault, really. Lorena had been pushed to hide the truth because of social pressure, the way Mexico was back then. She had been a victim too. Thelma helped me see that Lorena had been afraid society would think she was damaged goods. It made perfect sense. And now that I'm older, I've had to deal with some of those same issues. Life came full circle."

"Well, now you won't have to deal with those issues alone. I'm here to help." He gave her another peck on the forehead and held her close.

Where have you been all my life? Camila thought.

"How long have you been practicing law?" Gustavo asked, hungry to hear more of Camila's story.

"Going on six years. I was twenty-six when I graduated from the University of Houston Law School. Afterward I landed a dream job in Austin. That's where I met Paxton Thomas III, at a cocktail party. I thought we made a great couple. I was so wrong—I see that now. It's almost funny in retrospect . . . . I mean, talk about patterns and learned behaviors. I was doing the exact same thing my mother did."

"Do you enjoy being a lawyer? I never did," admitted Gustavo. "That's why I gave it up and got this job. I hated the litigation aspect of it. I was fighting at home with Vanessa, then I had to wake up in the morning and go fight opposing counsel, but not before fighting traffic to get down to *tribunales*. Always fighting something."

"I've had my ups and downs," confessed Camila, "like everybody else, I suppose. Lately, I've realized you have to have something to believe in, something to get you through the day. I believe I can really help Vicente, if they would just give me a chance . . . let me try the case the way I want to."

"You'll be great. I know it."

They kissed until their passions began to rise.

NINETEEN

"You wanted to see me, Your Honor?"

"Please, take a seat," ordered Judge Colt Yamamoto. He pointed to an empty chair. Barton Nutley already occupied a seat across from the judge. They were in his chambers.

"What's this all about?" Camila asked as she sat down.

"I wanted a status report. To see if the government and Mr. Aldama had reached common ground. "Where are we? Mr. Nutley?"

Nutley cleared his throat. "Ah, yes, Your Honor. Let me see . . . as you already know, the co-defendants in the same case as Mr. Aldama got eight years each for money laundering."

"And?" asked Yamamoto.

"The government has made a very generous offer to Mr. Aldama, way below what McKenzie and Barrera got. This in order to avoid a very public trial. As the court is aware, a straight-up money-laundering case could carry a sentence of up to twenty years in prison."

"What's the offer for Mr. Aldama?" asked Yamamoto.

"Sixty months."

Yamamoto seemed surprised. "Five years?! Well, that's a hell of a deal in a case like this."

"We think so," added Nutley. "And he doesn't have to plea to the money laundering. We're willing to let him plea to a simple 'failure to report cash' or 'bulk cash smuggling' which are less serious offenses. Take your pick."

Yamamoto directed his attention to Camila. "Ms. Harrison, is that right? Is there an offer of sixty months for your client on the table?"

"Yes, Your Honor," answered Camila. "There is."

"And is your client going to take it?"

"No, Your Honor. He doesn't want to."

Yamamoto considered Camila's response, but didn't say anything. He sat without moving, digesting the words.

Nutley interjected, "Your Honor, for humanitarian reasons, we are willing to reduce Mr. Aldama's exposure significantly, let him get credit for time served, plus good conduct. He'll be home in three years. Thirty-six months max."

Yamamoto's eyes grew wide. "Ms. Harrison, you can't beat that. That's a hell of a deal! You need to go back to your client and explain to him that he needs to take it. Stop wasting everybody's time, for God's sake. Why would you want to force a trial? What's your defense?"

"I've even offered," Nutley interjected again, turning to Camila, "to make some calls so after he finishes serving his sentence, ICE can expedite his deportation. There won't be any delays."

"Wow!" exclaimed Yamamoto. "Looks to me like the government is really trying to help your client, Ms. Harrison. Now it's up to you to make him see the light. You need to convince him to take this very generous offer. Why would he insist on making everybody waste time, money and judicial resources? Do you know what's going to happen at sentencing if he gets convicted in my court?"

"Your Honor, we believe a CI is involved and we're entitled to discover their identity, plus there's the issue of the traffic stop. The whole case should be tossed," Camila argued. "The illegally obtained evidence—in my opinion—also constitutes fruit from the poisonous tree."

"Look," said a very determined Judge Yamamoto, "let's say you're right. You know how this works: If we have a suppression hearing, the court is not going to suppress the evidence. You can object all you want and take it up on appeal, but by the time you perfect the appeal and get a hearing up in the 5th Circuit, four or five years will have elapsed. Your client could have been home by then. Taking the case to trial will have been a waste of time. And even if you won the appeal in the 5th Circuit, at the end of the day, the result is the same."

"It's not practical," added Nutley.

Camila felt as if she was being railroaded. She could not believe her ears. "What about the confidential informant? My investigator tells me he's transactional and we're entitled to discover his identity."

Yamamoto was starting to get really annoyed. "So what?! Let's say you know who it is, how does that change anything? That doesn't help your client in the slightest. The CI comes and testifies, you cross him, so what? They'll testify that your client was involved and knew what he was doing. The jury's still going to pop Mr. Aldama. CI or no CI, your client is screwed!"

"If, in fact, there happened to be a CI," clarified Nutley, raising his finger in the air. "And only if they were transactional, which is not what we have here. Now, let's talk hypothetically. If there was a CI and there was a trial that could very well force the government to burn him or her here, the entire world would get to learn his or her identity and we wouldn't be able to use him or her anymore, but that still doesn't help your client. So in the end, he's found guilty and a CI is now useless for no good reason. The jury, I'm sure, would find the CI very convincing, very credible, and they'll sock it to Aldama. If you put him or her on the stand, that's exactly what will happen. How does that help your client? How does that help anyone? It's like a terrorist tactic: If you're going down, take as many as you can with you."

"I don't care," answered Camila.

"Ms. Harrison," continued Nutley, "I'm not admitting that there is or isn't a CI. However, you know that there's value in keeping one's identity concealed. Not burning them has value to law enforcement. Any agency would rather keep working with a productive CI, have him or her continue to make cases for the government. You know how long it takes to develop or groom a CI? You should take that into consideration."

Camila sat there, arms crossed. "I'm entitled to discover their identity and call them to testify. You guys are trying to protect your friends, Burwell and Michaels. They screwed up because they just rolled over and never did any discovery, never bothered to push to discover the CI. I don't know why they didn't, but it's probably because they're too cozy with the US attorney's office."

Nutley looked at Yamamoto. Yamamoto looked at Nutley. Yamamoto was starting to regret the day he'd appointed Camila Harrison to the case. What had gotten into her?

Nutley let out a big sigh. "Look, just for today . . . you go and talk to Mr. Aldama. And if he takes the plea, I'll let him plea to forty-eight months—and we're done."

"I suggest you tell your guy to take it, Ms. Harrison," ordered Judge Yamamoto, staring straight into Camila's eyes. "They're bending over backwards to help him, and that rarely happens! Christmas is coming early this year for him. You need to go see him, then get back to Mr. Nutley before five this afternoon, and the answer better be a yes. Forty-eight months? Wow! With credit for time served and good behavior . . . he'll be home in a little over two years."

"But the offer is only good until five o'clock today. So if your client wants to get home soon to tend to his daughter," followed Nutley, "this is his chance."

"We're going to trial, Your Honor," Camila replied without a hint of hesitation, "that's what my client wants."

Yamamoto shook his head in disbelief. He threw his hands up in the air. "Why are you doing this, huh? You can't win. You really want to expose your client to twenty years? That's called legal malpractice, you know. The sentencing guidelines are now advisory. You know very well that I don't even have to follow them. I can do whatever the hell I want, and I'm telling you, I will pop him for the twenty, Ms. Harrison."

"You do what you have to, Your Honor," Camila answered. "And I'll do what I have to."

Judge Yamamoto was getting more upset by the minute. No one ever rebuked a federal judge. No one. "I'll have to report you to the state bar for incompetence. You'll never practice again, Ms.

Harrison. Do you want to be reprimanded again for the whole world to see? Was Austin not enough?!"

"Once your client lands in prison," Nutley added more fuel to the fire. "The jailhouse lawyers are going to have a field day. We'll be back in court on a motion for a new trial for ineffective assistance of counsel. His new lawyer will put you on the stand . . . it'll be quite a spectacle. Why do you want to do this? Have Aldama take the goddamned plea!"

"I can't, Judge. Sorry," said Camila. "He specifically told me he wanted his day in court."

Yamamoto looked frazzled. "You don't get to decide! Go tell your client what the offer is."

"I already know what the answer will be," replied Camila.

Nutley pushed the issue. "Time's running out."

Yamamoto tried another approach. "Okay, if that's the way you want it. See you in ten days for jury selection. Don't say we didn't warn you."

Camila grabbed her bag and exited his chambers. Nutley did not know what to make of Camila Harrison, the most brazen attorney to have crossed paths with Chief Presiding Federal Judge Colt Yamamoto. If Camila Harrison was supposed to be a down-and-out attorney, she sure wasn't acting like one.

TWENTY

After Nutley's menacing deadline had expired, Vicente Aldama was hauled to court again. He had been briefed by Camila the night before and now was ready to face the US government. It was time to get through the final pre-trial conference, test the waters.

Though prisoners in federal court always went to court after eating breakfast or lunch, Judge Colt Yamamoto had ordered the US marshal to bring Aldama to court on an empty stomach. It was time to increase the pressure, find a way to put screws in him, get him to plea. Make he and his counsel both get with the program.

Aldama sat in the holding tank, his stomach grumbling, waiting for the marshal to bring him into the courtroom. He remembered his daughter and parents. *Would Alicia still be alive by the time he got out . . . if he got out? Did he really have a shot, as his lawyer had promised? Or should he cut his losses and take the deal? Was it too late?*

Aldama closed his eyes as he sat in front of the iron bars now holding him prisoner. He tried to relax, to breathe in and out slowly. He tried not to think about how things might end, but it was impossible to put the nagging thoughts away. Could Camila Harrison deliver? Would he ever get out?

Aldama slowly opened his eyes, stood up from the concrete bench in the holding cell and took another deep breath. He said a quick prayer and did the sign of the cross.

It was time to begin.

"In the matter of the *United States of America v. Vicente Aldama,* please make your announcements," called out an angry Judge Yamamoto. "What says the government?"

Barton Nutley, the US Attorney for the Southern District of Texas, Houston Division, got up slowly, cleared his throat, adjusted his reading glasses and announced, "The government is present and ready, Your Honor."

"Ms. Harrison, what says the defense?"

"Present and ready," Camila announced.

"Let the record reflect that this is Case No. 2014-CR-3456-3, *United States of America v. Vicente Aldama,*" said Yamamoto. "This is the final pre-trial conference."

"Mr. Nutley," followed the judge, without missing a beat, "has the defense tendered the government discovery?"

"Yes, they have, Your Honor," answered Nutley.

"What about the witness list?"

"That too, Your Honor," added Nutley.

"How many witnesses will be called to testify on behalf of the government?" asked Yamamoto in rapid fire fashion.

"Five to seven. The arresting officer, the backup agents, the custodian of evidence, the government's expert on money laundering, the agents from OFAC, the co-defendants . . . that's about it, Your Honor."

Yamamoto was taking notes and, without looking up, asked, "And how many days will it take for the government to present its case-in-chief? Any idea?"

"Two to three days tops, Your Honor," answered Nutley.

"Have you provided the court with your proposed jury charge and *voir dire* questions?"

Nutley turned to Wyatt Fox, who nodded in the affirmative. "Yes, the government has tendered a flash drive with the proposed charge and jury selection questions."

Without wasting a single minute, Yamamoto asked, "What about the defense? Ms. Harrison, have you received all the discovery you need from the government to try the case?"

"For the most part," answered Camila, as she thought about raising the cell phone issue, but quickly decided against it. She would play her cards close to her vest. "I still need a ruling or a reliability hearing on the issue of the confidential informant. Other than that, I believe the government has complied with all of our discovery requests."

"Good, very good," said Judge Yamamoto.

"What does the court want to do regarding my motion for the discovery of the informant's identity and my motion to suppress the evidence? The grounds raised in our motion to suppress is that the traffic stop was done without probable cause. If the government is representing to us that there was no CI, then we would argue the stop was a 'pretext stop.' We would like a hearing on those two motions."

"That will be denied," Yamamoto replied.

"But, Your Honor, we're entitled to a hearing on the CI issue," protested Camila. "We have been asking about the confidential informant for weeks, and we've been given the runaround. I've asked for a hearing before and . . . "

"And we have asserted the Informant Privilege before," declared Nutley, suddenly interrupting Camila.

"Thus, the reason your request was denied, Ms. Harrison," said Yamamoto, smugly, "is that you have failed to convince the court you're entitled to a hearing on the informant issue. You haven't met your burden of proof. Without more, I can't give you a hearing. Let me ask you . . . "

"Yes?"

"Without telling me what your client has told you . . . no need to get into attorney-client conversations . . . but from what you've read in the file . . . "

"Okay? . . . "

"Do any of the reports you've read in connection with this case indicate that the informant was present during the traffic stop?"

"No."

"Is there mention of a tip coming in from a hotline, like Crime Stoppers?"

"No."

"Is there mention that the source or the informant was present when the vehicle was loaded with the contraband?"

"No."

"Is there mention that the source delivered the vehicle to the defendants at the pick up or drop off locations?"

"No."

"Or that the source packaged the money?"

"No."

"Or that the source runs the shop where the cars are prepped?"

"No."

"Or that the informant helped organize the operation?"

"No."

Yamamoto threw his arms up in the air. "Then you don't get a hearing. Don't you see? You have nothing, Ms. Harrison."

"Just because there's no mention," answered Camila, "doesn't mean it isn't true, Your Honor."

Yamamoto shook his head. "The CI has nothing to do with anything. The genesis of the arrest was the traffic stop, wasn't it?"

"Yes," interjected Nutley, "that's exactly right. A defective license plate light, for the love of God!"

Camila was quick with her comeback. "The agencies have been taught to conceal the identities of informants by not mentioning them anywhere in the case files. We, as defense attorneys, have to ask and ask and ask and ask until we get to the truth. That's the way it's always been. We have to push the issue, beat this horse to death until we get the real facts."

"I'm not convinced," said Yamamoto.

"Don't *you* see? No agency will give us their informants willingly. The Odessa Unit will not just roll over and give us a name. That's why we're entitled to a hearing on the issue . . . to ask questions of the HIDTA agents—under oath—so we can get to the truth!"

"Your request for a hearing, again, is *denied.*"

"Then I should be given more time . . . to better prepare."

"The request for a continuance will also be denied," shot back Yamamoto. "And we'll carry the motion to suppress with the trial. It's time to get this show on the road."

Camila could feel the pressure rising. "Then I need to build a record, in case there's an appeal."

Yamamoto thought about this for a second. The threat of allowing Camila Harrison to build a record of what the court would or would not allow her to do didn't sit too well with the judge. It could be grounds for a new trial, a chance for someone to challenge the unfairness of the system. A chance for the reviewing court to scold Yamamoto.

"Mr. Nutley," asked Yamamoto, "would you care to explain to Ms. Harrison why the identity of the CI is not discoverable, again?

Nutley cleared his throat. "It'll be my pleasure, Your Honor. Should I discuss *Rovario v. United States?* Or *McCray v. Illinois?* Where would this honorable court like me to start?"

Camila rolled her eyes. She was familiar with those two seminal US Supreme Court cases. She and Thelma had already discussed and dissected both decisions, line by line, word by word.

"Start from the beginning," Yamamoto admonished, with a hint of disdain toward Camila. "Maybe you need to give the defense counsel a refresher course on the law relating to informants."

Nutley smiled as he looked around the courtroom and acknowledged the spectators. "It all comes down to a balancing test. On the one hand," explained Nutley, "law enforcement agencies all over the country regularly use informants to develop criminal cases to conduct arrests and searches and testify at trial to prove a defendant's guilt. As such, law enforcement agencies like to protect their informants' identities to keep them from harm and to be able to continue using them to generate new cases . . . new arrests."

"Go on," said Yamamoto, hoping Camila Harrison would learn a thing or two.

"While the CIs are being protected, we as a society also recognize that an accused person has rights. The rights of the accused have to be balanced against the wishes of the law enforcement agency. An accused person has the right to confront his accusers, i.e. the informant. An accused person has a right to a fair trial— thus, the argument that he should have the opportunity to explore a witness' credibility and reputation for truthfulness, including the credibility and reputation of the informant. An accused person has the right to know if, in some way, the informant's identity, along with what informant knows, could be considered helpful to the defendant. If that's the case, then the informant's privilege takes a back seat in the name of fairness. The accused's right to cross-examine comes out on top."

Yamamoto was making faces from the bench aimed at Harrison, as if saying she should be paying close attention. He stepped in. "It's the old argument, Ms. Harrison. It's about allowing the flow of information to law enforcement in order to protect society versus the accused's right to a fair trial and his ability to mount a proper defense."

"I'm aware of that," interjected Camila. "With all due respect, Your Honor, I don't need a lesson on the topic."

"Please continue, Mr. Nutley," followed Yamamoto, "and don't interrupt, Ms. Harrison. What about Rovario and McCray?"

"The Rovario case had to do with an actual trial. The defendant made a significant showing that the CI's possible testimony was quite likely relevant and could prove helpful to his defense," said Nutley. "The Supreme Court concluded that the CI was really the only material witness who could contradict the federal narcotics agent because both the CI and the federal agent had been present when the arrest was made. In fact, it was believed that the CI could probably add to or corroborate the defendant's allegations that he had been entrapped."

"So," continued Yamamoto, "if I hear you correctly, Mr. Nutley, the court in Rovario found that the CI was the only other witness who could either bolster or challenge the credibility of the government's witnesses at trial, correct?"

"Correct," said Nutley.

"And what happened in McCray?" asked Yamamoto, happy to be dispensing tidbits of wisdom and legal knowledge to all the spectators in his courtroom.

"In McCray," added Yamamoto, "there was no trial. Prior to trial, the defense moved to have a suppression hearing and pushed to discover the identity of the CI who had alerted the cops that the accused was selling dope down at the corner. Defense counsel wanted the evidence thrown out, alleging that the arrest had been an illegal arrest."

"And what was the outcome?"

"They were not entitled to discover the CI's identity."

"Why?"

"Probably because the defense was not able to make a showing that the CI was transactional. They failed to show the CI's involvement, plus nothing casted doubt on the arresting officer's actions or credibility. However, had the CI been able to add to or detract from the officers' credibility, or if the CI had possessed information that could help the accused prove his innocence, then the outcome may have been different. However, that was never the case in McCray."

"What does all that mean for *you*, Ms. Harrison? For your client?" Yamamoto asked. "Do you know?"

"No." Camila crossed her arms. "But I can just imagine . . . "

"You have to make a showing. *You* have the burden of proof." Yamamoto cleared his throat. "That means that the court will carry along the motion to suppress with the trial, and I will rule on it after the government's case-in-chief has been presented. As far as the confidential informant goes, here's what I'm planning, Ms. Harrison."

Everyone connected to the Aldama case perked up.

"Since trial is less than a week away," followed Yamamoto, "and in the interest of fairness, we are going to have a closed hearing in two days on the issue of the informant. You better have your witnesses ready to testify and convince the court that the informant is discoverable, you hear? So far, that doesn't appear to be the case. Unless you can show the court that the CI has information which undermines the arresting agents' credibility, or that the CI can help exonerate your client . . . I just don't see it."

"Yes, Your Honor." Camila smiled, feeling relieved and reinvigorated. Yamamoto was finally starting to see the light!

"So, you better have your witness here to testify, Ms. Harrison," warned Judge Yamamoto as he stared down Camila and her client. "And whoever else you may need."

"What about the government, Your Honor?" followed Camila. "Will they have the Odessa agents here to testify?"

Yamamoto turned to Nutley. "Mr. Nutley?"

"We were not planning on it," he answered. "Ms. Harrison has the power to subpoena whomever she wants to, but she must issue her own subpoenas. I will say, though, she should subpoena the agents with sufficient notice . . . they may be away for training or on vacation."

Although Vicente Aldama understood and spoke English, he had been listening to the entire pre-trial conference through headphones as the court interpreter translated the proceedings in Spanish. He was well aware that his counsel was facing an uphill battle.

"Figure it out, Ms. Harrison," directed Yamamoto. "We'll see you on Wednesday at 3:00 p.m."

All parties began to collect themselves.

"We'll be in recess," Yamamoto said.

⁂

"What happened in there?" asked Aldama, sounding concerned.

He was back in the holding tank, Camila standing on the other side of the metal bars, explaining to him what was to happen at the hearing.

"We have them on the ropes," said Camila, pretending not to be worried at all. "You see how hard they're fighting us on the informant issue? They're worried. Even Yamamoto is bending over backwards to help Nutley."

"Is that good or bad for us?" asked Aldama.

"Oh, it's just more work, that's all. I think it's a very good sign."

"Do you think maybe we should go back and take the deal? What if things don't go our way?"

"Don't worry," replied Camila, "I've got other tricks up my sleeve."

"Are you sure?"

"I'm sure. Gosling is going to do a good job for us." She looked at her watch. "In fact, I better give him a call, schedule a meeting and get him ready for the hearing on Wednesday. We have to do a lot of prep work."

Two burly US marshals built like MMA fighters walked in.

"Is your client ready to go back?" they asked Camila.

"Give us one minute, please," she begged.

They turned around and exited the holding area.

Camila took a deep breath. "I'm sure after the hearing—after Gosling testifies and the government is ordered to produce the informant—Nutley will approach us and offer us an even better plea bargain. Trust me, I know how the game is played. If they were at sixty months, then forty-eight months, I'll bet they go lower . . . you just wait."

"Okay," nodded Aldama. His attorney appeared to have everything under control.

———

In the quiet of her car, Camila realized the seriousness of her predicament. Lines had been drawn in the sand, and she was about to go to war with the US government. It caught up to her all at once. She opened the driver's side door, stuck her head out and started vomiting.

Oh my God, she thought. *This is really happening!*

TWENTY-ONE

"Did you send out all the subpoenas for the hearing on the CI?" Thelma called from across the large table. "Do we know if the US marshal got to serve them on the Odessa agents?"

They were seated in the back of the Harris County Law Library, up on the fourth floor, in a quiet, isolated corner. Thelma was helping Camila prepare for trial, that and the hearing scheduled in two days to determine whether or not defense counsel was entitled to discover the identity of the CI. Things were happening too fast.

"I had Julio e-file the subpoenas," replied Camila as she glanced over her notes and the agents' names. "But I don't know if there was sufficient time to get them served. . . . We'll have to wait and see."

"Is Gosling ready to testify?" asked Thelma. "Is he prepared to be grilled and raked over the coals?"

"I think so. He's coming in tomorrow to do more prep work, give me copies of his latest findings. I spoke with him today and we exchanged notes."

"As soon as he provides you with his latest report," Thelma suggested, "you need to provide a copy to the US government, especially if you want to use that report during the hearing or the trial. You don't want Nutley to accuse you of trying to ambush him in the middle of the hearing."

"Don't worry," replied Camila, "whatever I get, I'll shoot them a copy."

Thelma peeked at her yellow pad and the list of things to do written on it. "Did we finish the proposed jury charge?"

"Check."

"And the special instructions and definitions?"

"They're all on the flash drive."

"What about jury selection questions?"

"Those are done too. We already gave copies to Yamamoto, remember?"

"That's right. Did you cross-designate all of the Odessa agents in our own list of witnesses expected to be called to testify?"

"Yes."

"Did we get Aldama the clothes he needs for the trial?"

"Yes. I went down to Walmart and bought him slacks, a dress shirt, a tie and dress shoes. I'll deliver them to the laundry sergeant at the detention center a few days before trial, make sure they know they're supposed to send him to court dressed in civilian clothing."

"Sounds like we're ready to go try this thing," Thelma said.

"Did you file your notice of appearance of co-counsel?" asked Camila.

"I'll e-file it tomorrow," answered Thelma. "I have to let the dean know I'll be out all of next week to sit second chair in the case."

Camila got serious. She pointed at all the law books and briefs and motions scattered around the table. "This . . . all of what you're doing . . . it really means a lot to me. I know you didn't have to. You could have said no."

"I wanted to. Besides, I don't think it'll be a problem."

"What if they don't like it?"

"Too bad. I can always find another job."

Silence.

"You'd do all that for me?"

"It's a sacrifice," followed Thelma, "no doubt about it, but you're my best friend, my sister. There's nobody else. I would hope you'd do the same for me."

"Why wouldn't I?" Camila got sentimental as she remembered how Thelma had always stood by her side, no matter the circumstance, no matter the tragedy. She thought of their college days and Dante. Through it all Thelma had been there, never once leaving her side, and never complaining. A true friend. Even when it came to planning her wedding to Paxton, she was there. In a sense, filling in for Lorena.

"Are you okay?" asked Thelma.

Camila smiled. "Yes. All of a sudden I thought of our time at Rice." She wiped moisture away from her eyes. She pulled the *Houston Chronicle* from her bag. "Anyways, have you seen the paper today?"

"I'm sure he's looking down on you, right now." Thelma said, she grabbed the paper and read the cover story. It featured a full-size, front-page article on the Odessa Unit. "Nutley doesn't play around, does he?"

"And here's the new *Texas Monthly*, and *USA Today* for good measure." Camila tossed the magazines on the table. "There's also a feature on *20/20* . . . slated for Sunday night, just days before jury selection. How do you like them apples?"

"Damn!" cried Thelma. "We have our work cut out for us. Talk about tainting the jury pool. Gosling better do a hell of a job at the hearing, otherwise I'd hate to think about what could happen. If we can't get a fair bunch, we might want to consider throwing in the towel."

"Not so fast," said Camila as she pulled a bottle of eighteen-year-old The Balvenie from her satchel. "Single malt—for Gosling. Hopefully this will motivate him to do a good job, a better job."

"I hope he comes through," said Thelma. "For your sake *and* Aldama's."

"He will, you just wait," followed Camila. "He's a pit bull. Neither Nutley nor Fox will know what hit them. They're going to go ape shit!"

They were walking to the parking lot two blocks down from the law library when a voice out of nowhere said, "*¿Abogada?*"

Thelma and Camila stopped dead in their tracks. They turned around.

"Yes?" answered Camila.

Thelma had no idea what was happening. She reached for the pepper spray in her purse, just in case.

"You said you were going to keep us posted," Angélica Dawson complained. She got in Camila's face. "And now we come to find out there's going to be a trial?!"

"I thought we'd agreed that you'd get Vince a plea bargain," interjected Mr. Dawson. "And we have to hear it from Vince's mouth that there's a trial starting . . . next week? What's going on?"

"Camila," said Thelma, "is everything all right? Who are these people?"

"They're Vicente's family. His sister and brother-in-law," said Camila.

The Dawsons ignored the introduction. They were quite upset.

"Vince called me collect last night," followed Angélica, "and told me what you were up to. I cannot believe you! We trusted you. I put my brother's life in your hands. We all agreed that a plea bargain was the way to go . . . and now this?!"

"Was there ever a plea offer?" asked Mr. Dawson. "Didn't we agree it was better to plea bargain the case? Precisely to avoid exposing Vince to a lengthy sentence?"

Camila gathered her thoughts. "Yes . . . listen . . . let me explain. We're pushing hard, and we're not done yet. Nutley—the prosecuting attorney—his initial offer was eight years, then went down to six. It's now down to forty-eight months. Pushing them to trial is actually working. Both co-defendants got stuck with an eight-year sentence."

"Forty-eight months!" exclaimed Angélica. "That's great . . . much better than the six years or so you thought he would get!"

"Of course. The lower the number the better." Camila said, relieved.

"You need to call the US attorney handling the case," ordered Mr. Dawson, "and tell him you'll accept the offer. We don't care that you think my brother-in-law can beat the rap. Are you listen-ing?"

"It's a . . . bit more complicated than that," stuttered Camila. "Because . . . "

"What's so complicated?" asked Angélica. "Pick up the god-damned phone and tell the prosecutor we'll take the deal. It's that simple."

"Yeah, all you have to do is pick up the phone," offered Danny Dawson. "There's nothing to it."

"Yes, there is," said Thelma, coming to the rescue. "The offer was only good 'til 5 p.m., yesterday. It's no longer on the table, folks."

Mr. and Mrs. Dawson could not believe what they were hear-ing. They looked as if they had been blindsided by a snowplow in July. They now turned their anger and frustration to Camila's sec-ond chair.

Mr. Dawson got in Thelma's face. "Who the hell are you?!"

"Leave her out of this." Camila pulled Mr. Dawson away. "It's *me* you're talking to. And let me say this—for a guy that professes to be a Christian, a missionary—you're sure acting like a big *pen-dejo!*"

The Dawsons looked at each other.

"So what's the strategy now?" asked an angry Mr. Dawson. "You *do* have a strategy, don't you? Are you pointing blame some-where else? Is there a smoking gun? An exculpatory video? Some-body else confessed to the crime? What? Why are we going to trial? Why? We don't get it."

"I only discuss trial strategy with the client," Camila shrugged. "Sorry, but I will tell you that the reason we're still pushing is to get the government to come back to the table with an even better deal. I have faith this strategy is going to work, but only if we *keep* pushing. Nothing ventured, nothing gained."

"And if they don't come back to the table?" asked Angélica.

"We try the case," interjected Thelma.

Danny Dawson was not having it. He pushed his index finger into Camila's chest. "How did you allow this to happen? How could you be so reckless? You're exposing our Vince to twenty years. And what about Alicia? My in-laws?"

Angélica suddenly realized she and her husband were the protagonists in what appeared to be a bad dream. "They'll all be dead by the time my brother finishes serving his sentence. Didn't you think of that?"

"Mr. Aldama is my client," replied Camila, "and he's a big boy. I'm going to do whatever the hell he tells me to do, not what sis or brother-in-law thinks is best. Not what family members may or may not suggest, either. I only listen to the client and, I'm sorry, but you're not him. Vicente and I are on the same page."

Camila grabbed Thelma, turned her around and continued walking toward the parking lot.

"You haven't heard the last of it, Ms. Harrison!" yelled Danny Dawson. "We're going to go visit with Vince tomorrow morning and we're going to make sure he fires you! You're not going to touch this case anymore, you hear?!"

"Yeah, that's right," followed Angélica. "You're off the case! We'll find him somebody else. Somebody who knows what they're doing!"

"Good luck!" Camila yelled back.

Thelma grabbed Camila and pulled her away. "*Ya, basta.* Let's go."

And just like that, the confrontation was over and the night went on.

TWENTY-TWO

Camila had called Gosling's cell number twenty times, and each time her call went straight to voicemail.

"Where are you? C'mon, pick up . . . pick up," she mumbled under her breath.

She was parked outside Gosling's office building. "Answer your goddamn phone! Where are you?! I have a bottle of single malt scotch for you. Don't you want it? C'mon, answer the phone!"

She was about to dial the number again when she noticed a female leaving the building. She bolted out of her car and rushed to the main entrance.

"Hold that door!"

The words on the glass door welcomed all clients to "Gulf Coast Investigative Consultants, LLC." The small office was locked and dark. Camila peeked through the glass door, squinting, trying hard to see some movement, a human shape, anything, when she noticed a stack of mail scattered about the floor of the reception area. It was as if the mailman had been steadily pushing the mail through the door slot, but nobody had been around to pick it up.

Man, this is not a good sign!

She Googled "Dennis Gosling" on her cell phone and found his home address. She was figuring out the quickest route to his house when she noticed another tenant exiting an office down the hall.

"Excuse me!" she yelled.

The man stopped. "Yes?"

Camila approached. "I'm looking for the investigator. Do you know if he's been in?"

"Mr. Gosling?"

"Yes. I've got something for him." She waved the bottle of scotch up in the air. "I'm a very grateful and thankful divorce client."

"I haven't seen him these last couple of days. I know he likes to go fishing down in Galveston. He told me he keeps a boat down there. I've seen the pictures . . . . You should try looking for him down there."

"You're sure he hasn't been around?"

"Not these last couple of days," said the man. "You want me to give him a message if I see him?"

"Nah," said Camila, "that's okay. Thanks."

He waved and headed down the hall toward the elevator.

Camila stood there, feeling the pressure starting to mount. The walls started closing in, like they had in Austin when Tim Zuckerman dropped the leaked-email bomb on her.

Oh, my God, why is this happening?!

The GPS map guided Camila to a duplex located in a suburb south of Houston called Sugarland. The two-story duplex faced Grant Boulevard. The place also looked deserted.

She got out of her car, went to the front door and knocked.

C'mon, c'mon. Where are you? Where did you go?

She knocked again and yelled Gosling's name. "Mr. Gosling, are you in there? Hello! Is there anybody in there? Can you hear me?!"

She tried peeking through the window, but the blinds were shut.

Waves of desperation were overtaking her. She pounded on the door.

"Dennis! It's me, Camila Harrison! Are you okay? Can you hear me? Open up! We need to talk. We have court tomorrow."

No response.

The porch light to the duplex next door suddenly came on.

Camila stopped and waited to see if a neighbor would appear. Finally, the door creaked open, and someone from behind the door said, "He's not home."

Camila went over to the door. "Hi, I'm a client of Dennis. Have you seen him?"

"He went fishing down in Costa Rica, said he wouldn't be back for a month. He asked me to look after his plants."

Camila's heart stopped. "Costa Rica? Wait, wait . . . you mean his boat The Costa Rica . . . down in Galveston, right?"

"Nah, his boat's name is The Bait-n-Switch. I'm sure he meant the country Costa Rica . . . down in Central America, ya know?"

Camila felt sucker-punched. She couldn't breathe. "Wait . . . wait . . . did he leave a number? In case of an emergency? Did he say if he was staying at a resort? With friends? Do you know?"

"He did mention something about a friend keeping a place in *Laahs Ahhrcahs* . . . The Arches? Some marina resort. He said he couldn't pass it up, had to go."

"*Los Arcos?*" Camila felt waves of rage and panic and confusion, all at once. She wanted to scream, but she forced herself to remain composed. "I see . . . . Okay . . . thanks."

The neighbor closed the door and turned off the porch light.

Camila was reeling. Deep down inside, she knew she was staring at a very costly mistake. She was fuming, cursing Gosling and his grand plans, when the neighbor's porch light came back on again.

The door opened.

"Wait! Are you Camila Harrison?" asked the sixty-something neighbor. "The attorney?"

"Yes!"

"Good. Wait right here."

The door closed again. After what felt like an eternity, the door opened again.

"Dennis left this for you, in case you came by," she said, handing Camila a small white envelope. "He said you would know what to do with it."

What the hell? Camila thought as she stood there, studying the envelope. *Okay, maybe this is it—the smoking gun, the silver bullet, cold fusion. Please, please God. Let it be something good. Por el amor de Dios, te lo ruego.*

She took a deep breath and hoped for the best as she tore into the envelope and pulled out its contents.

It was Gosling's bill.

"Fuck you, asshole!" screamed Camila at the top of her lungs. She crumpled the bill and tossed it into the bushes.

Camila was back in her garage apartment, trying to regroup. She debated on whether or not she should call Thelma. She opened her laptop and Googled marina resorts in Costa Rica. She found Los Arcos; a 1,500-acre, master-planned luxury resort with its own rainforest reserve. On the contact information page she found a 1-800 number. She dialed, planning on letting Gosling have it.

In Costa Rica the time was 9:00 p.m., an hour earlier.

"Los Arcos Luxury Resort, how can I help you?" said the woman with the pleasant voice at the other end of the line.

"Hi," said Camila, "I'm calling from Houston, Texas. This is Maria Gosling, the daughter of one of your guests."

"What's the guest's name?"

"Dennis Gosling," replied Camila. "Can you put me through to his room?"

There was silence at the other end. Camila could hear the guest attendant typing on a computer keyboard.

"Is he a guest at the *hotel*? Because I don't see that he's registered here . . . . Let me check something else . . . . Maybe he's staying at one of our villas."

More strokes on the keyboard.

"Ah, yes . . . here it is. Let me put you through."

"Thanks," said Camila, her suspicions confirmed.

Camila implored, *Pick up the phone, you asshole! Pick up the phone!*

But no one did.

⁕

"Calm down, calm down!" Thelma ordered from her end. "Take a deep breath, get ahold of yourself. I can't understand what you're saying."

Camila was on her cell, rushing to her office. "I have nothing! Nothing! I'm screwed. . . . What am I going to do?!"

"What happened? What's going on?" Thelma could tell Camila was falling apart.

"Gosling, my PI, he's gone . . . gone to Costa Rica. . . . I'm screwed!" bawled Camila. "Aldama will be popped for twenty years! And it's all my fault."

"Wait, wait, wait . . . our witness Gosling? What do you mean 'gone?!'"

"That asshole is fishing down at a resort in Central America!"

Thelma restrained herself. "We have a backup plan, right?"

"Gosling *was* it," cried Camila.

"But Gosling can't just disappear like that! Didn't he take the money from the court? Isn't he retained? Didn't you have him sign a contract when you paid him the $2,000 that Yamamoto gave you to hire him?"

"Not exactly," Camila mumbled, jamming on the breaks at a stop sign and purposefully banging her head on the steering wheel.

"Excuse me? Come again?"

"Yamamoto approved the money, but everybody gets paid when the case is over. When the case is *over*, Gosling submits his final bill. I was to submit my final voucher . . . and then we'd get paid. You kind of float the government until then. That's how it works with appointments in federal court these days."

"But he signed an employment contract, right? Something we can show the court? We have *that* nail to hang our hat on at least, right? Please tell me you had him sign a contract."

Silence.

"Well?"

Silence.

Still at the stop sign, Camila took out a tissue and blew her nose. "We never got around to it. I started preparing the employment agreement . . . but just never got it done. I put it in the file and forgot about it."

"*Aaay, amiga.*" Thelma was in shock. She could get a grievance too, because she'd agreed to help her friend and had already filed a notice of appearance as co-counsel in the case. She was now on the hook, just like her friend and their client.

"Camila! I can't believe how bad this is! But wait a minute. . . . It sounds to me like *they* got to him. How could that guy afford a trip to Costa Rica?"

"You really think so?" asked Camila, wiping her nose again. "But how?"

"That's a very good question."

"This is what happens when you screw with the government, I suppose," Camila guessed.

"You suppose right."

"So . . . what can we do?" asked Camila, hoping for a miracle. Begging God to enlighten Thelma Issa, Professor of Law, and the Sandra Day O'Connor Distinguished Professor of Advocacy Studies, one of the nation's highest honors bestowed on female law professors.

"Hell if I know, I'm just second chair."

TWENTY-THREE

It was Wednesday when Judge Yamamoto's clerk, Chloe, announced, "All rise. Hear ye, hear ye, hear ye! The Honorable Colt Yamamoto presiding. All having business before this honorable court draw near, give attention and you shall be heard. Long live the United States of America. You may be seated."

Judge Yamamoto emerged from a back door, climbed to his place behind the bench and greeted the parties. "Good afternoon. You all may be seated. Thank you."

The meticulous judge looked at his computer screen, then turned and whispered something to Jessica, the court coordinator. Jessica handed him two printouts. The judge adjusted his reading glasses, glanced at the two documents in his hand and then at his computer screen until he found what he was looking for. He then pointed at one of the marshals to remain inside the courtroom to keep an eye on Aldama. He signaled for the other to go outside and stand guard, as this hearing would be conducted behind closed doors.

"Okay, the court calls *United States of America v. Vicente Aldama, et al.* Case Number 2014-CR-3456-3. This is a hearing to determine whether or not the defense is entitled to discover the identity of a confidential informant. For the record, this hearing is being conducted behind closed doors and is not open to the public. Please make your announcements. What says the government?"

"Barton Nutley for the government," announced the pompous US Attorney for the Southern District of Texas, "The government's ready to proceed."

"Camila Harrison, on behalf of Vicente . . . "

Judge Yamamoto interrupted Camila and didn't give her a chance to finish with her announcement. It was time to put Camila Harrison in her place. "Mr. Nutley, please bring me up to speed. What are we doing?"

"This case is a money-laundering case, Your Honor. The Odessa Unit made a traffic stop south of Houston. The Tahoe being driven by the three co-defendants was carrying almost a million dollars in illegal proceeds. McKenzie and Barrera, two of the co-defendants, have already pled guilty. Ms. Harrison's client, Mr. Aldama, wants to go to trial. Ms. Harrison thinks she's entitled to discover the CI's identity. You graciously allowed her to have a hearing. That's why we're here. The government has asserted the Informant's Privilege," replied Nutley. "She's not entitled to discover the source's identity . . . that's our position."

Yamamoto appeared satisfied with the intro. "So, she now has to meet her burden, show that the informant has information that either bolsters or puts into question the Odessa agents' credibility, or that the CI possesses information that can help establish her client's innocence, correct?"

"Correct," answered Nutley. "She has the burden."

Nutley then turned to Aldama and gave him a cold look, as if dealing with a child molester. While waiting to hear Camila Harrison's announcement, he noticed that out of the two attorneys defending Aldama, Camila appeared the most worried, the most nervous.

Camila and Thelma were still standing at their table, waiting for a moment to finish making their announcements. Vicente Aldama was seated between them, still dressed in a green jumpsuit. His hands were cuffed and his ankles were shackled.

"Ms. Harrison," Yamamoto said, directing his attention to Aldama's defense team, "I see you have company. Would you introduce your co-counsel?"

Thelma took the opportunity to introduce herself. "Your Honor, my name is Thelma Issa. I filed my notice of appearance. I'm asking for leave to be Ms. Harrison's second chair. I'm doing this pro bono, Your Honor. I'm licensed in the state of Texas and in federal court. I'm just helping out, Judge."

"Jessica alerted me to your filing just now. Do you have any idea what you're getting yourself into?"

"Yes, Your Honor," replied Thelma.

"You've been warned," continued Yamamoto. "Ms. Harrison, are you ready to continue?"

"No," muttered Camila. "I mean . . . yes, but no. Your Honor, we have a problem . . . a problem that just came to my attention yesterday—last night, to be exact."

"What now, Ms. Harrison?" Yamamoto rolled his eyes, the carotid artery in his neck starting to bulge.

Thelma looked down. The ass-chewing was about to start.

"My witness for this hearing is unavailable. I'm sorry. We need more time. As I said, I just found out."

"We would object!" cried Nutley. "That's not the government's problem, Judge."

"What happened, Ms. Harrison? Who is your witness? Where *is* this witness?"

"It's the investigator I hired, Your Honor," Camila explained, blushing. "He skipped town. He knew he was supposed to be here . . . and he bailed on me and my client. If we could have a short continuance . . . postpone the trial . . . two short weeks. That's all we're asking."

"Denied!" yelled Yamamoto.

Nutley, Fox and Griffin were in a huddle, all smiles and giggles.

"Approach the bench, Ms. Harrison," ordered Yamamoto. "Just Ms. Harrison!"

Nutley, Fox, Griffin and the two other assistant US attorneys stopped dead in their tracks. They returned to the counsel table.

Thelma braced herself for what was to come.

Camila was mortified. She shuffled her way to the bench.

Her voice cracked as she said, "Yes, Your Honor?"

Yamamoto looked at his electronic recording officer and scowled. "This is off the record. You should have taken the deal, Ms. Harrison. There's nothing I can do for you or your client now. I warned you. Now it's too late. I'm going to have no choice but to sentence your client to the maximum, you hear? You understand what I'm saying? And this is nobody's fault but yours. When this is all said and done . . . I'm going to have you . . . " He stopped mid-sentence.

"Yes?"

"Back on the record," barked Yamamoto. He pulled back and said, "You're going to trial on Monday—informant, no informant, ready or not, like it or not, witness or no witness, you understand?"

She nodded like a child being scolded by the school's principal.

"Take a seat," Yamamoto ordered, waving her away. "Let's continue."

The electronic recording officer put his earphones back on and continued moving dials and pushing buttons on his equipment.

"Ms. Harrison," started Yamamoto, "do you have any other witnesses you can call?"

"No, Your Honor. I only intended to call the investigator."

"Did you subpoena him?"

"Didn't think I had to."

"Did you subpoena any other witnesses?" asked Yamamoto, ready to finish off Camila Harrison. "Somebody else who can help you make your case? The officers from the Odessa Unit? Other third parties?"

"We tried . . . the marshals were not able to serve any of the agents, there wasn't enough time, Your Honor. We think they got wind they were going to be subpoenaed and went into hiding . . . " She gave Nutley an icy stare, "or someone told them to stay away."

"I resent that!" cried Nutley, "what is Ms. Harrison insinuating, Your Honor? That the government is obstructing justice? Those are some serious allegations!"

"Drop it! I'm warning the two of you," Yamamoto scolded the lawyers, as he waved his gavel high up in the air. "Stop talking to each other. Address the court!"

"Yes, Your Honor," said the pair.

"Ms. Harrison, so, this exercise was a complete waste of time?" asked an angry Yamamoto. "*All* of this was for naught?"

Camila had nothing to say other than, "Sorry."

Thelma, over at counsel's table, looked miserable.

"This court has better things to do than deal with incompetent lawyers who are not prepared, who don't know what they're doing and who end up screwing their own clients. Ms. Harrison, you and Mr. Aldama better stop wasting the court's time, do we understand each other? Jury selection will be on Monday," Yamamoto reminded everyone, "I suggest you find a way to avoid the trial . . . . Cut your losses while you can. We'll be in recess!"

"All rise," ordered Chloe as Judge Yamamoto left the bench and stormed out of the courtroom. Meanwhile, the US marshals collected the defendant and whisked him away.

After Aldama had been removed from the courtroom, Nutley, Griffin, Fox and the other two AUSAs came over to Camila's table. It was a scene out of a National Geographic TV special, the part where a pack of hyenas is about to devour their cornered prey.

"You and your grandiose schemes." Nutley was smiling, almost salivating. "I hope you've advised your client to bring a toothbrush. He's going away for a loooooooong time!"

"Kiss my ass!" blurted out Camila.

The group laughed, thoroughly enjoying making Camila Harrison squirm.

After the courtroom fiasco, Camila called Gustavo Govela.

The three were regrouping in Sorelle's conference room office.

"What do you need me to do?" asked Govela, concerned.

"Can you spare an investigator?" asked Camila.

"Yes, he'll be here at 8 a.m.. Is that okay?"

"Thursday?"

"We might not have sufficient time," volunteered Thelma, "but I guess it's worth a shot. Otherwise, we have nothing."

Camila was exhausted, out of ideas and sulking. She excused herself and headed to the restroom. Govela and Thelma remained in the shabby conference room.

"Talk about a headache," blurted out Thelma. "This is not going to end well."

"Why are you doing this?"

"Doing what?"

"*This*," pointed Govela. "Why are you jumping into this case? It's unwinnable, don't you agree?"

Thelma thought about her answer. She chose her words carefully. "Camila needs a friend, but more than that, she needs someone to believe in her. That's why I'm doing it."

"Well, that's kind of you—"

"Camila has suffered a lot," followed Thelma.

"How so?"

"Has she told you about Paxton?"

"Not really."

"Dante?"

"She's only mentioned him in passing."

"He was killed by a drunk driver who fled the scene. He escaped back to Mexico and never faced prosecution."

"Really?"

Govela had searched Camila's name and happened upon some articles. In fact, he had recently gotten wind that his sources, down in Mexico City, had pick up the trail on Lazcano, the drunk driver that had killed Camila's fiancée. In a few weeks, Lazcano would be served with an extradition warrant, get taken into custody, and be shipped back to Houston to face justice. Govela would make sure of it. In any event, he hoped Thelma could provide additional details.

"Well," continued Thelma, "I'll let her tell you more, when she's good and ready. As for me, I'm very proud of her. She's a fighter despite everything that has happened. Anyone of us would have already called it a day."

"You're a good friend," said Govela.

Thelma's facial expression changed suddenly. "I am *mad* at Camila, however, for getting involved with that con man, Gosling. What a weasel!"

"How did she find him?" asked Govela. "Any idea?"

"Craigslist," followed Thelma. "He was the cheapest."

"I can't believe he left you guys hanging, just like that."

Thelma was turning various shades of red. "Gosling doesn't know what he's got coming. When this case is all said and done, I'll make it my mission to yank his private investigator's license."

"Is she going to be okay?"

"I hope so . . . ." Thelma paused. "I hope this trial doesn't push her over the edge. I know she's tough, but we all have our breaking point."

"I want to help," volunteered Govela. "She can use us both."

"I'm glad you feel that way. She'll appreciate it."

"Don't mention it."

"That damn Yamamoto . . . " Thelma stared at her hands. "You're supposed to get justice at the courthouse. Nowadays it's all about winning, getting the most convictions. It's about who's got the most money, the better lawyer, who's the most connected, the most powerful. That's why our courts are going to shit, I'm sorry to say. Our founding fathers would be turning in their graves."

Govela scratched his head, letting Thelma's words sink in. "Well, it's the same in most countries . . . that's the way it is in Mexico, too, although I shouldn't say it as a consular official."

Thelma started laughing, shaking her head. "Here we are, going up against the US government, the most powerful government in the world, but we only have two thousand dollars to hire an investigator and thirty days to prepare for trial. You see how ridiculous the whole thing is? Don't make me laugh!"

"The scales of justice are tipped . . . that's why our consulate gets involved . . . try for a little balance . . . "

"But the worst part," Thelma said, "is that I was the one who pushed Camila to stay on the case. She wanted to pass on it, decline . . . but Alan called me. We agreed to push her, but now I feel terrible. I feel like it's my fault she's in this mess."

"We need to help her. What kind of strategy can you put together for the trial? Any idea, now that Gosling is gone?"

"Based on Gosling's assertions, plan A was to push for the CI and get Nutley to offer our client a real good deal. It was risky, we knew that. Plan B has to do with the video in Aldama's cell phone."

"What's in it?"

"Exculpatory evidence, of course . . . " Thelma stopped mid-sentence. "But I can't say more than that, Camila would kill me."

Just then, Camila came back into the conference room. "Okay, I have a plan . . . ."

Sounding more put together, she announced, "Have the investigator meet me here at 9:30 a.m. I'll run down to the jail to visit with Vicente very early in the morning . . . go over a couple of things."

"What do you need me to do?" asked Thelma.

"I'll text you after I meet with the investigator. What's his name?"

"Nicolás Montanaro. We call him 'Monty,'" Govela said. "He's very good. He'll do whatever you ask him to."

"Okay," said Camila, trying to be back on top of things. "I'll text you with instructions, Thelma. We'll work all weekend."

"What about me?" Govela asked. "Can I help?"

"You've done enough, sweetie." Camila smiled. "And believe me . . . I'm very grateful. You and Thelma go home now, get some rest."

Govela picked up his car keys and cell phone from the oval-shaped conference table. "Okay, I'm out of here. Keep in touch, ladies. Let me know if you need anything else. I'm available 24/7."

He leaned over and gave Camila a goodbye kiss.

TWENTY-FOUR

"This is their list of witnesses that could very well testify at trial," Camila said, pointing at a paper in her hand. "Bergendahl, Batiz, Dale, Rico, Franco, Rabinovich, Wolf, Stephens, González, Nelson and Copeland. Do any of those names ring a bell?"

Vicente Aldama thought. "Only Bergendahl for sure. I think he was the sergeant in charge, if I remember correctly."

"You wouldn't know what role, if any, the rest played in the traffic stop? The arrest?"

"Bergendahl pulled us over. González was the first officer to arrive—I think, I'm not too sure. I don't know about the others. I was very nervous. I mean, many more agents showed up later . . . but I couldn't tell you who was who."

Camila paid close attention to Aldama's body language. She was having a hard time reading him this morning. He appeared distant, somewhat cold. Was he worried? Disappointed? Had he figured out that the *Titanic* was sinking and their strategy had backfired? Had he talked to his sister? Was she about to get canned?

"Another investigator is going to help with the case," Camila blurted out, faking a smile. "He'll lend a hand. We're going to be okay. Don't worry."

"Where's Gosling?" asked Aldama. "What happened to him? I thought *he* was going to help us?"

Camila's smiled turned into a frown. "I don't know. He took off at the last minute. I reallyly can't explain why he did that, believe me."

Aldama let out a big sigh and started to massage his temples. "Look, I know you wanted to help. I know you and your friend Thelma are trying real hard, but would you mind going back to Mr. Nutley and asking him if he would consider putting some kind of offer back on the table? I don't want to go to trial. I just don't have it in me anymore. Let's put an end to this."

Camila felt extremely guilty. "Are you sure?"

"Yes." Aldama locked eyes with Camila.

She looked down and reached for her yellow pad. "Okay, I'll reach out to Mr. Nutley. Now, going back to the cell phone issue . . . " Camila said, redirecting her client's attention, "you had it during the traffic stop?"

"Yes."

"And you're sure you guys took a video of the Tahoe's condition?"

"McKenzie and Barrera said it was routine. They called it 'insurance.' Why? I don't know . . . this was my first time doing this."

"Think . . . think . . . " Camila said, pushing her client. "What happened to it?"

"I guess the agents have it," answered Aldama. "I'm thinking that's what happened . . . I don't know."

Camila pulled a copy of Bergendahl's inventory sheet. It had been prepared prior to the tow truck coming by to pick up the Tahoe, after the cash had been removed. She went over it.

"Do you know why there's no mention of it in this inventory form?"

Aldama grabbed the inventory sheet and scanned it. "It should be there. They mention CDs, packs of cigarettes, lighters, coins, a radar detector . . . "

"Okay. After I leave here, I'll stop by the US attorney's office and ask to speak with Mr. Nutley. I'll let him know you want to plea."

"Promise?"

"Promise," Camila said, feeling guilty he'd had to extract a promise from her. It was her job to represent his interests, whether or not she believed in her ability to win.

⁓

Camila sat in the reception area. She was spent.

All her life, she'd been taught to do the right thing. That's how she'd been raised by Darin; follow the rules, don't cut corners, tell the truth; if you work real hard and keep your nose clean, you'll get ahead; don't steal, don't lie, treat others as you would like to be treated. Be yourself. Don't compromise your principles. Looking back, she had become an attorney, in part, because of these rules. She'd always liked rules—good things were supposed to happen to people who followed the rules, to people who chose what was right over what was easy. Those who picked good over evil. But Camila felt repulsed, angry, frustrated. She had had it with Nutley, Yamamoto and their system. A system where the average Jane or Joe had no chance.

She reached for a dog-eared *Time* magazine on the coffee table and made a mental note to ask about the roles of the government's witnesses. Since Aldama couldn't remember, and there were only four reports in the file, she needed to know why the US government felt compelled to put eleven witnesses on their witness list. She flipped the magazine open to a feature titled, "How the US is Winning the War on Drugs."

She rolled her eyes.

What a joke.

⁓

After a young staffer showed her the way, Camila knocked on the door to Wyatt Fox's office. The college intern quickly scurried away and left Camila behind to deal with the portly assistant US attorney.

"Come on in," shouted Wyatt from behind the piles of documents on his messy desk. "Take a seat." He looked distracted, glued to his computer monitor, watching a news bulletin. "Jesus! Have you heard?!"

"Heard what?" Camila asked.

"Un-freaking-believable!" exclaimed Wyatt. "You've gotta be kidding."

"What?!" Camila removed her courier bag and placed it on one of the chairs. "What are you watching?"

"There's a shooter at the state capitol in Austin. He's barricaded himself inside. Thank God the legislature is not in session. They're reporting five dead . . . many more wounded. He wants to know why his brother was sent to prison for insider-trading when members of our US Congress can trade on insider information and are immune from prosecution. The guy's had it!"

"He makes a valid point, don't you think?" Camila asked.

"Just another nutcase on the loose, if you ask me."

Camila came around Wyatt's desk to watch the images on the computer monitor. It was mayhem. "Don't you just love the second amendment? Maybe this isn't a good time," muttered Camila. "Should I come back later?"

Wyatt closed the tab on his computer screen. "No, it's okay. What do you need?"

"My client has asked me to come by and test the waters . . . "

Wyatt motioned for Camila to take a seat. "Test the waters?"

"He has instructed me to try and get him a plea offer," Camila answered. "He doesn't want to go to trial."

"Too late for that," Wyatt spat out, sounding fed up. "If he wants to avoid a trial he can plea cold to the judge on Monday . . . but he's not getting a deal from us."

Before Camila spoke another word, she looked around Wyatt's office, trying to put aside the enormous guilt she was feeling. She focused her attention on a lone framed picture on a file cabinet. It was Wyatt, forty pounds thinner, surrounded by DEA agents and Mexican marines, celebrating a drug bust. Marijuana bundles were stacked four feet high. The group was in front of an airport hangar, with Mexican navy helicopters proudly displayed in the background. At five-eleven, the slender Wyatt towered over his Mexican counterparts.

"Look, the whole thing is my fault . . . " Camila apologized. "Don't take it out on my client. I believed Gosling, and he played me. I should have seen it coming, but I was fooled."

Wyatt remained silent, his thoughts obviously somewhere else. He finally spoke, "There's nothing to talk about, Ms. Harrison. I have instructions from above. We're going to spank you in front of the whole world and then we're going to make sure Judge Yamamoto sends Aldama away for a long, long time."

"Okay. I just thought I'd ask." Camila got up slowly, reached for her bag and proceeded to exit Wyatt's office like a dog with its tail between the legs.

"Didn't you just leave?"

"I almost forgot . . . I was out by the elevators when I remembered," said Camila. "I received your updated list of witnesses. Can you tell me something?" She pulled her copy of the list from her bag.

"What do you want to know?"

"Sgt. Bergendahl conducted the traffic stop, correct?"

"Let me look at my notes." Wyatt typed on his keyboard, then opened the discovery file on the Aldama case. He focused on his computer screen. "Let me just . . . Odessa's reports . . . it says here . . . yes, Sgt. Bergendahl initiated the traffic stop."

"What about Agent Batiz?"

Wyatt looked at his notes again. "He was one of the backup officers."

"And Agent Dale? What can you tell me about him? What is his title in the department?"

"He's a narcotics officer. I don't think he had anything to do with the actual arrest. He was another backup, he may have helped inventory the Tahoe."

"After the money was removed? Or with the money?"

"After," answered Wyatt.

"And Rabinovich?"

"He may have interviewed McKenzie and Barrera."

"And Wolf?"

"He's just a supervisor. He's the guy that calls the assistant US attorney on duty to see if the case goes 'state' or 'federal'. He then makes sure the files are complete when they get submitted to the DA or the US attorney's office . . . the prosecutorial authority. And don't forget González . . . the K9 officer."

"Yes, I got that one. I'd figured that was his role, to sniff out the Tahoe . . . see if there were drugs."

"Correct. Now, we're not bringing Wolf and some of the others to testify, just so you know. Their testimony would be just more of the same. And we don't want to bore the jurors. If you wanted all of them here on Monday to testify, you should have subpoenaed them."

"Yes, I know. Don't remind me." Camila was beginning to see the complete picture. "So Wolf makes sure the files have all the reports, videos, photos, inventories, lab results, lab submission forms, witness statements, confessions . . . things like that?"

"Correct."

"And the custodian of evidence?"

"In this case," said Wyatt, "it was Rico."

"And Nelson and Rabinovich, what role did they play in all of this?"

"Rabinovich retired and moved to Puerto Vallarta, but that night . . . he had desk duty. Nelson transported the co-defendants to jail, got them booked."

"What jail was that?"

"When the cases go federal, they almost always bring them here to the Harris County jail . . . or the FDC."

"Okay, thanks," said Camila, seemingly satisfied with the answers. "That's all I needed to know."

She started to walk away, but then paused, turned around and came back into Wyatt's office.

"One last thing," she said.

"Now what?"

"Did all of the agents prepare reports? Or are there more reports that you haven't shared with the defense?"

"What do you mean?"

"There were only four reports in your file. How can there only be four reports when there were, like, ninteen agents involved in the case?"

"Ms. Harrison," said Wyatt, more annoyed than anything, "we've given you everything we have, trust me. There are no more reports. The 'A' file is the same as ours."

"Okay, sorry," apologized Camila. "I'll take your word for it . . . but can you do me a favor?"

"What is it *now*?"

"Can you just check?"

"Too late for that. You've got what you got. If you think we're withholding reports from you, then you should have brought that up to Judge Yamamoto when you had the chance. Now get out of my office and let me get back to work."

Camila got the message. "Thank you. I won't bother you again."

She turned and exited Wyatt's office. As soon as she was out of sight, Wyatt picked up the phone and made a call.

TWENTY-FIVE

The mock courtroom was located in an off-limits area in the basement of the highrise that housed the US attorney's office in downtown Houston. The whole thing was an exact replica of a federal courtroom except for the designated sitting area usually reserved for the public. The gallery was replaced by a large, rectangular room with one-way mirrors, where Nutley and his jury consultants could observe, take notes and provide feedback in anticipation of big trials.

It had been Nutley's idea to implement the use of the mock courtroom with focus groups whenever the US government went up against the super-lawyers from mega-firms hired to defend the Enrons, Washington Mutuals and FIFAs of the world. It was just another tool in their prosecutor's toolbox, and this time it was being put to good use to teach Camila Harrison a thing or two.

Nutley had learned that, by listening to and observing the mock jurors deliberate, he was able to identify effective or useless arguments. He could anticipate potential weaknesses in a case, such as the jurors not believing the agents, or whether some were having difficulty understanding the scientific or accounting principles discussed in open court or were confused about the evidentiary exhibits.

Other times, the jurors would make valid observations that no one, including Nutley, had ever even thought about, much less considered. Today, the mock courtroom was being used with one purpose in mind: Help develop the most favorable juror profile to be selected the following week. All that remained was for Nutley and his crew to fix minor details and fine tune the witness line-up. He would teach Camila Harrison not to mess with Barton Nutley—future Texas Attorney General.

"Mr. McKenzie," asked Wyatt Fox, "did you see Mr. Aldama give consent to Sgt. Bergendahl to search the vehicle?"

It was Friday when McKenzie found himself on the witness stand. Dot Griffin was playing the role of judge. In a separate room, the Odessa agents and Barrera awaited their turn to testify. From the box, a mock jury paid close attention. At the defense counsel's table, a file clerk from the US attorney's office wore a green jumpsuit, playing the role of Vicente Aldama. His defense attorney was Erin Gómez, an assistant US attorney working in the white-collar crime section.

"Yes," lied McKenzie, enjoying the role of party crasher, "Mr. Aldama gave verbal consent. I clearly remember . . . and it was voluntary."

Fox got right to the point. He was going for the jugular.

The "jurors" from the focus group were quickly impressed by the lead prosecutor's demeanor. With his direct, no-nonsense style, he'd grabbed their attention right away.

"Did you know the Tahoe was loaded with cash?"

"Yes," answered McKenzie.

"What about Aldama?" followed Fox. "Did he know?"

"Objection!" yelled Gómez. "Calls for speculation."

"Sustained," ruled pretend-Judge Griffin from the bench.

Without missing a beat, Fox moved on to another topic. He could come back to the last question later on when the defense least expected it or ask it another way. There was always a back door. "Who recruited you?"

McKenzie pointed at the file clerk pretending to be the defendant, "He did."

"Who is that?" asked Fox. "Do you know him by name?"

"Vicente Aldama," answered McKenzie. "That's him over there in the green jumpsuit."

The actor playing Aldama was shaking his head in disbelief. Even *he* doubted McKenzie's credibility. He couldn't believe the lies and distortions being thrown around the mock courtroom.

The jury appeared captivated by Wyatt Fox. He looked at his notes on the yellow pad he was holding in his right hand. He paused for effect. He then flipped the pages, as if looking for the question that would be Aldama's coffin nail.

"How many times did you, Mr. Barrera and Mr. Aldama smuggle money down to the Texas-Mexico border?" asked Fox.

McKenzie was feeling pretty confident. He would do whatever it took to help the government's case. The truth was no longer important. Getting a conviction, whatever the cost, was.

"Six times," McKenzie lied.

"And how much did each of you get paid to smuggle the cash?"

"Five thousand each, per trip," replied McKenzie.

"Pass the witness," said Fox.

Erin Gómez started her "cross-examination."

"Mr. McKenzie, what kind of deal did you enter into with the government to point the finger at Vicente Aldama?"

With mercy in her eyes, Gómez turned to look at her poor client. The members of the focus group playing the role of jurors inched closer to the edge of their seats. They were eager to hear the witness' response.

"I don't understand the question," replied McKenzie, playing dumb. Days earlier, Burwell had coached him to fully answer the government's questions, yet give the defense a hard time during cross-examination.

"Are you getting a reduction in your jail sentence in exchange for your testimony here today?"

"I . . . guess. . . . Yes . . . I think so," stammered McKenzie.

"You think so?!" She threw her arms up in the air.

"I mean . . . yes," said McKenzie, surprised that Gómez was really getting mad. Wasn't this nothing more than a *pretend* trial?

"Then what kind of reduction are you getting?" asked Gómez. "How many months is the government shaving off your sentence?"

"Twenty . . . four months, I think?"

"You think? You *think*?! Isn't it true that when you gave a statement to the arresting officers, you said this was your first time driving a car with cash to South Texas?"

"Well, yes," admitted McKenzie, starting to feel rattled, "but I was scared . . . confused."

"And now you're telling this good jury," she turned to look at the jurors, "that you, Barrera and Aldama had done other money runs?"

McKenzie started squirming in his seat. "Well, I . . . lied—to the cops!"

"Oh, so you lie, eh? You're an admitted liar, is that it?!" Gómez pounded counsel's table. "But today you want us to believe that what you're telling us here and now is the truth, is that it?"

"It *is* the truth," insisted McKenzie.

"Well," continued Gómez, getting ready to inflict more damage, "did you tell the arresting agents that you had no idea the car contained cash?"

"Yes."

"Because here, today—now—you're saying that the three of you *knew* the Tahoe had cash. So that was another lie, wasn't it?"

McKenzie was starting to get flustered. "But today I'm telling the truth! I swear." He locked eyes with the jurors. "You have to believe me. I swear I'm telling the truth. Yes, it's true that my lawyer got me a better deal if I testified against Mr. Aldama . . . but that's not why I'm doing this. I'm doing this because I got sick and tired of lying."

Gómez shook her head, looking disgusted and fed up. She was an exceptional actress.

If Wyatt Fox was mad as hell, he didn't show it. He maintained his composure, pretending that whatever McKenzie was espousing would not affect the ultimate result of a guilty verdict.

"This time I'm telling the truth," griped McKenzie again as he continued trying to justify his actions.

"Sure you are," replied Gómez, happy and satisfied with her performance. "That's what they all say."

Out of the corner of her eye, she glanced at the members of the focus group. They were all shaking their heads.

"Pass the witness," she announced.

Nutley also picked up on this from back in the observation room. No doubt about it, McKenzie needed a lot more work.

"I told you already . . . don't call me Nicolás. It's Monty, plain and simple," said Nicolás Montanaro, the investigator on loan from the Mexican consulate. He was a beanpole, tall and lanky, and one of those people of indeterminate age. Camila wasn't sure if he was twenty or forty. The only distinguishable feature he had was a large moustache. "Monty . . . plain and simple."

He wore khakis, a short sleeve shirt and waterproof hiking boots. Camila had met the investigator at the parking lot of Cloud 9, a popular smoke shop on Richmond Avenue. It was Saturday morning and she was following up on some of the things they had discussed, hoping some of the leads they had agreed to pursue were panning out.

Monty was leaning against the driver's side of his blue, 1969 Ford Mustang. "Since our last meeting, I've been talking to all my connections and they seem to agree that the CI thing is a bust. Either no one knows anything or it's a closely guarded secret or, my theory, is that Gosling was feeding you some bull."

"I just want you to focus on one last Gosling thing," indicated Camila. "Gosling did mention that there was a guy who used to work for the Odessa Unit but was no longer around, and AUSA Fox said Agent Rabinovich had left. I would like to find them both, if possible. But, then again, they could be one and the same."

"Do we have any names?"

"Gosling mentioned a guy named Beto Leal. I don't know if Gosling was pulling my leg or not, but the guy's real name could be Roberto, Humberto, Gilberto, even Robert. Not exactly sure. I would like to find out more. The US attorney's office isn't saying much. We need to find them. I just have a gut feeling."

"Any idea where I should start?"

"Beat the bushes. Here's a picture from an old newspaper I found the other day. That's the Odessa Unit after they took down a major drug operation some years back. Those are most of the guys working on the inside. They're posing with the drugs, cash and weapons. I wish I had more to help you get started."

She handed him the newspaper clipping with a large picture and names of the agents involved in the takedown.

He studied the picture. "This is a good start."

"One suggestion I have for you . . . " volunteered Camila, "what do you think about approaching some of the defendants Odessa took down over the years? There's got to be folks out there who are done with their jail sentences . . . back on the streets. I bet they know more than you and I could ever imagine."

"You're absolutely right." Monty smiled, folded the clipping and put it in his shirt pocket. "I'm sure Odessa's made a lot of enemies."

"Especially if they're crooked, which I suspect they are."

"Okay, let me see what I can do," answered Monty as he rubbed his beard stubble and played with his moustache. "Maybe something else will pop up. I'll make some calls, knock on some doors, hit the pavement. And I *will* check in with you, don't worry."

"Thanks," said Camila. "You can call me every hour on the hour if you want. I need to be informed, got it?"

"Got it," Monty replied as he opened the door to his car. "I think I'll start with an internet search. Ever heard of a website called *whosearat.com*?"

"No, what's that?" asked Camila.

Monty took his place behind the wheel of his car. "It's a website that lists all known informants and their handlers. In other words, for each informant listed, there's information on who they're working for. It's the largest online database of confidential informants and their agents. Maybe the informants that work with Odessa are already there. Who knows?"

"Is that even legal?" Camila looked puzzled.

"Sure is," said Monty as he fired up the engine. "The site's founder makes a valid point: If the government is keeping tabs on us, why shouldn't we be able to keep tabs on the government?"

"Never thought about it that way."

"It's a sound philosophy," smiled Monty. He slammed the car door shut, hit the ignition switch and punched the gas pedal. Monty was gone.

*　　*　　*

"Just got a call from our investigator," Camila was anxious to tell Thelma. "His contacts down in Mexico have not been able to find Rabinovich, but he thinks he's discovered what happened to Beto . . . the guy who also used to work for the task force but left on bad terms, remember?"

Thelma got curious. "And?"

"Apparently he didn't fit in very well with all the others. Last name is Carrillo, not Leal. Leal was another officer. He's trying to find out more . . . "

"Why did Beto leave?" asked Thelma.

"That's what we need to find out."

Camila had a hunch that maybe the way to defend her client was not necessarily the obvious, traditional way. Maybe it was better to try a different approach. Sure, every able-bodied defense attorney in town would raise the issue of the CI or illegal traffic stop, or argue that consent to search the Tahoe was involuntary, but maybe there was another way to attack the government. There had to be, and with luck they'd never see it coming.

If Odessa was a lawless task force, like many others around the country had proven themselves to be, or one-tenth as bad as the Panama Unit from South Texas, then somebody had to know their dirty little secrets. How could that somebody be flushed out? And where was Camila Harrison supposed to look? Or was the answer right in front of her, but she just couldn't see it?

"You and I should visit this Beto guy," suggested Thelma. "What else did Monty say?"

"He'll call back with more info. His source is making calls. Maybe we'll get lucky, get an address, and then we can go talk to him."

"Well," Thelma said as she looked at her watch, "his source better hurry. We don't have much time."

TWENTY-SIX

Known as the "Pearl of the Prairie," El Campo, Texas was a small community just sixty miles south of Houston. With eleven thousand residents and very little crime, it was the kind of place that fit ex-narcotics agent Beto Carrillo just fine. That was until Camila Harrison found him working as a loss prevention officer at the local K-Mart.

"Beto?" asked Camila. She poked her head into his small back office. "Are you the same Beto who used to work for the Odessa HIDTA Task Force . . . the unit headed by Sgt. Bergendahl?"

"Who wants to know?" asked Carrillo, turning his attention away from the wall of monitors showing various parts of the store. Camila could tell already he was a hard-ass. Even seated the man was a hulk, the kind of store cop who'd make you piss your pants if he caught you shoplifting. "Who let you in here?"

"I asked the manager," said Camila. "He said I could come on back. He was very helpful that Mr. Lambert. Gotta' love little Texas towns; everybody is so friendly."

"What do you want?" asked Beto, obviously bothered by the interruption.

"I'm defending a guy in federal court . . . Houston. They're charging him with money laundering. The Odessa Task Force conducted the traffic stop. I thought—"

"I haven't worked for those guys in a long time," Carrillo said, cutting her off. "When was your guy arrested?"

"Two months ago."

"I left Odessa almost a year ago. I don't know anything about your guy, sorry." Beto went back to his monitors.

"Why did you leave?" asked Camila.

"Personal reasons. Look, I really don't have anything that can help you, okay? All I ever did was work the evidence locker. Please leave. . . . Let me do my job, leave me out of it."

"I can subpoena you, you know," Camila said, studying his reaction.

"For what, Lady?! You're starting to tick me off!" he blurted out, getting to his feet. He seemed to fill the office all at once. "I already told you . . . I wasn't even there when your guy got arrested."

"Did Bergendahl work with CIs?"

"I don't have to answer that," Beto fired back. "I'm not on the stand, I'm not under oath . . . I don't have to talk to you. Now get the fuck out!"

"Do you really want me to subpoena you? Is that what it's going to take? I can put you on the witness stand . . . and, and, uh . . . ask you all kinds of questions. You'll be in front of a federal judge. You'll have to tell me anyway."

"Like hell I would."

"Are you telling me you're willing to commit perjury, go to prison for lying under oath?"

"Get out!" he barked, pushing Camila out of the office. After slamming the door on her face, he yelled, "And stay the hell out!"

⁂

"You know about Suzy Breeden?"

"What do you think?"

Ned Pruitt had landed in Austin an hour earlier, rented a car and driven to his covert weekend appointment at Hulse. He was now sitting across James Levinson, the firm's managing partner, who was staring at Pruitt with a worried look.

"James, you really think that in this day-and-age deep, dark, buried secrets can stay secret forever?"

"I . . . I don't know," stammered the managing partner, he was now white as a ghost, "I would think . . . that . . . well, maybe."

"C'mon, James, this is not the first time someone has come forward and accused a rich frat boy of raping a freshman? Now, maybe your son, Scotty, did slip Suzy the date rape pill or maybe he didn't? Who knows! Maybe it was a false allegation and the girl was trying to squeeze Scotty's rich father for a buck, or maybe not . . . "

Levinson gulped. His eyes wide with fear.

Pruitt continued, "What matters is that in the end, the case was settled—quietly, confidentially, under the table—and everyone went their separate way. No muss, no fuss. The matter was resolved among the aggrieved parties themselves. Without having to air their dirty laundry for the world to see. Catch my drift?"

"I think I do," Levinson replied.

"Are you going to call off the hounds?" Pruitt asked.

Levinson gave Pruitt a bemused look, "Or?"

When Pruitt and Camila had talked about finding something that could be used against Hulse to stop the firm dead in its tracks, never in a million years would the pair have imagined that Trey Collins would have dirt on Scotty Levinson. But then, Drew West had insisted that Camila continue to secretly advocate for him with Trey Collins and Collins had taken a liking to the down-and-out attorney. Many a long-lasting friendship had started that way. Crisis turned into opportunity. The attorney might hate his opponent while litigating his client's case, but once the case is over, those same two lawyers can become best of friends. As luck would have it, that had happened between Collins and Camila. And when Camila had opened up about her troubles back in Austin, Collins had been quick to come to her aid.

"Scotty can kiss his dream of becoming a doctor goodbye," Pruitt replied. "And, what is the public and your partners going to think when they find out that it was you who rushed Suzy to the hospital after Scotty alerted you that she wasn't waking up? That her breathing was labored? Because he had made her smoke marijuana, down half a bottle of tequila and slipped her the rohypnol? I'd hate to think what the DA is going to say. Can you imagine? That you knew of Scotty's drug use and allowed it? That he kept drugs in his garage apartment? Right under your very own nose?!"

Levinson was sweating bullets. "What do you want?"

"Leave Camila Harrison alone," ordered Pruitt. "That's all. Drop everything. And I mean everything."

"But . . . but," Levinson shook his head, "stuff is already in motion . . . "

"You're a smart man, James. That's why you are this firms' managing partner. I know you'll figure it out. Besides, I'm doing you a favor. I already took care of the State Bar. You just make sure people leave Camila Harrison alone."

"Okay," a reluctant Levinson agreed, "but let me ask you . . . "

"What?"

"How did you find out?"

"I'll answer your question this way," answered Pruitt, "why was Camila Harrison hired at Hulse in the first place?"

Levinson thought about it. He drew a blank.

"C'mon, James," said Pruitt, "it's not that hard."

"We hired Camila because she was resourceful and intelligent," answered Levine, "she'd get knocked down, get right back up."

"That's right . . . those are some of her best attributes," Pruitt winked, "but don't forget the most important one . . . "

"What is it?"

Ned Pruitt smiled at Levinson, "her uncanny ability to get lucky."

TWENTY-SEVEN

"Here's the latest," said Wyatt Fox as he presented several blown-up photos of a mustachioed man.

Nutley studied the man in the pictures. "Who the hell is that?"

"They call him Monty, but his real name is Nicolás Montanaro," explained Fox. "He's an investigator that moonlights for the Mexican consulate. Gustavo Govela loaned him to Harrison."

"*That's* the guy?"

"Yes, why?" asked Fox.

"Is he even licensed here in Texas?"

"Yes, he's licensed. Is he any *good*?" followed Fox. "That's the better question."

"I've heard the name and the love that precedes him," said Nutley, "but I had no idea that's what he looked like."

"Get this," said Fox, chuckling, "he's half Olmeca Indian and half Gringo. Can you imagine? Is that weird or what?"

"Be careful no one hears you say that," admonished Nutley. "We're going to have to treat him with kid gloves. God forbid some Native American ends up on our jury and they don't like the way we treat him while he's on the witness stand. Remember, he has 'the same constitutional rights as you and I.'"

"Got it."

Nutley tried to think back. "I've heard he's pretty good. His investigative methods are unconventional but effective. We need to neutralize him."

"How?"

"Well," said Nutley, "for starters . . . find out if there are any other prosecutors in our division who are half-Indian, half-Anglo. Put out some calls."

"What? Come again?"

"Half-Native, half-Anglo," repeated Nutley, "or some other combination like that."

"And?"

Nutley shook his head, not understanding why Fox was failing to see the very obvious, the big picture. "Ask them to come 'lend a hand.' We'll want him or her to sit with us at the counsel's table. We have to fight firewater with firewater here, cancel out their Indian with ours. Simple math."

"Okay," said Fox, finally seeing the light, "I'll make some calls."

"And find out if he's ever had a grievance against him or had his license suspended," ordered Nutley. "We need to know."

Thelma, Monty and Camila were in Thelma's kitchen. Poised and punchy, Thelma was conducting a mock cross-examination of Monty.

"Let's go over your training and a few other areas, okay?" asked Thelma.

"Sure," said Monty, feeling confident. He was seated on a wooden stool by the kitchen's over-sized center island. "Go ahead."

"What did you do to prepare for this case?"

Monty fidgeted in place and thought about a proper response. "I reviewed the witness statements, the police reports and visited the scene where the traffic stop took place."

"Anything else?"

"I spoke with folks with knowledge of the inner workings of the Odessa HIDTA Task Force."

"Why are you involved in this case? And in what capacity?"

"I'm a private investigator," answered Monty. "I was asked to check some things out."

"Are you licensed in Texas?"

"Yes."

"Can you work in Texas?"

"Yes," Monty answered, surprised that such a question would be asked of him. "Why?"

"How are you working in Texas?"

"My dad was a US citizen. Although I was born down in Veracruz, Mexico, I derived my citizenship from my father. I consider myself a US citizen, though I do contract work for the Mexican consulate."

"Have you testified in court before?"

"Yes, in state *and* federal courts. I've participated in about thirty jury trials during my career. Before doing contract work for the Mexican consulate, I investigated insurance fraud on behalf of various insurance companies."

"Tell us what some of your areas of expertise are."

"I have access to several online databases to search for individuals and find out if they have criminal histories, arrests, convictions, or if they've been sued or possess a professional license. I can do background checks, skip traces . . . surveillance. I'm familiar with tracking devices . . . surveillance photography . . . . Those are some of the areas I work in."

"On the legal side," Thelma continued, "are you familiar with legal concepts such as the law on search and seizure, the law on wiretapping or even Miranda warnings?"

"Yes."

"What are they?"

"The Miranda warnings?"

"Yes, what are they? Can you recite them?" Thelma asked.

"You have the right to remain silent. You have the right to an attorney. If you cannot afford an attorney, one will be provided for you . . . " He froze. "You have . . . the right . . . to . . . to . . . "

Monty appeared stumped.

Thelma became concerned. She looked at Camila. Camila dropped what she was doing over in the living room and inched closer to the kitchen.

"They're the Miranda warnings," said Camila, as she leaned against the stainless steel fridge. "You're missing the two others . . . what are they?"

"C'mon," Thelma encouraged him, "everybody knows them. If you watch TV, you know them."

Monty started turning various shades of red. He pulled a handkerchief from his pants pocket and wiped small beads of moisture off his forehead. "You have the right to remain silent. You have the right to an attorney . . . "

Thelma encouraged him some more. "Go on . . . "

"If you cannot afford an attorney, one will be provided for you. You . . . you . . . have the right. . . . Let me see. . . ." He started counting in silence with his fingers. "One, two, three . . . . What's the fourth one?"

Camila was now sporting a concerned look.

Thelma gave him a hint. "Anything you say . . . " She waited.

Nothing. Things got quiet, tense. The only sound coming from the clock up on the kitchen wall.

Thelma egged him on, "Can and will . . . does that ring a bell? Be used?"

"C'mon," said Camila, "you know this. Be used . . . ?"

"Against you!" he yelled, happy to remember. "Anything you say can and will be used against you." He let out a sigh of relief.

"And the last one?" Camila asked from the living room. "It's an extra one we have here in Texas! You have to know it."

"There's more?" he asked with a horrified look.

"Yes," said Camila, "we have a fifth one in Texas."

Thelma was now looking worried too. "What's the one you're missing? C'mon, Monty, you *have* to remember it. You know what Nutley is going to do to you if you don't know this? This is basic stuff!"

"It's not going to be pretty," added Camila. "He'll have you for lunch."

Monty wiped sweat off his forehead again.

"If you don't know it, the jury will not believe anything you say. I bet you even the jurors will know all the warnings," added Thelma. "They all watch *Law & Order* and *CSI*."

Monty started reciting the warnings again. "You have the right to remain silent. You have the right to an attorney. If you cannot afford one, one will be provided for you. Anything you say can and will be used against you . . . and. . . . And? C'mon, what's the fifth one? Think, think, think!"

"The most important one!" said Camila. "C'mon! You can . . . "

"You," interjected Thelma, "you can terminate . . . "

"The interview at any time," finished Camila.

"I'd forgotten about that one," said Monty. "Sorry."

Thelma tried another approach. "Okay, we'll come back and review the fifth warning. Let's try a different topic. Do you know what the good faith exception to the search warrant requirement is?"

"The what?" asked Monty, now even more confused. "The exception to what?"

"What are some of the exceptions to the warrant requirement?" asked Camila. She was now standing over Monty. "Do you know?"

"Plain view," answered the private investigator.

"What are some of the other ones?" asked Thelma, growing more concerned.

"Inventory . . . inventory . . . something," he answered.

"What else?" followed Camila.

"Those are all the ones I know," said Monty, sounding exhausted. "I'm sorry. It's been ten years since I last cracked open a book."

Camila and Thelma gave each other a look of grave concern, a look that screamed, *We're in trouble!*

The cross-examination prep session of Nicolás "Monty" Montanaro ended Saturday afternoon, and Camila did not waste a second reaching out to Govela to give him an update. She had to leave a message on his voicemail, but he called back not five minutes after.

"How's it going?" he asked.

"Not good," Camila answered. "We're worried about Monty."

"What happened? Is he giving you a hard time? Do I need to talk to him?"

"It's not that," replied Camila. "He's a good investigator . . . it's the other component."

"What do you mean?"

"He's going to get creamed when he takes the witness stand," explained Camila while massaging her temples. "He's very rusty on all his legal concepts. I'm worried."

"I had no idea. I'm so sorry."

"On the other hand, he's found Beto Carrillo and now he's on the trail to find Stephen Leal . . . so thank God for that."

"Where are you?" asked Govela.

"I'm heading home . . . long day."

"Can I stop by later on? I miss you. Seems like eons since I saw you last."

Camila, feeling a wave of butterflies invade her stomach, said, "I'd love that."

Camila sat at one end of the small dining room table littered with files, papers, empty coffee mugs and all other sorts of legal research related to her client's case. Govela sat at the opposite end. A half-consumed bottle of wine held a spot in the middle of the table. The mood was not joyful, but having Govela there to vent to made Camila feel less desperate.

"Maybe Nutley won't get into those matters," said Govela. "Maybe you can stay away from the stuff that might hurt the case during your direct examination of Monty?"

"Yeah, I know Nutley can only cross him on the stuff that was brought out on my direct," replied Camila, "but this is Judge Yamamoto we're talking about here. He's bending over backwards to help Nutley. He really wants to clip my wings and let his boys run roughshod all over my witnesses."

"Why do you think that is?"

"To send a message . . . the government always win, no matter what."

"Did you find out the CI's name? His identity?"

"Nope," sighed Camila, "Gosling was working on that. . . . Monty has tried, but we've only run into dead ends."

Govela shook his head. "I can't believe Gosling left you guys hanging."

"Thelma seems to think they must have gotten to him. He was getting close, they heard footsteps, got spooked and when I didn't take the deal they were offering and they realized that Gosling was on the verge of figuring out what was going on . . . he conveniently disappears. How do you like them apples?"

"Do you really think Nutley would stoop so low?"

"I don't know what to think anymore."

Govela sipped on the last of his wine. "What proof do you have? Those are some serious accusations, don't you think?"

"I wouldn't be surprised." Camila thought some more about his last comment. "All I know is that they're hiding something. I don't know what it is, but there's something fishy going on. Think about it: the other two co-defendants didn't make waves, pled out and got eight years. We could have taken the same deal, no sweat. That would have been the *easy* thing to do."

"And?"

"My guy and his family pushed me to try and do better. He really needs to get out, and the sooner, the better. Eight years is too long, and Alicia might die before then. I push to discover the CI as a pressure tactic. It works. The eight-year offer is dropped to five years. I hire Gosling and put him to work; the plea offer improves to just forty-eight months. Then I get called into Yamamoto's chambers. I'm cornered by Nutley and Yamamoto both . . . they want to strong-arm me into taking the deal, just abort the trial; now my client will serve something like two years . . . more or less."

Govela was listening intently. He reached for the wine bottle and refilled his glass. "*Really?* That happened?"

"Yup."

"Unbelievable."

"What does that tell you?" asked Camila.

He sipped his wine and thought about the answer, as if savoring the moment. He loved being in the company of a smart, beautiful woman. "That they want you to disappear. Don't come snooping around. Go away, quickly and quietly."

"That's right. Let sleeping dogs lie."

Govela looked amused. "Sort of throwing you a bone. 'Take it and go away.'"

"I don't like the way you put it . . . but that's exactly right!"

Govela grabbed the cork sitting on the table and studied it, then put it close to his nose and sniffed. "Would your client have taken the forty-eight months Nutley was offering?"

"Maybe . . . but now it doesn't matter," griped Camila, wishing she hadn't taken her client at his word when he said he wanted a trial, that she'd at least taken the offer to him. "There's no offer on the table anymore. It's either a cold plea or go to trial."

"Ouch! A cold plea, huh? That would mean your client pleads guilty to the indictment and Yamamoto sentences him, straight up—as per the sentencing guidelines, right?" asked Govela.

"Yes and no. The guidelines are no longer mandatory, which could be a double-edged sword. Yamamoto could still drop the hammer on him."

"I see."

Camila's guilt turned to anger. "Now, let me ask you: Isn't my client entitled to discover all the favorable evidence there is in order to mount an adequate defense?"

"Well, yes," admitted Govela, "those are the rules."

"And if there's evidence that casts doubt on the conduct of the officers who arrested my client, or if there's evidence that tends to discredit the agents' credibility, their integrity, am I not allowed to discover that?"

"I suppose."

"Of course, I am! I'm entitled to discover everything, whether it's good or bad, whether it helps me or hurts my case."

"I think you're thinking of the Michael Morton case," said Govela, "the new statute that says you get to see everything, the entire file. But that only applies to state court . . . to cases prosecuted in the state of Texas. I don't think the federal courts are as liberal. They're still using the Brady standard, where you only get to discover," he made air quotations with his hands, "'favorable evidence only' in the hands of the government. But maybe I'm wrong, I don't know. Have things changed that much?"

"It's all the same shit! If there's something you're hiding from me and my client, why is that? Why don't you want me to see it? Why are you trying to prevent me from getting my hands on it?"

"Because it helps your case."

"Duh! Of course it helps my case. And that's my point. It means it's favorable! My client's entitled to look at all the evidence. Why is the federal government still picking and choosing what I can and can't see? Why?! Why do Nutley and Yamamoto get to decide?"

"I can't answer that, but what I *can* say is this: You can do this. You've got what it takes to try the case. Show them bastards!"

"I just pray it was all worth it," said Camila as feelings of gloom and doom overwhelmed her again. She finished the rest of her wine. "Anyway, none of that matters now. You didn't hear this from me, but I figured out why they gave me the witness list they gave me. I'm onto them."

Govela poured Camila the last of the wine. They both raised their glasses in a toast.

"To Camila Harrison," said Govela, smiling from ear to ear.

"We'll see." Camila was shaking her head, not really feeling it. "It's in God's hands. *Que sea lo que Dios quiera.*"

Govela snuck out of bed and got dressed in the semi-darkness. It was Sunday. The time on the clock sitting on Camila's dresser read 5:30 a.m. Camila remained sound asleep under the covers.

He picked up his cell phone, car keys and wallet and went into the kitchen.

I'll call you later, he wrote on a small yellow pad in the kitchen. *Good luck on Monday. You're going to do great, I know it!"*
    Gus.
    X-O-X-O

TWENTY-EIGHT

It was 8:30 Monday morning when Camila pulled into the parking lot across from the federal courthouse. She looked in the rearview mirror to apply lipstick and fix her hair. She then reached into the backseat, grabbed her leather bag and the Aldama file and headed out, never even noticing all the news vans parked up and down a side street.

Once inside the courthouse, she was shocked to see Barton Nutley standing behind a podium, under the rotunda, flanked by his team of prosecutors.

"What's going on?" Camila asked a young man wearing a DEA windbreaker.

"Press conference. The Odessa Task Force just carried out the largest drug bust in the history of Harris County."

"What?!" Camila's heart skipped a beat. She could not believe what she was hearing. Nutley didn't play around.

"They took down an entire meth operation," said an older individual in jeans and army vest, "over the weekend."

The DEA agent added, "And seized ten tons of meth with an approximate street value of half a billion dollars. I'm so jealous. Those guys are the cream . . . "

Camila's heart started racing. Why was Nutley doing this?

Nutley took the podium and tapped on one of the microphones. "Are we on?"

A crew member behind one of the cameras gave him the thumbs up.

Nutley cleared his throat. "This weekend, members of the Odessa High Intensity Drug Trafficking Area Task Force, assisted by special agents from various other agencies, cornered and arrested forty-year-old Eusebio Teniente, a person with ties to the Texas Syndicate, a violent prison gang."

Immediately, hands shot up in the air.

Nutley paused and looked out into the crowd, but didn't call on any of the reporters. "Information obtained during Teniente's arrest led the Odessa agents to a warehouse at the Port of Houston, where a state-of-the-art meth lab was discovered along with several tons of meth, ready for distribution across the United States and Europe."

"Mr. Nutley, when do you expect the government to make more arrests?" asked a reporter with KHOU, channel 11.

"There's an ongoing investigation, that's all I can say. I'm not allowed to make any other comments." He paused. "But I can say this: if we uncover additional evidence pointing to other suspects, you can bet the brave men of the Odessa Unit will effect more arrests."

"Was he the mastermind?" asked another reporter from CNN.

"Teniente?"

"Yes."

"We're still reviewing all the evidence, but we suspect he was a key player in this drug-trafficking organization," Nutley explained, "one of the higher-ups."

"How come nobody at the Port of Houston noticed the meth lab?" asked a male reporter with Telemundo, a Spanish-language network.

"We're looking into that," said Nutley. "Due to the size of the operation, we believe port insiders were probably involved . . . "

Another reporter quickly jumped in. "Do we know who gave up Teniente? Someone had to point the finger at him, right?"

"I'm not allowed to discuss that, but thousands of tips come in every day on our hotlines. Some pan out, some don't. We almost never know who is making the calls."

"What can you tell us about this Teniente guy?" a female reporter asked.

Nutley grinned from ear to ear. "He has ties to the Texas Syndicate and an extensive criminal record. We should all be thankful that our Odessa special agents stopped him dead in his tracks. He's a violent criminal, but thank God he's off the streets now. We can all sleep a little sounder tonight."

More hands went up. "Are you running for Texas Attorney General?"

Nutley downplayed the question. "I love my job—keeping Texas and the USA safe. That's all I'll say on the matter."

Other reporters raised their hands. "What about the case that's set for jury selection this morning?"

"Will *you* be trying the case?" someone else asked.

"Yes, with the help of my team." He pointed out the team members by his side.

Flashes from cameras lit up the marbled foyer. Nutley, his prosecutorial team and the arresting agents continued smiling.

"If you're a criminal, you better not dare set foot in Texas. You've been warned!" finished Nutley as he wrapped up the conference, jumped aboard an elevator and yelled, "Don't Mess with Texas!"

He gave the crowd two thumbs up before the elevator doors closed.

<hr />

Angélica and Daniel Dawson were standing outside Judge Yamamoto's courtroom when Camila approached. They did not look happy.

Camila had had enough worry and surprises for one day. She marched right up to them. "Guys, listen. You have to trust me. Everything will be okay."

"Oh, yeah? How?" asked Mr. Dawson. "You don't have what it takes. I've read up on you. You need to surrender your license, go do something else."

"I have a plan. It will work."

He interrupted her. "You and I both know that you have nothing. We're stuck, and Vince is going to pay for your mistakes."

"My mistakes?!" Camila snapped back, getting in Mr. Dawson's face. "I didn't tell your brother-in-law to agree to move millions of dollars in drug money for a drug cartel, sir. I wasn't the one who got busted driving a Tahoe full of cash, sir. Or the one who decided to come into this country illegally. So then, how can all this be my mistake, huh?! I'm tired of idiots like you who refuse to see things for what they are and blame everybody but themselves."

Dawson glared at Camila, then pried his wife away and marched into the courtroom.

Twenty-six-year-old Vicente Aldama was dressed in beige slacks, a buttoned-down shirt and a brown blazer. As he sat in the courtroom waiting for the jury selection to start, he waved to his sister and her husband sitting out in the audience. He reminisced about life with Alicia and the little time he had spent with her lately.

"How are you holding up?" Camila asked, keeping an eye out for Thelma.

"I'm okay," replied Aldama, "I guess . . . . "

"We still have a lot of work to do," Camila added. "Thank God, we caught a break this weekend . . . I'll tell you more about it later."

Thelma walked into the courtroom and joined Camila at the counsel's table.

She leaned over to Camila. "Are you ready?"

"Yes. I'm praying we get lucky and, find the guy we've been looking for. We'll see."

"Have you heard from Monty?"

"Yes," whispered Camila. "He's been knocking on some doors, talking to people. He thinks he's getting . . ."

There were three loud knocks on the bench, and "All rise," yelled the US marshal. "Hear ye, hear ye, hear ye, the Honorable Colt Yamamoto presiding!"

"Thank you," announced Judge Yamamoto as he took his place on the bench. "You all may be seated. Are we ready to proceed?"

Barton Nutley went first. "The government's ready, Your Honor."

"We're ready," announced Camila.

"Marshal," Yamamoto called out, "where's the defendant?"

The marshal pointed out that the defendant was already seated at the counsel's table.

"Very well. Let the record reflect that the defendant, Mr. Vicente Aldama, is already in the courtroom," Yamamoto said, "sitting with his attorneys. Mr. Nutley, are there any pending issues we need to address prior to this morning's jury selection?"

"No, Your Honor," said Nutley.

"How about you, Ms. Harrison?"

"Motions *in limine*," Camila announced, clearing her throat. "And just *one* clearing issue. We're asking for leave to file a motion to transfer venue, since my client cannot get a fair trial in Houston. Just this morning, Mr. Nutley held a televised press conference . . . in this very courthouse . . . touting the accomplishments of the Odessa Task Force, Your Honor. And last weekend, all kinds of stories ran on social media and other platforms peddling Odessa's success. I don't think we'll be able to find impartial jurors. I'm sure the community feels, at this time, that the Odessa Task Force can do no wrong."

"Judge," cried Nutley, "this is an outrage . . . and I'm offended by such accusations!"

"Order!" yelled Yamamoto as he banged his gavel on the bench. "Ms. Harrison, I'll decide whether open-minded jurors can be found in the jury panel this morning. That's why I get to do jury selection and not the attorneys. You can file your motion for leave and ask for all the relief you want . . . but you know what the answer will be."

"Yes, sir," Camila said, disappointed.

"In my twenty years on the bench," added Yamamoto, "I have never granted a motion to transfer venue and I don't plan to start now. Unless something out of the ordinary happens between now and *voir dire*, I expect we'll be able to find twelve good jurors who can listen to all the evidence *before* they make up their minds one way or the other. Anything else?"

"No, Your Honor," said Nutley, glaring at Camila.

"No, Your Honor," she replied maintaining his glare.

"Very well, we'll take up motions *in limine* after jury selection. We'll be in recess! See you at 11:00 a.m. for jury selection. Let's wait for the panel to come up. The trial will start tomorrow, come hell or high water."

"All rise!" yelled the marshal. "This court will be in recess."

⸻

Barton Nutley was standing by the elevator when Blackwell approached, out of breath.

"What's wrong with you, boy?" asked Nutley. Together, they got on the elevator.

"They may have found Beto," replied Blackwell.

The elevator's doors closed behind them.

"Tell me something I don't know," Nutley said, smiling, unfazed.

Blackwell studied Nutley's face. "You knew? How?"

"You've got your sources and I've got mine." Nutley shrugged. "Anyway, don't worry. Beto doesn't know anything about the CI. There's nothing there."

Blackwell scratched his head. Nutley cracked a wicked smile. By the looks of it, Barton Nutley knew more than Blackwell could have imagined.

The elevator stopped. "We'll talk after the jury selection."

⸻

On Monday evening, Barton Nutley found himself eating popcorn straight out of a microwavable bag and sipping a Coke Zero with his feet up on his desk.

"I feel good about our jury," remarked Nutley, "how about you?"

"I agree," said Fox.

"And are we ready?" Nutley asked one last time.

"Yes, sir," the prosecutor answered, displaying confidence and bravado. "I've gone over Bergendhal's testimony, and the evidence has been pulled from the evidence locker. I have the pictures of the Tahoe's interior and its compartments. Plus, the two co-defendants have been taken to the woodshed and prepped. We have the bundles of money, subpoenas have been issued, motions *in limine* have been ruled upon by Yamamoto, and our money-laundering expert has been advised on what to say and prepped for days on end. Our custodian of evidence is also ready."

Wyatt was excited to help Nutley take the Aldama case to trial. There was no way a jury was going to acquit the defendant; it was an open-and-shut case. It was what Texas' lawyers called a "laid down" case, a case so simple, so straight forward, even a first-year law student could try it and get a guilty verdict.

"And she thinks she can win this thing, huh?" Nutley huffed.

"I don't think she's playing with a full deck," Fox said. "We've shown her the evidence. She knows it's overwhelming. I have no idea what the hell they're thinking."

"Maybe we've overlooked something," pondered Nutley, sounding a bit worried. "But what? I thought I had all my bases covered."

"Harrison's either crazy or has a silver bullet."

"That's what everybody thinks," said Nutley, "but if you want to know the truth . . . I think she's full of hot air."

Fox nodded his head, agreeing with his boss. "She's doomed. The co-defendants will say say that Aldama was the mastermind; he recruited them, paid them, told them where to pick up the car, where to deliver it, etcetera. Aldama was the logistics operator. He was a higher-up. It's going to be hard for the jury to believe he didn't know or had nothing to do with moving loads of cash."

"At what time is opening argument tomorrow?"

"We're starting at 10:00 a.m. because Yamamoto has two other hearings that morning. Remember when we used to pick juries on Wednesday," observed Fox, "and then commence trial the following Monday? I always thought that was better."

"Yes and no," replied Nutley. "When you do that, it seems like the trial is just dragging on . . . taking a long time and the jurors always resent it . . . it's a psychological thing, you know? But if you're a juror and the judge starts on Monday and he makes everyone finish by Wednesday or Thursday . . . and you're home for the weekend . . . then you'll want to serve again. That way it is fast, painless . . . efficient. It gives the appearance that the government is on top of things."

"I had heard that breaking for the weekend gave the jurors more time to go snooping around. Google stuff. Do research on the cases. Not a good thing."

"True. Anyway, let's be ready for anything and everything." Nutley rubbed his chin. "McKenzie and Barrera. We still sure they're heads are on straight?"

Fox smiled, thinking of another won case in the record books. "Barrera and McKenzie are ours, no question. Michaels and Burwell said the mock trial with the focus group really helped, plus they want their one-third sentence reduction so bad they can taste it."

"Good," said Nutley, relieved to know that everything was falling into place. "Let's hope they don't screw things up."

"And dont' forget they also want to be sentenced on the low-end of the guidelines . . . "

"Anything else?"

"That's it," said Fox.

"Well," Nutley said, "they better come thru."

TWENTY-NINE

It was a Tuesday morning and Camila Harrison felt a panic attack coming on.

She was standing alone, in a women's lavatory located on the fourth floor of the federal courthouse. While going over her opening argument, she had visions of Alicia swirling around in her head. She saw the Dawsons screaming, demanding a plea bargain, Aldama found guilty immediately after opening statements, Yamamoto pounding the bench, Nutley making a spectacle. It was all too much. Did she really think she had a chance?

Camila splashed some water on her face for the third time. She patted her face dry and threw the paper towel in the waste basket. She straightened her navy blue business suit, took a deep breath and composed herself. She studied her image one last time in the mirror. Could she and Thelma deliver a miracle? Would the recently selected jury of six women and six men side with her, with her client?

There was only one way to find out.

"Would the defendant please rise?" called out Judge Yamamoto. "Let's go ahead and re-arraign the defendant."

Vicente Aldama stood between Camila and Thelma. He turned to look at the jury, their eyes on him.

"Go ahead, Mr. Nutley," Yamamoto instructed, ready to get started.

Barton Nutley got up slowly, cleared his throat, adjusted his reading glasses and focused on the indictment in his hands.

"Case No. 2014-CR-3456-3, *United States of America v. Vicente Aldama, et al.* In the name and by the authority of the United States of America, the grand jury for the Southern District of Texas, Houston Division, aforesaid, duly organized and impaneled as such at the July term, A.D. 2014, upon their oath, do hereby present that Vicente Aldama, hereinafter 'defendant,' on or about the 16th of September, 2014, and anterior to the presentment of this indictment, did then and there, with the assistance of others, known and unknown, intentionally and knowingly, combine, conspire, confederate and agree together to commit money laundering in violation of Title 18, United States Code, Sections 1956(a)(1)(A)(i) and Sections 1956(a)(1)(B)(i)."

Nutley paused for effect.

"To the indictment, Mr. Vicente Aldama, how do you plea, sir? Guilty or not guilty?"

Vicente Aldama stared at Nutley, then turned and looked at the jury, and finally over in his sister's direction. He smiled and said, "Not guilty."

"You all may be seated," directed Yamamoto. "Let the record reflect the defendant has entered a plea of 'not guilty' to the indictment."

Nutley, Fox, Camila, Thelma, Aldama and all the others sat down. Sitting at the government's table was now an additional assistant US attorney, Madhaven Forbes, on loan from the Chicago US attorney's office. The Pakistani-American prosecutor had been brought in to 'lend a hand,' per Nutley's request to even out the playing field.

"Go ahead, Mr. Nutley," Yamamoto said, prompting Nutley to start his opening argument.

Nutley left the counsel's table, walked toward the jury box, planted himself squarely in front of the jurors and proceeded to deliver a standard, garden-variety opening argument—not the kind of argument someone contemplating running for Texas attorney general would deliver.

Camila picked up on this. Why was he holding back?

"You're up, Ms. Harrison," instructed Judge Yamamoto.

Camila's mouth was dry as West Texas, but she knew it was now or never. She turned to look at her client, then looked out into the crowd and noticed that Alan, Julio, Govela, Thelma's daughter and even Ms. Landry were all sitting in the gallery. Out of the corner of her eye she thought she'd caught a glimpse of her mother, Lorena, and Darin sitting together in the crowd.

What the hell? I must be hallucinating! she thought.

With her heart pounding furiously, she said a quick prayer and tried to swallow a bit of saliva, but there was none in her mouth. "May it please . . . the court . . . Mr. Nutley . . . Mr. Aldama, Mr. Fox . . . Mr. Burwell, Michaels, co-counsel . . . ladies and gentlemen of the jury." She cleared her throat and continued, "I'm sorry . . . I'm a little nervous . . . please forgive me. This is my first trial after being away from the courtroom for many years. I hope you'll excuse me . . . I'm a little nervous—oh wait, I already said that."

The demeanor of the female jurors softened and a couple of them even smiled and made eye contact with Camila.

"The evidence will show," continued Camila, "that two months ago, Sergeant Dwayne Bergendahl conducted a traffic stop involving a Chevrolet Tahoe. Riding in the Tahoe were Mr. Aldama, my client, and two other co-defendants, Bobby McKenzie and Roland Barrera. The traffic stop happened between Victoria and El Campo. You heard Mr. Nutley say that McKenzie and Barrera will be testifying for the government. The evidence will show that they have cut deals with the government in order to receive reduced sentences in exchange for pointing the finger, and the majority of blame with it, at my client. Their testimony, the evidence will show, cannot be trusted. Their testimony is highly suspect . . . "

Nutley sprang to his feet. "Objection, Your Honor. The government has made no such arrangement. That's misleading."

"Denied," answered Yamamoto. "Mr. Nutley, I believe Ms. Harrison is arguing that this is what she *believes* the evidence will show. Carry on, Ms. Harrison."

"Thank you, Your Honor," Camila said, turning to face the jury with more confidence. "Now, I don't know anything about McKenzie and Barrera, but I do know this . . . my client is going to testify, and the evidence will show that Agent Bergendahl has lied about the reason he made the traffic stop, about obtaining proper consent from the occupants of the Tahoe to search the vehicle and about other facts in connection with the way this case was handled . . . and investigated."

"Objection, Your Honor," cried Nutley, trying to rattle Camila's cage. "That's totally improper."

"Denied," shot back Yamamoto. "This is her opening argument. Go on, Ms. Harrison."

"Now . . . " Camila took a deep breath, then paused to gather her thoughts. She was starting to feel even less anxious. "Where was I? Oh yes!" followed Camila. "We concede that there was money in the Tahoe found in secret compartments. We concede that Aldama, McKenzie and Barrera were in the Tahoe. However, we believe the evidence will show that the traffic stop was done in an illegal manner, it was a pretext stop. The resulting search was also illegal. . . the evidence will show that Vicente Aldama never gave voluntary consent to the Odessa agents to search the vehicle. In fact, *you* will get to decide what to do about that."

Nutley could be seen whispering something into Wyatt's ear. The jurors noticed this. Wyatt was scribbling on his yellow pad.

Camila ignored the pair and continued delivering her opening argument.

"This was a pretext stop, plain and simple. We believe the evidence will show that my client's constitutional rights were not only violated, but violated as a result of lies, deceit and fabrications. And in this country, when the government violates our constitutional rights and guarantees—guarantees given to us by our founding fathers . . . written in the Constitution—then jurors, like you here today, have the right to send the government a message."

"Objection!" cried Nutley. "This is not a closing argument. This is the opening statement, Your Honor!"

"Stick to what the evidence will show, Ms. Harrison," ordered Yamamoto.

Camila quickly adjusted her delivery. "The evidence will show that the Odessa Task Force cannot be trusted. That this investigation was flawed and that Sergeant Bergendhal had no valid reason to pull the Tahoe over, thus making the traffic stop illegal. As a result of this shoddy investigation, you get to do something about that. But, most importantly, the evidence will show Vicente Aldama must be acquitted. Thank you."

Camila took her place at the counsel's table and sat next to her client she caught a glimpse of Govela sitting in the crowd. He winked at her.

<hr />

"Mr. Barrera, how was it that you met the defendant?" asked Barton Nutley without wasting a single minute.

"We met at a Buffalo Wild Wings. Oscar De La Hoya was fighting Manny Pacquiao . . . their bout was being televised."

"What year was that?"

"I think it was back in 2013. December, maybe? It's been a while," apologized Barrera, who had never met Aldama before that fateful day of the traffic stop. Barrera and McKenzie had been brought in to make sure the money got to its final destination, make sure the rules were followed.

"What happened at the Buffalo Wild Wings that led to you becoming friends with the defendant?" Nutley turned to look at Aldama with revulsion.

"We were sitting at the bar watching the fight," explained Barrera. "We started talking. He said he was from somewhere down in Mexico . . . "

"Objection, hearsay," said Camila.

But before Yamamoto could rule, Barrera finished his thought, " . . . and he came to Houston looking for work . . . to send money home to care for his sick kid."

"Sustained," ruled Yamamoto, then addressed the defendant. "Sir, we don't want to hear what other people said or the statements third parties made. The jury wants to hear about what you know, the stuff you have personal knowledge of . . . understand? Don't testify about he said/she said sort of stuff, got it?"

Barrera nodded his head as if he'd understood, but he was now more confused than ever. The last few days, during the prep rounds, he'd been instructed on what to say, what not to say, what to cover, what not to cover, how to say things, how not to say them, how to look at the jury, how not look at the jury, how to address the judge, how not to address the judge. It was impossible for him to remember everything. So, he did what came naturally. He shot a look at his attorney for an explanation, but Michaels just shrugged his shoulders. Barrerra was on his own. It was sink-or-swim time.

"And? Please continue," indicated Nutley. "What kind of work was he looking for?"

"Anything. He wasn't making much money mowing lawns. He needed something with better pay . . . that was all."

"Did he say anything else?"

Camila sprang to her feet. "Hearsay!"

Barrera turned and looked at Yamamoto. Yamamoto gave him a stern look.

"No, that was it. De La Hoya lost the fight. I gave him the number of a friend who was looking for help . . . the guy is in the roofing business. I think he went to work for him."

"How did you end up getting involved in the courier business . . . in the business of moving loads of cash?"

The jury was mesmerized by Barrera, who despite his twenty-eight years of age looked much younger than he was.

"Through a mutual friend . . . I can't remember the name . . . I think they call him Rufo?"

"Speculation," cried Camila.

"Sustained," answered Yamamoto.

Nutley pressed on. "Do you know Rufo's name?"

"No."

"About how many times have you gone on trips to South Texas with Mr. Aldama?"

"Several. Maybe more than five. Somewhere around there."

Aldama was shaking his head. This was a lie. Camila and Thelma leaned over and whispered in his ear to stop reacting, to stay composed. As hard as it was, he needed to try and keep a straight face. It was imperative.

"Was that in 2014?"

"Yeah."

"How would Aldama get in touch with you?"

"By telephone."

"What would happen after you got the call?"

"We would meet at a truck stop on the outskirts of Houston. Someone would deliver the vehicle we were supposed to drive. We'd get in it . . . and drive to South Texas."

"Do you think it's possible the defendant didn't know the car was transporting illegal cash?"

"Nah, not really." Barrera turned his attention to the twelve in the box. "We all knew what we were doing. Once we got to the Valley, we had instructions to go to a Target or Walmart. We had to call a number when we got there, leave the keys under the floor mat, get in another car and drive that other car back to Houston."

"Who is 'we'?"

"Whoever came along for the drive. There's like a pool of drivers and different sets of lookouts. You sometimes go on the road without knowing the other people."

"The cars you drive back . . . is there anything in them?"

"We don't know. They don't tell us, but I don't think so. If they were loaded with something, we would have been stopped at the checkpoint . . . and that never happened."

Camila started to get up from her chair and was about to lodge another speculation objection but refrained. Barrera's testimony was actually helping her case.

"In this case," continued Nutley, "do you recall the traffic stop?"

"Yeah."

"Who was driving?"

"He was," said Barrera, pointing at Vince.

"Why was the Tahoe stopped? Do you know?"

"Not really sure. We had been on the road for about an hour, when all of a sudden, this unmarked Dodge Charger started flashing its lights. We got pulled over. I think I heard there was a light that was out, the light on the rear plate. That's why we got pulled over. Guy came out of nowhere."

"Do you remember the agent's name? The guy who stopped you guys?"

"Bergendahl, I think . . . not really sure what his first name was."

"Fair enough," said Nutley. "How was it that Agent Bergendahl went about searching the Tahoe?"

Barrera turned to face the judge. "I heard Aldama give consent. By this time, other agents had arrived, and either Bergendahl or some other agent . . . I can't remember who it was exactly, Your Honor," he turned to look at the jury, "but they got consent from the driver. A few minutes later, a K9 officer arrived. The dog found the bundles of cash."

Nutley continued. "How much money did they find? Do you know?"

"It was a big amount . . . I don't know—I didn't count it."

There was a small wave of laughter in the courtroom. It died almost immediately following a look from Yamamoto. Nutley pressed on.

"A big amount, huh? Was it more than five hundred thousand? Eight hundred thousand? A million?" asked Nutley, turning around and glaring at Aldama.

"It was a lot," blurted Barrera. "All I remember is that the agents were really, really excited. I think Bergendahl said something about Christmas arriving early this year."

Camila noticed Burwell and Michaels huddled in conference. The jurors had also noticed the pair consulting with one another.

"I pass the witness," said Nutley, sensing that Barrera was starting to forget the rehearsed script and might begin to delve into matters that could hurt the government's case.

"Let's take a ten-minute break," announced Judge Yamamoto. "Ladies and gentlemen of the jury, we will now take a bathroom break. Don't go wandering off. Please follow the marshal and be back when we call you."

"All rise," announced the marshal.

The jurors marched single-file out of the courtroom through a side door. As soon as they exited the courtroom, Camila made a dash for the ladies' restroom.

"Christmas in September, huh?" That's how criminal defense attorney Camila Harrison started the cross-examination of Roland Barrera. "You're *also* getting an early Christmas present for your testimony here today, aren't you, Mr. Barrera?"

"What do you mean?" asked the witness, playing dumb.

"In exchange for your testimony, the government is reducing your jail sentence by . . . what? Another three years? Am I correct?"

"One-third . . . whatever one-third is," answered Barrera, " . . . of eight years."

"So you're catching a break, correct?"

He shrugged. "Yeah, I guess."

"After your arrest," said Camila, waiving a document, "you gave a statement to the agents at Odessa, didn't you?"

"Yeah," answered Barrera.

"And how well would you say that initial statement matches what you've said here today?"

"I don't know. I can't remember."

"You want to see your statement?"

"Sure."

"Not a problem," Camila paused, "but let's get a few things straight here. You never mentioned that my client had given consent. You never told the agents that you and my client had done other trips. And you never mentioned that my client would call you. Is that correct?"

Barrera started fidgeting on the witness stand. "I don't know . . . I guess I've had time to think about what happened that day."

"May I approach, Your Honor?" asked Camila.

"You may," said Yamamoto.

Camila left counsel's table and handed Barrera his statement.

"For the record, could you please tell us where in that statement you discuss the consent, the call and the other trips? Please . . . tell us. Tell the members of the jury where you discussed those things."

Barrera took his time and read his statement. After a few minutes of silent reading, he finally muttered, "There's nothing there."

Camila pressed on. "And the reason there's nothing is because the government told you what to say here today, isn't that the truth?"

"Objection!" yelled Nutley. "That's improper, Your Honor."

"Sustained," said Yamamoto.

"How is that improper, Your Honor?" asked Camila. "I'm entitled to know the basis for the objection. On what grounds is Mr. Nutley objecting?"

Yamamoto gave Camila a glare. "I've made my ruling, Counselor. Move on."

"What's the basis, Your Honor? How is my question improper?" repeated Camila. "This is cross-examination."

Yamamoto tried to keep his composure. "Ms. Harrison, this is not Evidence 101 . . . and I don't have time to educate you. Move on!"

"The government bought your testimony—isn't that the truth, sir?" blurted out Camila. "They told you to say those things in exchange for a reduced sentence, didn't they?!"

"Objection! Move to strike, Your Honor," said a frustrated Nutley.

Yamamoto turned to the jury and admonished them. "The jury will disregard that last question." He then turned to face Harrison.

"And you, Ms. Harrison," continued Yamamoto, "you're walking a fine line. Ask something relevant, and if you don't have anything relevant to ask, then sit down. Let's call the next witness so we can move things along."

"I'm not finished with my cross-examination, Your Honor," Camila complained. "I'm just getting started."

"Young lady!" yelled Yamamoto. "This is federal court and in federal court we don't have wide-open cross-examination. Your cross-examination must be narrowly tailored and specific to matters brought out by the government during their *direct* examination. You don't get to ask everything under the sun, moon and stars. You get what I'm saying?"

"Loud and clear," Camila snapped back.

"Then sit down!" ordered Yamamoto. "Mr. Nutley, are you ready to call your next witness?"

But before Nutley could provide an answer, Camila asked the witness a quick follow up question, "Mr. Barrera, you said there were several trips before to South Texas, do you recall that testimony?"

Yamamoto gave Camila an icy stare. Boy she was pushing his buttons. He let it go.

She ignored him.

"Yes," replied Barrera.

"And those other times," continued Camila, "my client would drive the vehicles loaded with cash down to the border? Is that what I just heard you say?"

Nutley suddenly leaned over and whispered something into Griffith's ear. Fox, Forbes and the others sat up straight.

"Correct," answered Barrera.

"Remember Mr. Nutley's question about my client knowing or not knowing if the cash was illegal, remember that question just a few minutes ago?"

"Yes . . . I guess..."

"And you said he had to know the cash was illegal, remember that?"

"Yes."

"How do you know the cash was illegal?" asked Camila.

"Well . . . well, it's from the sale of drugs," fudged Barrera, "I mean . . . "

"What drugs?"

"I don't know."

"Coke?"

"I don't know."

"Marijuana?"

"I don't know."

"Objection!" cried Nutley, "Where's the relevance, Your Honor?"

"Denied," shot Yamamoto.

Camila continued peppering Barrera. "Well, did you see anybody get paid for the drugs?"

"No."

"Were you present when drugs were exchanged for cash?"

"No, but I mean . . . c'mon."

"You don't really know, do you?"

"I'm sure it comes from the sale of drugs . . . "

"Are you sure?"

"Yes."

"Could it be money that belongs to an alien-smuggling organization?"

"Maybe."

"So, you don't really know, do you?"

"I guess not . . . but c'mon . . . isn't it obvious?"

"Now, let me ask you, if my client is in the country illegally," pressed Camila, "how was he able to come right back to Houston to do other runs? Remember that he's an illegal alien, with no legal documents. Would you care to explain that to the jury?"

"Objection!" yelled Nutley, "Calls for speculation."

"Sustained," ruled Yamamoto, "Are you finished Ms. Harrison?"

"Mr. Nutley opened the door when he asked the witness about the other trips to South Texas, Your Honor. I want this witness to explain how it is possible to accuse my client of driving to South Texas, on different occasions, and then drive back to Houston?"

Yamamoto was not happy with Camila injecting her own two bits. "Counsel, that's enough!" He gave her a stern look.

Thelma tried to signal Camila to tone it down. Besides, the jurors had probably already figured out that Barrera's story didn't make sense. No illegal alien, in his right mind, was going to drive to South Texas only to risk being arrested at any of the checkpoints as he drove back north. That would never happen.

"Pass the witness," announced Camila, as she turned and stared at Nutley.

"Nothing further," followed Nutley, glaring back at Aldama's counsel.

"Let's take a break before you call your next witness," ordered Yamamoto, as he nodded to the marshal to escort the jurors while they had their break.

<hr />

"Are you passing the witness at this time?" Yamamoto asked.

After the break, the trial had quickly resumed with the testimony of co-defendant, Bobby McKenzie. Seeing that Barrera had not performed as a witness for the government, Nutley had danced around some key areas pertaining to the traffic stop and the search of the vehicle. Nutley had McKenzie, instead, talk about Vicente Aldama. The less time McKenzie spent talking about the actual traffic stop, the defective rear plate light, and the Odessa Task Force, the less of an opportunity for Camila Harrison to inflict damage.

"Yes, Your Honor. Pass the witness," answered Nutley.

Bobby McKenzie smiled for the jury, oblivious to what was about to happen. He had spent the first few hours of his direct examination talking about his background, his education, his family, his work history and his criminal record. The jury had quickly figured out that he was a repeat offender, two-bit loser, who knew his way around the criminal justice system.

"Mr. McKenzie," instructed Yamamoto, doing his best to appear fair and even-handed, "I remind you that you're still under oath." Then Yamamoto nodded at Camila. "Please, Counselor . . . go ahead."

"Thank you," answered Camila as she grabbed a yellow pad and walked over to the podium in order to start her cross-examination. "Okay, let's see . . . "

McKenzie sat up straight, as did the jurors, ready for a contentious exchange.

"Mr. McKenzie," Camila started, "you too were offered a deal by the government, is that correct?"

"Yes," McKenzie replied, no sugarcoating to his response.

"Objection!" yelled Nutley, as he rolled his eyes. "Here we go again . . . Your Honor, this is totally inappropriate!"

Yamamoto stared at Camila as if saying, *Don't push your luck.*

Camila got the message and moved on. "You also gave a statement to the agents from Odessa, didn't you?"

"Yes."

"And in that statement, you said that you all had been asked by a man named Rufo to do the run. Do you remember that?"

"Yes . . . Rufo . . . I don't know his real name . . . might be Eduardo. Why they call him Rufo? That I don't know."

"But here," indicated Camila, "today, you said it was *my* client who appeared to be in charge. You testified earlier that *my* client appeared to be the organizer. Remember that?"

McKenzie started getting hot around the collar. "Yes . . . I think that's what I said." He shifted in the witness chair. He tried to get some kind of clue from Burwell, his federal public defender, but Burwell had his face buried deep in notes.

"Why did you tell the agents *then* you were working for a guy named Rufo, but *now* are telling the jury it was my client who was in charge? Why are you changing your story?"

"Well . . . um . . . . " He glanced at Burwell, but this time Burwell was doodling on the yellow pad in front of him, ignoring his client on purpose. Without any guidance from his counsel, he started getting more nervous. "Well . . . I've had time to think about the events of that night and I now remember what happened."

"Wait! That information was not fresh on your mind on the day you were arrested . . . but two months later, you suddenly remember new information? asked Camila.

"Uh . . . you know what I mean . . ." fumbled McKenzie.

"You mean you've had time to meet with the government . . . and you're testifying the way they want you to testify, isn't that right?" asked Camila. "You're changing your story. You're lying."

Nutley sprang to his feet. "Objection, Your Honor. Ms. Harrison is leading the witness and this is an area we're not supposed to go into. I'm asking for a jury instruction to disregard that last question."

Yamamoto banged his gavel on the bench. "Order, order! The jury is hereby instructed to ignore that last question and whatever the answer may have been. The jury is not to consider any of the last exchange." He then directed his attention to the attorney. "And you, Ms. Harrison . . . approach the bench!"

All members of counsel approached the bench. The judge covered the microphone in front of him and waved to the ERO to stop recording.

"What do you think you're doing?" asked an angry Yamamoto. "You keep getting into matters that we covered in motions *in limine* . . . matters you're not supposed to get into."

Burwell jumped up instinctively. "Your Honor, McKenzie opened the door when he said he's had time to think about it . . . " He caught himself and quickly sat down.

Nutley, Fox and Griffin gave him the look of death. Yamamoto did too. Forbes didn't care either way; he still couldn't figure out why he'd been asked to sit at a trial he found particularly boring. He was an appellate lawyer, after all. Trial work was just not his cup of tea.

"Exactly," added Camila. "I'm entitled to explore how well he remembers the events of that evening, and *any* reason he may be changing his statements, Your Honor."

"He *did* open the door," added Thelma as she stuck her hands in the fire for her first chair. "The rules allow her to cross-examine on those matters, Your Honor."

"Nobody asked you!" replied Yamamoto, visibly upset. "I'm warning you, Ms. Harrison, if you keep disobeying my directives, you're not going to like the outcome."

Before Yamamoto had a chance to say anything else, Camila snapped back, "I'm defending my client to the best of my ability. And if the court doesn't like it, then the court has to do what it has to do, and I'll do what I have to. I've had it with the court's meddling and its attempts to get me to stop fighting for my client."

"I'm going to find you in contempt. Is that what you want?!" whispered Yamamoto, his nostrils flaring. "How are you going 'fight' for your client when I throw your ass in jail, huh?"

Thelma grabbed Camila by the elbow and pulled her away
from the bench. She had to intervene before things really got out
of hand. "Sorry," Thelma whispered to Yamamoto. "It won't happen again, Your Honor."

"Let's get back on the record," Yamamoto barked. "Your witness, Ms. Harrison."

Thelma took her seat at counsel's table and Camila went back
to the podium. The prosecutors all went back to their places.
Camila resumed her cross-examination of Bobby McKenzie. She
was done with being pushed around.

"Did you meet with the lawyers in Mr. Nutley's office to prepare your testimony?" She ignored Yamamoto and looked over at
the twelve in the jury box.

"Objection!" cried Nutley, "How is that relevant?"

Over at counsel's table, Thelma could be seen shaking her
head and mumbling under her breath, "Oh no, here we go again."

"He testified," clarified Camila, as she now turned her attention to Yamamoto, "that he'd been offered a jail time reduction. I
want to know how that happened and when. The circumstances
surrounding that agreement: who was involved when that was discussed? And what exactly did he have to do to earn the jail time
reduction? The jurors are the judges of Mr. McKenzie's credibility
and they're entitled to know, Your Honor! What exactly was he
promised?"

Suddenly McKenzie blurted out, "we only did a mock. . . . "

Nutley sprang to his feet, "Your Honor?!"

"A mock trial, huh?" remarked Camila, as she turned and
looked at the jurors.

"Your Honor," cried Nutley, "that's all work product!"

"Stop!" barked Yamamoto, signaling McKenzie to stop.

"That's off limits, Ms. Harrison," Yamamoto scowled, his face
turning various shades of red, "ask something else. Let's move on."

Camila finally relented. Hopefully, the jury could see what exactly was going on between Barrera, McKenzie and Nutley's office. It
was obvious, the co-defendants' testimony had been bought and paid
for by the US government. She cleared her throat, "Mr. McKenzie,
did you see my client put the money in the vehicle?"

"No."

"Did you hear my client say the vehicle had money?"

"No."

"Did my client act nervous during the drive?"

"No."

"So, bottom line . . . you can't tell this good jury if my client knew or didn't know the Tahoe had cash. Isn't that right?"

"Correct."

"So, why would Barrera testify that my client knew. Any ideas?

"Don't have a clue," McKenzie replied.

Nutley looked disappointed. He was ready to walk over and punch Burwell. Why was McKenzie suddenly helping Aldama? This case was supposed to be a slam dunk!

"Pass the witness," Camila announced, ready to put the first two witnesses behind her and touch base with Monty . . . see if anything was happening out in the Odessa universe.

THIRTY

"Don't be so depressed, you're doing great!" said Gustavo Govela as he spooned red beans and rice up to his mouth. "You're doing the best you can with what you have. In my opinion, you're doing a hell of a job."

"That's right," interjected Thelma. "I hadn't seen you in action since moot court in law school, Camila, but let me tell you . . . I'm very, very impressed. You haven't lost your touch."

Julio put down his iced tea. "The jury loves you. Even your landlady can see that!"

"It is pretty obvious," finished Heather Landry, winking at Julio. This was not necessarily true. The jury was hard to read, but Julio and Heather Landry believed in the power of positive thinking and wanted nothing but positive thoughts to rain down on Camila Harrison.

Camila and her cheering section were sitting inside the Christ Church Cathedral, where the owners of Treebeards operated a location of their famous Cajun restaurants. The eatery was located a short walk from the federal courthouse.

"Can somebody tell me how it is that my mother and father ended up in the courtroom, sitting side by side?!" Camila stared intently at Thelma.

"Don't look at me," replied Thelma.

Govela gave her a blank stare, "I have no clue."

Julio avoided Camila's gaze. He kept eating his jambalaya, taking care not to look up while he chewed his mouthful thoroughly.

"Yes?" he asked, looking up from his plate. He could no longer pretend he wasn't feeling the group's stares.

"Well?" Camila asked.

Julio put down his fork, took his napkin from his lap and wiped his lips. "She called the office and said Cassie had given her your new work number in Houston. We got to talking . . . asked me how you were doing, the usual pleasantries . . . I guess I volunteered that you were super busy with this case . . . probably slipped out, you know what with the trial coming up and stuff."

"Is that right?" huffed Camila.

"I swear," answered Julio, "I had no idea she would show up in Houston to watch you in action, Camila. I swear . . . for real!"

"I think it's great!" volunteered Thelma, " . . . especially since it appears that Lorena and Darin have put aside their differences."

"You don't say." Camila checked her cell phone while picking at her pear, walnut and blue cheese salad. She was waiting to hear from Monty. She was dying to find out if he had been able to get a copy of the video and if anyone had looked at it.

"If it's any consolation, my parents never came down to see me try a case," followed Thelma. "I would have liked them to."

"We'll talk about this when the case is over," said Camila, bothered that her friends appeared to be keeping secrets. And at the worst possible time.

"Is your client taking the stand?" Govela asked, changing the subject.

"He's waffled back and forth. I don't know. This morning he was, but you never can tell. Things are changing minute by minute; confidences, testimonies . . . *allies*." She glared at the entire table.

"Uh, who do you think Nutley will call next?" asked Julio.

"Bergendahl," said Camila, "the Odessa agent who pulled the car over. That's my guess."

"Are you ready?" Julio asked.

"Oh yeah," Camila said, semi-sarcastically. "I'm just getting started."

"I know you have a lot on your plate right now," said Thelma, washing up next to Camila in the ladies' room. "But the reason Darin and Lorena are together is because Luis Pablo is sick. She reached out to Darin because she didn't have anybody *else* to turn to, FYI."

"How's that my problem?" snapped Camila, angry at the fact that Thelma had broached such an uncomfortable topic just as they were getting ready to go back into the courtroom. "You couldn't wait to tell me this, until *after* the trial?"

"Amiga," started Thelma, as she stared at the mirror and checked her teeth for food, "Luis Pablo needs a bone marrow transplant. And you, being his half-sister, might be a match. Lorena, she's desperate. She didn't want to bother you . . . but."

Camila didn't know what to make of it. She'd heard Thelma's words, but they just didn't register.

Silence.

Thelma continued. "Omar has made arrangements with his friends at M.D. Anderson, in case you decide to help out, get tested. I've been asked to whisk you away, after we break today or tomorrow—your choice. Once they obtain your bone marrow sample, they'll run various tests to see if you're a match."

"Wait, wait, wait . . . " Camila was now more confused than ever. "Slow down. You're going too fast. I'm in the middle of trial . . . did you guys not get the memo?"

"Darin also pulled some strings and was able to make arrangements for your brother to receive the bone marrow transplant here, at M.D. Anderson, if a match can be found. Apparently, when Luis Pablo fell ill, his adoptive parents felt it was important to reconnect with his biological mother. Luis Pablo's parents are now best friends with Lorena and Darin. Luis Pablo, his wife, his children and his parents are staying at a hotel in the Medical Center. The last piece of the puzzle is you."

Nothing that Thelma was saying was making sense in Camila's head. She continued to give Thelma a blank stare.

"But, of course, your blood and marrow have to match in order for the transplant to be done—and if you transplant, you'll need some days to recover. What do you say?"

"Is that why they are in town?" Camila stared down at the sink, trying to understand. She was now more confused than ever.

"Yes," said Thelma, "like I said, they've put aside their differences to help Luis Pablo. Let me ask you this: If you are going all out for Vicente Almada, a complete stranger, some guy you didn't know from Adam, why wouldn't you want to help your own brother? Your own family?"

Camila couldn't argue with that. She regained some of her composure.

"Okay," muttered Camila, calm with shock, "let's get in there and wrap things up for the day."

Thelma smiled.

<hr>

Monty was seated in a booth inside the House of Pies, holding a manila envelope in his hands.

"Hey!" said the voice.

Monty turned around. "Oh, I didn't see you come in. I was expecting Ms. Harrison."

"She's tied up in trial . . . " Alan slid across the booth from him. "But, I'm here. What did you find out?"

"Footage from Buc-ee's rest stop. The night shift . . . 6 p.m. to 2 a.m."

"Great! Did you look at it?"

"No, I barely got it."

"Care for a menu?" asked the waitress who was now standing next to Monty and Alan.

"Just water," Alan said. "I have to rush back to court, let Camila and Thelma know we got the video."

"Coffee." He turned back to Alan. "I also found the Tahoe. It was auctioned off, but I traced it to a used car lot in McAllen, that just sold it to a Mexican National. I have a friend who is going to drive across the border to Reynosa to go and talk to the new owner. Hopefully he'll be able to make contact."

A wide grin appeared on Alan's face. Things were finally starting to click. "What about Beto? The guy who used to work for Odessa. Any news?"

Monty sighed. "Yes, he's no longer working at the K-Mart. The manager gave me an address, and I plan on driving over to see if I can find him."

"I hear Nutley is burning through his witnesses pretty fast. There's a good chance the government might rest by tomorrow afternoon. Then it will be Camila's and Thelma's turn to put on their case-in-chief, and call witnesses. So, we need you to come up with something quick. We don't have much time."

"I better hustle, then."

"Yes, Camila wants you to keep beating the bushes . . . don't stop."

The waitress came by and set the coffee and water on the table, and left without a word. *If only the legal system was as efficient,* Alan thought.

Monty sipped his coffee. "What do they need the video footage for?"

"Camila wants to see if the video shows the 'defective' plate light, which is supposed to be the reason for the traffic stop. That vehicle's condition is key to the case."

Monty was scratching his head. "Well, I'm glad the video still existed. The cloud is a wonderful thing."

Alan said, "I hope your friend down in McAllen can find the Tahoe, check out those rear plate lights, just in case."

"Hey, and what if my friend finds the Tahoe and the light's out and there's nothing in the video . . . then what?"

"Aldama's fried. Might as well throw in the towel."

"So, if we show the lights are working just fine, then and now, is it a slam dunk?"

"Not quite. The judge still has to let the evidence in."

"What a mess!" Monty played with the coffee spoon, looking stumped. He lit up a second later. "Did you know that Beto's real name is *Gualberto?*"

"Really? How did you find out his real name?"

"I peeked inside the employee file when the manager was rifling through it, looking for an address. Anyway, I told the manger I was a half-brother of his, looking to patch things up."

"And he bought it?"

"Apparently . . ."

"That's smart. Anyway, I really have to run," said Alan. "I need to go look at the video. I'll have Camila call you."

"Sure," said Monty. "I'll be waiting."

THIRTY-ONE

"It's two o'clock, everyone ready to continue?" asked Judge Yamamoto of the trial lawyers present in his courtroom. Yamamoto looked refreshed, excited even.

Barton Nutley went first. "The government's ready, Your Honor."

"We're ready," announced Camila, stressed and bothered that she now had another thing to worry about. Luis Pablo! Why couldn't it wait?

"Ready," said Thelma, following Camila's lead.

"Marshal," Yamamoto called out, "please bring in the jury."

The marshal walked over to the other side of the courtroom, opened a door and disappeared down a hallway. After about thirty seconds, he came back with the group of twelve in tow. Everyone in the courtroom stood until the jurors sat down.

"You may all be seated," Yamamoto ordered. "Mr. Nutley, call your next witness."

"We call OFAC special agent Howard Copeland, Your Honor. He's testifying as an expert for the government. Mr. Fox will conduct the direct examination."

The DEA agent with expertise in laundering operations walked into the courtroom and took the witness stand. Agent Copeland appeared to be around thirty-five. He looked more like a hippie off the beach, with his long beard and long hair—nothing like a federal agent. He was sworn in and they started.

"Agent Copeland," Wyatt Fox began—he and Nutley had decided to alternate the direct examination of the government's witnesses, "are you familiar with the means and methods drug organizations use to launder drug proceeds?"

"Yes, that's my job. I'm part of the Office for Foreign Asset Control, a federal agency that disrupts and dismantles drug organizations by interrupting their ability to launder money."

"And as part of this task force, what do you do?" Fox asked.

"I conduct financial investigations and target businesses, enterprises, bank accounts and properties that we believe were obtained or purchased with illegal proceeds—usually drug money. Once we identify a target, we commence civil forfeiture proceedings to seize the accounts, businesses, land, whatever it might be . . . warehouses, mansions, even airplanes and yachts . . . and art collections to some extent."

"What are some of the most famous cases you've been involved in?"

Copeland grinned from ear to ear. "We just finished a case that began in Austin, but ended in Oklahoma, where we seized a race-horse-buying operation owned by the Zeta Cartel."

"Tell the jury a little more about that."

Camila got up and objected, "Relevance, Your Honor?!"

Yamamoto shot back, "Overruled . . . I want to hear more."

"I renew my objection, Your Honor," repeated Camila, "and I'll stipulate that the agent is qualified to testify as an expert on money laundering. There's no need to taint the jury with tales of glory, Your Honor."

"I resent that," Fox shot back, "and I object to the sidebar comment. Would you instruct the jury to disregard that last comment by Ms. Harrison, Your Honor?"

"Mr. Fox," followed Yamamoto, ignoring the objection, "since Ms. Harrison does not object to Mr. Copeland's qualifications . . . are you tendering the agent as an expert at this time?"

"Yes, Your Honor. We are."

"Okay," said Yamamoto, "let the record reflect there's no objection to special agent Copeland testifying as an expert."

"Thank you," said Fox.

"Please continue," ordered Yamamoto, eager to hear what Copeland had to say. "Tell the jury all about the racehorse-buying operation."

If Nutley was going to struggle putting away Aldama, Yamamoto was not. He was going to make sure Aldama got what he deserved and teach Camila Harrison a very valuable lesson.

"Well," continued Copeland, relishing the spotlight, "a family member of one of the organization's leaders bought this sprawling horse ranch in Oklahoma, and they were using drug money to buy, breed and train quarter horses. The family member had been a roofer working construction all his life . . . and now, all of a sudden, he and the wife owned a ten-million-dollar-a-year operation? It just didn't add up."

"Any other examples?" Fox asked.

"Again," complained Camila, "objection, relevance!"

"Overruled," smirked Yamamoto.

"Just recently," continued the agent, "my office seized a jet belonging to a Mexican public official. When he was in office, he was on the Gulf Cartel's payroll. And when we learned that he had bought the Gulf Stream with drug money, we seized it. The same with the other Mexican governors who bought investment properties in Miami, South Padre Island, San Antonio. We seized all of their condos, beach homes, even a couple of malls. Their names have been in the news. Those are some of the more visible cases we've been involved in."

"How do cartels launder money?"

"They buy legitimate businesses or smuggle their cash out of the United States. Once they have their money in Mexico, they usually use currency exchange outfits under their control to rinse the money clean, or they buy hotels and land . . . usually registered under a distinct corporation or a *prestanombres*."

"What's a *preestah noumbraas*?" Fox asked.

"A straw man or straw purchaser . . . someone who lends his or her name to be used as the official title holder, but everybody knows who the real owner is. We saw a lot of that with the last two governors of the state of Tamaulipas. They used their close friends and business associates as *prestanombres*—even relatives, and friends of their wives and such."

"Interesting."

"Of course, the governors were also laundering illegal kickbacks from government contracts. It hasn't always been drug money."

"But it's still illegal, right?" asked Fox, attempting to educate the jury. "Even if the kickbacks happened in Mexico . . . if the governors or politicians laundered their ill-gotten gains in the USA . . . it becomes a crime in the States, correct?"

"Correct. If you decide to launder your money in the USA . . . let's say you buy homes or businesses or stocks, and the money was obtained illegally—from anywhere in the world, not just Mexico, and not just from drugs—you've just become a target for prosecution in the United States of America," explained Copeland.

Fox turned and looked at Nutley, then at Camila Harrison. "Now, back to *this* case. Do cartels use secret compartments in vehicles to get the money out of the United States?"

"All the time. Just the other day, in San Diego, California, they pulled over a VW Jetta with three million dollars in Office Depot banker boxes in the trunk. These folks also stuff the cash in the gas tank, under the dashboard, inside the door panels, even inside the transmission, or inside the seats. Usually the vehicles come up full of dope. Here in Houston, the driver goes to a hotel, leaves the car keys under the floor mat. The driver stays in his room and another person comes and gets the car, takes it to a secret location. They don't see each other. It's basic compartmentalization."

"And then?"

"The guy who picks up the car takes it to a secret location— usually a body shop or mechanic—removes the dope and stuffs the compartments with cash. The car is then returned to the hotel. The guy waiting in the hotel room gets a call, then drives the car back to the border."

"To reiterate, does the driver know the individuals who retrieved the car from the hotel's parking lot?"

"What we've found is that the drivers have no idea where the compartments are located, how to get them open or who retrieves the car and where they take it to. Like I said, the whole operation is compartmentalized."

"Why is that?"

Nutley leaned over and whispered into his first assistant Dot Griffin's ear. He was worried that this line of testimony could hurt their case because drivers aren't aware of the specific location of the vehicle's storage compartments.

"When we've arrested the drivers," explained Copeland, "all they can tell us is that they know the cars have something stashed in them but they can't identify the other conspirators, the guys who loaded the vehicle. In most cases, the left hand doesn't know what the right hand is doing. We might take down part of the operation, but the other parts keep working to stay in business. These guys are pretty sophisticated as far as setting up systems."

"Let me ask you this," said Fox, switching gears, "do legitimate businesses use secret vehicle compartments to transport money?"

"I've never seen it happen . . . well, hang on—I misspoke." Copeland did a one-eighty.

"Excuse me?" asked Fox, eyes wide open.

"I've only seen it one time; a rancher in South Texas who didn't believe in banks. He kept some of his cash at home in a safe and some of it in his pick-up trucks in secret compartments. Some more of it was buried in different places. Turns out the guy was legit. Yeah, guy's name was Martin. Carl Martin."

Fox breathed a sigh of relief. "In your professional, *expert* opinion, do you believe the monies found in the Tahoe in this case came from illicit proceeds?"

"Yes."

"And why is that?"

"Objection!" cried Camila. "Calls for pure speculation."

"I'll allow it," replied Yamamoto.

"Because if the cash was legit, someone would have come forward with documents, receipts, deposit slips, bills of sale . . . something, anything showing how the monies were generated, where everything came from. Just like Carl Martin did. He fought us in court and was able to prove us wrong after money was seen poking out of his door panel in a routine traffic stop and he was arrested. That has never happened in this case. *Someone* would have come forward and said, 'Hey, that's my money, I can prove it! It's legit.'"

"Is that how we know?"

"Well," replied Copeland, "in this instance McKenzie admitted the cash came from the sale of drugs."

"Pass the witness."

"Agent Copeland," Camila began her cross-examination without wasting a single second, "if I hear you correctly, then it's true that oftentimes the individuals driving the cars don't know what's in the vehicles—is that right?"

"Well . . . I mean . . . yeah," stumbled Copeland. "Sometimes."

"Because that's how these organizations operate, right?" Camila continued in rapid fire fashion. "They 'compartmentalize.'"

"I guess . . . if you put it that way."

Camila started shaking her head. "Those were *your* words, Agent Copeland. 'The organizations compartmentalize.' Do you want the electronic recording officer to read back to you that portion of your testimony?"

"Judge," griped Fox, "she's fighting with the witness."

"Move on, Counsel," instructed Yamamoto. "Don't fight with the witness."

Camila wasn't having any of it. "You testified that the drivers drive and that's all . . . and *other* individuals prep the cars, isn't that correct?"

"Well, yes," said Copeland, "I did say that, but you're taking it out of context."

"And that the individuals who drive the cars often don't know who the individuals that prep the cars even are—and vice-versa, correct?"

Nutley, Fox and Griffin were in a huddle, trying to figure out a way to put the brakes on Harrison.

"Yes. I did say that."

"Oftentimes the left hand doesn't know what the right hand is doing, correct?"

Copeland looked over at Nutley for a clue, a signal, anything, but Nutley, Fox and Griffin were still in their huddle.

"Yes . . . uh . . . sort of."

"And the reason these organizations compartmentalize is so that if someone gets busted, then that person can't point fingers and the operation can continue to operate, correct?"

"I suppose."

"And in your experience," followed Camila, "who *usually* drives the cars? The organizer? The recruiter? The operation's manager?"

Copeland sighed. "The drivers are the low men on the totem pole," answered the agent.

"Why is that?"

"Because the brains of the operation aren't going to get caught driving cars with the dope or cash. . . . "

"And why is that?"

"Because they don't want to go to jail," Copeland said. "It's obvious. That's why they're the leaders and organizers."

"So, if the co-defendant, Barrera, testified that my client was an organizer or recruiter, in other words, a higher-up, that wouldn't be consistent with your testimony here today, would it? I mean, it wouldn't make sense in the regular scheme of things, right?"

Copeland hedged his reply. "I don't know what Barrera testified to, I couldn't say."

"I'll tell you what he said," replied Camila. "He testified under oath that Mr. Aldama was a recruiter. In your experience, would a recruiter be driving the vehicle himself?"

"I don't know . . . maybe."

"Are you sure? Didn't you just tell these good jury that the left hand doesn't what the right is doing?"

"I did."

"So, if Barrera said Vicente Aldama was a recruiter, manager and organizer, and also drives . . . would Barrera have been correct? Or was he making this up?"

"I don't know. Anything is possible."

"But in your professional experience," Camila pushed harder, "have you ever observed that to be the case?"

"No."

"And if McKenzie also said that my client appeared to be in charge, that wouldn't be accurate either, would it?"

"Don't know."

"Because *no* recruiter, *no* manager, *no* higher-up will put himself in a position where he can get busted with the money or contraband, correct?" asked Camila.

"I suppose."

"Well, that was your testimony, Agent Copeland. It wasn't mine."

"Okay, I see," followed Copeland.

"So McKenzie and Barrera were lying, isn't that the truth?" suggested Camila.

"I guess."

"Objection," cried Fox. "Defense counsel is mischaracterizing the testimony, Your Honor."

Fox then turned to Copeland. "Don't answer that."

"Sustained," interjected Yamamoto, who then directed his attention to Camila and said, "Are you going to ask something else, Counselor? I think you've already beat this horse to death. It's time to move on."

Camila figured it was time to change strategy. She would try, a technique lawyers sometimes employ to impeach the opposition's own witnesses.

"Agent Copeland," Camila continued, "when a traffic stop is conducted, must the officer conducting the traffic stop . . . must he or she have probable cause to pull the vehicle over?"

"Yes."

"And what is probable cause? Can you define that term for the jury?"

"The way I think of it is having reason to believe some violation of the law has occurred. It could be a violation of the Texas traffic code or the penal code or the transportation code. You have to be able to articulate the probable cause."

"What do you mean, 'articulate?'"

"Explain why you thought the law was violated. In the case of a traffic stop, for example, an officer can pull a vehicle over because they were speeding . . . not driving in a single lane . . . not using their turn signals . . . not using a seat belt . . . having a defective headlamp—anything along those lines. But there's got to be a good, valid reason."

"Can a vehicle be pulled over without any valid reason? Without valid probable cause?"

"Nope," said Copeland. "Unless the laws have changed, which I don't think they have. The officer must have probable cause. A valid, legal reason to conduct the stop."

"Do officers sometimes make up probable cause? Have you ever heard of something like that happening? Like a pretext stop?"

"Objection!" shouted Fox. "Speculation!"

"Overruled," Yamamoto said, surprising the hell out of Camila and Thelma. He threw them a soft ball, but Camila knew not to get comfortable. It was to give the jurors and the folks in the audience the appearance of impartiality. "I want to hear this."

"Not to my knowledge," answered Copeland. "Never heard of such a thing."

Camila thought about asking the question another way. "Hypothetically speaking . . . *if* an officer pulls a car over for an invalid reason, with no probable cause . . . let's say the officer pulls the car over just because he didn't like the way the driver looked or because the driver was black, he had a 'gut' feeling . . . whatever."

"Okay . . . "

"Are you following?"

"Yes. What is the question?"

"*If* that's the case . . . what do you call a traffic stop like that?"

Fox jumped up. "Objection, calls for a legal conclusion!"

"I want to hear this," ordered Yamamoto. "Officer, what do you call that?"

Copeland turned to look at the jury, at Fox and then at Yamamoto. Finally, he muttered, "An illegal stop."

Camila smiled. "Thank you, Agent. And, just to clarify, what happens to the evidence resulting from an illegal stop or an illegal search or illegal detention?"

"Usually gets thrown out," replied Copeland, "without the evidence . . . there's no case."

"Thank you, Agent," said Camila. "Pass the witness."

<hr/>

Barton Nutley took the reins again and called K9 Officer Ron González of the Wharton County Sheriff's Office to the stand instead of Bergendahl. The fourth witness in the government's case-in-chief was a young, muscular sheriff's deputy who still believed that he—and he alone—could make a difference in the War on Drugs.

He practically beamed with passion and ideals. Although he did not belong to the Odessa Task Force, he would often be called to assist other agencies when looking for narcotics. González testified that he had been taking a break inside Prasek's Hillje Smokehouse, south of El Campo when he'd heard a request for K9 assistance over the radio. He had arrived at the site of the traffic stop in a few short minutes. It was dark. Sergeant Bergendahl had pulled over the Tahoe just over on the side of the highway.

"Officer González," Nutley continued, with the air of an actor performing a well-rehearsed play, "when you pulled over to the side of the road, what did you see?"

"There were two individuals sitting in the back of Agent Bergendahl's unit, and a third individual sitting on the front passenger side."

"Were they arrested?"

"I didn't see any handcuffs or anything. I'm sure Agent Bergendahl asked them to sit in his cruiser for safety reasons."

"So they wouldn't jump him?"

"Objection, calls for speculation!" yelled Camila.

"Sustained!"

"Do you know why Agent Dwayne Bergendahl had the trio in his unit?" followed Nutley.

"No, not really, but it *could* have been for safety reasons."

"Fair enough," said Nutley. "Now, did you talk to Bergendahl?"

"Yes."

"What did he say?"

Camila objected, "Hearsay!"

"Sustained," ruled Yamamoto.

"What was your job function there?" Nutley asked.

González turned to look at the jury. "As I said earlier, I heard the call over the radio for a K9 unit—Odessa looking for assistance. I came over with Rocky, my K9, with the express purpose of checking for narcotics, weapons, cash or any other type of contraband."

"Did your K9 alert you to anything?"

"Yes. At first, all we knew was that Rocky had hit on *something*, but we didn't know exactly what it was."

"And what did it turn out to be in the end?"

"Cash."

"How much money was hiding in the Tahoe?"

"I can't answer that. I didn't count it, sir."

"Nothing further," said Nutley.

Camila stood up and headed for the podium.

"Officer González, did you get consent from any of the occupants to search the vehicle?"

Nutley got up, was about to object, but let it go.

"No, ma'am, I did not."

"Do you normally have to get consent to use Rocky to sniff out a vehicle?"

"To sniff out a vehicle, no, no consent is required. To search, yes. We need consent. It's preferable and recommended," answered González, "so later on there won't be any issues. It's always best."

"When *wouldn't* you have to obtain consent first to search a vehicle or someone's luggage?"

"At an international port of entry or a checkpoint," explained Deputy González.

"Other examples that you might think of?"

"When the contraband is in plain view," he said, "or if the defendant is already arrested. Usually we inventory the vehicle before it's towed away by the wrecker. It's called a 'search incident to a lawful arrest.'"

"And what happens if the contraband is not in plain view and there's no consent or arrest? Can you still have Rocky sniff out a vehicle . . . let's say on the side of the road?"

"To sniff, yes. To search, that's a different story, unless of course, as I said earlier, we're in an airport or a port of entry. There, we can search and don't need consent or warrant."

"Can you stop someone for a traffic violation and make them wait an hour until a K9 unit arrives to sniff the car?"

Deputy González shook his head. "No . . . and that's why when your client was pulled over, I was at the scene within minutes. Law enforcement is not allowed to prolong the stop for no reason, while a K9 unit arrives."

"Can you get a search warrant *just like that*?"

"No, we have to develop probable cause . . . be able to articulate that some crime has been committed, then draft an affidavit, show it to a judge. The judge reads it and he or she decides if there's enough grounds, enough probable cause, to sign the warrant."

"In this instance, was an affidavit prepared?"

"Not that I know of . . . . But, I want to say, Agent Bergendahl indicated that the occupants had consented to a search."

"And you believed him?"

"Yes . . . I had no reason not to. I was acting in good faith."

"So, to clarify, you just took him at his word?" continued Camila. "*Without* checking first if it was true or not that Sergeant Bergendahl had *good consent*?"

"Objection," cried Nutley. "If counsel wanted to complain about the consent obtained in this case, she should have raised the issue. But she didn't, so that issue has been waived. Let's move on. That point is moot, Your Honor."

"I did file a motion to suppress!" replied Camila. "That's why I'm asking. We're carrying it along with the trial."

"I'll sustain the objection," said Yamamoto. "Let's move on, Counselor."

Camila was getting upset. Nutley and the Judge were double-teaming her.

"Did Agent Bergendahl tell you why he'd stopped the Tahoe?" Camila asked.

"I couldn't really say," said González. "All he said was that we had consent, and based on that representation, I put Rocky to work. I really don't know what happened before I got there."

"You do agree, don't you, that in order to use the K9, you would have to have good consent?"

"Only," said the deputy, "if Sergeant Bergendahl had already issued a ticket, or warning . . . or whatever . . . and the purpose for the traffic stop was over . . . but yet he insisted in detaining the vehicle until a K9 unit arrived . . . then I would have needed consent from the owner of the vehicle to sniff the Tahoe. It comes down to the duration of the stop."

"Wait," said Yamamoto.

Deputy González turned to face the judge, "Yes, sir?"

Yamamoto was now taking over the examination, "Let me ask you, Deputy González. Just so the jury understands. There's a traffic stop. And if there's no K9 involved, the officer that stopped the vehicle would need good consent or a warrant to search vehicle, correct?"

"Yes, sir, unless there's contraband in plain view."

"Okay, I got that," Yamamoto continued, "now, assume we have another traffic stop. K9 unit arrives immediately thereafter. No consent is needed to sniff out the vehicle, correct. And just so we're clear, a sniff is different than a search, correct?"

"Yes . . . a sniff is a whiff . . . once the dog hits . . . we now have probable cause to do the search because there's contraband in the car . . . without a hit form the K9, we would need a warrant or consent to search, or have some kind of exception to the warrant requirement."

"So," Yamamoto declared, "in this case you happened to arrive at the scene within minutes after the call came in?"

"Yes," answered Deputy González.

"Now," continued Yamamoto, "if you arrived an hour after the traffic stop had happened and the occupants refuse to give consent to search to the officer that pulled them over for the traffic violation and also the occupants won't consent to a dog sniff, and there's no contraband in plain view. What happens then?"

Deputy González thought for a minute, but then answered, "We would have to let the occupants go, or go get a warrant to be able to search the vehicle."

"Why?" asked Yamamoto, as he turned to look at the jury to see if they were following.

"Because the reason for the encounter or 'traffic stop' is over! The driver has been ticketed or given a warning. And we're not allowed to detain someone for long periods of time to go get the K9 or a warrant. The stop has to be brief."

Yamamoto turned to Camila, "You may continue, Counselor."

Camila gave Yamamoto a fake smile, then turned her attention to the witness, "Where were we . . . so, to pull over a car, any car, you must observe the driver having committed some sort of violation or illegality, is that correct?"

"Yes, you would need to have probable cause," answered the deputy, "a belief that the law has been violated in some way."

"What happens if the agent or officer manufactures probable cause? In other words, makes up some sort of excuse to stop a car just to see if he can find something? Can you tell this jury?"

"I guess if the judge that hears the case decides it was a lame excuse . . . then the evidence gets thrown out . . . the defendant walks."

"Is that because the evidence was obtained illegally?"

"Yes."

"It would be what the call," Camila made air quotation marks, "fruit of the poisonous tree, wouldn't it?"

Nutley shot up like a missile. "Your Honor, I'm going to object! These are the same questions opposing counsel asked of Agent Copeland. I think the jury knows what happens when there's a bad traffic stop. Can we move on—for the love of God?"

Yamamoto nodded his head in agreement. "Counselor, do you have any other areas to cover? Let's move on."

Camila, again, ignored Yamamoto. "I'm sorry, Deputy González . . . I didn't get your answer."

González shrugged and answered, "Something like that . . . if it was a bad traffic stop, whatever evidence was obtained . . . gets tossed out. Without evidence, there's no case. But that's not what happened here!" shot the deputy. "Let's be clear."

"Sure . . . whatever you say," said Camila. "Pass the witness."

Camila appeared satisfied with González' responses, but deep down she was fuming because Yamamoto would not let her try the case like she wanted.

***

Gustavo Govela's loft was small and comfortable, though sparsely furnished. It was located on the sixth floor of Greenridge Towers, nestled between Westheimer and Richmond, the two principal avenues running west some eight miles from downtown to the Houston border. The street noise filtering into the bedroom made sleeping difficult. Govela sat up in bed and checked his cell. He had a missed call.

He reached for the pack of cigarettes. After lighting one, he blew out the match and tossed it into the ashtray on his night stand. He opened the bedroom's sliding doors and stepped outside onto the balcony, then punched the number into his phone and waited for an answer.

From his balcony he could see the sparse late-night traffic on Westheimer. Probably employees going home after a nightshift in the restaurant business, or partyers leaving one of the numerous stripclubs around the Galleria area—Centerfolds, Rick's or Marfreless. Places he used to frequent until he met Camila Harrison.

"Hello?"

"Camila," said Govela, "sorry I'm calling at this hour . . . I just noticed I had a missed call from you. Is everything all right?"

Down below, Govela could see the graveyard shift; one crew cleaning the pool while another resurfaced one of the four tennis courts under large, portable spotlights. He puffed on his cigarette and wondered if he would ever be able to quit. He'd been smoking off and on since he was a teen—maybe it was time to get on the patch.

"I just wanted to thank you for lending your moral support," said Camila. "And for lending us Monty."

Govela perked up. "Oh, yeah?"

"Yes," said Camila, "he was able to pull some strings and get us the video."

"Good, good. I'm glad things are working out." He took another drag. "Does it help your case?"

"Yes, there's some good stuff in there. Nutley is not going to know what hit him."

"How was it possible that they missed it?" asked Govela.

"They been focusing on the traffic stop and the CI," explained Camila, "or maybe they knew. It's possible that Barrera and McKenzie told the government what happened at Buc'ees, but if that came up, that would also open a new can of worms."

"Like?"

"What happened to a certain piece of evidence that shows up in the video? Maybe Nutley thought it was better to leave things 'as is.' Hope the defense wouldn't think to look in all the dark corners."

"That makes sense," said Govela.

"The only problem now," Camila continued, "is that one of the witnesses we really needed to talk to, a guy I had located and talked to, has gone missing. Maybe they got to him too."

"We already had this conversation, baby. Do you really think Nutley is capable of engaging in witness-tampering, obstruction of justice?" Govela flicked cigarette ash to the parking lot below.

"That's what I'm trying to find out."

"And Thelma, what does she have to say about all this?"

"Not much. If she's worried, she's not letting it show, and she hasn't complained one bit. To tell you the truth, I think she's happy to be in the courtroom. There has been no shortage of fireworks, that's for sure."

"Can I stop by, again, tomorrow?

Camila thought about it. "And watch me act like a fool?

"Yes, my *beautiful* fool."

THIRTY-TWO

Sergeant Dwayne Bergendahl took the witness stand. He removed his Ray-Ban wayfarer glasses, swore to tell the truth, adjusted the microphone in front of him and smiled to the jury. Bergendahl appeared to be in his early forties, in good shape, with the aura of an ex-military man.

Although usually prosecutors like to *start* their presentations with the arresting officers, in this instance Nutley thought to put Bergendahl fifth in the line-up. He would be the first witness Wednesday morning, a perfect way to start the day; let the Barrera and McKenzie debacle become nothing more than a distant memory in the 'jurors' minds.

"Can you hear me okay, Agent?" asked Nutley from the podium.

Despite looking healthy, Bergendahl coughed and adjusted a hearing aid in his right ear. Once finished, he nodded that he was ready.

"I'm sorry, Agent. Was that a yes? You'll have to speak. If you just nod your head, the court reporter won't know if it's a yes or a no," indicated Nutley.

The agent nodded his head and answered, "Okay . . . *yes*." He appeared annoyed, bothered to be testifying at all.

"Were you working US Highway 59 back in September 2014?"

"Yes," answered the agent in a smoker's rasp.

"And during that patrol, did you initiate a traffic stop on a 2012 Black Tahoe with plates ZTA 911?"

"What?" strained the agent, struggling to comprehend what Nutley was asking. "Can you repeat the question?"

"Judge," Camila interrupted, "can you advise Mr. Nutley to stop leading the witness?"

"Is that an objection?" Yamamoto asked.

"Yes, Judge, it's an objection," replied Camila. "Leading the witness. Mr. Nutley is testifying for the witness."

"Due to the unusual circumstances surrounding this witness' condition—hearing loss as the result of an IED explosion while serving in Afghanistan—the court will give Mr. Nutley and the witness some leeway. Please continue, Mr. Nutley."

"Can I have a running objection?" asked Camila. "That all of the government's questions are leading and not allowed?"

"Denied," replied Yamamoto.

"Then let the record reflect our objection, Your Honor," said Camila. "The defense objects to counsel for the government testifying for the witness. This is an abomination and it violates the spirit of the federal rules of evidence."

"It will be noted," Yamamoto remarked, appearing amused by Camila's irreverent use of the word "abomination."

"Very well," Nutley continued, clearing his throat and adjusting his glasses. "And what was the reason for stopping the Tahoe? What was the probable cause?"

Bergendahl cupped his ear, while attempting to hear the question, until he managed to figure out what Nutley was asking. He then turned to look at the jury and explained, "The . . . light . . . one of the lights on the rear license plate . . . it was out."

Nutley repeated his answer, making sure the jury was paying attention, "You mean one of the rear plate lights was out?"

Bergendahl nodded. "Yes, that's right."

"And did you make contact with the driver, Mr. Aldama?"

Bergendahl shook his head "no."

But Nutley was casually nodding "yes," as if telegraphing the answers to the witness.

"Judge," cried Camila, "I have to renew my objections. Can you please instruct Mr. Nutley to stop testifying *and* giving signals to the witness? This is totally improper. The jury needs to hear the *witness* testify . . . not Mr. Nutley. Can you also instruct the witness to answer?"

"Don't testify for the witness, Mr. Nutley," admonished Yamamoto.

"Can you point out Mr. Aldama, the defendant in this case?" Nutley asked again.

Agent Bergendahl did a cursory inspection of the courtroom, first over to the jury box, then in the opposite direction. After about twenty seconds, he finally pointed in the direction of Camila's counsel table. "That's the driver: Vicente Aldama."

"Let the record reflect that Agent Bergendahl has identified the defendant, Your Honor," called out Nutley. "He's sitting between Ms. Harrison and her co-counsel, and he's wearing khakis, a tie and a blue blazer."

Camila could not believe Nutley's impudence. She shot up like a rocket. "Judge, I object! Mr. Nutley is again testifying for the witness. Let the witness describe the articles of clothing, for God's sake. That's why it's called witness identification, not US attorney identification. What's the criminal justice system coming to?!"

"Please behave, Counselor," Yamamoto warned Camila. "Just make your objection . . . you don't need to rant and rave. I expect you to behave like the professional you are supposed to be."

Camila was aghast.

Nutley resumed his direct examination. "Take your time, Agent, there's no rush. Look around carefully and see if you can describe the clothing the defendant, seated between Ms. Harrison and her co-counsel, is wearing."

"Judge," griped Camila, still standing up, "now Mr. Nutley is coaching the witness. Why doesn't Mr. Nutley just get on the witness stand and testify himself? He might as well at this point."

"Enough with your antics!" Yamamoto yelled. "Ms. Harrison, if you don't refrain and start acting accordingly, this court will take matters into its own hands. Do we understand each other?"

Thelma leaned over to talk with Camila. She whispered into Camila's ear, "Just let it go, Camila. Stop fighting or Yamamoto will find you in contempt and throw your ass in jail. Please sit down and get ahold of yourself."

"Let's move on," ordered Yamamoto. "The witness made his identification. It is what it is."

Nutley did not look happy with the way Bergendahl was testifying. Although he looked fit and trim, his hearing loss made him look like he was lying, trying to cover up something. His performance could quite possibly change the outcome of the case. This was something Fox had obviously not prepped hard enough for. When the case was over, he would have a word with Wyatt Fox, let him have it. Why had this rather apparent detail been overlooked? There would be hell to pay.

"Okay, Agent, are you telling the jury that the reason for the stop was that the plate lights were out?"

The agent started coughing but managed to utter the word "Yes" for the benefit of the jury.

"So, you pulled the SUV over for having no lights, and then you found the money. . . . Is that it?" asked Nutley, worried that Bergendahl was starting to fall apart. He needed to get him off the witness stand quickly.

"Objection: asked and answered!" announced Camila.

"Sustained."

"Excuse me," said Bergendahl as he coughed into a handkerchief he was holding in his left hand. "Sorry about that. Yes, that's what happened."

"Let's take a break," said Yamamoto. "Ten minutes. We'll be in recess."

"All rise for the jury!" ordered the marshal.

⁂

Once the jury was out of earshot, Yamamoto summoned Nutley and Harrison to the bench. Naturally, their respective co-counsels and obligatory entourages followed.

"How much longer do you have with this witness, Mr. Nutley?" asked Yamamoto.

"I just wanted to go over the consent part," said Nutley. "Get him to testify that he obtained consent from Aldama."

"He's not doing a very good job," pointed out Yamamoto. "Is he sick? What's wrong with him? Do you know?"

"Maybe Mr. Fox can better answer that question, Your Honor." Nutley turned and shot daggers at the lawyer. "Wyatt?"

"Uhm . . . well. You see," stuttered Wyatt, "Agent Bergendahl is dealing with some health issues, that's all. That's why he seems a bit . . . what's the word? Distracted. But he *can* continue."

"Well," Yamamoto declared, this is starting to look like a train wreck . . . "let's finish up with him. Quickly. How many more witnesses after that?"

Nutley looked at Griffin. She was in charge of getting witnesses to the courthouse and having them wait outside until they were called into the courtroom.

"Judge," answered Dot, "after Agent Bergendahl, we just have the custodian of evidence and the agent that transported the defendants to jail."

"We can finish with our presentation of witnesses by this afternoon, Your Honor," said Nutley. "We don't have to call the agent who transported the defendents."

Yamamoto looked at the clock hung behind the jury box. It was 11 a.m., and to get to a decent stopping point on this Wednesday they would have to continue quickly.

Oh, that's not good. Camila became concerned when she heard that the government would be wrapping up their case soon. This was not what she'd expected would happen.

Yamamoto turned to face the US marshal. "Marshal, please bring in the jury. Let's continue."

⸻

Bergendahl continued testifying under Nutley's direction. For the most part, despite his unexplained medical condition, he stuck to his story. He had pulled the Tahoe over because of a defective plate light, called for a K9 unit and, just to be safe, obtained verbal consent from the driver, Vicente Aldama. The defendant was obviously an operator and money launderer who needed to be taken off the streets, once and for all.

"Are you passing the witness at this time?" asked Yamamoto, looking and sounding somewhat disappointed with the government's errant "star witness."

"Yes, Your Honor," smirked Nutley, trying to conceal his anger and dissatisfaction.

"Ms. Harrison," followed Yamamoto, "are you ready for your cross-examination?"

Camila cracked a wide smile, ready to pounce on Bergendahl. "Yes, Your Honor. As a matter of fact, I am."

Yamamoto turned to face Bergendahl. "Agent Bergendahl, I remind you that you're still under oath." He then turned to Camila. "Carry on."

Camila walked up to the podium. "You testified earlier that one of the license plate lights on the SUV was out, correct?"

Agent Bergendahl nodded his head.

"I'm sorry . . . was that a yes?" asked Camila as she turned and looked at the jury.

The agent nodded again and finally uttered the word, "Yes."

"Are you sure that a plate light was out on the Tahoe?" asked Camila as she turned to look at the jury again. This time, she focused on the three male jurors sitting in the front row.

The agent nodded again and muttered a subdued, "Y . . . Ye. . . . Yes."

"At this time," announced Camila, "I would like to introduce into evidence a copy of the security footage from the night in question obtained from Buc-ee's . . . the truck stop south of Houston, Your Honor."

"Objection." Nutley sprang to this feet. "The video has not been properly authenticated and the government was never provided with a copy in discovery. The government has not had a chance to see the contents of the video, either."

"This is impeachment evidence, Your Honor. We were just made aware of its existence last night. We can view it together in your chambers, if you'd like, Judge," said Camila, turning to face the jury. "The video it's highly exculpatory and shows Bergendahl lied."

"Unless Ms. Harrison subpoenaed the custodian of evidence for Buc-ee's," interjected Nutley, "that video doesn't come in. There's no foundation. No proper authentication. And right now, it's *my* witness who is on the stand. This isn't even the proper time to offer the video as evidence. She should save it for her case-in-chief."

"I disagree," countered Camila, raising her voice for all to hear. "First of all, this is cross-examination! And the defense should be allowed to show the jurors that Bergendahl is lying. This video clearly shows that the Tahoe's lights were working."

"Both of you," signaled Yamamoto as his patience was wearing thin, "approach the bench!"

Again, the entire entourage approached. Camila could not contain her excitement. Bergendahl had been caught. Nutley would have to eat his words, and the jury would start to see the magnitude of Odessa's corruption. All that was left to do was for Camila to get the video admitted into evidence so that she could play it for the jury.

Yamamoto would have none of it. "I should throw you in the slammer for making those comments, Counselor. I get to decide if the evidence in the video is exculpatory or not. You're tainting the jury with your comments, and the court does not appreciate that. Your behavior is borderline idiotic."

Camila got in Yamamoto's face, but did not raise her voice. "With all due respect, *Your Honor*, I've had it with the court bending over backwards to help the government, *and* Your Honor's continuous bullying. This video right here . . . this exculpatory video," she waved it in front of his face, "clearly shows that the Tahoe's plate lights were working that night. The stop was a pretext stop, Bergendahl was just fishing, profiling, and the evidence obtained by Odessa should be thrown out. The court knows that this was either a bad traffic stop, or there was a CI that snitched on the defendants and that's why Bergendahl knew and decided to go after them that night. A CI, which I may add, we were not allowed to discover, and which makes this a very unfair proceeding . . . a mockery really. And to make matters worse, you're letting Mr. Nutley and the government get away with it!"

"You're walking a fine line!" whispered back a fuming Yamamoto. "I've had it with your suppositions and innuendos, Ms. Harrison."

"I resent that last comment, too," cried Nutley, trying to appear composed. "How could the government know anything if this is the first time we even found out a video existed?"

"The court," added Camila, "said we would carry along my motion to suppress with the trial. I'm sorry the court doesn't approve of the way I've chosen to try the case, but I have to provide evidence that the traffic stop was nothing more than a pretext stop. The record has to show the stop was illegal and this video proves that. Plain and simple."

Yamamoto looked up from the huddle in front of the bench. He realized the jury could probably hear portions of their heated exchange.

"In my chambers!" ordered Yamamoto. "All of you!"

He waved to the marshal to take the jury.

"We'll be in recess!" shouted Chloe.

"What the hell is in that video?" asked Yamamoto, now scratching his bald head. "Would you care to explain?"

"It is the Tahoe at Buc-ee's," she said. "The video is date- and time-stamped. This is the real deal, Your Honor."

Forbes stood by Yamamoto's desk alongside Thelma, Fox and Griffin, all of whom were anxiously waiting to learn more about the video's contents.

"And?" Yamamoto asked, prodding further.

"The occupants are getting gas and when Barrera gets back in the Tahoe, my client climbs into the driver's seat and turns on the ignition . . . all the lights come on, including the rear plate lights. The video is clear as day."

"Are you saying Bergendahl lied?" Yamamoto asked.

"He sure did," Camila gloated. "He's been lying since day one. That's why he is being cautious, guarded even, during testimony. There's nothing wrong with him. He knows he's been caught. The earpiece is just a misdirect, meant to garner sympathy with the jury, Your Honor."

"Wait, wait, wait!" Nutley interjected, quickly thinking on his feet. He wasn't going down without a fight. "None of that matters . . . Besides, the Tahoe isn't registered to McKenzie, Barrera *or* Aldama."

"And?" asked Yamamoto.

"They have no standing to complain, Your Honor!" Nutley then recited the law on searches and seizures. "McKenzie and Barrera have already pled. They would have had standing to challenge a search of *their* persons, but not the Tahoe. But even then, they didn't do that. They waived that. The contraband was not found on *their* persons, anyway, so that point is moot. And not only is the point moot, they could have complained if, and only if, the search of their persons had arisen from an initial illegal stop, which is not the case here."

"So, what are you saying?" Yamamoto asked.

"What I'm saying, Colt," Nutley turned various shades of red. "I mean, Your Honor, sorry."

Camila and Thelma were shaking their heads. The camaraderie between Nutley and Yamamoto was getting in the way of a fair trial.

"There's a difference between the search of a car and the search of the defendant's person!"

"And why is that important?" Yamamoto asked.

"Because Aldama complained about the search of the vehicle," indicated Nutley.

"And that is the reason I filed a motion to suppress!" interjected Camila.

"But" continued Nutley, "*only* if he can show that he has standing to challenge that search. And he would most definitely have standing to fight the search *if* he owned the Tahoe, but it's not even registered in his name! Besides, he consented anyway!"

"That's not entirely correct," remarked Thelma, "a person who borrows a friend's car can also have an expectation of privacy according to the 4th amendment, Your Honor. There's case law on that."

"Who is the Tahoe registered to?" asked Yamamoto.

Fox volunteered the answer. "Your Honor, the Tahoe is titled under the name EXP Enterprises. We checked out the business. It doesn't exist."

"Figures," muttered Yamamoto.

"Despite all that, Your Honor. We take exception to Mr. Nutley's analysis," continued Camila. "Even if it's not his Tahoe, the US supreme Court has said that there are instances where a driver can have an expectation of privacy in a car, even in a rental, or a vehicle belonging to someone else."

"It doesn't matter . . . " Nutley cried, shaking his head in disagreement, "Bergendahl was going to search the Tahoe anyway . . . the schmuck had a fake driver's license! In Texas people get arrested every day for driving with fake or invalid licenses. Once the driver is arrested, Bergendahl has authority to search the car! So, this little exercise . . . whatever you call this thing we're doing here in chambers . . . doesn't add anything! It's just a waste of time, in my humble opinion."

"But the analysis has to start at the beginning!" Thelma pointed out, shaking her head. "Your Honor, we need to focus on the reason for the traffic stop. Was there really a plate light that was out? Or was Bergendahl targeting this car? And if so, why?"

"Look! So, he doesn't have standing," Camila continued. "Who cares?! This is impeachment evidence, Your Honor! It can still be used for another purpose . . . to impeach Mr. Nutley's star witness, Bergendahl! Attack his credibility. We don't have to use the video to argue that the stop was illegal. We should be able to use it to show that Sergeant Bergendahl has no creditability. *And* we're entitled to an instruction in the court's charge so that when the jury starts deliberating, they'll know that they can consider the agent's transgressions and, if they so choose, they can also disregard his entire testimony. So, what do you have left?"

"What do I have left? I'll tell you what I have left! The fact that there was almost a million dollars in the Tahoe," snapped Nutley, as he got in Camila's face. "The jury can draw a reasonable inference that these guys are money-launderers, warm bodies in the trafficking business!"

"I'll decide what happens," Yamamoto stepped in. "Let's see the video . . . here, give it to me."

Camila handed the DVD to Yamamoto. The judge inserted it into his desktop PC. Everybody gathered around his desk.

On the computer screen, the black and white footage showed the Tahoe pulling up to Pump 6, far away from the main entrance. All the lights appear to be working fine. An unknown individual quickly gets out of the SUV and walks out of frame. A few seconds later McKenzie and Barrera appear in the frame. Barrera climbs in while Aldama circles around, cellphone in hand, videotaping the Tahoe's condition. Seconds later, McKenzie reaches for the gas pump and starts fueling them up. Everything looks normal, banal, the standard operation of a fuel stop. Finally, McKenzie finishes pumping gas while Aldama climbs in on the driver's side and turns the ignition. All the lights come on, including the rear license plate light.

"Oh my!" Thelma sighed.

The room fell silent.

Yamamoto was in a contemplative mood. "I'll tell you what I'm going to do," he said. "We're going back into the courtroom and I'm going to allow Ms. Harrison to develop her cross-examination a little bit better. Then she can re-urge the admission of the video into evidence. At that time, I'll make my ruling."

"Judge," complained Nutley, who by now looked and sounded nervous, "we're walking on thin ice here. This is setting a dangerous legal precedent."

"Ms. Harrison should be able to use the video," explained Yamamoto, "at a minimum as impeachment of evidence. Maybe it doesn't come in to show there was no legal basis for the traffic stop, I don't know. But for impeachment purposes . . . I'm inclined to let her use it."

"Judge," said Camila, "we have another problem?"

Jude Yamamoto rolled his eyes, "What is it now, Ms. Harrison?"

"You see the cell phone being used to record the Tahoe's condition?" Camila pointed out, "We want it. Where is it?"

"Mr. Nutley?" asked Yamamoto, "Where is the cell phone?"

"This is the first time I hear of it," mumbled Nutley, "there was no mention of it in the file. I would have to ask . . . see if one of the agents picked it up."

"I need you to find out what happened to it, Mr. Nutley," ordered Yamamoto, "Mr. Aldama should have access to it, especially if there's exculpatory evidence stored in it. Particularly, in light of the fact that we're carrying along Mr. Aldama's motion to suppress the evidence resulting from the '*so called*' illegal traffic stop."

"I'll ask," Nutley gulped, hard.

Camila and Thelma both looked at each other and smiled. Yamamoto appeared to be coming around, faced with strong evidence for their side, and Camila Harrison was about to hit her stride. It was about time.

Forbes, Fox and Griffin were surprised, and Nutley was ready to come unglued, shaking his head in disbelief. Why wasn't Judge Yamamoto helping?

"Let's get back to the courtroom," ordered Yamamoto, "we're wasting a lot of time."

The lawyers entered and took their places back at their respective tables. The jury was brought in and the trial resumed.

"Please continue, Ms. Harrison," Judge Yamamoto requested.

"Agent Bergendahl, I want to talk about probable cause, okay? Are you with me?"

"Yes," said Bergendahl. He fidgeted in his seat until he found a comfortable spot.

"Before stopping the Tahoe on September 16, 2014, had you or any member of the Odessa Unit conducted any type of surveillance on my client or the co-defendants?"

Bergendahl appeared surprised by the question. "Surveillance? No, of course not."

"And you," Camila continued, "never obtained a warrant to search the Tahoe, correct?"

"What do you mean?"

"You never prepared an affidavit, took it to a judge, who then signed a search warrant, did you?"

"Duh, of course not. I didn't have to do that," answered Bergendahl smugly. "Your client consented to the search of the vehicle ."

Camila was nodding her head, pretending to agree with the agent. She then turned to look at the jury to make sure she had their full attention.

"And is it your testimony that there was a defective rear plate light? Is that true?"

"Yes."

"And prior to the traffic stop in September, you had never previously had any dealings with my client or either of the two co-defendants, had you?"

"Nah."

"And you understand," Camila pressed forward, "do you not, that it is you . . . the government, that has to prove that the search of the Tahoe was valid . . . constitutional. You understand that?"

"Yes, of course."

"And you never observed my client or the passengers loading the Tahoe with the bundles of cash that were seized, did you?"

"Nope."

"You never saw my client or the co-defendants at a car garage giving instructions to others on how to prep the car with the cash, did you?"

"I think it's obvious. . . . No. I did not."

"How much time elapsed from the time you obtained the purported consent to the time Deputy González arrived with his K9?"

"Wasn't long . . . I can't remember exactly."

"After you pulled the Tahoe over, did my client provide you with a driver's license?"

"A fake driver's license which . . . " Bergendahl stopped mid-sentence and turned to address the jury, "wait, it was not fake for all intents and purposes . . . it was actually a valid driver's license but it wasn't his . . . it was somebody else's . . . he was pretending to be that other person . . . which ultimately warranted an arrest, and once Mr. Aldama was arrested for using somebody else's license, the Tahoe could be searched and inventoried at will. It's called a 'search incident to a lawful arrest.'" Nutley, Fox and Griffin breathed a big sigh of relief. Bergendahl at least had grounds to search the Tahoe, despite defense counsel's protestations. Whether or not Bergendahl *should* have stopped the Tahoe if all the lights were, indeed, working . . . well, that was another story.

Camila was not thrilled with the way Bergendahl had answered her last question, but she was not showing it. She pressed on. "But first—whether or not the search was incident to a lawful arrest—the traffic stop had to be legal, isn't that correct?"

"I'm sorry, what?"

"The traffic stop had to be legal first. Isn't that true?" asked Camila.

"The traffic stop was legal. A rear plate light was out."

"If you say so. What about the other two? Did they provide you with their IDs?"

"Yes."

"Did you run their drivers' licenses? Did anybody come back with any issues?"

"Yes, we ran them. No, there were no issues."

"Did you ask them if there were weapons or contraband in the Tahoe?"

"Yes."

"And what did they say?"

"They all answered in the negative."

"So, what drove you to search the Tahoe?"

"Look," said an aggravated Bergendahl, "I already told you, I was gonna arrest your client anyway. Driving with someone else's license pretending to be that person is a felony in Texas. Aldama was as good as 'arrested.' And I was gonna search the Tahoe no matter what—consent, no consent. And don't forget there's the good faith exception. You might not like it . . . but it is what it is."

"Argumentative!" Camila objected. "Move to strike."

"Sustained," ruled Yamamoto.

"Were the defendants carrying weapons?"

"Nah."

"How many other vehicles from the task force responded that night, do you recall?"

"Eight or nine units . . . I think. More than five, I'm sure."

"Was there a cooperating witness or a confidential informant who had given you or members of the Odessa Unit information regarding the Tahoe or the people driving it?"

"Objection!" cried Nutley. "Where does the opposing counsel think she's going with this?"

"Sustained!" announced Yamamoto. "Ms. Harrison . . . please don't go there, okay?"

Camila ignored Yamamoto and proceeded to cover more ground, anticipating that soon Yamamoto would allow her to introduce the video into evidence, then she would let up. "Prior to the day of the traffic stop, Agent Bergendahl, had you obtained information that Mr. Aldama was purportedly in the courier business?"

"No."

"When you first approached the Tahoe on the night in question, did you notice anything out of the ordinary? Anything that would indicate that the Tahoe had been tampered with? That it had secret compartments?"

"Nah, nothing like that."

"Was there anything in plain view inside the Tahoe that would indicate it was transporting bundles of cash. Things like scales, or wrapping paper, rubber bands. Anything?"

"No, there was none of that."

"Anything that would raise a red flag that the individuals were involved in some sort of criminal activity?"

"Not at that point. Nah, nothing."

Camila switched gears. "So let me get this straight . . . if you were going to arrest my client for the issue with the driver's license, would McKenzie and Barrera have been free to go?"

The question threw Bergendahl for a loop. He thought about it. "They were momentarily detained . . . "

"In your patrol car? In the back seat? Unable to get out? Is that what you call 'momentarily detained?'"

"Yes, that's right. For *my* safety . . . and uh . . . their safety."

"Just so we all understand . . . your cruiser . . . can people open the back doors from the inside?"

"No."

"So McKenzie and Barrera couldn't leave, even if they wanted to, even though at this point they had done nothing wrong and you hadn't seen anything that would have alerted you to any criminal activity? You'd already decided they were guilty of something and you'd already arrested them, isn't that the truth?"

Nutley got up to object. "Your Honor, McKenzie and Barrera are not on trial here. What difference does it make whether or not they could have driven off, or not, or whether they were detained or arrested, huh?"

"Overruled," said Yamamoto, "I want to hear this."

"Well," said Bergendahl, "they were just detained. That's all. You say 'arrested,' but I say 'detained.' It was just a short detention, while we investigated, and the K9 unit arrived."

"Investigated what?"

"The Tahoe!"

"But why? Did anybody say or indicate that there was contraband in there?"

"Well, no," answered Bergendahl.

"Then what was there to investigate?"

"Aldama had a fake license, remember? He was going to be arrested, and we were gonna inventory the vehicle. That's how it works!"

"You could have released the vehicle to either McKenzie or Barrera. Isn't that the truth? *They* both had valid driver's licenses."

"Could have, should have, would have," snapped back Bergendahl. "This here is Monday morning quarterbacking, Counselor. I have to make split-second decisions when I'm out there—in real-time—on the side of the expressway. They're one-second judgment calls. I want to see you try it."

"When did you first find out that my client's driver's license was not his?" asked Camila.

"I don't know," answered Bergendahl.

"Well, you called them in, didn't you?"

"Yes."

"Did you call the licenses in before you *detained*," Camila put quotation marks in the air, "the three of them in your cruiser? Or did you call after?"

"I really couldn't tell you," said a flustered Bergendahl, "but this I know. The driver's license was not your clients."

"Well, did that license come back with any issues?"

Bergendahl fudged, "I don't know, but I probably made a note . . . it should be in my report."

"Well," answered Camila, "that's why I'm asking you. None of this fake driver's license business is discussed in any of the reports contained in the government's file!"

"Objection!" Nutley complained, "This has gone too far, Your Honor. All of this is irrelevant!"

Without issuing a ruling on Nutley's objection, Yamamoto banged his gavel on the bench, "I agree. Ms. Harrison, are you almost done?"

"I just have a few more questions, Your Honor," Camila answered.

"Well, move it along, Ms. Harrison," said Yamamoto, "I think the jury has heard enough."

Camila turned her attention back to Bergendahl, "Please humor me," Camila said, "it took Deputy González at least ten minutes to show up with his K9, correct?"

"Correct."

"And all that time you had Barrera, McKenzie and my client restrained in your unit, is that right?"

"Right."

"So, in essence they were arrested."

"Detained," corrected Bergendahl.

"Well, let me ask you this, when they were in your cruiser were you talking to them?"

"Yes."

"Where you asking questions?"

"Yes."

"Did you read them their Miranda warnings? When they were as you say . . . *detained*, and not *arrested*," Camila again put air quotation marks on the words to make a point to the jury, "before you obtained consent to search the Tahoe?"

There was a collective gasp in the courtroom.

"No, I never did that," admitted Bergendahl.

"You put them in your cruiser and *then* you obtained consent. In essence, you were taking a confession from them, without reading them their Miranda warnings. Which is what you're supposed to do once you arrest someone, isn't that the truth?"

"They were not arrested. I keep telling you: They were *detained*," muttered Bergendahl.

Camila was ready with a comeback. "If they had told you they'd rather wait in the Tahoe, would you have let them?"

"Uhm . . . no . . . I would have ordered them to get into my unit."

"So, you were going to restrain their movements?"

"Yes, I detained them while I investigated," replied Bergendahl.

"That's no different from ordering a suspect to lie face down on the ground, is it? You're controlling their movements, their free will. That's what you did when you put the co-defendants in your cruiser. You forced them to stop the Tahoe, despite the rear plate lights working, and without any reason to arrest McKenzie and Barrera, you stuck them in your cruiser hoping the K9 would hit on something, isn't that correct? You were fishing!"

"You're crazy!" Bergendahl said, fuming at the nostrils. "That's not what happened."

Camila wasn't having any of it. "They were listening to your authority, your position, sir. It's no different from having your weapon drawn and pointing it at their heads!"

"They were detained!"

"Who had the keys to the Tahoe?"

"I had them in my pocket," Bergendahl replied without giving it much thought. "Why? That's not important."

Camila thought otherwise. "If Barrera or McKenzie had asked for the keys back, would you have given the keys back to them? Allowed them to drive away?"

Silence.

"We're waiting for your answer, Agent Bergendahl," Camila reminded him. "Had McKenzie and Barrera asked for the keys . . . would you have let them go? Given them back their keys?"

The agent looked at Nutley, then at the judge, then at the jury. A hush fell over the courtroom. The jurors leaned forward, waiting for the answer.

"Were you going to return the keys to them?" Yamamoto asked. "What's your answer, sir?"

"Not until the temporary detention had concluded," answered Bergendahl, fudging, "or until after the K9 had sniffed the Tahoe."

"So, the answer is no," clarified Camila.

The witness just shrugged.

"Would you instruct the witness to answer, Your Honor?"

Yamamoto gave Bergendahl a stare.

"No, I said no."

"Your Honor," announced Camila, smiling, turning to look at the jurors, waving the DVD in hand, "at this time, we would like to introduce into evidence the surveillance video from Buc-ee's . . . for impeachment purposes only."

Nutley was quick on his feet. "Objection, no foundation!"

"Sustained."

Nutley knew it was time to bring the jurors back into focus. "Your Honor, for the record, unless Ms. Harrison is prepared to bring the custodian of evidence from Buc-ee's, that DVD should not come in. Furthermore, I remind the court that the Tahoe was not registered to Aldama. It was not his, so he has no standing to complain about the search. And besides, he was arrested for identity theft . . . for having someone else's driver's license. Secondly, McKenzie and Barrera never raised those issues. As such, Ms. Harrison has no valid grounds to complain about anything. This is all smoke and mirrors. She wants to lead the jurors down this magical rabbit hole just to confuse them. A red herring, that's all."

"I'm aware of that," said Yamamoto. "Anything further, Ms. Harrison?"

"Yes, I move to admit the video, Your Honor," she said, flustered.

"Denied," shot back Yamamoto.

"This is crazy!" Camila yelled, reaching her boiling point. "I'm trying my best to defend my client, and the court insists on bending over backwards to help the government! Whatever happened to an even playing field?!"

"You should have subpoenaed the custodian of evidence, Counselor." Judge Yamamoto banged his gavel on the bench. He looked as if he was about to explode.

"You're crazy!" cried Camila, losing her composure. "The video is impeachment evidence. By its own definition, impeachment evidence is evidence that could not have been anticipated. If it cannot be anticipated, then how do you expect someone to have the custodian of evidence on the sidelines, waiting, ready to testify?!"

"Okay, Ms. Harrison. I've been more than patient with you . . . but now you've crossed the line. You're in contempt! Marshal, arrest her and take her to the holding tank!"

Silence took over the entire courtroom.

"Go ahead!" yelled Camila. "And while you're at it, why don't you and Mr. Nutley go find my client's cell phone! Find out who the hell is hiding it, and why?!"

"Enough!" yelled Yamamoto, banging his gavel on the bench. "Marshal, please remove Ms. Harrison from the courtroom."

The marshal walked over to Camila and took her arm. She continued as he led away, "If this is what has to happen because I have to fight for my client with my arms tied behind my back, then so be it."

"We'll be in recess!" yelled the marshall instinctively. "Please, all rise for the jury."

Another marshal got the message and quickly escorted everyone out of the courtroom.

───────────

Nutley and Yamamoto found themselves in chambers, discussing the little-known phenomenon called "the bully in the courtroom." Often times, juries feel sympathy for the attorney getting pounded by either opposing counsel or the judge in a case. Whenever that happens, jurors most always side with the abuse victim, no matter the evidence. It is a way for juries to right a wrong and to send a message to abusive prosecutors, judges and trial attorneys. Jurors don't like bullies.

And neither do the courts of appeals, for that matter. Many cases have been reversed on appeal because of judges abusing the lawyers appearing before them. There have been well-documented cases of the abuse suffered by lawyers and their clients at the hands of the judiciary.

"So, what do you want me to do?" asked Yamamoto from behind his desk.

"I'm thinking we should let her out," offered Nutley. "If we don't, then the jury could take it out on the government, or the court of appeals might reverse the verdict if there's a conviction."

"But she's disrespectful, and I'm sick and tired of her shit, Bart," countered Yamamoto. "Nobody disrespects a federal judge and gets away with it."

"All I'm saying is that we need to be careful. Even if you make her co-counsel finish the case by herself, the jury will know that Harrison is in the slammer, being held against her will. And that won't sit well with them. In fact, they could very conclude that the whole system is rigged, and we don't want that. Jurors will feel that you're punishing her for doing her job, because she's fighting for her client tooth-and-nail. That's the wrong message to send."

"I hear what you're saying." Yamamoto leaned back in his chair and thought for a moment. He didn't like what he was hearing, but he knew Nutley was right. Let the attorneys do whatever the hell they want, and you get labeled a softie. Run your court with an iron fist, demand respect and professionalism, and you get labeled a bully. It was all the media's fault!

"You know, Bart," Yamamoto started, "when I appointed Harrison to this case . . . I did it to help her. Every now and then, I ask my staff about who hasn't gotten an appointment in a while. I wanted to be fair, you know? *Her* name came up. I was reluctant at first, because I had heard of her struggles, and yet, there I was . . . trying to help a young colleague."

"No good deed goes unpunished," said Nutley, rubbing his chin.

Yamamoto gave him a sagging smile. "Indeed."

"Apologize?" Camila shot back from inside the holding tank, "when the court grants my motion to suppress . . . I'll apologize."

"Here we go again," muttered Nutley.

She was in an area where defendants in custody wait for their cases to be called. Nutley, Fox and Yamamoto were on the outside side of the cell, looking in intently. A marshal kept watch from a corner.

"What's your excuse now?" demanded Camila, "you saw the video! Or, are you blind? It's clear as night and day that Bergendahl is lying!"

"You can take it up on appeal, Ms. Harrison," Yamamoto said, "and you'll probably win, for that matter. Your client still has that legal remedy available to him."

"But how is that fair?" Camila asked.

"Who said life was fair," Nutley said, mocking her. Fox chuckled.

Yamamoto shook his head.

"Look, I'm willing to forego having a show-cause hearing so that the trial can resume," indicated Yamamoto, "if you only apologize and promise to behave in the courtroom. Otherwise, you'll have to spend the remainder of the week in custody, until we have the hearing next Monday and the court figures out what to do with you. I could force your co-counsel to finish the case. Is that what you want?"

"You wouldn't dare," hissed Camila. "I was appointed to represent Mr. Aldama . . . she's just helping."

"Don't try me!" yelled Yamamoto.

"Besides, you don't want an apology," snapped Camila, "you want me to bow to you, bow to the government. I'm not about to do that, Your Royal Highness!"

Yamamoto's eyeballs were about to pop out of their sockets. His carotid artery became visible on the side of his neck, blood pressure rising.

Nutley jumped in. "Counselor . . . why are you being so stub-born?"

"Just apologize," followed Fox, "so we can get on with the show . . . finish it once and for all."

"That's right," said Yamamoto. "I haven't sent the jurors home yet." He looked at his watch. "It's only noon time. There's four more hours we can put to good use."

Fox added, "We'll only call one more witness, Ms. Harrison. You can start with your case right after our case-in-chief."

"Hell," said Yamamoto, "if it looks like we can finish today, we'll work late. I'll bring dinner for the jurors . . . get them started on their deliberations. Maybe we'll even get a verdict *tonight*, before Thursday."

Over in the corner, Camila could see Thelma and Alan trying to peek into the holding cell area, but the marshal shooed them away.

"I'm willing to set aside my finding of contempt," added Yamamoto, "if you just apologize. Believe me, you don't want to have a show-cause hearing on Monday. If we have to go through with the hearing and I make a finding of contempt, then I will have to fine you a significant amount, or worse, order you to serve additional jail time to purge yourself of the contempt. You don't want that, do you?"

Camila didn't know what to do. On one hand, she couldn't help her client if she was sitting behind bars. On the other hand, she did need to stall, extend the trial at least a couple more days or even the weekend. *I could still subpoena the custodian of records for Buc'ees. Try to get the video admitted into evidence that way*, she thought.

"You'd love nothing more than for me to just roll over and die, wouldn't you? Well, I've got news for all of you . . . I'm tired of playing nice, assholes!"

"Watch your language," Nutley said.

Fox stodd there, like a statue. Watching the exchange.

"Yeah," ranted Camila, "I know about *all* of you. You don't think I know . . . ." She focused on Yamamoto first. "You don't think I know that the only reason you got this job was because you couldn't hack it in the real world? That your father-in-law gave a five-million-dollar donation to Clinton's presidential campaign when he ran Anglo Energy & Metals?"

Yamamoto grew angrier by the second, but bit his tongue. Some of what she said was true. His well-connected father-in-law had convinced the senator from his home state to whisper the name Cole Yamamoto into Clinton's ear some years ago.

Camila then focused on Nutley. "And you? What's your story? I'll tell you what it is . . . "

Nutley gazed away, not sure what was about to happen.

"You, Barton Nutley," Camila pointed at him, "the only reason you've gotten this far is because your grandfather was a US Congressman. You would have never landed a job with the federal government if it wasn't for your grandfather pulling some strings to get your criminal record expunged . . . isn't that right?"

"What are you talking about?" asked Nutley. "You're crazy!"

"Crazy my ass! You were caught crossing the border with peyote when you were a college student in El Paso, don't you remember?"

"I don't know what you're talking about!"

"Of course you don't," Camila exclaimed. "Why would you be held accountable for your actions? The high-and-mighty Barton Nutley, future attorney general of the state of Texas. Give me a fucking break!"

Yamamoto had had enough. He turned and looked at the marshal. "Take her to the county jail until I figure what to do with her."

Yamamoto, Nutley and Fox turned around and marched out of the holding cell area.

<hr />

It was Thursday evening when Thelma got to visit Camila at the Harris County Jail. Camila looked to be in good spirits, all things considered. She wore her orange jumpsuit with poise.

"How's Vicente?" asked Camila from the other side of the glass in one of the attorney-client interview rooms of the jail.

"He's worried but I think I calmed him down," Thelma said into the receiver. "I really need you to talk to you about something else. Alan and I had a chance to speak with Yamamoto and he has agreed to order the marshals to take you to M.D. Anderson tomorrow, Friday, for a bone marrow biopsy."

"What?! Are you serious? *Tomorrow?* But, I haven't even decided if I want to be part of that."

"Look," said Thelma, "you sacrificed yourself to get us the extra time. I get that. Now, I don't know if Vicente's sister and brother-in-law appreciate that or not, but that's another story. All you need to know is that Alan, myself, Nutley and Yamamoto spent all day today figuring out what to do with you. Yamamoto was going to send the jury home and have them come back on Monday, after bringing you back tomorrow, Friday, and knocking out the show-cause hearing, but . . . "

"But?"

"Nutley filed a last-minute motion to sequester the jury and put them up in a hotel from today, Thursday, until Monday, instead of sending them home."

"Why would he do that?"

"Why not?"

"That's crazy!" said Camila with a look of disbelief.

"It's a double-edged sword," said Thelma, "but I can see the reasoning behind it. On the one hand, Nutley and Fox want to limit their access to computers, newspapers, so they won't be able to do research. On the other, I'm sure they will figure out that it was the government who filed the motion to sequester and it was Nutley that wanted to separate them from their families and loved ones. Maybe they will be pissed at the Government. It's a risky move, but it could also work to our advantage."

"And what did Yamamoto do?"

"He agreed with Nutley," explained Thelma, "then, after the hearing on the motion to sequester, all the attorneys and Yamamoto spent the rest of the afternoon trying to figure out what to do with you and when to resume trial. There were lengthy discussions about me and Alan taking over. Another proposal was to bring you back Friday, carry along the hearing for the show-cause till after the trial, and let you finish trying the case. Alan thought Monday would be better and pushed to resume the trial next week. Ultimately, Yamamoto believes it's you who has to finish the case. It's you who has to fall on your sword if things go south for Mr. Aldama and he gets convicted."

"So, are you going to help Luis Pablo?"

"Do you know how painful a bone marrow extraction is, Thelma? How much it hurts? I'm not mentally prepared to go through something like that. Not right now, anyway."

"And I think Yamamoto knows that," sighed Thelma, "you should have seen him smile, his eyes lit up. He's all for it and wants you to have it. He could hardly contain his excitement when we floated the idea . . . "

Camila protested. "That psychopath . . . he has no right."

"Look, you want to spend the entire weekend in jail, or take a little trip to M.D. Anderson; a nice, hot shower, TV, a telephone, decent food to eat?"

"Shit, I'm not ready . . . you don't understand."

"You will be under the custody of the marshals, of course . . . there will be one assigned to you the whole time," Thelma explained. "Omar will meet you over there . . . your family will be waiting for you . . . "

"But, but . . . "

Camila felt dizzy. The room was spinning. Not only was she worried about the trial and the threat of sanctions, but now she had become an unwitting test-subject for bone marrow and soon would have to come face-to-face with Lorena. It was inevitable.

Camila let out a big sigh. "I need you to get in touch with Monty . . . find out if *he's* found Beto . . . who you'll also need to talk to. And find out if Monty learned anything about Stephen Leal, the other guy that went missing. We have to catch a break . . . and make sure we get Buc'ees custodian of records served with the subpoena."

Thelma looked at her watch. "Yamamoto said we would have the show-cause hearing on Monday and the trial will resume on Tuesday."

"Right. So we have Friday, Saturday, Sunday *and* Monday," said Camila. "Call Gustavo if you need another pair of hands or eyes on this. We're out of time."

"What else?"

"I'm sorry you'll have to work the whole weekend," apologized Camila. "Believe me, I wish I could be there."

"Don't worry. Alan is going to represent you at the hearing. Hopefully Yamamoto will have cooled off and you'll do *your* part. Just apologize. Okay?"

"Okay."

"The hearing will be at 10 a.m. Anything else?"

"Nope," Camila said, "just work with Monty. He has to be ready to take the stand by Tuesday."

"Hey, did I tell you I got a call from my nephew? You made the news."

"Your brother's kid? Freddie? The news?"

"Yes," explained Thelma. "He's in college, majoring in criminal justice. He's a real news junkie. He wanted to know if that was the same Camila Harrison he knew to be my best friend."

"Did you explain to him you were trying the case *with* me?"

"Yes," Thelma said. "In fact, he said his roommate was friends with a guy who owns a shooting range where the guys from Odessa come in for target practice. When I leave here, Freddie and his roommate are meeting me for dinner. There might be something there. Speaking of dinner . . . how's the food in here?"

"I'll survive," Camila replied. "Just stick to the game plan."

━━━━━━━━━━━━

Despite the fact that the trial had been postponed, some of the things that were happening in the courtroom bothered Barton Nutley. Immediately after the hearing on the government's motion to sequester the jury, Nutley had summoned Griffin and Fox to his office. He had come short of firing Dot and punching Fox. Why had no one bothered to obtain the surveillance video from Buc-ee's and where was the cell phone that Aldama had used to record the Tahoe's condition? Why wasn't it noted in the inventory sheet?

Why had nobody caught this?! Dot had been quick to remind Nutley that she had warned him that all of the cases put together by Odessa had issues. And that if someone had dropped the ball, it had been Fox and not her.

After Nutley had chewed his troops out, he had placed a call to Bergendahl. The two of them got into a heated exchange, with Bergendahl insisting he had found no cell phones during the traffic stop. He had ended up accusing Nutley of being a bully and a sorry excuse for a politician.

"And you're a sorry excuse for a lawman!" Nutley had countered, "You need to take early retirement, quit while you're ahead."

After the contentious call, and slamming the phone down on Bergendahl, a sense of trepidation had taken hold of Nutley. Could there be more surprises, more curveballs coming his way? He was not one to quit in the middle of battle. Much less, allow a talentless paper lawyer get the best of him.

Nutley's breathing got heavier, his jaws clenched, his focus sharp as a laser beam. He picked up the phone and called the private cell number of Houston's Mexican Consul Rodolfo Canseco.

"Rudy? This is Barton Nutley with the US attorney's office here in Houston."

"What can I do for you, Bart?" asked Consul Canseco, surprised to hear Nutley at the other end of the line. He hit the record button on his cell phone.

"You need to speak to your boy, Govela."

"Why?"

"I hear he's gotten close to a lawyer you might know . . . Camila Harrison."

"Oh, yeah," said the consul, "we've heard of her. My office has been helping one of her clients, Vicente Aldama."

"Did you know Mr. Govela has been providing assistance . . . and they're using one of your investigators to help him?"

Consul Canseco cleared his throat. "I'm aware of that. That's what we're supposed to do, Bart. That's why we are here, in case our nationals find themselves in trouble . . . that's our mission."

"Well, that needs to stop," ordered Nutley.

"Can't do that," replied Consul Canseco.

"You want me to send INS to Monty's home and arrest his live-in girlfriend. You know she came over on a tourist visa and never left. She's overstayed her visit."

"Ha ha ha," laughed Canseco. "What's the matter, Bart? Are you losing your touch in the courtroom? Are you worried the government might lose? Please don't make empty threats."

"You take it any which way you want," yelled Bart, "but you make sure you talk to your boys over there."

"What's the matter? Is Camila Harrison kicking your ass? You're not getting desperate, are you?"

"The hell with you, Rudy!"

Click.

THIRTY-THREE

"Mrs. Issa, this could very well be the one witness Ms. Harrison wanted to talk to, the one we've been looking for."

Thelma had left home early Saturday morning and found sanctuary inside the library of her law school. She and Monty were going over the investigator's latest findings. Thelma had given Monty a play-by-play of everything that had transpired down at the courthouse during the trial; the fireworks, the witnesses, the heated exchanges in chambers, Camila being thrown in the holding tank and then county jail. Now Monty was bringing Thelma up to speed on the Beto-Stephen connection.

"I found Beto. He is now working at the Walmart in Wharton, you know, just south of Houston."

"Sure, I know where Wharton is."

"Anyway," followed Monty, "turns out the security company he was working for transferred him to the Walmart. They were shorthanded over there. He doesn't really want to open up *himself*, but after much cajoling, he said the guy we really want to talk to is Leal."

"What if he's feeding you a lie."

"Don't think so."

Monty looked around, making sure nobody was within earshot. When he felt confident that no one was listening, he leaned across the large table. "Before I left, Beto let it slip that he had heard that most of the Odessa agents were skimming money from the seizures. The rate of seizures were so frequent, and there was so much money, that it was impossible to track. He also said that he'd heard that Bergendahl . . . was dangerous."

"He heard? That doesn't help us. We need somebody that saw these guys do it, don't you see?"

"Well," replied Monty, "that's just it. I think he knows, but if he admits that or that he saw these guys skimming the cash, he will be called in as a witness . . . and he wants no part of it. So, he's distancing himself."

"He's being smart . . . he knows if he testifies that *he heard* . . . that's not going to fly in court."

"Without more, no one will want to call him as a witness," answered Monty.

"How are we going to find Stephen Leal?"

"I don't know. But it makes sense," said Monty. "The guys that get busted, they're not gonna make waves if a portion of the money is missing. They're worried about their own necks, not recouping their money. So, it's the perfect crime. Who's gonna know they're skimming cash? Who's gonna raise a stink?"

"Nobody," Thelma answered.

"So here's what I'm thinking: a two-pronged attack. First, I need to find out about this Stephen character. He appears to have fallen off the face of the earth, but Beto said something that might point me in his direction. Secondly, I found a guy who was busted a few years ago by Odessa and he's willing to sit down with me. Apparently they did a number on him and he also happens to know of two other guys that also had a run-in with Bergendahl. Bergendahl and the agents kept some of the kilos that were later resold to a rival gang. The CI helped Bergendahl put together the transaction. The story goes that, when they busted someone, if there was no money, only drugs . . . they would keep a portion to resell down the road."

"The CI again, huh?"

Monty nodded. He gave Thelma a look. "Guy's all over the place. Chances are that's why Odessa fought so hard to keep the CI's identity hidden. The guy knows *too* much. But here's a question: Could there be more than one confidential informant?"

"I'm sure. How many, who knows?" Thelma pondered.

"Yup, that's often the case," said Monty.

"How are you holding up, baby?"

Gustavo Govela had gone to visit Camila Harrison after she had returned from her exam at M.D. Anderson Cancer Center. They were sitting across from each other, in a large room divided by a thick wall of glass, used for friends and family members to visit inmates. They were talking on the phone in their assigned partition.

"You're very brave, Camila. How long is Yamamoto going to keep you in here, do you know?" he asked.

"There's a show-cause hearing on Monday. Trial is supposed to resume on Tuesday . . . we'll see what happens."

"And if he finds you in contempt?"

"Thelma might be forced to try the case without me," answered Camila. "I'm hoping that Yamamoto will reverse course and let me out after the hearing. I need to be there for my client, he's counting on me."

"I can't believe Yamamoto is doing this to you," said Govela. "He's such an asshole."

"I deserved it."

"You were just fighting for your client . . . how is that bad?"

"They don't want you to fight. They don't want you to question anything. And, of course, they want you to respect the ringmaster, which I purposefully didn't do. I really insulted him, *and* everyone else . . . opposing counsel . . . I had to do it. We needed the time to finish preparing our case."

"But . . . " Govela looked worried, "what if Yamamoto *doesn't* let you out? What if he throws the book at you, fines you to high heaven?"

Camila reached out and touched the glass that seperated her from Govela. She gave him a half-smile. "Don't worry, I'm going to give Yamamoto my sincerest, abject apologies on Monday. He wants to get this over with, and letting me get back on the case is the best and fastest way to do that."

"You want me to try and talk to the judge?" offered Govela. "That way you don't have to spend the weekend here?"

"No, sweetie," Camila replied, "that would be the worst thing you could do. You could be charged with obstruction, or worse . . . extortion. Don't even think about it."

"What if I go to the press . . . have them write a story. The public has a right to know."

There was a pause.

"Just call Thelma," Camila instructed, "see what *she* needs."

"Are you sure about all this?"

"Yes. Check in with her and make sure she's talking to Monty. If you really want to help . . . that's what I need you to do. Make sure Monty keeps working and make sure he's talking to Thelma. Those two need to communicate."

"Okay," said Govela, "I'm on it."

"Thanks for coming by. This means a lot. Can you have the guards send my parents in when you leave?"

"Sure thing," said Govela wondering what had changed betweeen her and her parents. Weeks earlier, they had been estranged from each other.

THIRTY-FOUR

Camila Harrison sat alone in Chief Presiding District Judge Colt Yamamoto's courtroom, waiting for the show-cause hearing to start. In accordance with Yamamoto's instructions, the marshals had brought the attorney to court shackled and in handcuffs at 8 a.m. The hearing was not to start for another two hours.

Where is everybody? Camila thought when she looked around the courtroom and noticed it was completely empty except for her and the marshal keeping an eye on her. The young marshal had seated her inside the jury box and then went over to sit by the door leading to the holding tank in back. He winked at Camila and then immediately frowned, as if apologizing for what Yamamoto was putting her through.

She smiled back at him. She understood. He was just doing his job.

When Judge Yamamoto finally assumed his place at the bench, he opened a file sitting in front of him and started reading from it. "Let's see, the court calls The Matter of Camila Harrison. What are the parties' announcements?"

"Good morning, Your Honor," announced Alan Sorelle from the counsel's table, where Camila was now sitting. "I'm representing Ms. Harrison at this show-cause hearing. I've filed my notice of appearance."

"Where's Mrs. Issa?"

"Thelma's not here. She's getting ready to take over the case should there be a need for her to do so," explained Alan.

"I see . . . " said Yamamoto.

Alan added, "I think she's expecting the trial to resume tomorrow."

"Good morning, Your Honor," interjected Nutley from the prosecution's table. "We're here to assist the court."

Yamamoto looked at Camila. "Ms. Harrison . . . do we need to go through a full hearing? The ball is in your court. I ask again, is there a need? I mean, I think everyone here would agree that you should be found in contempt . . . that's really not the issue . . . the issue is how are you going to purge yourself of the contempt . . . do you follow me?"

"Yes, Your Honor," muttered Camila.

"Let's go off the record," ordered Yamamoto.

The electronic recording officer pushed some buttons and turned off his recording machine.

"Hearing, no hearing, I am going to make a finding of contempt . . . now I don't have to act on it," explained Yamamoto, "I can hold off on the imposition of the fine or the jail time. I can have my law clerk prepare the order finding you in contempt, but I don't have to sign it . . . I can sit on it for a while . . . so the contempt won't be actionable. . . . Do we understand each other, Ms. Harrison?"

"Completely," Camila replied.

Camila continued standing up, the butterflies playing havoc with her stomach. Here she was, about to do the unthinkable: kiss Yamamoto's ass and apologize to Nutley. She tried hard to keep her anger in check.

At that moment, Yamamoto made a signal to the marshal, who left his post and came over to the defense counsel's table to remove Camila's handcuffs and shackles. He looked over at the ERO officer and signaled him to get back on the record.

Camila waited for the marshal to finish. "Thank you, Your Honor. I don't think it's really necessary for us to have this hearing. I was completely out of line and I apologize for my behavior. I acted in a very unprofessional manner."

"Mr. Nutley? What do you think?" the judge asked.

"Doesn't sound like a heartfelt apology, Your Honor," said Nutley, rubbing it in. "I mean, she's made a *spectacle* of these proceedings."

"Ms. Harrison?"

"Uhm, yes," Camila continued, "I'm really, *really* sorry. I know I disrespected this court, the jurors, the government and I'm here asking for forgiveness. I lost my composure in the heat of battle, something that should never happen. I'll go to anger management classes when the case is over, or do community service, whatever the court orders. Anything, just please don't send me to jail again. The weekend was enough, Your Honor. Please, I've learned my lesson."

"Are you willing to pay a fine . . . or do you want to go back to jail to purge yourself of the contempt?" Yamamoto asked.

"Ten thousand dollars would be an appropriate sum," volunteered Nutley. "Sometimes you have to hit people where it hurts . . . "

Yamamoto gave him a glare, as if saying to keep quiet. Truth be told, Yamamoto would rather have Camila Harrison pay a fine than to have to sentence her to more jail time. There was a case to try and she needed to do it. It would be completely unfair to have Thelma fall on the sword for the situation that Camila Harrison had created.

Camila cleared her throat. "I don't know, Your Honor. I haven't closed on the sale of my Austin home. I really don't know . . . Maybe you've heard? I lost some big deposits on a wedding . . . a wedding that didn't happen."

"It's either a fine or jail time," Yamamoto said as he made some notes in the file. "You choose."

"Can I have a minute to speak to my client?" asked Alan, interrupting the exchange between Camila and Yamamoto.

"Sure," the judge quipped.

Alan leaned over and whispered something in Camila's ear. After a minute in conference, Alan announced, "I think we have a proposal for the court's consideration, Your Honor. My client would like to address the court."

"What is it?" Yamamoto asked, curious.

"Ahem, Your Honor," Camila struggled to find the right words, "I'm willing to waive my fees for the entire case. It's at least ten thousand dollars in attorney's fees . . . probably more."

Yamamoto's eyes popped wide open. He flashed a smile. "I like that! Very original . . . very practical."

Nutley shook his head, disappointed.

"Mr. Nutley?" Yamamoto said. "What do you think? That's hitting Ms. Harrison in the pocket, don't you think?"

"I suppose."

"So you're saying," Yamamoto followed, "that you, in essence, are doing the case pro bono? Since you won't keep any of the money you would have otherwise received. Is that what I'm understanding?"

"Yes, in essence," said Camila. "I mean, Uncle Sam will issue a check to pay me, but I'll return the money to the court. It'll be put back in your court's registry, Your Honor. I'll work for free."

"Pretty much," Alan mumbled. "Yes . . . pro bono."

"Then I will make a finding that Ms. Harrison was out of order. That a finding of contempt is appropriate in this case. However, the court will hold off signing the order to make the contempt actionable and, instead, will allow attorney, Camila Harrison, time to finish the case and time to pay. The court will further order that Ms. Harrison be released today, and shall remain free, pending payment of ten thousand dollars to purge herself of the contempt." Yamamoto looked over at Chloe to make sure she knew what language to put on the order. He appeared satisfied that a compromise had been reached. "And Ms. Harrison will also be ordered to submit her payment voucher at the end of the case, right away. The check Ms. Harrison receives from the government, all of it, she will endorse and deposit into the registry of the court to purge herself of the finding of contempt. Only then will the court sign a final order purging Ms. Harrison of contempt. Are we clear?"

"Yes," said Alan.

"Ms. Harrison," Yamamoto pointed out, "do we understand each other?"

"Yes, Your Honor. At what time do we resume with the trial tomorrow, Your Honor?" Camila asked.

"Mr. Nutley," followed Judge Yamamoto, "how many more witnesses do you have left?"

Nutley looked at Fox, but Fox was busy writing something on a yellow pad. "I think we only have one witness left, Your Honor, the custodian of evidence."

"So, if we start at 10 a.m., does the government expect to finish with its case-in-chief before lunch?" Yamamoto asked.

"That should do it," Nutley explained.

At that moment, Chloe handed Judge Yamamoto a note. He read it and announced. "We have a scheduling issue. We'll resume the trial on Wednesday. Tuesday's shot, unfortunately. I've been asked to conduct hearings and decide whether the State of Texas is entitled to a preliminary injunction to stop the White House from expanding portions of the DACA program."

"Wednesday?" asked Nutley, disappointed again.

"It's contested," replied Yamamoto. "It will take all day."

"Wednesday it is," said Camila, sounding relieved.

She turned and gave Alan a thankful look, patted him on the back and whispered, "Thanks for agreeing to stand in."

The marshal immediately came over, handcuffed and shackled Camila, but not before taking care that the cuffs around her wrists weren't hurting her. He then proceeded to escort her out of the courtroom.

Yamamoto addressed the marshal before the young man exited the courtroom. "Finish processing Ms. Harrison. She's to be released today."

"Yes, Your Honor," replied the marshal.

"Hold on a minute," said Yamamoto as he signaled the marshal to wait before hauling Camila away. "Ms. Harrison?"

Camila turned around. "Yes, Your Honor?"

"How's that brother of yours?"

She gave Yamamoto a warm smile. "We're optimistic I'll be a match, Your Honor. Thanks for asking."

"Good luck," Yamamoto replied, "we'll be in recess!"

The marshal finished escorting Camila out of the courtroom.

Thelma Issa's waterfront property in Clear Lake was located twenty-five minutes from downtown Houston. It had been built in the Spanish Mediterranean style with comfort in mind. It was a six-bedroom, four-bath, three-story structure with its own pier, boat slip, boat lift and a rooftop terrace with the best view in the area. Dr. Omar Issa's forty-foot sailboat was moored at the pier.

Camila sat at the dining room table eating a ham and cheese sandwich, Alan next to her. Thelma sat opposite the two.

"Can either one of you bring me up to speed?" asked Camila. "Did you have a chance to meet with Monty? What's the latest?"

Alan and Thelma looked at each other but didn't say anything. Finally, Alan broke the silence. "Thelma wants to tell you something."

Thelma gave Alan a glare.

"What's going on? Is there a problem?" Camila asked.

"Yes," said Thelma, "there's a problem."

"What is it? Does it concern Monty?!"

"Sort of," said Alan.

"You see," Thelma said, rubbing her hands together, "Monty found Beto . . . "

"And?"

"Well," continued Thelma, "Beto wouldn't say much, but he did point us in Stephen Leal's direction."

"That's good, right?" Camila nodded with a big grin across her face.

"Yes," said Thelma, "and no."

"Yes and no?"

Alan said, "Something happened to Leal."

"What?!"

"He's dead," finished Thelma. "Stephen Leal committed suicide. Beto was pulling our legs. He played us."

Camila gritted her teeth and pounded the table with a fist. Thelma came over and put her arms around her, trying to comfort her.

"When?!" Camila asked. "Is he sure he found the right guy? Who has a phone? Let me call Monty. I need to hear this for myself."

Alan reached for a manila folder and handed Camila a newspaper clipping. It was Stephen Leal's obituary. "Here you go. His obituary was published in some obscure local newspaper that's not online."

Camila grabbed the clipping and studied it. "How can this be? I can't believe this. We have nothing! Nothing, I tell you . . . Jesus freakin' Christ!"

"Look," Alan said, "maybe a miracle will happen. Maybe we can still pull a rabbit out of our hat. We're still alive, aren't we?"

Camila was devastated. She shook her head, trying to comprehend the magnitude of their problem. "How? With what?"

"Maybe the jury will feel sorry for us," suggested Alan.

"Why would they do that? I've ruffled a lot of feathers. They probably hate me *and* my client. And now they're sequestered!"

Camila buried her head in her arms. After about a minute, she composed herself and pushed away her sandwich and can of soda. She looked out toward the bay. A silence fell over the trio.

"Maybe Yamamoto will win the case for you," Alan muttered. "I've seen it before. One time, I tried a case in front of Judge Hester, he was mean, *mean*. He kept pounding on me and on my client, for the entire trial. I couldn't get an objection sustained . . . but all of the state's objections were sustained. Everything I said was overruled. I couldn't even get my exhibits admitted . . . nothing was going my way. And guess what the jury did?"

"C'mon, Alan! That's not realistic," admonished Thelma. "You're not helping."

Alan ignored Thelma and continued his story. "Surprise, surprise. The jury went my way anyway. Despite all the instructions in the jury charge, despite the lost exhibits, despite all the evidence against us . . . the jury felt bad and they sided with me and my client. It could happen. You never know."

Camila was tired and fed up. "Thanks, Alan, but I think we all know what's going to happen."

"Monty is still out there," Thelma added, "pounding the pavement. Last he checked in, he was on his way to talk to a couple of guys that were busted some time ago by Odessa. Maybe we'll get lucky."

"Let's face it," Camila sighed, "we've run out of time. One day isn't enough. It's over."

"For the life of me, I can't believe no one has tattled on Bergendahl and his boys in Odessa before," Thelma said. She worked at applying color to Camila's roots along her hair line.

"You would think that, right? After all these years?"

It was late Monday afternoon. Alan had already left, Thelma and Camila were sitting in the bathroom, worried about the trial resuming in less than forty-eight hours.

"If Beto knows something," Thelma volunteered, "and he sent us to Leal . . . I wonder if he knew that Leal had died? Why would he send us to him if he knew he was dead, knowing we would just come back to hound *him* again?"

"Did they keep in touch?" wondered Camila.

"I bet you he didn't even know," Thelma suggested. "Maybe we should pay him a visit."

Camila twitched. "I feel like we're chasing our tails. And now, we have to figure out how to subpoena the custodian of records for the cloud service provider for Buc'ees . . . some outfit in California? Give me a break! Oh, and don't forget the cell phone, a key piece of evidence that mysteriously disappeared . . . an issue that I've let go because I didn't want to piss off Yamamoto anymore than I already have. What else could go wrong?"

"What are you saying?"

"It's over. Let's just finish the case. Whatever happens . . . happens."

They sat in silence looking at their reflections in the mirror, lost in their own thoughts. Both wondering if there was something or someone that could help them turn things around.

"You're doing this for Alicia, remember?" Thelma reminded Camila. "We have to push through. This isn't *really* about justice for Aldama or exposing Odessa, anymore. This is about Alicia, bringing her daddy home to say goodbye."

"I guess you're right," mumbled Camila, as she remembered having to say goodbye to Dante. He was the love of her life and losing him had been the hardest, most painful thing she had lived through. Now, ten years later, Lorena's actions had started to make sense. She realized her mother probably had felt like she was losing Camila to Dante, in the same way she had lost Luis Pablo to the world. That is why she had refused to give them her blessing to marry. Looking back, it was obvious Lorena had been unable to let Camila go.

"If we're going to do this," Thelma continued, "just promise me one thing."

"What is it?" Camila asked, trying to get her head back in the game, while putting away the painful memories.

"Don't fight with the remaining witnesses. Don't fight with Nutley and the judge or anybody else. You can come across as an angry, bitter woman."

"I am angry and bitter," replied Camila. "That's how I feel. My life went to shit because I was careless and now look at me!"

"I get it, I know," answered Thelma, "but you still need to tone it down. Promise me you'll do it."

"I'll try, I promise. It's just that something comes over me and I can't control it. I'm still pissed at Paxton, at Bergendahl, Nutley and the whole thing . . . "

"Trust me," Thelma shook her head, "we all get that you're angry. Really, we do. You've made your point. Now it's time to let it go."

THIRTY-FIVE

"Think, think!" Monty said to Vicente Aldama in one of the attorney-client interview rooms inside the federal detention center. It was right before closing time; in a few minutes, the guards would come around and ask all the lawyers and visitors to say goodnight.

"I can't remember what I did with my cell phone," Aldama replied, "or what happened to it. I've racked my brain for days, trust me."

"Okay," said Monty, "let's go back. You took a video of the Tahoe with your cell."

"That's right."

"And your reason for taking the video?"

Aldama turned to look at Monty. "The guys I was with told me that it was a way to protect us against false traffic stops," he said. "They said that's how it's done. That it was a good idea . . . just in case."

"And everything was working?" Monty asked.

"Yes," answered Aldama, "all the lights . . . the turn signals, brake lights, plate lights . . . the Tahoe was perfect."

"Man, that's just what we need!"

"Why are you so intent on trying to find my cell phone now?"

"You know what happened . . . Yamamoto is not letting the defense introduce the surveillance video into evidence," the investigator explained, "because we don't have the custodian of evidence from Buc-ee's, they're out of state. But if we find your cell, since *you're* the owner, you can help us get it admitted into evidence. It would go to prove that there was no valid reason for the traffic stop. Bergendahl had no probable cause, has been lying all along. The evidence should be thrown out . . . and you walk. Hopefully!"

"The feds should have it!"

"They claim they don't know what happened to it. Is it possible that you could have dropped it at Buc'ees? When you were getting into the Tahoe? Or did you drop it at the location where Bergendahl pulled you over?"

"I really don't know," said Aldama, "I guess it could have fallen out from one of my pockets, maybe . . . "

"Think! Think back! What could have happened to it? Did you see Bergendahl pick it up? The others? Who has it? Where did it end up?"

"I wish I knew!" Aldama replied.

THIRTY-SIX

Alan, Camila, Monty and Thelma arrived at Alan's office before six in the morning on Tuesday. Now that the trial was about to resume, Camila and her team needed to regroup and figure out a last-minute strategy. They were out of time.

"Anything on the cell phone?" asked Camila. "Was he able to remember? Any idea where it ended up?"

They sat in the conference room. Parts of the Aldama file were scattered all over the table.

Thelma was shaking her head, "I can't believe the government doesn't know what happened to it. Just doesn't make sense."

"I'm gonna go back to Buc-ee's," announced Monty. "Maybe he left it there that day, somebody picked it up and turned it in. It could be waiting for us in the lost and found. It's a long shot . . . but at this point it's worth a try."

"Camila, when you looked at the inventory report," asked Thelma, "did they mention anything about the co-defendants' personal property? Do you remember?"

Camila rifled through a stack of papers and pulled out a copy of the inventory report generated by Odessa's custodian of evidence. She studied it. It was signed by Bergendahl. She then noticed two small markings on the bottom right-hand corner. They appeared to be somebody's initials: *A.F.* "No mention here of any cell phones . . . only the $850,000 in bundles."

"How incredibly convenient," observed Alan as he pulled the phone from his pants pocket and checked the latest stock tips.

"Maybe Bergendahl kept the cells," suggested Thelma, "in order to go through them, pluck their contents, develop other leads and even wiretap other targets."

"It's possible," said Monty, "and if he did that, he'll never admit it."

"This is so frustrating!" cried Camila, ready to bang her head on the table. "*So* aggravating. I hate this!"

"Here's what I propose," said Thelma. "Monty, you go on back to Buc-ee's like you planned . . . see what you can find."

"Okay," said Monty.

"But don't spend too much time down there. If they don't have it, come back here fast," ordered Thelma. "And stay in touch. We'll have our phones on."

"Okay."

"Where did you say you talked to Beto last?" asked Thelma, trying to put together a plan of action.

"At the Walmart in Wharton. It's an hour drive."

"Okay," she said, "Camila and I will head on over there, see if we can talk to him again."

Camila interrupted. "We should call Freddie, your nephew, Thelma."

Thelma, Alan and Monty looked at each other.

"Why?" asked Thelma.

"He's savvy with computers . . . maybe he can help us do a search on the internet," Camila said.

Thelma scratched her head, confused. "And what can he do at this stage in the game?"

"While you and I go talk to Beto," recommended Camila, "I'll have him look up Beto and Stephen Leal on Facebook and all the other websites he can, see who their friends are. Maybe there are others who worked for Odessa. Maybe Beto is protecting somebody else. I would like to find out, do some cross-referencing, check everything. You see this?" Camila showed Monty and Thelma the copy of the inventory sheet and the initials A.F.

"A.F.?" Monty wondered.

"*Exactly!* Who is A.F.?" asked Camila.

"Okay, I'll call Freddie on the way. I just hope it's not too late," Thelma said as she gathered her keys and purse and watched Camila do the same.

＊＊＊

While on the road, Thelma's nephew had touched base with them and simultaneously started a deep search on all social media. It turned out that Gualberto "Beto" Carrillo, was also known as "Wally." Freddie, the internet-sleuth, had cross-indexed Wally's friends, acquaintances and relatives with other markers. He'd noticed that someone named Armando appeared to be a common denominator between Odessa's Facebook Page, Beto, Leal and Bergendahl. It was a lead worth exploring. He'd immediately conveyed this new piece of information to Camila, right as she and Thelma were pulling into the Wharton Walmart.

Camila tapped the window of Beto's patrol car. He was parked under a tree in the parking lot, napping.

Beto opened his eyes, yawned and slowly rolled down the driver's side window of his white Ford Focus. He was a bit annoyed.

"What do you want now?" He let out a big yawn.

"Oh, nothing," said Camila. "I just wanted to tell you that I had a chance to talk to your pal, Armando. We straightened things out."

Beto's eyes grew wide, but he didn't say anything. Had they really found his cousin?

Camila continued fishing: "Oh, yeah . . . he explained everything. Anyway, he said he was moving to Austin."

"Austin? Are you sure?"

"That's what he said," Camila replied, baiting him.

"Mando hates Austin. He would never leave the dude ranch he's working at. Besides, his wife's from Brenham . . . born and raised. Are you sure we're talking about the same Mando? *The* Armando Franco?"

"I'm sure," Camila said. "But it doesn't matter. My guy took the plea anyway. We didn't need you *or* Mando. We were in the middle of the trial when the government approached us and offered us a sweet deal. We decided to throw in the towel . . . wrap things up."

"And you came all the way to Wharton to tell me that?" Beto asked, still confused and trying to make sense of what he was hearing.

"Oh, no. My friend Thelma . . . " Camila pointed at her friend sitting in the white Range Rover about ten parking spaces away, "she lives here in Wharton. We came by to pick a few things up from the store . . . when I recognized you sitting in the patrol car. Just wanted to chew the fat. We're making margaritas and enchiladas for lunch, celebrating now that the case is over. Come join us?"

"Good . . . good," stammered Beto. "Over . . . that's good. Finally, huh?"

"Anyway," continued Camila, "it was nice seeing you." She started walking away, then stopped, turned around and came back.

"*Now* what?" He said, rolling his eyes.

"Did you know Stephen Leal was dead?"

"Ha, ha, ha . . . " A big smile appeared on Beto's face. "Yeah . . . I knew. And you have to admit . . . it worked, huh? You left me alone *and* lost more time. Can you blame me?"

"No, I guess I can't," Camila replied. "You sly fox, you . . . Wally, Beto . . . whatever your name is."

She started laughing, then turned around and hopped into the Range Rover.

"Found him! Go, go, go!" Camila ordered as soon as she got into the vehicle.

"What happened back there?" Thelma asked.

"He was covering for his cousin, Mando. The guy works at a dude ranch in Brenham, Texas. We just have to find him!"

"Here," offered Thelma, handing Camila her iPhone, "Google 'dude ranches in Brenham.'"

Camila texted Freddie to ask him to find out more about Mando, aka Armando Franco, before she skimmed the search results. Who was he married to? What was his wife's maiden name? Who owned the ranch where he worked?

"It'll be about a two-hour drive to Brenham," remarked Thelma. "Should we split up?"

"What do you mean?"

"You can drop me off in Houston, and while you head to Brenham. I'll try to find the dude ranch—pinpoint its location for you. Plus, I can start researching how we can convince Yamamoto to let him testify. I might have to have some briefs and motions ready . . . and there's just not enough time."

"You're assuming that I can even convince this Mando to lend us a hand, get him to come testify."

"Why wouldn't he?" Thelma glanced at the speedometer. They were doing ninety, flying past all the other traffic. "Remember, even if he agrees to testify, Yamamoto might not allow him to, just like he kicked the surveillance video out. I have to be ready to argue that, as a rebuttal witness, he needs to be allowed to take the stand. But I need to have the case law to support our position. I have to be ready to preserve that issue in the event of an appeal."

"Are you saying Nutley will argue he's not a 'traditional' rebuttal-type witness?"

Thelma set the cruise control at ninety-five miles per hour. She pulled out her Viper radar detector from the glove compartment and set it on the dashboard, then handed Camila the power plug.

"Exactly . . . because, by doing what we're doing . . . we now know of his existence in advance. But there's another issue that we need to get ready for."

Camila threw her arms up in the air. "Man! Practicing real estate law was so much simpler than this! What's the new issue?"

"Nutley only has one witness left. Once you find out what Mando knows, we better pray that the last witness for the government talks about whatever it is we're trying to get in with Mando. Remember, rebuttal witnesses are allowed to testify, but the scope is limited. Yamamoto won't let you bring out anything and everything under the stars."

"Oh my God, you're right! And that's assuming this Mando guy would even get to testify."

"Let's keep our fingers crossed."

Camila smiled at her best friend and let out a big sigh.

Thelma punched the gas pedal. They were now doing one hundred.

THIRTY-SEVEN

The atmosphere in Alan's borrowed conference room could be best described as chaotic but positive, with a spark of excitement. The latest developments in the case had both Monty and Thelma in good spirits. Also, Freddie was checking in with the legal team every twenty minutes with his latest discovery, update or interesting fact. As soon as Thelma received the news from her nephew, she would text Camila the information.

Monty was busy on the phone when Govela showed up to the war room, unannounced. Thelma didn't notice as she was glued to the computer screen, reading an appellate opinion dealing with rebuttal testimony. She'd been busy whipping up briefs and motions most of the late morning.

Govela tossed his car keys and government-issued cell phone on the conference table and sat down. "How's it going? Can I help?"

Monty waved at him and carried on with his conversation.

Thelma turned around and greeted him, "Hey."

"Where's Camila? Is she okay?" asked Govela.

"Oh, yes," said Thelma. "She's out running an errand."

Monty covered the mouthpiece and yelled from across the room, "We found him." He gave Govela a thumbs up.

"Who? Who did you find!?" Govela asked, infected with the excitement of the moment.

"The missing link," blurted out Thelma, "the real deal."

Govela scratched his head. "Is that where Camila went? To talk to this missing link?"

"Yes," Thelma answered. "She's on her way to a dude ranch in Brenham. We think they've been hiding this witness from us, but now we have him in our sights."

"And what do you think this new witness can possibly know?" asked Govela.

"That's what we want to find out. He's got to know about the CI." Monty volunteered.

"Wow, the CI. You're getting close, huh? Hey, are you guys hungry, thirsty? I can run to Starbucks. That way you can keep working. Don't let me interrupt."

"Yes, yes," Thelma said, still glued to the monitor. "I'll have a cappuccino. . . . "

"How about you, Monty?"

Monty was consumed with whatever he was doing and simply waved to Govela that he was fine. He seemed to be trying to set up a meeting with someone who had served three years in prison and was currently living at a halfway house, wrapping up the remainder of his sentence.

"Okay," Govela said. "I'll be right back." He picked up his keys and cell phone and headed out the door.

On the way to the dude ranch, Camila received a text from Thelma that concluded that A. F. was indeed Armando Franco, the missing link. She found an old group picture of Odessa agents online, posing after a large drug seizure and he was in it.

Camila pulled up to the main house of the Rio Tinto Ranch, got out of her car and approached a college-aged woman in Wranglers and a white T-shirt, a woven straw cowboy hat on her head.

"Can I help you?" asked the young woman.

"I'm looking for Mando . . . or you might know him as Armando Franco," said Camila.

"Mando," the girl thought for a second. "He's out with a group of riders right now. They're out on the trails, left in the morning." She looked at her watch. "But they'll be back in an hour or so. Why don't you wait over in the dining hall?" She pointed at a screened-in, wooden structure on top of a hill about fifty yards away. "That's where we'll be serving refreshments and snacks to them."

"And Mando will be there?"

"Sure."

"And you have no problem with me talking to him?"

"You're not a process server, are you?"

"No, I'm not."

"Then, sure," she said, "you can talk to him."

THIRTY-EIGHT

"Who are you?" a thirty-year-old cowboy asked Camila. He, too, was wearing Wranglers, along with boots, a western shirt and a cowboy hat. He was playing with a pair of leather gloves in his hands.

"Camila Harrison. I'm a lawyer. I practice in Houston." She handed him a business card.

"You here to set up a corporate event? The group sales are handled by Sherrie. That's the girl in the front office."

"I've met Sherrie."

"And?"

"That's not why I'm here," answered Camila.

"What do you want?" He looked her over from head to toe.

"I've been looking for you for a long time," said Camila, unsure of whether she should dive right in or slowly work her way up to it. "You're great with the guests . . . I saw you interact with them back at the dining hall."

"It's a job."

"You used to be a narcotics agent, right?"

"Who said?"

"I saw the pictures in the newspapers. You worked for the Odessa HIDTA Task Force, right?"

"I wanted to be an agent."

"Something happened?"

"Yes."

309

"Listen," said Camila as she pulled out a picture of her client and his daughter, Alicia, "I'm here because I need your help. I'm not going to beat around the bushes . . . "

"I don't think I can help you," said Franco, cutting her off, but he still looked at the photos Camila had handed him. "Besides, I don't know these people. I've never seen them. I worked in the evidence locker as a custodian of evidence."

He handed the pictures back to Camila.

"I understand." Camila put the pictures back in her large manila envelope. "Honestly? I didn't expect you to know my client . . . or his daughter, Alicia."

Franco looked out into the distance, over the rolling meadows, trails and woods. "That was another time, another life . . . I don't care to relive it."

"No?"

"You know what it's like to have your dream stolen, your spirit crushed?" asked Franco.

Silence.

"Will you help me?" begged Camila, ready to drop to her knees, if necessary. "Would you just give me five minutes?"

"Let's proceed," ordered Judge Yamamoto. "Who is the next witness for the government?"

"Your Honor, the government calls Agent Adrian Rico to the stand."

Thelma leaned over, past Aldama, and whispered to Camila, "This is our only chance."

Wharton Police Officer Adrian Rico was administered the oath by Judge Yamamoto. After the agent swore to tell the truth, he placed a paper grocery bag he'd been carrying under his left arm on the floor, sat down in the witness chair and adjusted the microphone in front of him. Rico was a forty-year-old Hispanic with bad knees and a large beer belly. One could easily tell his best years were behind him. Rico was the main custodian of evidence for the Odessa Task Force.

AUSA Wyatt Fox addressed him from the podium, "Officer Rico, what is your job title with the Odessa Task Force?"

"I'm the principal custodian of evidence for HIDTA."

"Can you tell the jury what the word HIDTA stands for?"

"Sure," answered Rico, "HIDTA stands for *high intensity drug trafficking area*. . . . "

"Are there other HIDTA task forces in the State of Texas?"

"Yes. There's actually several of them throughout the country."

"And as the custodian of evidence, what do you do? Would you care to explain to the ladies and gentlemen of the jury?"

Rico turned to face the jurors. He flashed a warm smile. "I receive the evidence that comes in from the field. I inventory it, catalog it, confirm it's linked to the proper case and correct defendants. I make sure nobody tampers with it and take it to court in the event that there's a trial. I make sure the chain of custody is unbroken. And when the case is over, if there are no more appeals or writs or what have you . . . I make arrangements to dispose of it."

"How is the evidence disposed of?"

"The narcotics are sent to an incinerator, an outfit near Houston in a secret location certified by the federal government to meet certain standards. The operators cremate the stuff, so it turns to ashes and there's nothing left."

"And where's the evidence locker for the Odessa Task Force?"

"Inside the Wharton Police Department. It's kind of in the middle of things, since Odessa patrols the corridor between Victoria and Houston."

"What about weapons? What happens to the weapons that are seized?"

"Those are destroyed, then sold for scrap," answered Rico. "There's also another governmental contractor that disposes of the guns and ammo. That's what *they* do."

"And money? What happens to the money seized from illegal activity?"

"The money is divided among the various police departments and agencies that make up the Odessa Task Force. It's then used by the departments to buy equipment and body cams and new patrol units and such." He smiled at the jurors. "You could say we share in the spoils."

Some of the jurors smiled back.

"What's the makeup of Odessa? Do you know?"

"We have members from various sheriff's departments across several counties: Victoria, Jackson, Wharton and Fort Bend. I also know that some police departments also lend a hand. For example, I work with the Wharton PD even though I'm assigned to the Odessa Task Force."

"And who pays your salary?"

"We get our funding through various grants, both state and federal."

Fox appeared satisfied with his answers, then switched gears. "Did you receive evidence in a case involving a cash seizure which occurred on September 16, 2014 north of Victoria, Texas?"

"Can you be more specific?" asked Rico.

"Currency seized from a 2012 Chevrolet Tahoe . . . "

"Oh, yes."

"Do you remember the incident?"

"Yes, I remember the $850,000 that was seized that night." Rico was smiling proudly. "That was a pretty good-sized bust."

"How did you know it was $850,000?"

Out of the corner of her eye, Camila glanced at Thelma. Thelma did the same back to her. This was the opportunity Aldama's defense team was looking for.

"I counted it," said the custodian of evidence.

"When did you count it?"

"When the agent who processed the Tahoe brought the cash to Wharton PD, I received a call in the morning that there had been a seizure the night before . . . that the money was on its way."

"And how was it packaged?"

"Rubber banded in small bundles. Each bundle had been carefully vacuum-sealed."

"What else can you tell us about this seizure?"

"The bundles were all hundred-dollar bills."

"And how is that significant?"

"Because we know, through years of experience, that when you're talking about hundred-dollar bills, like in this case, a million dollars weighs just around twenty pounds. *And* it doesn't take up very much space."

He picked up the paper grocery bag from the floor next to him and showed it to the jury. He then quickly set it down.

Camila was about to object since the evidence had yet to be admitted, but she let it go.

"Who processed the scene in this instance?"

"Agent Bergendahl, I'm pretty sure," said Rico as he reached for his reading glasses. "But if you give me a second, I'll be able to tell you for sure."

Camila, Thelma and Aldama looked over at the jury. They were glued to Agent Rico. He seemed to have struck a chord with them.

The witness put on his reading glasses, then reached for the paper grocery bag again and read a small sheet of paper that was stapled to the sealed bag.

"It was Bergendahl," replied Rico, pointing to the sheet of paper. "It says so right here, and it's also dated. There's a time noted on the tally sheet as well, along with Bergendhal's initials. It also has my initials right over here," he continued, "where I received the evidence, the date and time."

"Who is Bergendahl with?"

"He's with the Fort Bend County Sheriff's office. He's on loan to Odessa, but he's pretty much the senior agent on staff . . . the one who calls the shots."

"Has the bag been tampered with or unsealed in any way?"

"Not that I know of," Rico said.

"How can you be sure?"

The witness placed the paper grocery bag in front of him. "You see this red, plastic tape right here?" He pointed at the strip holding the bag shut.

"Yes," said Fox.

"If it had been tampered with, this strip of tape would show it. This is a very special kind of tape. Once it's put on a paper bag . . .

it can't be removed without destroying it. It also has the agent's initials and my complete name written on it. Once it's removed, the name of the custodian receiving the evidence that's written on it will become deformed, as well as the agent's initials."

"So . . . has anybody tampered with the evidence bag—to the best of your knowledge?"

"No. The tape is intact," answered Rico, still pointing.

"To the best of your knowledge, was the chain of custody broken in any way?"

"No. Bergendahl processed the scene . . . he took pictures, made an inventory and then put the bundles in the evidence bag. He filled out the tally sheet; the tally sheet was signed by him and another witness. In this case, it was Agent . . . " Rico looked at the tally sheet until he found what he was looking for. "Here they are . . . the other initials . . . "

"Whose initials?"

"S. L. Stephen Leal . . . another custodian of evidence Stephen Leal," said Rico.

"And then what happened?"

"Once Bergendahl brought the evidence into the station—into the evidence locker room, to be more precise—we sat down. We made sure the evidence, in this case the bundles of cash, in the evidence bag matched what was being reported in the tally sheet."

"Did you count the money?"

"Yes, we opened the evidence bag and counted the money with special currency counters we have back at the PD. It was $850,000."

"Why are the bundles still vacuum-sealed if you counted the money?"

"We always take pictures during the entire process, and we vacuum-seal the money after we're done counting so nothing is lost . . . no evidence disappears. The bundles are put in a plastic evidence bag, like a Ziploc bag, and then all of that goes into the paper sack."

"And then what happened?"

"We then stapled the tally sheet to the paper sack and sealed it with the red tamper-proof tape. Both of us signed and wrote our names or initials on the tape. The paper sack was then booked into the evidence locker. There's a log we keep. All part of the chain of custody."

Camila and Thelma were scribbling furiously on their yellow pads, getting ready for the cross–examination.

"Would you open this evidence bag for the jury?"

"Certainly," said Rico.

As he opened the paper bag, the red tape broke. He reached inside for the bundles of cash. All in all, there were nine bundles of cash, each one vacuum-sealed.

"How much money is there again?"

Rico smiled. "This right here is $850,000 US dollars."

"Do you have a picture of the bundles . . . those bundles right in front of you now, Agent Rico?"

"Yes. Yes, I do," from inside the same paper bag, he pulled out a couple of Polaroid photos. "These Polaroids were taken the same day the evidence was deposited into the locker room. There's a picture of us counting the money."

"Do they accurately reflect the bundles of cash . . . in the same condition they were in on the day in question?"

"Yes."

"Move to admit the Polaroid pictures, Your Honor. We'll mark them as exhibits 10, 11 and 12."

"Any objections?" asked Yamamoto.

Camila stood up. "No objection, Your Honor. "

"They'll be admitted," said Yamamoto.

"Pass the witness," followed Fox, smiling as he approached the jury box and published the three Polaroid pictures to the jury.

Camila got up and went to the podium. "Agent Rico," she started, "you said you were the principal custodian of evidence for Odessa, is that correct?"

"Objection," Fox yelled in an effort to rattle Camila. "Leading."

But before Yamamoto could say anything, Camila replied, "Of course it's leading, Your Honor. This is a cross-examination."

Yamamoto gave her an icy stare but agreed with her, albeit reluctantly. "Overruled."

"You can go ahead and answer," Camila instructed the witness.

"Yes, I'm the custodian for Odessa," said Rico.

"The principal custodian," clarified Camila. "Which means that there's more than one, isn't that correct?"

Fox sprang to his feet. "Objection! This is outside the scope of my direct examination, Your Honor. Counsel is not entitled to get into matters that weren't brought out during direct examination."

"We disagree, Your Honor!" Thelma said, jumping into the fray. "These matters *were* brought out, Your Honor! I know because I wrote it down. And I quote Mr. Fox asking the witness, 'Question: Officer Rico, what is your job title with the Odessa Task Force? Answer: I'm the principal custodian of evidence for HIDTA.' That was his answer. He stated quite clearly he was the principal custodian of evidence, Your Honor."

Nutley jumped in. "Your Honor, I'm sure that's not what Agent Rico meant."

"Is there an objection?" Camila asked, ready to move on. "Your Honor, can you make a ruling so I can continue with my cross-examination of this witness?"

Yamamoto tried to remain calm and restore order in his courtroom. "First, no double-teaming. Only Mr. Fox and Ms. Harrison can object and respond. They're the ones who have the floor, got it?"

"Yes," replied the attorneys.

"I do remember the word 'principal,'" said Yamamoto. "I have to agree with the defense counsel. I'll allow the question, but only to establish that there may have been other custodians."

"Thank you, Your Honor," said Camila, who immediately returned to face Rico. "Who else worked in the evidence locker, Agent Rico?"

"Judge!" cried Fox. "This is not the same question as 'Who were the other custodians,' Your Honor. There's a big difference . . . and we object. That was definitely not brought out during my direct examination."

"Rephrase your question, Counselor," ordered Yamamoto.

"If you were the principal custodian, who were the other custodians that assisted you, Mr. Rico?" asked Camila.

Nutley, Fox and Griffin were in conference, strategizing how to best stop Camila Harrison from getting into forbidden territory.

Rico thought it over for a few seconds and gave his response: "Mando, Stephen, myself . . . that's it."

"When you say 'Mando,' do you mean Armando Franco?"

Nutley and Fox were about to object, but Griffin made them sit down.

"Yes," replied Rico.

"And Wally . . . is that the same Gualberto Carrillo, also known as Beto?"

"Yes, but Wally preferred to patrol. He rarely worked the evidence locker."

"Stephen Leal . . . was he also a custodian of evidence?"

"Yes, he was," said Rico, nodding, "on occasion."

"How so?"

"He did double-duty. Sometimes he was out in the field, doing traffic stops, busting people, and sometimes he was on call when I had time off."

"Why is that?"

"Because crime never stops, but we do need to rest." He smiled. "So, on the days I was off, others would cover for me."

"And that's why Wally, Mando and Stephen got to work in the evidence locker room."

"Correct."

"Do they still work for the Odessa Task Force?" Camila asked.

Fox couldn't help it. He shouted, "Objection! This is clearly outside the scope of direct examination, Your Honor."

"Sustained!" ruled Yamamoto.

"Isn't it true that Armando Franco also signed off on the tally sheet prepared by Agent Bergendahl? Are those his initials on the tally sheet?"

Rico inspected the sheet still stapled to the grocery bag. "Yes, there's an 'A.F.,' but I couldn't really tell you if they're Mando's."

"How many other agents were there that *you* know of with names matching the initials A and F?"

Rico stared at Nutley as if looking for clues, but Nutley was in conference with Griffin. "Just Mando," he said.

"If A.F., or Mando . . . Armando signed off on this tally sheet, he witnessed the evidence being collected, is that right?"

"Yes, I guess so."

"Do you know why the government did not list Mr. Franco as a witness in this case, why they didn't want him to testify?"

"Objection!" cried Fox. "The government doesn't need four custodians of evidence to prove its case, Your Honor. I am asking that the question be stricken from the record and that the court give an instruction to the jury that they're not to assume anything by Ms. Harrison's petulant suggestions and false innuendos . . . "

"Ladies and gentlemen of the jury," said Yamamoto, "you're not allowed to consider that question whatsoever, for any reason, or its implications. I'm also ordering that the question be stricken from the record."

Camila carried on. "Is Mr. Franco still working for Odessa?"

"No."

"How long has it been since he stopped working for the unit?"

Rico fudged his answer. "Six, eight weeks . . . maybe."

"And why did he leave, do you know?"

"Objection! Relevance?" interjected Fox.

"Sustained," said Yamamoto.

"Was he tampering with the evidence in the locker room?"

"Who? Mando?"

"Yes," answered Camila.

"Objection! Odessa is not on trial, Your Honor. It's Vicente Aldama who's on trial here today!"

"I'm entitled to explore this line of questioning, Your Honor," Camila argued, "because Agent Rico testified that his job is to make sure the evidence is safe and untampered with. And the jury is entitled to know if Mando was fired because he was tampering with the evidence in the locker room. If so, did he tamper with any *other* evidence? Or even the evidence in *this* case, for that matter?"

"Objection! This is totally improper," cried Fox. "Counsel is grasping at straws, Your Honor."

"I'll ask another question," volunteered Camila. "Don't worry. Agent Rico, was Stephen Leal a good agent?"

"The best," he answered.

"And Wally? Gualberto, also known as Beto? What kind of agent was he? Was he reliable? Honest? Competent?"

"Yes . . . yes, he was. They all were." Rico said.

"Even Franco?"

"Even Franco. Never had any issues with any of them," said Rico, making sure that Odessa's image and reputation stayed intact.

Nutley nodded discreetly from a distance, as if approving of Rico's performance.

"They were all honest?"

"Yes . . . very, very honest."

"Like *you*?"

"Um . . . haha," snickered Rico, "I suppose . . . like me."

"And they were credible?"

"Yes?"

"And they performed their work with diligence, honesty and integrity?"

Nutley, Fox and Griffin were now back in a huddle. Where was Harrison going with this? What was she trying to accomplish? Certainly, all these accolades would *help* Odessa's credibility in the end, wouldn't they?

Fox did not wait for Camila to continue asking questions, not those kinds of questions, anyway. "Judge," cried Fox, "can we move on? I think we've established *ad nauseam* that the other custodians were honorable and credible."

"Judge," replied Camila, "I never interrupted counsel during his direct. At least, not with frivolous and meritless objections. I would object to Mr. Fox's needless delay tactics and sidebar comments."

"Are you almost done with your cross-examination?" Yamamoto asked, ready to clip Harrison's wings.

Harrison knew she didn't have much time left. "Agent Rico," Camila pressed on, "how do you know there was only $850,000 in the Tahoe?"

"I couldn't tell you," said Rico.

Camila was impressed with his honesty. "Is that because you only inventory what gets delivered to you?"

"Correct. I trust that all the evidence seized out in the field makes it to the locker room," he answered.

Fox interrupted. "Objection! Relevance?"

"Your Honor," said Camila, "Agent Rico testified earlier that he has to keep the evidence safe, make sure it's not tampered with. This is stuff that was already covered in direct examination. I'm just cross-examining the witness on the same topic."

"I'll allow it," said Yamamoto, surprising Thelma, Camila and even their client. "But, start wrapping up."

"You wouldn't know," Camila offered, "if some of the evidence seized out in the field never made it back to the locker room. Is that a fair statement?"

Nutley, Fox, Griffin held their breath.

Thelma waited with anticipation. Depending on Rico's answer, Mando Franco would get to testify . . . maybe.

Camila noticed Nutley was looking for something in the gov-ernement's file. A look of concern was plastered over his face. Agent Rico, on the other hand, was obviously bothered by the last question. He resented it and was starting to get angry. "Listen to me, Ms. Harrison. The agents that work at Odessa—all of them— day in and day out . . . they all put their lives on the line. They do this because they love this country and they want to keep it safe. We refuse to let the bad guys win. So how dare you suggest the HIDTA unit is crooked? No agent would be so stupid as to ever think of skimming monies or drugs. Odessa only works with the best of the best. We're the good guys, got it? How dare you!"

Camila pretended to be embarrassed by her own audacity. "Got it," she answered and turned to look at the jury and the prosecution's table. She then smiled at Thelma. "We all get it. Pass the witness."

"Mr. Fox," said Yamamoto, "anything else from this witness?"

Fox looked at Griffin and Nutley. They shook their heads. They were relieved that Rico had held his ground.

"No, Your Honor," Fox replied. "The government rests."

THIRTY-NINE

"Call your first witness," ordered Yamamoto.

"We call Vicente Aldama to the stand," announced Camila, turning to look at her client.

Aldama left the comfort of the defense counsel's table and headed to the witness stand. The defendant swore to tell the truth, the whole truth and nothing but the truth.

"Introduce yourself to the jury," instructed Camila.

"Vi . . . Vicente Aldama," stammered the defendant. He fixed the microphone in front of him.

"Where are you from?"

"A fishing village down in Mexico. It's called Los Higueros, near the border of Veracruz and Tamaulipas, on the Gulf Coast."

"Are you going to tell this jury the truth?"

"All of it," Aldama said as he turned and locked eyes with Judge Yamamoto. "Everybody needs to hear it."

"You admit that you were hired to move whatever it was the Tahoe was carrying, do you not?"

Aldama turned and looked at the jury. "Yes."

"Why did you do it?"

"I have a daughter who is sick."

"What's her name?"

"Alicia."

"How old is Alicia?"

"She's nine. She suffers from ALS."

"Also known as Lou Gehrig's disease?"

"Yes . . . that's another name for it."

"May I approach the witness, Your Honor?"

"You may," said Yamamoto.

Camila handed Aldama two small pictures, while Thelma used the courtroom's projector to display the same pictures onto a big screen for everyone to see.

"Is that Alicia?"

Aldama got teary-eyed. "Yes. That's my Alicia."

"Who takes care of her while you're over here in Houston working?"

"My parents. They're there in the picture . . . by her bedside."

Camila studied one of the pictures. "Can you describe your home for the jury?"

The jurors were glued to the pictures up on the screen.

"It's a mud hut with dirt floors and sticks for a roof. A one-room shack, but my baby *does* have a hospital bed. I sent my folks money so they could buy it for her. With the money I used to send, they would also buy her medications and take her to the doctor . . . hours away, in Tampico. She will need a tracheotomy, soon. Without it, she will die."

"Is that why you came to Houston to work?"

Aldama's head was hanging low. "Yes. I snuck across to find work and to keep my Alicia alive. Someone at work knew of my predicament. They said I could make good money if I drove a car down to the border. That was gonna be the money for Alicia's treatment. That's why I did it. If she doesn't get the tracheotomy. . . .her situation will turn fatal. Her mother already abandoned her—us. . . . I was not going to abandon my girl. I'm all she has."

"Move to admit the pictures, Your Honor."

"Was the government provided with copies prior to trial?" asked Yamamoto.

"They sure were, Your Honor," explained Camila. "It was part of our reciprocal discovery packet."

"Mr. Nutley," inquired Yamamoto, "any objection?"

Nutley sprang up. "No, Your Honor."

Nutley, Fox and Griffin knew the real battle was ahead. The way Rico had testified, he'd left the door wide open, and who knew what Camila Harrison would push through.

"They'll be admitted."

"May I publish the pictures to the jury?"

"You may."

Camila handed the female juror closest to her the pictures of Aldama's family. She gave them a few minutes to pass them around and inspect them, and then returned to her direct examination.

"Could you have driven many more vehicles to the border, as McKenzie and Barrera claimed?"

"No."

"Why not? Please explain to the ladies and gentlemen of the jury why that was impossible."

"I'm here illegally," clarified Aldama. "I was going to do one trip, get paid and go home, never come back. I was planning on getting my Alicia the operation she needed, so she wouldn't die."

"I still don't understand," said Camila.

Aldama focused on the jury. "I knew that driving to South Texas meant I would not be able to come back up to Houston."

"Is that because of the checkpoints?"

"Correct."

"So, if McKenzie and Barrera testified that you all had done these trips before . . . what does that tell you?"

"They're lying. *They* may have done the trip before, but not with me. For me, it was a one-shot deal. I was gonna go back home, to Mexico. I couldn't have come back to Houston even if I wanted to . . . I have no documents."

Camila shook her head. "No papers."

"Correct."

"But you had a driver's license?"

"Yes. McKenzie and Barrera gave it to me. I have no idea where they got it. They said they had lots of them and that I looked like the guy in the photo. I was supposed to memorize the information on the license," explained Aldama.

"Let's talk about the traffic stop, okay?"

"Okay," answered Aldama.

All of the jury members suddenly sat up straight and started paying closer attention. Nutley, Fox, Dot and Forbes noticed this. They also sat up straight.

"You heard Agent Rico testify that the Odessa agents are the best of the best. They're honest and truthful . . . and what have you . . . "

"Objection!" cried Nutley. "Odessa is not on trial here. It's this defendant who's on trial, Your Honor," he said, pointing at the witness.

"What's the objection?" Camila asked.

"What *is* the objection?" followed Yamamoto.

"The objection? The objection is . . . " Nutley muttered, "Irrelevant and prejudicial!"

"Overruled," said Yamamoto.

"You still remember my question, Mr. Aldama? Were members of the Odessa unit who testified lying?" asked Camila.

"Yes."

"And was Agent Bergendahl lying when he said he stopped the Tahoe because there was a broken plate light?"

"Yes, he was lying."

"And how do you know that?"

"Because McKenzie and Barrera had me video the Tahoe's condition before we left."

"So . . . it appeared like they knew what they were doing."

"Yes. They'd done the trip many times before, it was obvious. They asked me to use my cell phone to shoot the video. All the lights were working; brake lights, stop lights, turn signals . . . everything. McKenzie and Barrera didn't want any trouble."

"Where's that cell phone now? Do you know?"

Aldama shook his head. "I wish I knew . . . I'd figured the agents kept it. I don't know what happened to it. Just like I don't know what happened to my wallet, my chain and locket with Alicia's picture . . . and my cash—fifty bucks, to be exact."

"Let me show you this tally sheet," continued Camila as she handed Aldama the exhibit, "does it mention your cell phone, wallet or your chain and locket?"

"No," Aldama replied, "it does not."

"And you're sure you had a cell phone, a wallet, some cash and the chain and locket?"

"Absolutely. In fact, the fake license was in my wallet. I don't know why there's mention of one thing, but not the other," Aldama speculated.

After that last answer, Camila glanced over at the prosecution's table. Nutley, Fox and Griffin could be seen scribbling and exchanging messages on their yellow pads.

She had asked the question for a reason. It was an important point that needed to be made: if irrelevant items such as these were missing, then other things cash, drugs or weapons were also very likely to go missing.

"Now, let me ask you, did you know the Tahoe had cash?"

"I knew these guys moved money, I'm not going to lie. How much was in there? I couldn't tell you. No idea."

"Did you know what you were doing was wrong?"

Aldama started tearing up. "Yes, I know I did wrong and I've made my peace with God." He paused and wiped the moisture away with his shirt sleeve. "If He doesn't want me to see my little Alicia again . . . then there's nothing . . . I . . . can . . . do."

"Would you like some tissues?" Camila asked.

Aldama waved her away. He finished using his shirt sleeve to wipe the tears. "I'm okay."

"How much is your daughter's operation? How much does it cost, do you know?"

"It was three thousand dollars for the hospital . . . eight thousand for the surgeon. I was promised twenty thousand dollars to drive the Tahoe to Brownsville . . . that was all gonna be for Alicia and her aftercare."

"If she doesn't get the operation . . . how long would she have to live?"

Aldama started sobbing. He put his head between his hands. "Doctors said nine or twelve months, maybe. Soon, she will no longer be able to breathe on her own."

"I can't imagine what you must be going through, Mr. Aldama," said Camila. "It's obvious you love your little girl very, very much."

All Aldama could do was nod. His emotional pain was obvious.

The jurors, one and all, seemed to have been affected by Aldama's heart-rending testimony.

"Just a couple more questions, Mr. Aldama," Camila said, bringing her client back into focus. "Who was going to pay you?"

"McKenzie and Barrera had instructions to call a number. So they could pay me, or that's what I thought."

"Let me stop you. Who is *They*?"

"Don't know. Whoever would answer their call, I guess. I was told someone would come meet us at a Walmart parking lot, pick up the Tahoe and pay us right after the call was made. Then we would go our own separate ways."

"How much money was really in the Tahoe? Do you know?"

"No clue."

"Who could tell us? Any idea?"

"Maybe McKenzie and Barrera know the real owners of the money."

Camila appeared satisfied with her client's answers. "Have you been honest with the jury?"

"Yes."

"You have told the truth?"

"Yes, the whole truth. *Todita la verdad*." He did the sign of the cross, kissed his fingers and then looked up to the heavens.

"Pass the witness," announced Camila.

Aldama's defense team soon learned that Nutley wasn't going down without a fight. There was no need to cross-examine Aldama on what Harrison had already asked. Nutley was prepared to push the boundaries, see how much he could get away with *outside* the scope of Harrison's direct examination. Nothing would please him more than to have his way with Aldama, to cut him up and skewer him through like a shish kabob.

"Mr. Aldama," started Nutley, "you admit, do you not, that you have violated the criminal laws of the United States of America?"

"Yes, sir. I did," answered Aldama. "I admit that."

"First, you entered the United States illegally, did you not?"

"Yes, sir."

"You didn't have permission to be in the United States, correct?"

"That's right. I didn't have a visa, if that's what you're asking."

"Or a passport, right?"

Aldama turned to Yamamoto. "That's right. No passport either."

"And when you started working in Houston . . . you didn't have a work permit, did you?"

"No work permit, sir. You're right."

Camila got up to object. "Judge, just to be fair. I should object to all these matters, because none of them were brought out during my direct examination. However, I want the record to reflect that, I'm not objecting in accordance with Mr. Aldama's promise to this jury," she looked at the jurors, "he promised to be completely truthful. And as such, he will not waffle or avoid answering any of Mr. Nutley's questions. But just for the record, this line of questioning is totally improper and outside the scope of direct."

"Are you objecting?" Yamamoto asked, looking confused.

"No, Your Honor," said Camila. "I just wanted to make a point . . . for the record. Hopefully the court gives me the same courtesy if need be."

"Ha! What courtesy?" asked Nutley.

Camila was ready to make a point. "To ask questions—dumb questions . . . for the sake of asking questions," replied Camila. "Questions that have absolutely nothing to do with the direct examination. We're just asking to be treated the same. That's all."

She sat down.

Yamamoto gave Camila a stern look, but then instructed, "Carry on, Mr. Nutley."

"And you didn't pay any taxes on the income you made during those six years while you worked here in the USA, did you?"

"No, sir, I did not."

"Were you using somebody else's fake papers?"

"Yes, sir, I was."

"Did you pay into Medicare or Social Security?"

"No, sir. My employer . . . Driller Construction USA . . . I think it's a subsidiary of Schreiber Oil and Gas Limited—I want to say it's owned by the Vice President of the United States . . . "

"Objection! Non-responsive."

"They paid me cash, under the table," Aldama muttered. "That's the truth."

Yamamoto admonished the witness. "Mr. Aldama, if there's an objection, you're supposed to wait until the court makes a ruling, you hear?"

"I'm sorry, Your Honor. I didn't know."

"The previous response will be stricken from the record," ordered Yamamoto, "and the jury is instructed to disregard it."

Nutley resumed his cross–examination. "And you know, do you not, that helping somebody do something illegal, like conspiring to transport illegal cash to get it out of the country, is a crime that can subject you to a lengthy jail sentence, right?"

"Now I know that," clarified Aldama. "At the time I was told if something happened I would probably get probation. I had no clue the penalties were so severe."

Aldama looked at the jury and shrugged.

Nutley smirked. "And you agree with me, do you not, that you conspired with McKenzie and Barrera to help launder currency . . . and that that money came from drug trafficking?"

"I don't know for sure if the money came from drug trafficking, sir. But I did suspect we were doing something illegal. There's no denying it."

Nutley pushed for the answer he was looking for: "But you did conspire with the other two co-defendants to drive the Tahoe to South Texas, correct?"

"Yes, sir, I agreed to help drive."

Nutley paused and looked at his notes. After about thirty seconds, he moved in for the kill. "Let me ask you this: If you were me, in charge of enforcing the laws of the United States of America . . . and I was you," Nutley said, to the dismay of Fox and Dot.

"If I was a federal attorney?" asked Aldama.

"Yes," replied Nutley. "If you were in my place . . . and I was in your place . . . what would you want to see happen to me?"

"I . . . I . . . " mumbled Aldama. He was not prepared for such a question, but he had to be honest. That was the implied covenant he had made with the jurors.

Nutley clarified his question. "What would you do to me for coming into the country illegally? Or if you'd caught me working without a permit? Overstaying my welcome? Not paying taxes? Laundering money? Helping a drug-trafficking organization move millions in currency? Conspiring with others to violate the anti-laundering laws of this country? You want me to keep going?"

"No, sir. I got it."

Nutley stared at the witness. Silence fell over the courtroom. "What would you do to me, Mr. Aldama? I ask you."

Aldama hung his head low. He was struggling with the loaded question.

"Your Honor," pushed Nutley, "would you instruct the witness to answer the question. It really is a simple question."

Yamamoto stared at Aldama.

The jurors waited in anticipation.

Aldama finally muttered, "If I was you . . . and you were me . . . I'd send you to prison, for a long time."

"No further questions," Nutley announced, satisfied with his on-point performance.

FORTY

"Call your next witness," ordered Judge Yamamoto.

Thelma got up from her chair slowly. She looked around the courtroom, smiled at the jurors and announced, "Your Honor, the defense calls private investigator Nicolás 'Monty' Montanaro."

Camila turned to look at Nutley's table and caught him looking back. She winked at him. He squinted as he stared hard at Camila, and then frowned. This was it, Nutley knew; she was about to throw her best punch.

"Approach the bench!" ordered Yamamoto out of the blue. The judge then turned his attention to the Electric Recording Officer officer and spoke to him off the record.

Camila, Nutley, Thelma, Fox and Griffin gathered at the bench conference.

Yamamoto locked eyes with Thelma. "Mrs. Issa, what exactly are you having Mr. Montanaro testify to?"

"Monty? He'll testify as to his qualifications, experience and involvement in the case," she whispered.

"*Like?*"

Fox, Nutley and Griffin inched forward.

Thelma added, "The things he uncovered. You know . . . general, basic information."

"He better not get into matters dealing with a confidential informant," admonished Yamamoto. "I'm warning you."

"He knows that's off limits, Your Honor," Thelma replied.

Yamamoto then waved everybody back to their seats. "Back on the record. Please continue, Mrs. Issa."

Thelma walked over to the podium, planted herself firmly in front of it, put on her reading glasses, gave her notes one last glance and began. "Please introduce yourself to the ladies and gentlemen of the jury."

"My name is Nicolás Montanaro," said the investigator, "but my friends call me Monty."

"Did you assist in the investigation of this case so as to help prepare the defense of Mr. Aldama?"

"Yes, I did."

"And what sort of training are you required to undergo to be an investigator in the state of Texas?"

"You cannot have any criminal history, for starters," explained Monty, "and you have to be mentally competent. You don't have to have a college education necessarily . . . but it helps, especially if you want to open your own agency. You have to either take a two-hundred-hour course, or have worked investigations for at least a year . . . like an apprenticeship. And you have to pass a background check and then apply and pay for the license."

"And how did you gain *your* experience? Or did you do the two-hundred-hour course?" asked Thelma.

"I came up in the insurance business. I started working for an insurance company in high school—back in New Mexico. Eventually, I was assigned to the investigations department and got to work with some folks who were really good. I did that for *ten years* . . . until I became the senior investigator. Then, one day, I woke up and decided I wanted to do a different kind of work, plus I wanted to live somewhere else; away from the desert and near the coast. That's how I ended up doing contract work for the Mexican consulate here in Houston."

"And you've testified in court before?"

"Yes, many times."

"For both defense and plaintiffs?"

"Correct."

"I'm curious: where are you from?"

He smiled at the jurors. "Aghhh, that always comes up. Glad you asked. My mother was Olmecan Indian, and my father was a crazy gringo who used to import vanilla beans from Veracruz, Mexico. He was from New Mexico and would travel to Veracruz to buy the beans to make vanilla extract for cooking. You may have seen the bottles . . . La Especial brand. That used to be his company. Anyway, I was born in New Mexico, but was raised in both places; Veracruz and the USA."

"So *that's* how your parents met?"

"Judge," complained Nutley, "is counsel ever going to ask something relevant here? About the case, perhaps?"

Yamamoto warned Thelma, "We don't have all day, Counselor. Let's move it along, please."

Thelma looked at her yellow pad. "Okay, let's dive right in, shall we?"

"Okay," replied Monty, smiling from ear to ear.

"What did you find out about the Odessa Task Force? Does it reek of corruption like the Panama Unit down in South Texas?"

"Objection!" yelled Nutley. "This is improper, Your Honor. There's no foundation. And—once again—Odessa is not on trial. I repeat, it is Vicente Aldama who is on trial!"

"May I reply, Your Honor?" Thelma asked, timidly.

"You may," said Yamamoto, "but first approach the bench." All the attorneys approached the bench simultaneously.

Thelma spoke first. "The government opened the door when Mr. Nutley was examining Agent Rico and Agent Rico said, on his own, without any pressure, that the guys from Odessa were honest, and reputable and honorable. Well . . . that's not entirely true."

"I remember something to that effect," said Yamamoto, rubbing his chin. He remembered Thelma Issa from his teaching days. He was proud of his former student, who now was a law professor. "Rico *was* tooting Odessa's horn, wasn't he?"

"Yes, he was" Thelma continued, "and part of a juror's job is to determine the credibility of all the witnesses. Your Honor knows it is the jury who gets to gauge their veracity. And right now, they think that what Bergendahl and Rico—who are members of Odessa, remember—said must be the Gospel . . . the honest truth.

We're prepared to give the jury another version, so they can have a complete picture and then make up their minds. They should be allowed to figure out who is telling the truth . . . and who is not. As it stands, the court is aware that Bergendahl lied."

"Your Honor," Nutley intervened, "there's no foundation. This is improper . . . and the defendant was caught with almost a million dollars in illegal cash, drug money. That's who is on trial here, not the law-abiding heroes that work for Odessa!"

"Overruled," Yamamoto said, smiling. "I'll allow it. Please sit down, Mr. Nutley. Continue, Mrs. Issa."

Thelma returned to the podium.

Nutley knew that had it been Camila Harrison asking the questions, maybe Judge Yamamoto would have sustained his objection.

Monty didn't wait for any coaxing from Thelma. "There have been several lawsuits against Odessa for all kinds of abuses and false arrests, even illegal searches."

"Can you be more specific?" Thelma asked.

"For example . . . they've gone to the wrong house, weapons drawn, without warrants, while searching for a suspect, who, it turns out . . . is not there because it's the wrong house!"

"And what happened?"

"They tore the house upside down, put the homeowners and children in handcuffs, and when they realized their mistake, they tried to cover it up."

"And then?"

"They got sued for violating people's rights. There's been at least three such lawsuits, what they call 'Section 1983' actions. Others never made it to court because they were settled privately, without making waves . . . under the table, so to speak."

"Do you have case numbers? The names of the plaintiffs? How do we know what you're saying is true?"

Monty pulled out several folded sheets of paper from his coat pocket. "Here are the docket reports for each of the cases that were actually filed."

"When you say 'cases that were actually filed,' what do you mean?"

"That there may have been other instances where the parties let it go, didn't file lawsuits."

Nutley got up to object. "Your Honor, this is not evidence. That last point is just hearsay . . . totally unreliable."

"Care to respond, Counsel?" asked Yamamoto of Mrs. Issa.

"I think if you allow me to ask Mr. Monty one question, that will clear up any confusion on the part of the government, Your Honor."

"Go ahead," said Yamamoto. "I want to hear this."

Nutley, Forbes, Fox and Griffin were back in a huddle. Nutley emerged and said, "Your Honor, can we take a five-minute break?"

"After the next question. I want to see what Mr. Montanaro has to say," replied Yamamoto.

Nutley sat down, not liking what he was hearing.

"Mr. Montanaro, look at the docket reports," ordered Thelma, "and tell us the names of the litigants, the case numbers and the locations where those lawsuits were filed, please."

Monty unfolded the papers, found his place and started reading. "This one is *Roberta Scott v. City of Wharton and Dwayne Bergendahl, et al* . . . Case No. 12-CV-135. It was filed in federal court in Victoria, Texas. Another one is *Javier García Moreno v. Fort Bend Sheriff's Department, Odessa HIDTA Task Force, et al* . . . it was filed in Corpus Christi, Texas. And this final one, *Claudia Moore v. City of Sugarland, et al*, was filed here, in Houston . . . in federal court. You want the case numbers?"

"No, that's okay," said Thelma. "Were you able to tell what happened in each of those cases?"

At the mention of the Moore case, Yamamoto perked up. "Mrs. Issa, I think you've made your point. The jury has heard enough, let's move on."

The defense had learned that the Moore case had been litigated in front of Judge Yamamoto. This piece of information explained why Yamamoto had wanted the Aldama case to go away. The task force was a thorn in the government's side, something the Honorable Judge Colt Yamamoto had known all along. It was inevitable that sooner or later the public would catch on. It was a PR nightmare.

"Thank you, Your Honor," said Nutley, sounding relieved, if for a moment.

"What else did you find out?" Thelma asked.

"Some agents weren't reporting or turning over all the contraband seized," Monty answered.

"May we approach the bench, Your Honor?!" begged Nutley.

"Come on up," ordered Yamamoto, and then, turning his attention to the jurors, he said, "Let's take a ten-minute break while the attorneys confer."

"All rise for the jury!" ordered the marshal. "We'll be in recess!"

"I'm going to cut you off, Mrs. Issa," said Yamamoto. "You're starting to stray into dangerous territory."

Camila's temperature was rising. "You can't be serious, Your Honor! Agent Rico opened the door and you're not going to let us do our job? Why do you insist on tying our hands? How is that fair?!"

"Watch it!" yelled Yamamoto. "Look, Mrs. Issa has already made her point, Ms. Harrison. The jury has figured out that the Odessa Task Force has issues. Why beat a dead horse?"

Thelma grabbed Camila by the elbow and pulled her back. They needed to be smart about how to handle Yamamoto and Nutley. The last thing they needed was to anger Yamamoto and risk him not allowing Camila to call the next witness.

"Not a problem, Your Honor," Thelma said, happy to accommodate the court. "I'll wrap it up. But to be fair, if Mr. Nutley opens the door during his cross-examination, I should be allowed to address those issues or clear things up."

Yamamoto looked at Nutley. "That sounds fair. Mr. Nutley, what do you think?"

"Fine!" huffed the US Attorney for the Southern District of Texas.

The rest of the day was spent with Monty on the witness stand. Nutley was careful and astute in the way he cross-examined Montanaro. He focused mostly on the investigator's credentials, training and education. Afraid to get into matters that would allow Aldama's counsel to come back and destroy what was left of Odessa's credibility, Nutley treaded lightly.

Miraculously, Monty had managed to regurgitate all of the Miranda warnings to Nutley without any problems. The only hiccup came when Nutley covered Monty's knowledge and understanding in the area of "Surveillance Law," but after a quick redirect by Thelma, she'd been able to rehabilitate Monty's credibility. Whether the investigator's testimony alone had changed jurors' minds was still up for debate.

Two hours later, after Monty had left the witness stand, Judge Yamamoto called it a day and asked the parties to have their proposed jury charges ready by the morning. Since there appeared to be only one witness left to testify for the defense, there was no need to subject the jurors to more punishment. Yamamoto instructed the parties to be ready to deliver closing arguments after lunch. He expected the jury to start deliberations by 3 p.m. He wanted the court to receive the verdict, one way or another, before the end of the day.

FORTY-ONE

"Good morning," announced Yamamoto. "Are we ready to proceed?"

It was Thursday morning and the courtroom was packed. The jury was in the box. The government's lawyers were sitting at their table. Julio, Alan, Mrs. Landry and Freddie, plus Thelma's old colleagues and students from the Houston Pan American School of Law had come to watch the spectacle. Over in one corner of the courtroom, Camila's parents, Darin and Lorena, sat side by side, holding hands. Gustavo Govela sat next to them.

Camila and her client, however, were sitting at their table alone. There was no sign of Thelma anywhere.

Yamamoto noticed this. "Ms. Harrison, where's your second chair?"

"Good morning, Your Honor," replied Camila, calmly. "Mrs. Issa is outside, Your Honor."

"But we're supposed to start right now," replied Yamamoto, "or is she not planning to assist in Mr. Aldama's defense? She needs to be here."

"She probably got sidetracked, Your Honor."

"Doing what?"

"She's probably still talking to a reporter," explained Camila. "I'll send Julio to fetch her."

Yamamoto raised an eyebrow. "A reporter?"

Camila motioned for Julio to get Thelma. She then turned around and continued explaining. "Yes, Your Honor. A reporter from the *New York Times* and maybe even a blogger, too, if I'm not mistaken. I want to say the reporter's name is Nora Edelstein, and the blogger is Lou Mowbray. She covers stories dealing with police corruption, he writes about legal issues. They heard about the case and the Odessa unit and decided to cover it . . . I guess."

Yamamoto showed his displeasure. "Are they planning to come and sit in the courtroom?"

"I guess," said Camila. "I don't know."

"Your Honor!" cried Nutley. "The rules of ethics prohibit attorneys from discussing any aspect of any case with outside sources while the case is being tried. It can have a prejudicial effect on a jury . . . and . . . "

Right at that moment, Thelma walked into the courtroom with Mowbray and Edelstein in tow. The pair sat down in the back of the courtroom, near Camila's parents.

"Sorry about that," Thelma said as she took her spot at the counsel's table. "Ms. Edelstein stopped me out in the hallway, Your Honor. She wanted to know if you had your own rules regarding reporters in the courtroom. I explained to her that I was unaware of any local rule prohibiting the media from reporting from inside the courthouse and that your chamber rules were silent on the topic. That's all."

"You didn't discuss any aspect of the case with her?" asked Yamamoto.

"No, Your Honor," answered Thelma, "of course not. In fact, I've never met Ms. Edelstein or Mr. Mowbray before."

Yamamoto seemed bothered by the sudden presence of the reporter and blogger in his courtroom, but he was eager to finish the case. It was time to move it along. "Call your next witness!"

"We call Armando Franco," called out Camila.

The marshal went outside to call the witness.

Nutley shot to his feet. "We object, Your Honor. We had no notice the defense was going to call this witness. This constitutes an unfair surprise, a trial by ambush. This is a grave injustice!"

"We just found him. He's a rebuttal witness," Camila replied. "One of the evidence custodians for the Odessa Task Force . . . one that the government conveniently left out when they listed their witnesses for this case at the trial's beginning."

Camila turned to see if Edelstein and Mowbray were paying attention while the marshal delivered the witness to the witness stand. Judge Yamamoto signaled for Franco to wait, not to sit down yet. The twelve jurors were all focused on Franco, who sported a western suit and boots.

"Since this trial started, Your Honor, we've come to find out that there were a few custodians of evidence; Rico, Leal, González and Franco. But the government conveniently only gave us Rico. Why was that, I ask you?"

"Judge!" cried Nutley. "I resent the accusation . . . "

Camila waved a stack of documents in her left hand. "This morning, Your Honor, we e-filed our brief in support for allowing this rebuttal testimony. We just found this witness and he *is* a rebuttal witness as defined by the Federal Rules of Criminal Evidence . . . what some would call a 'textbook example.'"

Yamamoto glanced over at the reporter, busy writing things on her pad. He then glanced at the jurors, who were murmuring among themselves. He then turned to his computer screen and saw the electronic filing Camila had just discussed.

He was still shaking his head when he spoke. "Agent Rico opened not one door, but *several* doors when he took the stand. He also put the Odessa unit on a pedestal."

"But Judge," muttered Nutley, "this isn't right . . . ."

"Mr. Franco," ordered Yamamoto, "please come up and raise your right hand. Let me swear you in."

Nutley fell into his chair.

Camila began. "Mr. Franco, how long did you work for the Odessa High Intensity Drug Trafficking Area Task Force?"

"Three years."

"And during those three years, did you work the evidence locker room?"

"Yes."

"You no longer work for Odessa?"

"That's right. I left some time back."

"Now, let me show you this tally sheet. Are these your initials?"

"Yes, A for Armando, F for Franco."

"How much money was seized the night indicated on the sheet?"

"One million eight hundred and fifty thousand dollars."

"And did you write that figure on this tally sheet: one million eight hundred and fifty thousand dollars?"

"Yes, I did."

"You're sure . . . that the money added up to one million plus."

"Yes."

Camila gave him a look. "To be *extremely* clear, you wrote that figure: one million . . . eight hundred and fifty thousand. Correct?"

"Yes."

"So this would mean . . . that Sargeant Bergendahl and the agents working with Odessa that night on September 16th, 2014—you included—seized almost *two* million dollars?"

"Yes."

"Are you sure it was close to two million dollars and not eight hundred and fifty thousand?"

"I'm sure."

Camila stood at the podium. She rubbed her chin. She turned to look at the jurors. "Eight hundred fifty thousand is still a lot of money, isn't it?"

Franco nodded. "Yes. Yes, it is."

"Thanks. That'll be all. Pass the witness."

<hr />

Nutley could not comprehend what was happening. Why had Camila Harrison stopped her direct examination of the witness midway, so suddenly? It didn't matter. His instincts took over. Nutley went on the offensive right away.

"Sir, do you know what can happen to you if you commit perjury?"

"Yes."

"And what can happen? Please tell the ladies and gentlemen of the jury."

"I could go to prison. That's why I wouldn't do it. I'd rather quit my job first than do something illegal . . . or commit perjury."

"And here, this morning, you've sworn to tell the truth, have you not?"

"Sure did."

"You were sworn in by Judge Yamamoto?"

Franco shifted in his chair and turned to look at the judge. "Yes, I promised and swore to tell the truth, the whole truth and nothing but the truth."

"And when you were on the force, you had also taken an oath, had you not?"

"Yes, I took the oath of honor."

"Now, I want to ask you something. When you took that oath of honor, you promised never to betray your badge or your profession, did you not?"

"Yes, sir."

"And you swore to never compromise your integrity or your character, isn't that the truth?"

"Yes, I did swear to that *and* to never betray the public trust."

Nutley turned to look at the jurors, make sure they were paying attention. "And you also swore to hold yourself accountable for your actions, correct?"

"Yes, sir. And I also promised to uphold the laws of the United States, the laws of the State of Texas and whatever agency I got to work for."

"But, here, on this tally sheet . . . you placed your initials, correct?"

"Yes, sir."

"I mean, these *are* your initials, right?"

"Yes, sir."

"Armando Franco?"

"Yes, sir."

"Not 'Mando Franco,' but 'Armando Franco.' You with me?"

"That's right, that's my name. Those are my initials: A. F."

Nutley waved the tally sheet up in the air. "And you, along with Bergendahl and the others, by placing your names and signatures here, you're all saying that what's written on this tally sheet is the truth, are you not?"

"That's correct."

"Now, several weeks ago, when you and Sgt. Bergendahl were processing the scene involving this defendant, and you processed the Tahoe for evidence, inventoried the contents found at the scene . . . by signing this tally sheet, you were swearing that the items on the sheet were the truth, did you not?"

"Yes, sir."

"In essence, you were saying everything was accurate, right?"

"Right."

"And by attesting that the tally sheet was correct, you were, in essence, swearing . . . just like you did here today . . . that you were telling the truth, correct?"

"Yes."

"Now, let me ask you something else."

"Okay."

"You do understand the importance of telling the truth, do you not?"

"Yessir, I do."

Nutley was shaking his head. "I don't think you do, Mr. Franco, but I will tell you. This trial is to get to the truth, and this good jury is here to hear the truth—because a lot is at stake. People's careers, reputations and even their future are on the line here today. Everybody here is relying on your oath. You see that?"

"Yes, sir. I understand completely."

"I don't think you do." Nutley shoved the tally sheet into Armando's hands. "So, which is correct?"

Franco stared at the tally sheet. "With all due respect, sir . . . you have to understand . . . let me explain."

"No, sir," Nutley snapped back, "I get to ask the questions, you hear?!"

Franco sank into his chair. "Okay . . . yes, sir. My apologies."

"You want to barge in here and destroy the good reputations of many special agents who risk their lives and limbs day in and day out to keep our highways and communities safe, to keep the drug dealers out and the money launderers behind bars. You, sir . . . you now want to come in here and say that on the night of September 16th, 2014, the Odessa Task Force seized one million eight hundred and fifty thousand! So, which one is the lie?!"

"Sir, if you would . . . "

"Now you're telling us it was one million and eight hundred-fifty thousand, when this tally sheet, with your initials on it, says otherwise. This tally sheet says eight hundred and fifty thousand only."

Franco grabbed the tally sheet and studied it. "They lied, sir."

"They lied?! No! You lied! You come in here, and now you want to be the hero by any means necessary."

Franco gave Camila a stare, but Camila didn't flinch.

Nutley continued pounding on Franco. "So you come in here and you want everybody to believe what you're saying is true. But it's not . . . because *you're* the liar!"

"This tally sheet . . . " Franco held it out.

Nutley snatched it from him. "Do you realize the magnitude of your lying? Can you see that?"

"If you'd let me explain . . . " Franco shrugged. There was no getting through to Nutley.

"You swore on this form that the Odessa Task Force seized eight hundred and fifty thousand dollars. You signed it."

"But that's not what I wrote," blurted out Franco.

"But you signed it along with the others," Nutley pointed out. "These are your initials, are they not?"

"Yes," replied Franco, "but that's not what I wrote."

The jurors inched closer to the edge of their seats. So did all the members in the audience. Yamamoto did too. The tension in the room was reaching its boiling point.

"For the love of God, don't you know when to stop?!"

"That's not what I wrote, sir. If you'd *just* let me explain."

Although the little voice inside Nutley's head kept telling him to be careful, to tread lightly, his ego had gotten the better of him. "What do you mean that's not what you wrote?!"

Nutley was not prepared for the answer. Suddenly, something registered in his brain and a look of total disbelief came over him. Over at the prosecution table, Griffin, Forbes and Fox had stopped breathing. They could sense what was about to happen. A strange quiet engulfed the entire courtroom. It was as if time had stood still.

"I didn't write a dollar sign. I just wrote in the numbers '1-8-5-0-0-0-0.' Sgt. Bergendahl changed the number 1 to a dollar sign. Let me show you," Franco took the tally sheet from Nutley's hands. He quickly pointed at the paper. "The first 1 was changed to a $. They kept the extra million, Rico, Sarge, . . . the others."

"The others?"

"That's why I quit. I didn't want any part of it. It was too much for me."

There was a collective gasp in the courtroom, but the witness' words failed to register in Nutley's mind. Yamamoto looked confused. Had the witness single-handedly exposed the rampant corruption of the ill-conceived drug interdiction task forces?

Nutley was barely able to mumble, "You mean this was not a number sign . . . ?"

"That's right," said Franco. "Sergeant Bergendahl made me *change* the '1' to a number sign, Rico knows."

The collective gasp turned to whispers and moans and groans. Judge Yamamoto banged his gavel on the bench. "Order! Order in the courtroom!"

"Oh c'mon! Do you really expect us to believe that?"

"I'm telling the truth!"

"And what happened to the rest of the money?"

Franco shrugged. "You'd have to ask Sarge . . . and the others."

"And how do you remember it so clearly? What you've just told us here is nothing but lies and lies and more lies!"

"They're not lies, sir. This happened back in September."

"Hell yeah they're lies, you insolent perjurer! Let's see . . . where's the proof?"

"I kept a copy." Franco reached for his wallet and pulled out a folded piece of paper. After he unfolded it, he waved it in front of jury. "See, this is a print out of a photo I took of the original tally sheet . . . the one that had the true figure. You can tell it's the same tally sheet because they're date-stamped and the initials are exactly the same. The only difference is that one has the 1 . . . and the other now has a dollar sign. It's clear, the 1 was turned into that symbol."

"Objection," cried Nutley, trying to appear composed. "This is hearsay!"

"I also took pictures. They're in my phone." Franco reached into his pants pocket. Do you want me to show you?" He pulled out his cellphone.

"Sustained," said Yamamoto, knowing full well that, at this stage in the game, sustaining the objection was futile.

"I even took a selfie with all the bundles of cash behind me. I did that when Sarge wasn't looking," Franco blurted out.

"Why would you take pictures?"

"For protection," said Franco.

"Protection?"

"Yes," Franco answered. "You see, all my life, I just wanted to be a policeman, a good cop, and when the opportunity came to work for HIDTA, I jumped on it. The job was right up my alley, what I always wanted to do. But then reality set in; the captains and sergeants in the task force weren't accountable to anyone and there was no oversight. They started cutting corners. No one was watching, they had no one to report to, and I started getting worried. At first, the guys were just skimming a couple thousand . . . here . . . there . . . then it was more. Then it was hundreds of thousands *and* drugs and weapons. The seized drugs . . . Sarge started selling to rival gangs for more money. So, yeah, every time Sarge told me to change things, I kept copies. This wasn't the first time Sarge, Rico and the others kept a stash for themselves; that's why I left."

"And you expect us to believe you?"

"Look," added Franco, "after Sarge started selling portions of the seized dope to rival gangs, members of the task force started receiving death threats. Why do you think Beto left? What do you *really* think happened to Stephen Leal?"

"You're lying!" Nutley yelled, getting in Franco's face.

"I don't care what you believe, sir!" Franco shot back at Nutley. "All I know is that all I ever wanted to be was a cop, you get me?! A good cop, one of the white hats, and now that's been taken from me. Do you think anyone will hire me now that the entire world knows I came forward? There's a code, a code of silence, and I've broken it."

Nutley tossed his copy on the floor and announced, "I have no further questions."

Yamamoto addressed Camila. "Ms. Harrison? Anything?"

"We would move to admit the copies of the photos of the tally sheet and the selfie into evidence, Your Honor," replied Camila. "Defendant's exhibits numbers 4 and 5."

"Anything else?"

"May we publish defendant's exhibits 4 and 5 to the jury, Your Honor?"

"You most certainly may," Yamamoto replied. "Anything else?"

Camila stood in front of the jury box, handing over the copies of the pictures to the jurors for their viewing. "Yes, one last thing. Mr. Franco, what would Sergeant Bergendahl do with cell phones taken from the defendants. Do you know?"

"He'd go through them. If there was stuff that would help the case, he would submit them into evidence. If there was stuff to hurt the case, he'd scrub them clean and toss them in the trash."

"Thank you, Mr. Franco. That is all, Your Honor."

"Okay. Defendant's exhibits number 4 and 5 are admitted," ordered Yamamoto. "Mr. Nutley, anything else from the government?"

"Not from this witness," said Nutley.

Yamamoto then turned to the witness. "You're excused, sir."

FORTY-TWO

After Nutley delivered the government's closing argument, Camila Harrison left the security of the podium and, instead, planted herself in front of the three female jurors sitting in the front row of the jury box. She focused on them.

"On the coast of the Gulf of Mexico, in the Mexican State of Veracruz, there's a little fishing village called Las Higueras. It is near the Colipa River. It's a little, tiny town with almost eleven hundred inhabitants. Because it is so close to the gulf coast most of its residents eke out a meager existence by fishing the gulf's waters. Also, most of the residents are of Indian lineage. Of Olmeca descent, to be exact . . . kind of like Mr. Montanaro, the investigator you heard from during the trial. In fact, many of the residents of this tiny fishing village still speak their native Indian dialect as well as Spanish. People in this village live in shacks and huts and there are no fancy hotels, hospitals, exclusive shopping centers or restaurants, and, of course, there are no jobs, which means there are no opportunities, educational or otherwise. It is lonely and isolated. If you need serious medical attention, you are better off traveling to Tampico or the Mexican Capital."

Camila paused and turned to look at her client. She then continued.

"This is where Vicente Almada was born. He is the younger of two children. His older sister, Angélica . . . " Camila stopped and pointed her out in the crowd. The jury turned and caught a glimpse of her and Danny, holding hands, in the back of the court-room.

"Met a young Christian man doing mission work in Veracruz and fell in love and married. Danny is from Dallas. That is where they live, with their two children. Now, both Vicente and Angélica were born in poverty. And my client, although he barely managed to get a third-grade education, learned to fish and when he left home in search of a better life so that he could help provide for his loved ones, learned to work in landscaping, demolition and roof-ing. He even learned the English language. Vicente Aldama is a hard worker. Yes, he's been living in the United States illegally, but he's never once asked for a handout. He's never once asked for food stamps, or welfare, or tried to milk the system. And other than being sent back to Mexico once, he's never been convicted of a crime.

"Now, let's not forget, that Vicente also became a father at the young age of seventeen. When Alicia was born, she appeared to be a normal, precocious, healthy baby. Later on, as Alicia grew, Vicente and Alicia's mother discovered that Alicia was sick. After difficult trips to Tampico and the Mexican Capital, and numerous rounds of doctor visits and appointments, Alicia was diagnosed with ALS. It became such a burden caring for Alicia that her own mother abandoned her and my client. However, despite all the hardship, all the ups and downs, Vicente made the decision to never abandon his daughter. He was not going to give up on her and he was going to do whatever it took to take care of her and provide.

"Therefore, he decided to leave Alicia's side in order to go work and make money to provide for her and her medical care. It took an enormous amount of courage to leave. He risked life and limb to come to the US in search of work, so that he could send money home to care for his sick daughter. And all these years, while he was working in the States, he was keeping out of trouble and sending his money home, every week, without fail."

Camila paused and glanced at her notes on her yellow pad.

"Now, sometime back, Vicente received word that Alicia was not doing well. So, he did what any other parent who loves his children would do . . . he dropped everything and went back to Las Higueras to check on his daughter . . . "

This time, Camila stopped mid-sentence and glanced over at her own mother, Lorena. Lorena beamed a smile. Camila felt herself getting emotional, but quickly forced herself to remain composed.

"Back at home, Vicente receives terrible, devastating news. Little Alicia's throat muscles are being affected by the ALS . . . she's going to need an expensive procedure to help her with her breathing and will also need a ventilator to stay alive. Vicente decides to head back to the United States. He needs to continue to work in order to save money, so he can provide his daughter with the medical care she desperately needs. He gets arrested by Border Patrol and is deported back to Mexico. Now, some of us might give up right there and then. I know that if it was me, I may have called it a day. I would have gone back home and would have tried to keep Alicia as comfortable as possible. But Vicente, my client, is not one to quit. And he sneaks back across and makes it to Houston, where he finds work in construction. And he keeps working to try and save money to get her the operation she needs. But it is not enough. And when he hears that Alicia is getting sicker and that her breathing has become labored and more difficult, in an act of desperation, he agrees to drive the Tahoe back to the border. And this is when Vicente Almada's world collides with the Odessa Task Force."

Camila turned and faced Judge Yamamoto, "How much time do I have left, Your Honor?"

"Fifteen minutes," replied Yamamoto.

"Now, we'll get to talk about the agents that run the Odessa Task Force, and the corruption that runs rampant within its ranks," continued Camila, "and it's going to take a lot of courage for you, as jurors, to deal with the fact that this task force, made up of rogue elements, needs to be held accountable. And this gets me to my next point, something we need to cover, now that you've met the real criminals . . . think about this."

She pointed at the empty witness chair.

"Odessa's transgressions would have never surfaced, if not for Armando Franco, who came here and told you everything he knew about the Odessa unit. Also, think about the courage it takes to do something like that . . . for Mr. Franco to come forward and know that he would be black listed and never be able to work in law enforcement, ever again. He's now known as a whistleblower among law enforcement because he chose to do the right thing. Think how hard that must have been . . . to choose to do the right thing. The easy thing would have been . . . just keep quiet, deny that he ever witnessed anything and simply turn a blind eye. Today, I'm asking you to have the courage to do the right thing, instead of the easy thing. Today, my client, Vicente Aldama, begs you not to turn a blind eye. Please, whatever you do, do not simply *turn and look the other way* . . . "

Camila paused and let the words sink in. She focused on the female jurors.

"Today it's your turn to show courage. It is your turn to do the right thing. You get to choose. You have the power. By your verdict, you will let the world know that juries are either nothing more than the government's 'rubber stamp,' or juries can actually make a difference and help preserve the integrity of the criminal justice system. It's up to you, the jury. That's how important your decision will be here today. So, don't take it lightly. Don't turn a blind eye. Don't give Mr. Nutley the satisfaction and Sergeant Bergendahl a *'free pass.'*"

This time, Camila turned and pointed at Mr. Nutley and his posse. She then glared at Yamamoto.

"Because if you do that, it means that you're complicit, that you don't care that there's flagrant corruption in the government's ranks and that you're willing to accept their behavior. You don't really want to hold *your* government accountable. It means that you are guilty of willful blindness. Do you know what willful blindness means? It's all around us. Look at the banks and the housing meltdown in 2008. Everyone knew the banks were selling fraudulent, worthless, security-backed-mortgages but no one did anything about it. Look at the Catholic Church when it swept under the rug, decades of sexual abuse, and everyone turned a blind eye. Look at the gun violence plaguing our country and our children, getting killed left and right! Yet no one in Washington has the courage to do anything about it and, we, as a society—you and I included—let it go and hope somebody else fixes the problem. That, my friends, is willful blindness!

"Now, some people are willfully blind because they are in fear. Others don't think they can make a difference. Others don't want to be thought of as snitches or whistleblowers."

Camila now focused on the men jurors.

"So, I ask you, are you also going to turn a blind eye? Are you going to let Bergendahl get away with it? Are you going to have the courage to do the right thing? Or are you going to be one of those jurors that knows that something is wrong, but chooses not to speak? Chooses not to do anything about it? Are you going to show courage?"

Yamamoto interrupted Camila. "You have seven minutes, Counselor."

"Thank you," Camila replied, and continued with her closing argument, "now, today I ask you to be fair to both sides—not just to the government, but to the defense as well. My client is not asking for special treatment. We're not asking for sympathy or charity. All we want is for you to be fair; do what's right. Step up to the plate and be brave."

She walked over to her client and stood by his side.

"Mr. Aldama took the stand and told you the truth. He did not hide and he did not run. All his answers were truthful, honest and heartfelt. He could have invoked his constitutional right to remain silent but he didn't? He chose to face you, to come clean because even though he did what he did, and it happened to be a crime under the laws of our country, we all know *why* he did it. He did it to save his little girl, Alicia, or at least try to, and that took a lot of courage."

Camila signaled Thelma to put Alicia's pictures up on the big screen.

"Mr. Aldama did what he did in a moment of desperation, not because he's your typical criminal, but because he's a father trying to save his little girl's life."

Camila then signaled to Thelma to switch images and put the copies of both tally sheets up on the screen, that way the jurors and the audience could compare the original tally sheet and the one Bergendahl had tampered with.

"Can you live with yourself knowing that you could have sent Odessa and the government a message, but, instead, chose to do nothing? I would hope that you put my client's behavior on the scales of justice and weigh his actions against the government's actions. If the scales tilt lower for my client because his behavior was more criminal than the government's . . . then find him guilty. But if Bergendahl is the biggest crook, then set Mr. Aldama free."

Camila paused to see if what she said was sinking in. She stood there with her arms spread out like the scales of justice. She then turned and gave Nutley a quick look before turning back to face the jurors again.

"So, if the transgressions committed by the government, by the agents who are *supposed* to keep us safe and uphold the law, to look after us and make sure our constitutional rights are protected . . . if those transgressions weigh more heavily on their side and my client is less culpable . . . then I ask you to let my client go home to see Alicia, say his goodbyes. Allow him to hold his daughter again before she dies because that's exactly what is going to happen. It's tragic, but it's the truth. Without money, she will not get an operation and death is certain."

Camila bit her lower lip. Some of the jurors were getting emotional, as was Vicente Aldama. He was wiping away tears with his shirt's sleeve. Camila looked out into the gallery; there was not a single dry eye in the courtroom, save for those of Nutley and his team. They were stoic, pretending not to care.

Camila walked back to the podium. She picked up the tally sheet that had been tampered with. "Now, here's the problem, ladies and gentlemen. We have a government that wants you to overlook its faults, pretend nothing happened and send my client to prison. They don't want you to question anything. They want you to follow . . . and not think . . . or feel . . . *that's* what Mr. Nutley wants. And that's because that's the way things are 'supposed to be' and 'have always been,'" she said, putting air quotation marks around the words. "And if the government says so, then supposedly you need to do it. No questions asked. You're supposed to turn a blind eye."

Camila got quiet and started shaking her head, looking disgusted. In her right hand, she held the altered tally sheet. She walked over to Nutley's table and faced him. Nutley avoided her gaze. She then turned and looked at the female jurors.

"*And you say, 'No sir!'*" She slammed the exhibit down on the table in front of Nutley, Fox, Forbes and Griffin. "*Not today!*"

The loud noise made Nutley, Fox, Forbes and Griffin jump up.

"Today, you take this courtroom back. Today, you send a message to the government. You tell them, 'It's over. You're done.'"

Still hovering over the government's table, she continued. "With your verdict, you will send Mr. Nutley and his boys down at Odessa a loud message. You'll tell them that they will no longer be able to run roughshod over people. Imagine they did this to you; allow these thieves to just come into your house, throw you to the ground, search your house and handcuff your wife and kids, because they know you can't do anything about it. You will keep quiet—take it . . . never say a thing. Turn the other way. And these are the agents at Odessa that are supposed to be putting away the bad guys. But, it turns out, they're really just like the bad guys themselves, except they're worse because they have weapons and they hide behind a badge—and the press, which calls them heroes. They're untouchable. Because *they are* the federal government."

Camila got quiet again.

"Except, guess what?"

"What?" mouthed back a juror, obviously enthralled, as if Camila Harrison were speaking directly to him.

Nutley was really worried now. Were the jurors with Camila Harrison?

"Except," continued Camila, "they're *our* government. They work for *us*. They don't work for themselves. Don't let them forget that. And don't you forget that, either. They work for *us*. For you and me."

Camila paused, took a deep breath. She gathered her thoughts. It was time to bring it home.

"It's time to hold the government accountable. It's time to hold Odessa accountable, and Rico and all the others who were skimming and stealing and lying."

"Objection," said Nutley. "The government is not on trial here. It's the defendant who's on trial."

Yamamoto ignored him. "Overruled. Please continue, Ms. Harrison."

Nutley sat down.

"Should we just allow the government to play by a different set of rules, to disregard our constitutional rights? To cheat and lie and steal? Should we not hold them accountable? Or will you, by your verdict here today, send a message to the government that you will not tolerate a government of cheats and scammers . . . scoundrels. That you expect better than that? You see, the only way the government will pay attention is if you acquit Mr. Aldama. If you don't acquit Mr. Aldama, you know what the US attorney's office will say? They'll say that juries are stupid . . . that they do what they're told. That guys like Bergendahl can pull a fast one and no one will say a thing."

Camila paused and reached for the court's charge, flipped through it and found what she was looking for.

"Judge Yamamoto read to you the court's charge. These are the questions you will have to answer when you start your deliberations. There are definitions in here and instructions over here."

She pointed at a specific paragraph. "This, here, is the instruction I want you to pay closest attention to," Camila said, pointing to a section on the court's charge now being projected onto the wall-mounted screen in front of the jury box.

Evidence has been received which tends to show that a government witness may have lied or engaged in unlawful conduct, including the failure to safeguard the defendant's constitutional rights.

From this, you may infer, though you are not compelled to do so, that the defendant's, Vicente Aldama's, right to have access to all exculpatory evidence may have been violated.

You may give this inference as much force and effect as you think it should have under all the facts and circumstances.

"What does it all mean?" Camila followed. "Think about it this way: Would you like a jury to convict you or your loved ones based on an investigation procured through lies, through manufactured evidence? Racial profiling? Made-up excuses?"

"Objection," shouted Nutley. "There's no evidence that there was any racial profiling."

"The jury will recall the evidence. Overruled," answered Judge Yamamoto. "Please sit down, Mr. Nutley."

Camila began: "Here's the real danger, members of the jury. Everybody knows that our jails are full of innocent people who were convicted on false identifications. Every day, the newspapers are full of headlines about people who have been exonerated based on newly discovered evidence. Our jails are full of people who were wrongfully convicted as a result of bad police work, coerced confessions, planted evidence, mismatched finger prints and even false identifications.

"In fact, if you read the papers, you'll find stories about our Texas legislature making restitution in the millions to those individuals who have recently been exonerated. Individuals who spent fifteen, twenty, twenty-five years in prison for crimes they did not commit. If you, as the jury, choose to look the other way, then the real danger is that such shoddy investigations will become the norm. It will be considered okay to lie and make stuff up just to get a conviction. If that's the society you want to live in, well, then do nothing. Find my client guilty and go on living your lives. Who cares?! But if you want to make a difference, send a message. You know what you need to do. You need to find my client not guilty, and while you're at it, tell Nutley and his agents that, if the government wants us to play by the rules, then the government must also abide by the rules. Neither the governement nor Odessa get a free pass."

Camila sighed for effect. "Two wrongs don't make a right."

Judge Colt Yamamoto allowed the jury to start their deliberations at 3:00 p.m. Camila, Thelma and the group walked across the street to the park to wait on the verdict after packing up their belongings. Camila's parents had decided, instead, to head to the Starbucks across the park and call to check on Luis Pablo.

Gustavo sat down on a park bench next to Camila and hugged her. "You did a great job. He was lucky to have you all in his corner."

"I agree, I think you did a hell of a job, Camila," echoed Alan. "Getting back in federal court when the cards were stacked against you took a lot of courage. You and Thelma were stellar, you both should be very proud."

"I don't see how the jury can come back with a guilty verdict," Thelma said. "Maybe a hung jury, but not a guilty one."

"I think you are getting an acquittal," followed Julio, ever the optimist.

"I just want it to be over," Camila replied. "Whatever has to happen . . . let it happen. I'm ready to move on."

Out of nowhere, Aldama's sister Angélica appeared, followed by her husband Daniel.

The group invited the pair to sit down at one of the other benches.

Daniel Dawson spoke first. "Angélica and I wanted to apolgize to you, Ms. Harrison, and to thank your entire team for a great effort. We don't know what will happen to Vince, but now I understand why you all did what you did."

Angélica interjected, "I'm glad you exposed those bastards. At the time, we couldn't see the whole picture, but now we know. Now, it's in God's hands and we trust in him and we know he'll take care of my brother, one way or another."

"Thank you. It was an honor and a privilege to have represented Vicente. He's a good guy," said Camila.

FORTY-THREE

"We have a hung jury," Judge Yamamoto declared. "They're stuck."

Nutley, Camila, Fox and Griffin were all in the judge's chambers trying to figure out what was going to happen next. It was Friday and still there was no verdict. Thelma was back at the law school getting her students ready for finals.

Yamamoto handed the lawyers a slip of paper. "Here, take a look at this."

The note read:

Judge, we're six "guilty," five "not guilty," one undecided. We've been deadlocked for two days. What if we can't decide? What happens next? And what will happen to the Odessa cops? Are they going to prison? If we send Aldama to prison, shouldn't those guys go to prison too?

"I'm going to Allen Charge them," Yamamoto said, "see what happens. Here, take a look at it."

Members of the jury:

Please continue to deliberate in an effort to reach a verdict that can dispose of this important case. This trial has been expensive in time, effort, money and emotional strain to all sides. If you fail to agree upon a verdict, the case will have to be tried again. Any future jury must be selected in the same manner and from the same source as how you were chosen, and there's no reason to believe the evidence will be any different the second time around.

If the majority of you are in favor of a conviction, those of you who disagree should reconsider whether your doubt is reasonable. On the other hand, if the majority of you are in favor of an acquittal, the rest should ask yourselves whether or not you should perhaps reconsider your position.

Remember, no juror is expected to give up on his or her beliefs or convictions, but it is your duty to agree upon a verdict if you can do so. However, if the evidence fails to establish guilt beyond a reasonable doubt, the defendant should be given a unanimous verdict of "not guilty."

Take as much time as necessary to continue your deliberations.

"It's okay," answered the lawyers, each one thinking the indecision favored his or her position.

⸺⸺⸺⸺⸺

"They've had the entire weekend to think about it," Judge Yamamoto said, "and we still don't have a verdict."

It was noon on Monday, and the jury had now deliberated for three days straight. Despite all that time to consider the facts, they were still struggling. The latest jury note revealed that they were now eight "not guilty," one undecided and three "guilty." And although they could not agree on a unanimous verdict, the one thing they could all agree on was that they wanted to go home.

"What do you want to do, Judge?" asked Nutley.

"I'm thinking of declaring a mistrial," Yamamoto said. "What do you think, Ms. Harrison?"

"I think they should continue to deliberate," Camila answered, trying to figure out how to play her last card. "My client merits a decision either way. He shouldn't be put through this ordeal again on the weight of such flimsy evidence: an illegal traffic stop and blatant official misconduct."

"Let's bring in the jury," Yamamoto ordered.

"I understand that you were unable to reach a verdict, is that correct?" Yamamoto asked the jury forewoman. She was a smartly dressed, forty-something executive.

"That's right, Your Honor."

"You don't think more time will help?"

"Oh, no. As of last count, we still had disagreements with four undecided jurors and others flip-flopping back and forth. We're never going to agree, Your Honor. One thing we all do agree on, however, is that Odessa should be investigated."

"Very well," Yamamoto said, ignoring the foreperson's last comment. "The court will declare a mistrial. The jury is excused."

The twelve jurors followed the US marshal back to another room in order to retrieve their belongings and then head home.

Camila, Aldama, Nutley and Fox stayed behind in the court-room.

"Okay, the defendant will be remanded to the custody of the US Marshals Service. The retrial of this case will be in sixty days: January 15th for jury selection and January 22nd for the trial itself. If any of you need to take up any matters between now and then, please file your motions. This court is now in recess."

After the mistrial, Nutley, Fox and Camila were caught together in the same elevator. To say the atmosphere was tense would be an understatement.

"I think you should dismiss the charges against my client, in the interest of justice," said Camila, breaking the ice.

"I will do no such thing," snapped Nutley. "Your guy's a scum-bag. He deserves to rot in jail."

"Do you really want to do this again? With the Odessa guys under federal investigation?"

"What investigation?" asked Nutley.

"Are you that stupid? What do you think is going to happen? Didn't you see the reporter and the blogger in the courtroom?" Camila sighed. "Please . . . you need to take those blinders off."

"The hell with you!" shouted Nutley.

Fox was staying out of it. He just leaned back and watched.

"Okay, we can talk about this later. I know you're tired. What's your cell number?" Camila asked. "Can I have it?"

"It's 832-855-5555," blurted out Fox instinctively, then covered his mouth, half-embarrassed. He wasn't thinking straight. For the last two weeks, he'd been getting less than two hours of sleep a night. He was drained.

Camila reached for her cell, plugged in Nutley's number, started typing a text message, and attached the audio file of the conversation between Nutley and the Mexican consul Rudy Canseco and hit the SEND button. She smiled. "That should do it."

A second later, Nutley's cell phone started vibrating in his coat pocket. He reached for it, looked at the screen and noticed the attachment. He made a frown, then opened and read the accompanying text message. Then he read it again one more time. Finally, after about five seconds, a horrified look came over him.

"Where did you get that?"

"Don't worry about it. Let me know what you want to do. If you want to discuss it in private. . . . Really, whatever you want. We have lots of time."

Right then, the elevator stopped on another floor and Nora Edelstein, the *New York Times* reporter, jumped in. She nodded to the lawyers as if to say hello.

"Or maybe you'd rather discuss it publicly," said Camila as she eyed-balled the reporter standing to her left, across from Nutley.

Nutley's eyes grew big. He gave the reporter a look of death.

"You let me know," followed Camila and announced, loud enough for Edelstein to hear, "I've got plenty of dirt to dish out about this bust and the Odessa crew . . . and your office, Nutley." With that, she exited the elevator.

Nutley jumped out after Camila and pulled her into the men's bathroom down the hall. He leaned against the door, desperate to shut Camila up.

Camila was not pulling any punches. "Who the hell do you think you are? Let me out of here."

"I don't know what you've got," Nutley replied, "but . . . "

"I'm sure," Camila challenged him, "Edelstein would love to get a hold of this story. She gave me her number too, you know? Hell, I don't think she's even left the building. I'm going to call her right now."

"Don't do that!" screamed Nutley. "Please . . . what is it you want?"

"If I don't say anything," Camila explained, "I won't be able to live with myself. You'll go on about your business, as if nothing happened. It'll be business as usual down at the US attorney's office."

"What?! What do you want, for God's sake?!"

Camila stared into Nutley's eyes. He had panic written all over his face.

"I'll do anything," said Nutley. "I mean it."

"I want all charges against my client dismissed, right now," ordered Camila. The tables had turned. Camila Harrison had Barton Nutley in the palm of her hand.

Nutley thought about it. He was struggling with the idea of losing face, losing to a fledgling lawyer over what should have been an open-and-shut case involving a rinky-dink wetback courier. "Okay, but you put a lid on it—no press, no talking to the *Times*. Odessa's bad news, they should get what's coming to them. Just keep me and my office out of it. If you can live with that . . . I guess I can."

"You've got a deal, Nutley," Camila said, jumping at the opening. "I want it to happen now. Let's get back to the judge."

"Yeah, yeah, you've got it. Now let's catch Yamamoto before he leaves for the day, you bitch!"

"I love you too, Nutley."

"What do you mean you want the marshal to bring Aldama back from the basement?" asked Judge Yamamoto, looking confused. "I ordered the retrial for January. The last thing I want to do is get back on the bench. You guys tired me out!"

"Your Honor, the government has thought better about pursuing the charges against Mr. Aldama," said Nutley. "We don't object to the honorable court granting Ms. Harrison's motion to suppress the illegally obtained. . . . "

"The evidence," followed Camila, "well, you saw it, Your Honor."

"So, the government is asking the court to go along and grant the defendant's motion to suppress?" Yamamoto asked.

"Correct." Camila smiled, hardly able to contain her emotions.

"Well," clarified Yamamoto, "after watching the Buc'ees' video, I have to admit, I grew somewhat concerned with what I witnessed. . . . "

"With the new information about tainted evidence and corruption among the government witnesses, there'd probably be another mistrial or even an acquittal," confessed Nutley. "I'm having my office reopen all the cases made by Bergendahl . . . review them, and if there are discrepancies, well . . . we'll have to address those."

Camila said, "It's the right thing to do, Your Honor. . . to preserve the justice system." She winked at him.

Yamamoto leaned back in his chair and stared at the ceiling, trying to make sense of Nutley's sudden 180. After a long pause, he grumbled, "Okay, let's go into the courtroom and put some things on the record. One less case on my docket." He pressed the intercom button and said, "Chloe, call the marshals, and have them bring Mr. Aldama back to the courtroom. Thanks."

"Ms. Harrison opened my eyes," declared Nutley. "Someday, when I become governor, I'm going to push to make these task forces more accountable, mark my words."

"You'll make a fine governor, Mr. Nutley. But first we have to get you elected as the next Attorney General of Texas, wouldn't you agree?" Camila smiled.

"That's right," smiled Nutley, "first things first."

"Ms. Harrison," Judge Yamamoto announced, "do you want to put anything on the record?"

Camila Harrison, Vicente Aldama and Barton Nutley were standing in front of the bench, near the podium, waiting for Yamamoto to sign the order granting the motion to suppress the evidence and the dismissal of charges.

Camila cleared her thoughts and spoke. "Judge, I would kindly request that the court order the US Marshal Service to contact Immigration and Customs Enforcement today. That way, my client can sign his voluntary deportation and be on his way back to Mexico immediately."

Nutley nodded his head. As soon as Camila finished, he declared, "The government would like to join Ms. Harrison in said request, Your Honor."

Yamamoto looked surprised, but he didn't say anything. "Very well, it will so be ordered. Anything else?"

"No," replied both Camila and Nutley.

"Very well," indicated Yamamoto as he signed the documents sitting in front of him. "Both orders have been signed and the criminal indictment against Mr. Aldama is no more."

"Signed with prejudice, Your Honor?" asked Camila.

"With prejudice," replied Yamamoto.

Aldama hugged his attorney.

"You're going home," said Camila.

"Thank you," cried Aldama. "Thank you, Your Honor."

"Go take care of your daughter," said Yamamoto. "Good luck to you."

The marshal escorted Aldama away as Judge Yamamoto banged his gavel on the bench.

"We'll be in recess," Chloe announced.

Yamamoto started heading back to chambers, when he stopped midway and turned around. He addressed Camila, "Counselor . . ."

"Yes, Your Honor?"

"Do you want to keep getting appointments?"

"You really mean that, Judge?" Camila asked, surprised.

"People need a real fighter on their side," said Judge Yamamoto, "someone who is ready to push and push . . . no matter how uncomfortable it gets . . . until the truth comes out. That's how the system's supposed to work."

"I'd be honored," said Camila, unable to comprehend how it could be that Judge Colt Yamamoto did not hold a grudge against her.

"Good," said Yamamoto, "you'll be hearing from me." He marched out of the courtroom.

Nutley stood there scratching his head.

Camila Harrison exited the courtroom. She felt like a brand new person.

Also by Carlos Cisneros

The Case Runner
Carlos Cisneros
2008, 368 pages, Clothbound
ISBN: 978-1-55885-510-6, $24.95

Winner, 2009 International Latino Book Award—Best Mystery Novel–English

In this legal thriller set on the Texas-Mexico border, a young lawyer is caught up in a wrongful death case involving insurance fraud, theft and maybe even murder.

The Name Partner
Carlos Cisneros
2010, 352 pages, Clothbound
ISBN: 978-1-55885-594-6, $24.95

Named to the Texas Library Association's 2011 Lariat Reading List: Best 2010 Adult Fiction

In this hard-hitting and timely novel about a drug company that puts its shareholders' profits over safety, South Texas attorney Guillermo "Billy" Bravo struggles with his reponsibilities to his client, his family and his own personal ethics.

The Land Grant
Carlos Cisneros
2012, 320 pages, Trade Paperback
ISBN: 978-1-55885-706-3, $16.95

Winner, International Latino Book Award, Best Mystery; Finalist, 2012 Foreword Reviews' Book of the Year Awards